TRUTH of EMBERS

BOOK 3

DRAGONSWORN

CAITLYN MCFARLAND

OLIVER HEBER BOOKS

Cover design by Hannah Sternjakob

Edited by Kristy S. Gilbert, Kate Rene Gleason

Published by Oliver-Heber Books

0 9 8 7 6 5 4 3 2 1

For Mom and Dad.
Without you, I wouldn't be who I am.
Because genetics.
But also because of your hard work, time, wisdom,
laughter, tears, and love.
Thank you.

CHAPTER 1

RHYS

Hell was not a place of fire. It was a place of ice and darkness.

A place of pain.

Rhys ap Ayen, King of the Eryri dragons, knelt in mud. He wore his human form, and snow melted by the flames of his magic formed a puddle that soaked into his knees and the toes of his boots. Arctic air whistled over the top of the narrow chasm in which he'd chosen to isolate himself. Not too far from the camp, but hidden from the sky by an overhang in case Owain's scouts flew overhead. He didn't want them to see the glow of his fire when he lost control—when he could no longer bear Kai's torment.

Kai?

Kai Monahan, his mate, wept inside his head. He pulled her close through the bond that connected them, despite the agony. Owain had given her to an air Draig this time. The man had tied Kai to a metal frame and was sending bolts of electricity through her, increasing the current until her muscles spasmed and her throat was raw from crying out.

Rhys slammed his fists into the mud. It sizzled and smoked. Tongues of flame licked over his hands. *Hold on,* cariad. *It will be over soon. I'm here. Hold on.*

She didn't reply. For fifteen or twenty minutes, she'd been beyond words. He could sense her fighting to not throw herself into him, to hold on to her anguish so he wouldn't feel it.

So Rhys wouldn't be tempted to give Owain what he wanted: Rhys's life.

Tonight, Rhys would take Owain's life instead.

Let me take your pain, Kai. Please.

She wouldn't.

Nothing he could do. She was in agony, and there was *nothing* he could do.

The weight of it bore down on him until his forehead almost brushed the churned earth. He sucked in air and loosened shaking fists as if he could breathe for her starved lungs, relax her rigid muscles. This was the last time. It had to be the last time.

She screamed.

Oh, Stars. Let them stop.

Thirteen days she'd been screaming. Weeping. Begging. Only constant guarding and sometimes physical restraint had kept Rhys from flying to Cadarnle to give himself to Owain and end her suffering. If it hadn't been for the vision his Seeress sister, Seren, left behind after *her* abduction—which had occurred during the same battle—he would have.

He would rather die than let Kai go through this.

Snow crunched as Morwenna, arrived from Eryri only hours ago, paced across the canyon mouth a dozen feet away. Normally Cadoc would've been standing guard. Since he'd broken the curse that forced him to attack Rhys on sight, Cadoc had stuck to Rhys's side like a barnacle. But everyone in the vee —the small military unit he'd trained and lived with since childhood—knew the cold bothered Cadoc's maimed hand. Despite having just arrived after the week-long flight from Eryri, Morwenna had volunteered.

Another shock ripped through Kai. Rhys dug clawed fingers into wet earth, and a primitive, animal sound forced its way past his lips. He tried to send her comfort, but he was as bare as a scraped hide. There wasn't much left to give.

But he had to try. This was his fault. He'd trusted Jiang—handed Kai right to her and watched them fly off. Too late, he'd discovered the jade dragon wasn't only a spy, she was also Owain's heartsworn. If Kai died, Jiang would be the undisputed Queen of Dragons.

Not...your...fault, Kai grated. He could feel the strain it took for her to form words. *Jiang's fault. Owain's. They...are going...to die.*

Rhys bared his teeth. *A few more hours, then by your hand or mine,* cariad, *it will be done.*

No answer but venomous hate, a shudder, another cry. Rhys bit the inside of his mouth to hold in an answering howl, tasting the salt and copper of blood.

Two weeks of torture had changed Kai. She wasn't broken, but she'd been boiled down. Her gentle awkwardness and carefree attitude had been stripped away, replaced with flashes of visceral fear and stunning rage. He'd tried to save as much of her as he could. If— *When* he brought her out of Cadarnle, he hoped he could salvage at least part of the woman he loved.

The shocks stopped. A moment later, Kai's fear lessened, her fury-shot dread ebbing bit by bit, like a lowering tide.

It was finished. For now.

Rhys tried to rub away the headache gnawing at his temples, but all he did was smear rapidly chilling mud over the side of his face. *Kai?*

They'd drawn close enough that he could sense her body

shake, how she tried not to weep in relief or feel gratitude toward Owain's henchmen for not hurting her anymore. *Still alive. I just...need a minute.*

Fighting his instinct to wrap her up tighter, Rhys relaxed his hold on their connection and let Kai pull away.

Now, if today was like every other day in Cadarnle, Owain himself would clean her up. The thought of his cousin touching his heartsworn drove Rhys almost as mad as the torture. That he dared lay hands on her, that he pretended to soothe and comfort her and assure her none of this was her fault, poor girl, but Rhys's. That Owain could touch her at all, when Rhys could not.

Perhaps, at this moment, a little distance was for the best.

Rhys had stayed with her after torture enough to know what was happening. Owain would carry Kai to the bed, which was in the same room where they tortured her—a demented space that was half lavish guest room, half dungeon. He'd prattle on about how necessary her pain was. How her suffering served the greater good, because the more Rhys felt her pain, the more likely he was to take Owain seriously, to give himself up so Kai could be safe.

When Owain had taken Kai, he'd given Rhys fourteen days to turn himself over. If he didn't, Owain would execute Kai. Publicly, grotesquely.

Worse, Owain had insinuated, he might not. He might keep Kai, and keep hurting her, for years. Either way, Rhys's time to bargain was coming to an end.

Though the sun didn't rise this far north in winter, Rhys had become precisely aware of the passage of time. It was the thirteenth morning, and everything was nearly ready.

Twelve more hours.

In twelve hours, Rhys's army would attack Cadarnle, and they would win. Seren had seen it.

A bolt of pain from Kai snatched Rhys's mind back to the dungeon bedroom. He reached for her, but Owain and his henchman were gone. The cut had come from the old Quetzal woman who took care of Kai's wounds. She'd sliced Kai's arm just below the elbow, drawing out blood she would use to heal any internal injuries. She was gentle, and her soft ministrations took away much of Kai's pain. Then the woman left, and Kai was alone.

Relief swept through him like the arctic wind, and with it, exhaustion.

It'll be over soon. Kai's voice was empty and matter-of-fact. Her emotions, once so vibrant, had muted. She'd locked them somewhere so deep even he couldn't find them. He doubted she could either.

Mud squelched when Rhys shifted his weight, but he heard it as if from a distance. *By tomorrow morning, I will have you out of there. When the battle starts, make sure to barricade the door.*

Her dulled emotions spiked into something sharp and icy: fear for him. Knowledge of what his capture and death would mean. Not only for dragons, but for the human race—for her family.

What if the vision was wrong? she whispered into his mind. *You should go home. Forget me. The Council can probably figure out how to re-heartswear you once I'm gone. Or maybe when the mantle is fixed you can do it yourself.*

No. He wasn't the one being tortured. He had no right to say he was suffering. But to witness it—to *know* the extent of her pain and be unable to save her from it—that was a torture all its own. *I won't leave you.*

Something stirred in her. Sadness? Regret? She put it down so fast he couldn't tell. *You can't die. You're the only one who can save the damn world.*

One side of his mouth curved. *I will save it. Tonight. And if I don't, Deryn can. She's more than capable.*

Thank the Ancients for that. He'd sent his sister home to Eryri literally kicking and screaming in the company of Evan—their vee-mate and Deryn's lover—and several guards. Even so, Rhys had to use the power of the mantle to make sure Deryn wouldn't come flying back to help him. If Rhys died, Deryn would inherit that power, and it would be her job to keep it from Owain. As long as either he or Deryn lived, the war would not be lost.

Kai didn't appreciate his feigned flippancy. Doubt crept into his mind, and Rhys shifted in the mud again. Wetness was climbing up his thighs and calves. Behind him, Morwenna let out an impatient sigh.

What time is it? Slowly, Kai's Wingless healing abilities and the Quetzal blood magic eased her pain. Her stranglehold over her emotions relaxed, and she lessened the distance between them.

Getting on to midmorning.

It's New Year's Eve.

Yes. For some humans, anyway.

He felt her rising panic that she wouldn't see another year. Another holiday. Might not ever see Rhys or her family—

You will. He wished he could touch her, smooth the tension and worry from that line between her brows, from the tight corners of her mouth.

She thrust her rising emotions into that mental vault and slammed the door. When she spoke, her feelings were muted again, giving her thoughts a flat, hard edge. *I'm going to sleep for a little while.* She hesitated, softening. *I love you. Whatever you're planning, be safe.*

Rhys had to push away a few of his own emotions. He

didn't want to let her go, but she needed rest, and he needed to make sure his army was ready. *I love you. I'll see you soon.*

She didn't respond.

Rhys inhaled, coming all the way back to himself in a puddle on a frozen island some few hundred miles from Cadarnle. He wiped his hands on his coat and glimpsed his filthy palms. The bottom halves were scarred with countless half-moons where his nails had pierced the skin, all created since Kai's capture.

"Why do you do this to yourself?"

Rhys started. Morwenna stood near the entrance to the little gully, her hand clamped around the hilt of a slender sword sheathed at her hip. Her short, sleek brown hair was pulled half up into a topknot, sharpening her foxlike features. Despite the weather, she wore only fitted pants tucked into boots and a loose shirt tucked into the pants, completing the outfit with a wide belt at her waist. Like him, she was a fire Draig. Cold couldn't touch her.

Rhys gritted his teeth against the ache of muscles left too long in one position and pushed to his feet. He staggered to a pile of unmelted snow and used it to scrub what mud he could from his hands and clothes. "She needs me. I won't leave her."

"Is that why you insist on putting yourself through this? Because she *needs* you? What a clichéd, male thing to say. Maybe if I was weak you would've had a harder time tossing me aside."

"Kai is not weak." Rhys put a hand against the wall of the canyon to steady himself. Orange flames sparked at his fingertips. "And this is not the time."

Morwenna's voice softened. "I understand that you want to save her. She's necessary for the future. I even stand by you, or I would have left and joined the rogues when Ashem's Wingless let me out of the cells."

Rhys's jaw tightened, and not only because she'd called Juliet King "Wingless" instead of using her name—though if Ashem, their vee commander and Juli's mate, heard her, he'd be apoplectic. He was sensitive about Juli these days.

But Morwenna had plenty of reason to leave. To hate Rhys, both as a terrible friend and a negligent king. He'd hidden Kai from her because he knew about Morwenna's feelings for him, and, like a coward, he hadn't wanted to deal with the messiness of that. Then, when she'd been accused of being a spy, he hadn't stood by her. "Morwenna—"

She slashed the air with her hand. "You don't need to sit here and suffer because she's suffering. Close your mind to her, Rhys. You're barely functional. We need a king. A leader. Not a martyr."

The small flames at his fingertips flared, scorching the stone. "You would have done the same for Iain," he said, naming her mate who'd been dead for ten years. "You know what it's like to love like this."

She shook her head. "I know how mad being heartsworn can make you. Take it from someone who has been heartsworn and then lost their mate, the feelings you have for Kai aren't *real*. They're lust and obsession and infatuation. Don't let the magic cloud your good sense."

"You're wrong." If she'd ever questioned her love for Iain, this was the first Rhys had heard of it. Ancients knew she'd had to claw her way back from the brink after his death. "I love Kai. Magic or no."

Morwenna's face turned sour. She shrugged. "I suppose you'll never know."

Rhys spoke through gritted teeth. Knowing how he felt about Kai without a heartswearing bond would mean they'd been sundered. Owain had sundered Rhys's parents, and his father had ended up dead. "You and I and the entire world had better hope not." He took a breath, seeking composure and not finding it. "Go back to camp. I need a minute."

"I'm not leaving—"

"I said *go*."

There must have been something in his voice. Fraying edges. Desperation. Rage, maybe. Instead of arguing, she glared, then stalked out of the ravine.

Rhys stepped out from beneath the ravine's overhanging wall and tipped his face to the stars, which were so numerous he felt he'd traveled back two hundred years, before humans clouded the air and lit the night. He reached out to Kai again, whether to comfort her or himself, he wasn't sure.

She'd fallen asleep.

She tended to sleep most of the time Owain wasn't torturing her or parading her around Cadarnle. Rhys worried about what that meant, just like he worried about the way she'd begun to shut away her emotions. The way she flinched whenever anyone—torturer or not—touched her.

He ran a hand through his hair and smoothed it down again. She was all right for the moment, and brooding would accomplish nothing. He forced his thoughts away from Kai, focusing on plans for the rescue.

They nearly hadn't gotten everything together in time. It took weeks to fly from the island in the Bering Sea where Kai had been kidnapped to Eryri in the South Pacific, and then weeks again to go from Eryri to Cadarnle in the Arctic Circle. He couldn't make the trip there and back and meet the ultimatum deadline. So he'd sent the wounded home and called out five more vees, plus Morwenna and Juli. They had joined him not long ago. He was ready to attack.

As he went over the plan again, the shaky burn of adrenaline from Kai's torture faded, replaced with cool, steely focus. To boost his confidence, Rhys reached into a pocket and pulled out an egg-sized sunstone—the record containing the vision Seren had around the time of her capture. In a stroke of luck only he could have, Cadoc had found it while searching the site of Seren's abduction. She must have dropped it when she was taken.

Rhys rolled the gem in his palm. False fire gleamed orange and red in its depths. Unable to resist checking one more time, Rhys let his mind go blank and sought the faint vibration of magic coming from the stone. The world blurred and darkened. Images flared to life in his mind's eye.

Rhys stands face-to-face with his father. Ayen speaks. "Y Ddraig Goch ddyry cychwyn." The red dragon will rise again. A golden dragon statuette tumbles from Ayen's mouth—the Sunrise Dragon artifact created by the Ancients, which could heal the mantle and end the war.

Flicker.

A white viper coils around a snowy raven, constricting until delicate bones snap. Beside the snake, a golden canary sings in a cage. Flames rise up and race through the grass, surrounding the viper. He releases the raven, and the flames consume him.

Flicker.

Mount Snowdon—the Eryri of old—stands against a black sky, riven in two. The earth shakes. With a grinding shriek, the mountain crashes into itself. When the dust clears, the mountain is whole.

Flicker.

All the dragons of the earth stand on an island half buried in the sea, battling a rising tide. In a rush, the dark ocean swallows them all.

Rhys released the sunstone, and it splashed into the mud at his feet. Cursing, he bent to retrieve it.

The vision was as it had been. No new details. No insights.

Stars, he hoped he was interpreting it correctly. He'd had

plenty of practice helping Seren parse the visual riddles her power showed her over the years, but he didn't have Seren's instinctive gift.

As well as he could guess, all of it had to do with the end of the war. The vision of his father meant that Ayen had known the location of the Sunrise Dragon—an artifact lost since before Rhys's birth. As his father had been dead for a millennium, that part of the vision wasn't helpful.

The snake and the birds, however—that had given him everything. The viper was Owain. The flames were Rhys's army. If he attacked Cadarnle while Owain held Kai and Seren, Rhys would win. Owain would die. The civil war that had dragged for a thousand years would end tonight. Owain would never control the full power of the mantle. Never have the chance to command every dragon on Earth to slaughter until humans were at the brink of annihilation. Which, of course, would lead to retaliation with bombs and drones and every weapon in the modern human arsenal.

Dragons would not win that war. No one would.

Rhys stowed the stone in his pocket and tried not to think of the last image. All the dragons trapped, drowning. Dying because they could not defeat the tide that could only be the rise of humanity against them.

If he won, humans wouldn't even know they existed.

One thing at a time. Shaking off a tendril of misgiving, Rhys stepped clear of the steaming mud his out-of-control magic had created onto frozen dirt, then into calf-deep snow. Outside the ravine, the snow rose in drifts up to his hips. It melted at his touch, but the slog to camp was wet and less than enjoyable.

He passed the sentries, stopping only long enough for a Wonambi soldier to ensure that he wasn't an assassin using illusion magic as a disguise, then entering the camp. The tents had been pitched in concentric circles, growing smaller the farther he walked toward the center. As he walked, he called for the vee commanders to assemble at his tent.

Time to make final plans.

His army wasn't large by human standards, but the coming clash *would* be the largest dragons had seen in living memory. Larger, even, than the one two weeks ago over the Bering Sea.

The plan was reckless, but worth it if Kai came home safely.

Unbidden, Morwenna's voice entered Rhys's mind. *The feelings you have for Kai aren't real. They're lust and obsession and infatuation. Don't let the magic cloud your good sense.*

He shook his head. His feelings for Kai were real, and soon, he'd have her back.

Tonight, his struggles would end.

CHAPTER 2
KAI

K ai smiled at the man who was going to murder her.

Owain's booted footsteps were quiet as he crossed to the bedroom half of her torture chamber. Declining to rise from the ebony-inlaid table where she sat, Kai raised her water goblet to him. The necklace-fine chains around her fingers hissed as they slid across the jewel-encrusted gold.

She suppressed a frisson of fear at his presence. He'd already had his people hurt her twice today—electrocution in the morning and a beating in the afternoon. Despite her pretend nonchalance, her breathing quickened and went shallow. *Not again. It can't be time again. Please.*

She slid the semitransparent shield she'd learned to make between herself and Rhys. Like the heartswearing version of a one-way mirror, she could still feel him—a connection she needed desperately—but he would only be vaguely aware of her, as if she'd fallen asleep. He didn't know that Owain threw in extra torture sessions. Or that she hadn't eaten for four days.

She was pretty sure most of the time he thought she was asleep.

But if Rhys was going to fight a battle tonight—to win, and get her out of here—she couldn't let her panic distract him.

Owain stopped across the table, studying her with his awful, pale eyes. "Good evening."

Please! The word almost escaped. But begging had never stopped him before, so Kai bit her tongue. Rage, disdain, the fire that spun like a hurricane inside her, barely held in by those fine chains—that was all she would feel. Not the fear. Not that harrowing, hollowing, sick-making terror.

Better to feel nothing than feel that. Like packing herself in ice, she grew more numb every day. Owain crossed his arms, rumpling the navy-blue fabric of his long, high-collared coat. "Tell me, Kai. How much does Rhys ap Ayen love you?"

Kai raised an eyebrow and made herself take a slow swallow from her cup. She pictured the look on his face when Rhys's army appeared in the constantly dark sky. Then she pictured his face when Rhys killed him. "Enough to kick your ass."

Owain chuckled politely, like he was a good host and she'd made an unfunny joke. "If he's going to save you, he's cutting it close."

Kai flicked a glance at the thirteen vertical lines she'd carved into the fancy pastoral mural on the wall. Tonight was New Year's Eve. Over three months since she'd found dragons in the Rockies. Almost the same amount of time since she'd heartsworn to Rhys, one of two claimants to the title King of Dragons. Six weeks since she'd given up her life as a more or less normal law school dropout and traveled to the South Pacific seat of Rhys's kingdom. Three weeks since she'd allowed herself to admit she'd fallen in love with him. And thirteen days since becoming the "guest of honor" in Owain's underground arctic stronghold.

Her gaze wandered back to the man in front of her. Tall,

blond, handsome Owain. A man who wore the veneer of civilization like celebrities wore ceramic teeth. Bright and perfect on the outside, insides better off unseen.

"Where's Jiang?" Kai asked. Owain was bad enough, but at least—strange as it was—Kai could tell torture made him uncomfortable. Jiang, though... Kai suspected watching the torture made it easier for her to forget that Kai was the "other" queen. The person who would take everything she wanted if Rhys won the war.

No. *When* he won the war. In just a few short hours.

"Busy." Owain's lip curled, but so slightly that Kai almost missed it. From what she'd seen, Owain and Jiang's relationship was more about mutual benefit than true affection. Unfortunately, that seemed to work for them. "I'm more interested in the whereabouts of my cousin." The corner of his mouth quirked up.

That smile. It was Rhys's smile.

Kai's breath hitched. With that smile in front of her and Rhys's presence at the back of her mind, it was almost like she could look into his starfire-blue eyes. Touch the warm, red scales of the indicium that wound over the right half of his body. Feel the storm-heavy pressure of his presence surrounding her like a blanket. Safe, protected.

After two weeks of his constant presence in her mind, feeling what he was willing to sacrifice, basking in his goodness, Kai loved Rhys so much she could hardly bear it. But safety was an illusion, and thoughts of Rhys threatened the disassociation that was the only tolerable state of mind since she'd become Owain's captive. Thinking of him inevitably led to the idea that she might never see him again, and that would break down the door behind which she'd locked her fear and pain. Not just break it down, splinter it into microscopic bits.

So she locked her love behind it too.

"I've told him not to come." Kai set her goblet on the table with a *clank*. "Is that all you wanted to talk about?" The movement jarred her shoulder, and she hid a wince. The beating had been brutal.

At least Rhys didn't know about it.

Owain pulled out the simple, elegantly carved wooden chair across from Kai and sat. "No."

A wave of blond hair fell into Owain's eyes, and he brushed it away with an elegant hand. Kai thought that he might be the most handsome man she'd ever seen. In a cold, plastic sort of way. He was definitely the most charismatic.

So like Rhys, yet so very opposite.

She gave him another empty smile. "What, then?"

His sigh was rueful. "I can't say I'm looking forward to your death. If it comes to killing you, know that I will regret it far more than I will regret killing him."

"Comforting." Despite her belief in Rhys, a chill slid down her spine. Death. She was twenty-four years old.

She locked down her emotions before they could overwhelm her.

"Is it?" Owain leaned back, his posture one of such undeniable authority that the wooden chair suddenly seemed a throne. "The Seeress had a vision."

A pithy response withered and died in Kai's throat. A vision. Of all the things that could throw off Rhys's plans, this was the one she'd feared the most. She tried to swallow, but her mouth was bone dry. "Oh?"

Owain's eyes found the mural Kai had scratched the days into, and his brows drew together. "She saw a great battle over Cadarnle. Naturally, hearing such a thing might happen made me more cautious. And I'm glad it did, as my scouts found an entire army camped three hours' flight away early this morning."

Her one-way shield slipped before she could stop it. The door that held back her emotions gave a little, and terror oozed around its edges.

Kai? Rhys's voice held no comfort. Not when that smug look on Owain's face was telling her she would never see him again. *What happened?*

Kai wrung her chained fingers under the table, twisting until it hurt. She used to click her carabiners when she was nervous. Now that wasn't enough. Not that she would have been able to click them anyway. Owain took her carabiners on the first day. Just like he took the gold necklace Rhys gave her and gifted it to Jiang. Bastard.

Flippancy annoyed Owain the most, so Kai shrugged, but her shaking voice betrayed her. "If you know where he is, why haven't you attacked?"

She kept her eyes focused on Owain while she answered Rhys. *He knows. Rhys, he found your army. He knows you're coming.*

Rhys swore. *What does he know? Find out. If we get in the air now, we can get there before he's had time to mount a defense.*

Kai told him about the scouts and Seren's vision. Rhys sent her a thread of comfort, then his thoughts turned to everything he had to do. Strike camp, organize the vees, find Ashem...

"You think I'm lying?" Owain rubbed the outside of his right eye. Kai suspected he'd picked up the habit from wearing an eye patch. A necessity until recently, since Rhys —with Kai's help—had burned that eye out of its socket three months ago. But Owain hadn't had Seren in his possession for more than an hour before he'd forced her to heal it for him.

Poor Seren. The Seeress was incredibly powerful, but still so defenseless. Kai took another drink of water, wetting her tongue enough to speak normally. "You aren't answering my question."

Owain narrowed his eyes. "I dislike repeating myself. The *only* reason I haven't ended this war in ice and blood is because *this is not my war.* My war is with humans. The more dragons I lose fighting Rhys, the fewer dragons I have to fight the real enemy. I haven't attacked because I have chosen not to."

Kai didn't flinch at his anger, but she couldn't stop the blood draining from her face. He'd never hurt her with his own hands, but there was always a first time.

Owain rested his elbows on the table and laced his fingers together. "Let me tell you about the vision. I hope you're listening, cousin, because this is a good one."

Kai got Rhys's attention through their bond. He stopped shouting orders, mentally leaning in close.

As if he knew he had Rhys's attention again, Owain nodded. "In hours, Rhys and fifteen vees will attack Cadarnle. There will be a battle. Many will die." A pause. "Including me."

Everything went still. In Kai's mind, Rhys might as well have turned to stone. It was the same vision he'd seen.

The seal over her emotions loosened, leaking hope. Maybe she could live. See Rhys again. Juli.

Her family. If she could even see Ashem scowling at her, that would be something. This could work. Rhys would come, save her. Owain would die, die, die like she'd pictured so many times.

Owain smiled. She saw a flash of his teeth, white like a shark's. "I see that pleases you. But you might want to tell him this: I won't die until after I've killed you. The vision was quite clear."

The seal fell back into place. Her hope turned brittle and sharp, like broken glass sliding across her heart. Good things turned wrong cut so much deeper than things that were bad from the beginning.

Maybe they shouldn't believe him. He'd found Rhys's army, so there clearly *had* been a vision to show him that. But that didn't mean he was telling the truth about the rest. Except Kai knew there had been other visions. Visions in which Owain ripped out the beating heart of a white raven.

It can't be true. Rhys's whisper was stricken.

It can. Kai's voice sounded dead, even to herself. *He's sitting right across from me. He could kill me right now, and there's nothing either of us could do.*

Owain reached across the table and took Kai's cup. He tipped the rest of its contents into his mouth. "My ultimatum stands. If a dragon so much as twitches from that valley, my scouts will tell me, and you die, Kai Monahan. If Rhys comes to me alone, however, they'll escort him here so we can...execute our transaction." He set the cup down. "Or he can go home with his army and leave you to your fate."

In her mind, Rhys let out a wordless rumble of hatred. His mind was flying through all the possibilities, but hopelessness was creeping in. All of their planning, wasted. He had no time. There was *no time.*

If Kai hadn't been numb, she would've panicked with him. She thought about running, as she had countless times before. Except Owain had planted some kind of magic device under the skin at the back of her neck that would blow her head off if she went anywhere beyond her room without him or Jiang.

Don't come, Kai whispered to Rhys.

His panicked thoughts froze. Rhys's presence wrapped around her, so achingly close to physical that his absence was agony. *I would rather die saving you than live into eternity knowing I didn't try.*

His closeness was suddenly too much. *Rhys. You cannot*

come here. There's so much more at stake than me. Than us. She was going to die.

I'm not going to—

Someone knocked on the door. Owain called for them to enter, and Kavar came in. Tall and broad, with bronze skin, shaggy black hair, and silver eyes, he looked painfully like Rhys's second-in-command and Juli's heartsworn, Ashem.

They were identical twins, after all.

Which was why, unbeknownst to Owain, Juli had ended up heartsworn to Kavar as well. And that was all kinds of messed up.

Kai watched Kavar, wondering in a disconnected way how he'd escaped from Rhys's prison the same day she'd been kidnapped. For someone who'd set Kavar up to be captured, Owain had been awfully glad to see him back.

Kavar bowed. Kai found that odd. Ashem almost never bowed to Rhys unless it was a formal occasion. And Ashem liked rules. Kavar, from what she'd seen, not so much.

"Majesty, Queen Jiang discovered a pair of traitors attempting to contact Rhys. They were apparently supposed to get the Wingless girl out of Cadarnle tonight in exchange for being taken to Eryri and given his protection."

The Wingless girl. Kavar never used her name. It was hard to feel bad about hurting something when it didn't even have a name.

Owain didn't look so happy now. "Where are they?"

Kavar flinched. Nothing more than a twitch of his hand, but Kai noticed. Usually Kavar was so cavalier about everything. Not this. Why?

Because he could read Owain's mind. He knew what the white dragon was planning.

Kai pulled at the fine chains over her fingers. To make Kavar flinch, it would have to be very, very bad.

"Jiang had them taken to the arena. She's waiting for you."

Owain rose, speaking through gritted teeth. "Why don't they understand? If I cannot end this war, our people will fall."

"If you try to exterminate humans, your people will fall," Kai retorted.

"The only person who is going to fall here is you if Rhys doesn't call off his army and give himself up." Owain wrapped hard fingers around her arm and hauled her upright. Kai gave an involuntary cry of pain—it was the shoulder that still hurt from the beating. The bone had probably been fractured.

Luckily, thanks to the accelerated healing of a Wingless, the pain had mostly faded. Until he grabbed her.

"What are you doing?" Kai tried to pull away, but Owain held her fast. Fear oozed from beneath the door that trapped her emotions. He wasn't going to wait for Rhys. He was going to kill her right now.

A muscle jumped in Owain's chiseled jaw, and his defined cheeks flushed with rage. "They wanted to save you. I think it's fitting that you watch their punishment."

Don't panic, cariad. *Owain believes himself a man of honor. He won't do anything to you until our time is up.*

Hard advice to take when she could feel Rhys coming apart at the seams. *What are we going to do?* Kai asked.

Let me think. We still have time. It's just past dinner. We have all night.

But there was no time for a new plan—not one that would work—and they both knew it.

CHAPTER 3

CADOC

Cadoc finished his flamecalling ritual, stood, and began to throw clothing and other necessary items haphazardly into a bag. Two bags sat open on his cot. The one filled with clothing was for the rogues to take to the cave where they would rendezvous—supposing they weren't all dead. The other held a tightly coiled riding harness and a first aid kit. Seren's champagne-colored pearl, wrapped around his good wrist, caught on a button. Cadoc swore and unwound the golden chain, stuffing it into his pocket.

He cursed the cold that made the shattered bones in his hand ache, cursed the darkness that made time feel interminable. Had they only been in the camp for two weeks? It felt like a fucking eternity, and he had nothing to do but imagine what Owain might be doing to Kai.

To Seren.

Now their carefully laid battle plans were shot to hell, and Juliet King had sprung an idea on them all that was more or less suicide.

Cadoc had agreed to it in an instant.

The pricking buzz of magic washed over his skin. Grateful for the distraction, he used his good hand—the hand Owain hadn't frozen and then crushed with his boot—to fish the sing-stone from his pocket and hook the curved line of silver and quartz over one ear. *Yes?*

What are you doing, wind-for-brains? It was Deryn, Rhys's younger sister. Future queen, if tonight didn't go well.

Preparing for my death.

Damn it, Cadoc! Deryn's voice, even in his head, was annoyed. Affection for the prickly little harridan filled his chest with warmth. Cadoc had never had siblings of his own, but thanks to Deryn and Rhys, he'd never felt the lack. *I can't get ahold of Rhys or Ashem. Tell me what's going on.*

If only he could think of Seren like a sister.

Owain knows about the army. If we move, he'll kill Kai. Cadoc thrust thoughts of Seren to the back of his mind and searched for his daggers. Snatches of music wandered through his brain, minor chords that sounded like a death march. He pushed those away too, wishing his subconscious would realize he'd never play again and stop tormenting him.

What? Deryn squawked.

Cadoc located the daggers beneath the cot, tossed one onto the bed, and strapped the other to his thigh. It was difficult to do one-handed. *Ashem went to locate the scouts so we know which direction to fly. Rhys is understandably distracted.*

Deryn's response was tense. *What are you going to do?*

Cadoc felt the ghost of a grin cross his face. *The only thing we can, love. Ditch the army and save our compatriots ourselves.*

Frustration washed through the singstone. Cadoc imagined Deryn in Eryri, tall and lethal, long auburn hair sweeping behind her as she paced her rooms. It would kill her not to be able to come.

Finally, she spoke. *Tell Rhys I'll kill him if he dies.*

Cadoc's smile tightened. *For you, anything.* He picked up the second dagger.

There's something else. Deryn sounded uncertain. *But never mind. It doesn't matter tonight.*

Cadoc let the pretense of humor drop. *What is it?*

Gethin. I hate him and I want Rhys's permission to dismiss him and his father from the Council. The whole time he's been filling Powell's seat, he's harassed the Wingless and spouted his antihuman rhetoric. He smirks whenever he sees me, and when I shout at him, he tries to placate me by bringing me bottles of mead. I threw the first one out the window and nearly broke the second over his head.

Cadoc's inner fire flared at the thought of Powell's son, Gethin. His grip tightened on the hilt of his blade. Aside from a king and queen, the dragons were ruled by the Council, which consisted of two dragons from each of the ten clans, two representatives from the Wingless, and—because Rhys insisted on it —Deryn. Powell was the councilman from Clan Draig, which was Cadoc's own clan, made up of dragons who had the power to control one of the four elements.

Powell was also an antihuman, anti-Wingless bull of a man who only followed Rhys because he didn't like Owain's plan of an all-out human/dragon war. Gethin, if anything, was twice as prejudiced as his father. When Powell came north with the fifteen vees, his son took his seat in the Council, which wasn't good for anyone. Cadoc was convinced that Gethin would gladly go to war with humans, and the only reason he stayed with Rhys instead of deserting for Cadarnle was the fact that his father, as a councilmember, had more than a little power. Owain didn't have a Council. If Gethin went to him, he'd be no one.

Gethin wasn't the kind of man that enjoyed being no one.

You can't kill him, Cadoc said with resignation. *Rhys can't afford to lose Powell's support. Besides, Powell is with the army. He'll be home in a week and you can go back to being irritated at him instead.*

Silence for a long moment. Then, *I suppose that's what I called to hear.*

Cadoc considered the second dagger once more, then stuffed it in with his clothes. A one-handed man didn't need two weapons. *Trip Gethin and pretend it was an accident. That will make you feel better.*

Deryn laughed, then turned serious. *I've missed you, you idiot. Keep him safe. Keep yourself safe too.*

Only if you do the same.

She snorted. *Yes. Because things are so desperately deadly here. Have Rhys get in touch as soon as you've got them.*

I will.

Deryn ended the call, and Cadoc took the singstone from his ear. Life was better since his curse had ended, but Ancients, he wanted to go home. He wanted everything to go back to the way it had been before.

Once they rescued Kai and Seren tonight, everything would. Unless, of course, they were all dead. Then what he wanted wouldn't matter at all.

CHAPTER 4

SEREN

Oblivion faded, and Seren cried out, reaching for it. Instead, the real world imposed itself onto her mind, all heat and chills and flickering light.

Her consciousness slipped and slithered back into her skull, trailing the clinging, suffocating muck of visions.

So many visions.

She rolled weakly onto her side and tried to vomit, but nothing came up. Her head throbbed and her sight was ringed in black, confining her field of vision to what was directly in front of her. Her mouth tasted like death.

"We are here to wash the Seeress," said an imperious female voice. "King Owain demands her presence imme-diately."

Seren closed her eyes. She couldn't see who was speaking anyway, not with the heavy gold-embroidered velvet curtains pulled around the canopy bed on which she lay.

She heard a whiny, "She is an oracle, not a trophy."

If she'd had the strength she would have bared her teeth. The whine belonged to the old turtle-faced man who had been "taking care" of her since her arrival in Eryri. She refused to learn his name.

"The king will see her," the woman said.

The man complained again, but his protests were lost in a rustle of skirts and the slap of slippered feet against stone. The curtain was torn aside, and she flinched away from the blazing fire in the fireplace that took up one entire wall of her room.

Her eyes adjusted to see the sneer on the woman's face. Seren wasn't sure who she was. Seren had female attendants to help her take care of her necessary business—which she was only allowed to do twice a day between visions—but they were usually juveniles. This woman was twice as old as Seren, at least.

The woman put a hand over her nose. "Eugh." She half turned to the juvenile girl behind her and said, "Make a note for me to send girls down here more often. The smell."

Seren's cheeks heated and tears burned her eyes. She tried to sit up, but was too weak to manage anything more than a twitch. She wished she'd been born someone else. Anyone. Human, dragon.

Anyone but the Seeress.

She'd never wished for that before, and it made her ashamed.

A juvenile male lifted Seren and deposited her on a chair. If the chair hadn't had arms, she would have fallen off. Helpless as a babe, she slumped and stared at the people around her.

The older woman's stern face softened. "This is no way to treat the Seeress." She jerked her head at the young male and the old turtle-man. "Get those bedclothes out and have them washed. Send for new ones."

The old man and the young male left, leaving only the woman and the juvenile girl.

They bowed, pressing their fingertips to their forehead.

"Lady Seeress. King Owain requests your presence at an...ah..." She looked ill. "An event. I'm afraid it's been put together in a hurry. We're to wash you and take you up to the main cavern as soon as possible."

Seren shivered. Owain had visited her frequently since she'd come to Cadarnle. Usually, he came only to speak with the old man and collect visions. Visions, which, Seren gathered, were growing increasingly obscure and useless the more they drugged her.

Good. Maybe they would burn the ability out of her. Maybe she would even live through it. She could escape with Kai. Go back to Eryri. To Rhys and Deryn.

And Cadoc.

The woman was still talking. The word *execution* cut through Seren's mental fog. If she could have moved, she would've shot to her feet.

"Kai?" Seren croaked. She hadn't heard her own voice in days. Or weeks? How long had she been here? The old man never spoke to her. "He's going to kill Kai?"

The woman's friendly expression chilled. "No. The son of the Usurper has until tomorrow morning to claim his mate. Owain caught a pair of traitors who were attempting to free the Wingless. He's going to make an example of them."

Something sparked in Seren, like fireworks just behind her eyes and a subtle, tingling pressure all over her body.

Premonition.

She struggled to remember which vision she'd had that might fit this moment, but there were so many that she couldn't recall.

Too weak to speak anymore, Seren allowed the woman and girl to strip her and lower her into an enormous metal tub. Her gaze fell on her ribs. She'd never been able to count them before. She'd always been softer, rounder. The drug they used

29

to keep her having visions constantly didn't allow her to keep down much food. Between that and the seizures, her softness was melting away like wax beneath a flame, and she hated it.

They washed and dressed her without speaking, then the younger one helped Seren drink water laced with herbs and fed her the smallest bit of broth.

Seren hoped they gave her long enough that she could keep it down this time.

When they were done, they called the muscular juvenile back in and had him carry her to a palanquin—a ridiculously ornate open chair with plush red cushions—carried by four juveniles. Once settled, Seren turned to thank the woman and her helper, but they had already disappeared.

The men lifted the palanquin onto their shoulders and started down the hall, accompanied by the old turtle-man, who muttered about lost time and doubling her dose as soon as she returned. Seren's stomach lurched and she tried to protest, but couldn't muster the energy to speak loud enough to be heard.

It was so good to feel moving air against her face and to be out of the stifling heat of her room. The halls were wide and twice as tall as a man, their walls a dark gray stone laced with veins of ice and gold. As little as she'd been out and about, to Seren, Cadarnle was like an organized anthill. All the halls were straight and everything seemed to have some kind of order, but she couldn't figure out what it was.

Despite everything, Owain's stronghold was a place of breathtaking beauty.

They emerged into the huge, ice-roofed cavern filled with all the things one might expect to find in an underground city—shops, places to eat, a huge underground hot spring where dragons swam in the water—and at its heart, an amphitheater that was already filled with most of the thousand-ish dragons who called Owain king.

They entered the amphitheater and set her chair down with a small *thump* beside Owain. He and Jiang sat on thrones overlooking the sand. Owain inclined his head. "Lady Seeress. Your light illuminates."

Seren gathered her strength to speak. "My presence...does not make...whatever you're about to do...acceptable."

Beside him, Jiang snorted and tossed her head. The golden charms dangling from her bun flashed in the artificial light of the white fireballs that hung high overhead, brightening the room. "The people don't know that. Good luck getting enough breath to tell them."

Seren opened her mouth to offer what retort she could, then caught sight of the figure behind the thrones. "Kai!"

Her brother's mate appeared nearly the same, if pale—small and athletically slender with black hair that fell down her back in waves, sea-green eyes turned to the ground, a smattering of freckles across her nose.

Then Kai lifted her eyes to meet Seren's, and the Seeress bit back a sound of dismay. Those eyes were so empty. She wondered if anything was the same at all.

Seren dropped her gaze. It was a good thing Rhys and Kai had opened to each other through their heartswearing bond a few weeks before. Without it, even if they were rescued, Seren had the sense that no one would be able to reach deep enough to find the place Kai had hidden herself.

CHAPTER 5

KAI

S eren looked awful, Kai thought. Like a wasted shadow of her former smiling, kind self. Her red-gold hair might be damp from a bath, and her clothes might be immaculate, but that didn't hide the half circles beneath her eyes, dark as bruises. Worse, it couldn't hide their haunted look. Rhys would not be pleased.

Despite waiting nearly an hour for Owain to arrange whatever he was going to do to the dragons who'd tried to help her, there had been nothing but radio silence from Rhys since Kai had left her rooms. Was he packing up his army? Would he leave her? Would he leave her and Seren both?

Kai steeled herself. She *wanted* him to leave her. That meant he would be safe. She felt for Seren, but Owain wouldn't outright kill *her*.

No matter what happened, Rhys had to be safe.

"Come up here, Kai," Jiang said.

Kai hesitated, which earned her a prod from Kavar, who stood guard behind the thrones. She went before the carved stone seats and dropped to her knees. Kai might have found a way not to break, but that didn't mean she invited pain. And as much as she loathed bowing to Jiang, not bowing meant a public whipping.

Three of those had been enough.

"They're coming." Jiang's voice was smug. "Turn around so you can see."

Kai turned, still on her knees, but refused to look at the arena. The platform with Jiang's and Owain's thrones perched directly in front of the risers in which a thousand other dragons were seated, about eight feet above the black sand. High enough to ensure they wouldn't miss one second of the bloody action below.

Owain was fond of gladiatorial competition. Not to the death or anything. Like he'd said, he wanted his soldiers to be alive for war with the humans. But he thought that violent combat *nearly* to the death was the best training any of them could get.

Owain rose and pulled Kai to her feet. "Come. Let the traitors see who they're dying for. Give them that, at least."

At last, Kai couldn't help but look. Four guards restrained a man and a woman right below the platform. The captives, an average-looking pair who would've been in their forties if they were human, were both struggling and pleading in Welsh, which Kai could identify, but not understand without Rhys to translate. Because of the Welsh, she assumed they were Clan Draig. She couldn't see their indicia well enough to tell which of the four elements they commanded.

Owain growled something at the male captive, also in Welsh.

Desperate to be anywhere else, Kai let her thoughts wander. For all it was endangered in the human world, Welsh was the lingua franca of dragons. Probably because both of their kings spoke it. Kai remembered Ffion telling her once that each clan of dragons had ruled throughout their history. In a detached way, she wondered if that meant the language they used changed based on who the ruling clan was.

The man and woman cried out, derailing Kai's determinedly distracted train of thought. Owain spoke again, cutting them off. The arena went utterly silent. Dragons sat on the edges of their seats.

The looks on their faces raised the hair on the back of Kai's neck.

Owain smiled, then spoke. "DEWCH YN DDRAIG A LLADD EICH GWR."

Though Kai couldn't understand his words, they carried a power that resonated through her bones and into her head.

He'd used the mantle.

A collective intake of breath from the crowd. The male captive dragon went bone-white. The woman let out a horrible cry.

Owain gestured at the guards, and they released the two captives then ran for the seating area of the amphitheater.

That didn't bode well. *Rhys?*

It took him a second, but he answered. *I'm here.*

She replayed the memory, focusing on Owain's words. *What did he say? What can I do to help them?*

Rhys "watched" the memory. Disgust and sorrow seeped through the bond. *There's nothing you can do.*

But what did he say?

The man and woman were staring at each other now. The woman was shaking. The man had stepped back from her. She clenched and unclenched her fists. Kai could actually see sweat dripping down her face. Whatever Owain had commanded the woman to do, she was resisting with all her strength.

He told her to become a dragon...and then kill her mate.

35

Kai's hand flew to her mouth. The ever-present chains around her fingers bit into her lips.

Owain sat on his throne. "Now, Wingless, sit and watch what happens to those who try to help you."

Kai ignored him, frozen at the edge of the platform. He hadn't bothered to try using the mantle on her since bringing her to Cadarnle. As Wingless and not a true dragon, it had no effect on her.

Kai. Rhys again. *There's nothing you can do. He's going to die.*

Vivid as life, an image flashed through her brain. Rhys, struggling out there on the arena floor.

Rhys, forced to kneel in front of Owain. Rhys, his blood seeping into the black sand as Owain killed him.

The image knocked the wind out of her. For an instant, she let herself feel the pain of it. *Rhys, I'm asking you again. Go back to Eryri. Please.*

Kai—

The sand around the female dragon rippled. She fought the transformation, but power collected around her in a crackling storm.

Two guards stood directly below Kai. Each man had a dagger in a sheath at his belt. She wasn't the best fighter—not compared to a dragon who had been training a thousand years or more—but she would have surprise on her side. She might be able to grab a dagger.

Too bad she'd never be able to get to Owain with it. It would take too long to climb back to the platform. If she went for the prisoners instead...

She couldn't save them from death, but she could prevent the atrocity Owain had engineered because of her.

Kai stood, ready to leap. She didn't make it. Owain—closer

than she'd realized—snatched her by the neck of her shirt and yanked her back. "What do you think—?"

A roar ripped through the amphitheater. Without warning, the female transformed. In place of a chubby, middle-aged woman, there curled a gorgeous dragon with mirrorlike scales and transparent wings.

An air Draig. Just like Ffion.

Just like the dragon who had tortured Kai that morning.

The man still knelt on the ground. The sand whirled around him in tiny black dust devils raised by a wind that wasn't there. He shouted something at the female, tears in his eyes.

She lunged, snapping jaws over unresisting flesh. Blood sprayed between her teeth. Bones crunched like breaking celery.

Dead.

Just like that.

The female dragon, released from the command of the mantle, opened her jaws and made gagging sounds. She shrank back from the shredded body of her mate. With a keening wail, she lunged at Owain—and straight at Kai.

Owain let go, and Kai leaped from the platform. The dragon's claws whistled by her ear, and she rolled as her body hit the sand. Owain lifted his hand and blasted the female dragon with magic so soul-chillingly cold that even Kai—despite the distance and her fire magic—could feel it. The female shrieked and jolted away from the icy magic, and Kai had to roll again as the dragon fell to one side, thrashing.

Owain had frozen one entire side of her chest. *Rhys!* Kai's internal voice shook.

Stay back. It will be over soon. He encircled her again, and this time she let him, imagining the warmth was his arms.

Pretending for a heartbeat that he was there. That he could truly keep her safe. It was her new favorite fantasy.

The female writhed on the ground. Owain was still spraying her with cold from the platform. Frost clouded her silver scales, unfurling like ferns up her neck and down toward her heart. A slow, cruel death.

It wasn't right.

As she had the night she'd saved Rhys from being killed by Kavar, Kai was moving before she realized it. She jumped over the wildly whipping silver tail and charged for the guards below the platform. Now that the female had become a dragon, stabbing her with a dagger would be like poking her with a needle.

Good thing the guards also held spears.

The guard on the end didn't see Kai until it was too late. She snatched the spear from his loosened hand and pivoted, sprinting for the dragon. Timing her jump, she landed on the female's head, grabbing a horn to keep from being thrown. Between beatings and not eating for a few days, Kai was weak. When the adrenaline wore off, she was going to feel this.

But as soon as the dragon caught sight of the spear in Kai's hand, she went still. *Please,* she whispered.

Kai had an instant of uncertainty—she had killed twice before, but only in self-defense.

This felt more important, even than saving her own life.

"*Stop!*" Owain howled. "She *will* suffer!"

But in this, Owain could not touch her.

Kai plunged the spear through the female's eye with a nauseating *pop*. The silver dragon drew breath, as if to scream again. Then the spear sank deep, deep into the soft tissue of the brain.

She went limp, as dead as her mate.

Kai's hands shook. Her feet were damp with the fluid that

oozed from the dragon's eye. She fell from the huge silver head and landed crouched in the sand, steadying herself with one hand before slowly rising again.

A blow knocked her sprawling onto her side. Stars burst in front of her eyes. Owain had jumped down from the platform and loomed over her, breathing heavily. Kai could hear Rhys in her head and realized he'd been shouting at her the whole time, telling her not to do it, to keep herself safe.

She didn't care. She'd done the right thing. Besides, what was Owain going to do? Kill her?

Owain kicked her in the ribs. Kai heard a *crack* and yelped like a whipped dog. She held up a hand toward Owain. She wanted to tell him to stop, but she couldn't breathe. One of her ribs was broken.

By now, she knew the feeling well enough.

It will pass. It will pass, she chanted to herself as her vision went black around the edges. The door closed over her fear shuddered, and all her drowning emotions threatened to escape. Here was pain. Always pain.

Owain drew back his foot again, and Kai closed her eyes, bracing herself. This was the first time Owain himself had struck her, but even if she could run, that would only make it worse.

The expected kick never came. Kai opened her eyes. Owain stood over her, clenching his fists, nostrils flaring. After a long moment, his neutral mask snapped back into place. He reached down and hauled Kai to her feet. Her broken rib shifted and she cried out, but bit off the sound. Maybe too literally, because her tongue started to bleed.

"When I am punishing someone, you do not interfere," Owain hissed.

Still reeling, half out of her mind with pain, Kai gasped, "After tomorrow it won't be a problem."

Owain nodded, as if that was just so. He shouted something in Welsh to the dragons in the audience—dragons who were staring, every single one of them, at Kai. Then he dragged her toward the stairs that led out of the amphitheater.

Kai nearly passed out from the agony of the forced march, but pride burned hot inside her.

The white dragon might kill her tomorrow, but at least she hadn't gone down without a fight.

CHAPTER 6

ASHEM

A shem scowled at the snow that covered everything in a cold, wet blanket: the tents, the ground, the trees. Even from the sky it stretched as far as he could see, from the valley where Rhys's army was camped all the way to the low mountain peaks nearly invisible against the star-flecked horizon.

He landed just outside the camp and called the change, diminishing into his human form. The fog of darkness around him dissipated and left him ankle-deep in melting white fluff. Not for the first time, he was grateful that the clothes he'd been wearing as a human reappeared when he shifted forms. There weren't many things that could make his mood worse, but being naked in the snow would have been one of them.

Ashem? Juliet prodded his mind, sending a spiderweb of cracks through the careful avoidance he'd attempted to cultivate. She'd arrived at the northern camp with Morwenna while he'd been scouting the best route for the army to take. Once Owain had revealed that he knew about the army, Ashem's mission had become to locate Owain's scouts. It had taken him longer than it should have.

Rhys had filled him in on the new plan—Juliet's plan—when Ashem stopped to rest. He hadn't been surprised to find out she suggested it. Only at how his own mate could come up with a plot made entirely of all his worst fears.

Juliet brushed his mind again, but Ashem didn't respond, only slogged into the camp, which was as busy as a kicked anthill, and toward his tent. They hadn't seen each other since Ashem left Eryri two weeks before to investigate whatever Owain was doing in the Taklamakan Desert, but he'd see her soon enough. Sunder him if he knew what he was going to say. Do. He'd forgiven her for kissing Kavar. What she'd done after that...he didn't know if he could.

Not that he would have done any differently, had the situation been reversed. Love made him a hypocrite.

Ashem kicked up bursts of powdery snow as he approached his tent, trying to force his thoughts in line, focus on the tasks he needed to finish before—

"Ashem?" A chill breeze wafted past, bringing with it the scent of chamomile.

He went rigid. Reminded himself he hadn't forgiven her. He lifted his gaze, a steely voice prepared. He would be curt. Cold. If she saw the anger, she would not see the hurt. The fear.

Juliet stood just inside his tent—one of the only ones still standing—and held open the flap. She was bundled in pink and blue, her short, pale hair poking out from beneath her sensible hat.

So herself. Familiar. Beloved.

Despite his intention to be hard, his voice came out a choked whisper. "Juliet." He closed his mouth and mind over the words that tried to follow. *Why? Why did you set Kavar free from Rhys's dungeons? Why did you promise yourself to him?*

He knew why.

She'd been so desperate to help Kai. That, he could under-stand. Kai was Rhys's heartsworn—she was necessary both so Rhys could function and for the continuation of his bloodline. More importantly, he reminded himself, Kai was Juliet's best friend.

Owain trusted Kavar. His brother was in a unique position to help bring Kai home. Freeing him should have been enough to guarantee his cooperation. But nothing was ever enough for Kavar—he'd had a price.

Juliet.

She'd agreed to live with Kavar for six months of each year. When Rhys had seen Seren's vision of their army winning the battle, Ashem had been relieved beyond words. He'd assumed that meant they'd never pay Kavar's price.

Now they would have to.

An uncertain smile crooked one corner of her mouth and she clasped gloved hands in front of her. He was surprised she still wore them, since magic provided by fire Draig kept the air inside the tents comfortably warm. "I missed you."

Ashem was unable to fight a surge of bitterness. Beyond heartsworn, he and Juliet were *pledged*. He belonged to her completely, but she no longer belonged only to him.

Juliet made a disgusted sound. "Really? This is what we're going to do? I haven't seen you for weeks and you're giving me the silent treatment?"

Though the speech had begun indignant, Juli's voice wavered toward tears at the end. She marched up and stood so close he couldn't move without touching her. "I told you I was sorry."

"Apologies change nothing that has been done." He inhaled her scent on the frozen air and resisted the urge to gather her soft, intoxicatingly beautiful body into his arms, to hold her against him, kiss her until the rest of the world dissolved into insignificance. He wanted to hold her and forget. He'd resolved not to break things with her the way he and Kavar had broken. Why could he not just take her in his arms? Tell her he loved her?

She made a frustrated sound. "What do you want from me, Ashem?"

He opened his mouth to speak, but could not find the right words. What was it about love and the pain of losing it—or thinking he might—that twisted him up until the only thing that could comfort him was the person who had hurt him to begin with? He'd vowed never to feel that way again, after Kavar.

And yet, here he was.

Juliet's full mouth—Ancients, that mouth—turned down in a frown. "I know you're angry, but Kavar is Kai's only hope."

"Don't think for one second you'll get him to betray Owain. Not unless you are prepared to give far more than you've agreed." At his tone, the dragons nearest them suddenly decided they had somewhere else to be.

"That's what you're worried about?" Her arms went around his middle, and he tensed. Juliet closed the distance between them. When she leaned her head against his shoulder, his arms pulled her close without his brain's consent. Closer, until she was tight against him, bodies hard against each other, his cheek rested against the top of her head, and his heart was trying to wing its way out of his chest.

"I'm not going to give Kavar the things I've promised only to give to you. Even he isn't awful enough to expect me to sleep with him."

"You don't know my brother."

She snorted, puffing steam into the air. "I believe we're fairly well acquainted. Consider that maybe you're the one who doesn't know him. It's been a thousand years since you were close. Kavar and I don't speak often, but when we do... He's not happy with Owain. He says that he is. He thinks that he is, but he hasn't forgotten that Owain basically gave him up to Rhys to boost Jiang's credibility in Rhys's court. Owain didn't *know* Rhys wouldn't kill Kavar when he was captured—he might even have expected Rhys to. Owain betrayed him, and Kavar knows that. If you want to win your brother back, now is the time."

Ashem stepped away and stared down at her. Then he shook his head and strode into the tent.

She followed. "Don't you look at me like I'm crazy. He's your brother. And the only other Azhdahā left in the world. You should be on the same side."

"Don't come on the mission tonight."

The words tore from him, and they both froze. Juliet came to stand before him. "My deal with Kavar doesn't begin tonight."

Ashem hadn't meant to speak, but he couldn't call the words back, so he might as well keep going. He cupped her face in his hands and tried—almost successfully—to keep his voice steady. "He will try to keep you."

Instead of answering, Juliet pushed him gently backward toward his cot. He didn't resist. When it hit the back of his knees, he sat. She tugged off her gloves and tossed them on the floor. "About tonight. I have an idea, and you..." She sighed. "You are *really* not going to like it."

"*Juliet*—"

She cut him off with a kiss. Despite everything, his hands went to her waist and he yanked her down onto his lap. Her mouth was warm, pliable, eager. She had her coat off in the next second, then his. Then her hands were sliding across his bare chest and he'd missed her so badly...

Damn him, she never would've been able to fog his brain

like this if it hadn't been so long since he'd seen her. He'd never been so easy to manipulate before. He tried to read her mind, first through the heartswearing bond, then with Azhdahā magic. The first she clouded. The second, she easily blocked. Since becoming heartsworn to both him and Kavar, her power had increased exponentially. She was, perhaps, the strongest magic user in the world. At least until the mantle was healed.

"Juliet," he said, holding her back when she tried to kiss him again. "What idea am I not going to like? I already know about your idea to get into Cadarnle."

"No, this isn't that." She sighed. "How long until we leave?"

He calculated the time. "Half an hour."

She slid her fingers into his hair. "Then let me tell you in twenty-nine minutes."

The last of his anger broke. If he knew her—and he did—he could guess what she wanted to do.

That meant this twenty-nine minutes might be all he had of her for a long time.

Letting go, he opened his mind. Hers rushed in to meet him, and then for a while, there were no more words. He stripped her slowly, marveling how the cold air pebbled her skin everywhere before she had him undressed as well. Then she was beneath him, his skin warming hers as he kissed and stroked her, as her nails dug into his back, leaving scratches that he welcomed. Any mark, any token to remind him she was his.

She wrapped her legs around him, opening for him. He slid inside her, and it was like coming home. She was the only thing that made him feel whole.

They moved together, pressure building at the base of his spine as she arched and gasped beneath him. Flawless. His own personal goddess. Their minds clung to each other, and Ashem reveled in their pleasure, lost himself to it until they were both breaking and muffling their cries against each other.

When they were finished and had caught their breath, he shifted them so that he was on his back and she lay on his chest. She snuggled into him, and he stroked her back, and raged at the future he could not control.

"Ashem..." She pulled back from him, sensing his anger, even though she had to know it wasn't directed at her.

He'd lost Kavar because they were both too stubborn to stop driving each other away. He couldn't lose Juliet, too.

I love you, jāné del-am, he whispered into her mind. *When you're with him, don't forget.*

I love you too. She tipped her face up and kissed him, and her cheeks were wet with tears. *No matter who is in my mind, my heart will always belong to you.*

CHAPTER 7

RHYS

Rhys's breath misted in front of him as he surveyed his team, all of whom huddled a few dozen yards from the perimeter of the camp. He couldn't take many. Owain's scouts were watching, and no one could be missed.

Ashem, Cadoc, Morwenna, me, Juli. Four dragons and one super-powered Wingless.

His eyes swept the line again. He kept expecting to see Deryn. Going into a fight without her made him feel as if he was missing a talon, but it couldn't be helped. When this was over, he would be glad to see her again.

Kai was sleeping off the aftermath of her actions in the amphitheater. She and Seren had been Owain's prisoners for thirteen days. Thirteen days of torture. Of Rhys waking in the middle of the night to her screaming in his head. Thirteen days of sick helplessness. Of no sleep. Of Kai drifting further away from him the more she was hurt.

No more.

He had never hated Owain before. He'd never truly

wanted him to suffer. Now he would gladly peel off those white scales one by one and watch his cousin bleed out in the snow.

"You're clear on the plan?" Rhys asked, keeping his voice low.

They responded that they were. Snow crunched beneath booted feet, and a girl approached from the direction of the tents. Until two weeks ago, Tharah—a Wonambi female barely out of her juvenile years—had been a rogue who followed his murderous mother. Before Mair had fallen, Tharah had switched sides.

Not for him though, Rhys thought as Tharah smiled at Cadoc. She gave the black-haired bard—former bard—a sharp nod. "The Wonambi are ready with the illusions."

Cadoc's eyes shot to Rhys, and he inclined his head. Cadoc said, "Give them the signal." Tharah turned and wove away through the tents.

Watching Cadoc, it occurred to Rhys to wonder, not for the first time, why the curse that made Cadoc lose his mind and fly into a murderous rage every time he saw Rhys had broken. They had Cadoc back, and Rhys was glad for it, but no one could explain why. When they returned to Eryri, he would have to consult with Citlali, a Quetzal councilwoman who was an expert in blood magic.

A dragon roared, and Rhys had a dizzying moment of dissonance because the roar sounded exactly like his own. It was supposed to. The Wonambi—a clan of illusion-casting dragons native to Australia—were very good at what they did.

At the center of the camp, Rhys—or the dragon enchanted to look and sound like him—roared again, threatening to demolish the few standing tents, and dripping flame from his open jaws. Dragons began to transform all around him in a circle, as if to cage the raging king.

Now, Ashem said into all of their minds.

Juli's eyes went wide and unfocused—a sign that she had cast a barrier around Rhys and his companions. Any eyes that might look for them would slide away, rendering them effectively invisible.

The battle in the camp intensified as a dragon enchanted to look like Ashem appeared, trying to reason with the false Rhys. The true Rhys transformed, reaching for the fire that burned along the outer edges of his being. His mind expanded, his perceptions refining and shifting.

He became the dragon.

You ready, boyo? Cadoc stood next to Ashem, his maimed front foot curled into his lean red-orange body. On his other side, Morwenna lashed her tail back and forth, clearing a swath of snow. Her scales were red, but in the night she looked nearly as black as Ashem.

Let's move out before the show stops. Ashem's eyes glinted gold in the cold light of the northern stars. Rhys couldn't see Juli's barrier, but the dragons huddled close together to make sure they stayed inside. Behind him, the false Rhys leaped into the sky and tried to fly toward Cadarnle, only to be pulled down again by half a dozen others.

Rhys helped Juli—who was so bundled in cold-weather gear she could hardly move—pull a flying harness over Ashem. It took her a few minutes to buckle the leather straps with gloves on. By the time she was finished, Rhys was ready to change back into a man and do it himself.

Kai. He was going to get Kai. The thought stung his bones like the bite of a thousand ants. He was going to wake up from the dream of Kai in his head and be with her again. They were so close. The imaginary ants surged beneath his skin until his scales crawled with need to get into the air and make that moment *now*.

Juli climbed up Ashem's side and settled in the saddle,

pulling down her flying mask. The stylized lioness face suited her. Rhys had Kai's white raven mask and another harness in a bag that he strapped around one wrist. Cadoc carried an empty harness as well. None of them expected Seren to be capable of flying, after what Kai had communicated.

Juli ran her gloved hand over Ashem's scales. *Let's bring them home.*

Ashem unfurled his night-black wings and leaped into the sky with a spray of snow. Rhys and the others followed, forming a truncated V. If the weather held, they would arrive at Cadarnle in three hours.

If he hadn't betrayed them, Kavar would be waiting.

Back in the camp, Rhys's army would continue the illusion that the Council was forcibly dragging Rhys back to Eryri, an idea they'd given him when they threatened to do it for real. They'd subdue the dragon playing Rhys, then break camp and head for the South Pacific. If things played out how they should, Owain's scouts would report that Rhys had abandoned Kai. Owain would relax his guard.

And Rhys would be in Cadarnle.

If, instead, Owain was waiting for them because Seren had foreseen this as well, Rhys would give himself up in exchange for Kai and his friends' lives. He would die, and Deryn would inherit his half of the mantle. She and Kai could carry on the war. Win.

Though if Rhys had a choice, he'd prefer to live and enjoy his life with his mate and his family for a long, long time.

CHAPTER 8
KAI

Owain had thrown Kai into her rooms without a word and slammed the door, drowning her in blackness. Twenty minutes later, she still couldn't move.

Rhys sighed into her mind, considerably calmer than he had been the last time they'd spoken. *You should have left them alone.*

Kai concentrated on breathing. It hurt so much. *You would've done the same.*

A pause, then, *Yes.* Then love. So much love it threatened her control.

He was doing something, but he wasn't letting her see what it was. In fact, he'd been doing things since Owain broke the news that he knew about Rhys's army. Rhys, for whatever reason, was hiding it from her.

Might he actually leave?

What are you doing? she asked.

I think you know.

She hated when he was cryptic. Being in each other's minds was wearing, at times, because of the lack of privacy. But it by no means meant she knew every single thing he was think-ing. *Rhys, it's all right if you're leaving. Just...tell me. So I can mentally prepare.*

How did a person prepare for death? Kai closed her eyes and pressed her forehead to the cool stone floor. She didn't want to die, she wanted to see Rhys again. The sun. Her family.

The thoughts pained her. So she shut them away. She was ice. She was stone.

I am not leaving you. He was frustrated. *Ancients, Kai, how could you even think it? You would never leave me if things were reversed. I'm on my way.*

He couldn't mean it. Owain knew he was coming. If he attacked with his army, she would die anyway. There was no way to win.

She tried to make her own mental voice hard and cold, but it wavered. *I would. Go home, you stupid lizard. You have to save the world.* Replaying the scene in the arena and unable to help herself, she added, *I can't watch you die.*

Cadarnle was crawling with guards and magic security. Not to mention that even if he did get to her, she had the thing in her neck that would detonate if she left her rooms without Owain. It would have to be cut out, and the thought made her want to cry.

More pain.

He didn't even have the decency to be angry. *You forget,* cariad, *without you, I'm not worth much.*

Kai snorted, then winced at the lance of pain through her torso. Among dragons, only heartsworn pairs could have chil-dren. That meant without her, Rhys couldn't have an heir, leaving him with no one to pass the mantle to. Some of the Council—some morons like Powell—might say that he wasn't worth much without her.

You are worth everything.

He didn't respond with words, only love.

Kai couldn't breathe right or move without jarring her ribs, so she lay on the floor where she'd fallen, arranging herself as comfortably as she could. Time passed in fits and starts—she wasn't sure how long. Rhys didn't say much, but he stayed with her.

Even if he went to Eryri, she knew he would stay with her until the end. How many hours until it came? Seven? Eight?

The door opened. Kai tensed, wondering if she'd severely overestimated her remaining time. The wall fires that dragons used to light their caves flared to life all around, illuminating the craggy face of Patli, the old woman who tended Kai's wounds. Not Owain or Kavar.

Not quite time to die.

Patli tutted at the sight of Kai on the floor. "You must stop making him angry."

Kai groaned. "I couldn't just stand there."

The old woman tutted again and bent to help Kai to her feet. "This is going to hurt."

Kai inhaled sharply through her teeth as the Quetzal woman helped her to bed. "Thanks," Kai said when she was settled, her voice high and weak.

Patli made a shushing noise and muttered something in the Nahuatl language the Quetzals spoke, then pushed up Kai's shirt.

The skin over her ribs had bloomed into a spectacular display of bruises—a sight made even more impressive because Owain had kicked her across her indicium. The colorless scale pattern that swirled over the left side of her torso made the dark purple-and-blue of the bruise shimmer like diseased flames.

Patli pushed Kai's head back onto the pillow, and Kai didn't resist. The woman went to work assessing the extent of Kai's injuries, muttering again.

"How is Seren?" Kai asked.

Patli sighed. "I try to get her to eat, to drink, but she keeps nothing down. Owain allows the man in charge of her to dose her with that potion so she is always having visions. It's made of diluted Azhdahā venom. It kills her a little each day."

Kai pressed her lips together. Of course Owain would be stupid enough to kill the Seeress in trying to get visions out of her. Poor Seren.

Patli continued, "After your show in the arena, Owain let the idiot in charge give her a double dose. Wants visions delivered to him as they come to make sure none of them have to do with Rhys coming for him before you die. She'll be useless for days."

Kai hated herself for still wanting Rhys to stay away, even if it meant Seren suffered longer. "How can you follow him? He made a heartsworn dragon murder her mate! You're heartsworn. Can you imagine?" Kai's throat closed, once again seeing Rhys in her mind's eye, ruby scales grayed and lifeless against the black sand. Maybe it was a good thing he was so distracted.

"Owain was a good boy," Patli said quietly. "For a long time, he was a good king. His mother was the best queen our people have in living memory. Ayen lied and manipulated his way into the crown. It is Owain's by right."

Kai had never understood monarchy. Just because a parent was good at something didn't mean the child would be. Owain was a perfect example. According to Rhys, Owain had spent his younger years obsessed with dark magic, which led him to murder a handful of dragons in the name of magical discovery.

Heartbroken and unable to stand the thought of putting a murderer on the throne, Owain's mother, Rigani, had gathered a coalition of the greatest dragon magic users alive. They had found a way to change the magic of the mantle so instead of going to Rigani's closest blood relative, Owain, it went to her brother Ayen.

Rhys's father.

Rigani had meant to break the news to Owain, but before she could, she'd died—killed by humans.

The mantle went to Ayen, who took his place as king.

Unbeknownst to Ayen, however, Owain had retained a small part of the mantle. With the help of the mate Ayen had mistreated—Rhys's mother, Mair—Owain used that bit of power to sunder Ayen's heartswearing.

Then he'd attacked.

In agony from the sundering, Ayen hadn't been able to defend himself. He'd died, and in murdering him, Owain gained a full half of the power of the mantle. The other half had gone to Rhys, who barely escaped Owain's attack with his life. If Owain could kill Rhys and Deryn, he would be able to bend every dragon on Earth to his will.

For Owain, that meant war against all of humankind.

Kai stifled a cough. "So you'll let a monster control you because he's got the right mother?"

Patli took out an obsidian knife and made a precise, stinging cut on the inside of Kai's elbow.

"Ayen was not a good king. He did not rule better than Owain. But I think, and some of my people begin to think, that his son—however he came to power—might be the better option."

Kai's eyes widened. "You'd support Rhys?"

"No. Owain's way will save our people. Without him, the humans will overrun us, and there won't be any dragons left. It is harsh, but right."

Though her voice was gentle, her words were like Owain's boot to Kai's ribs all over again.

Patli held her hand above the cut on Kai's arm and made a

grasp-and-pull motion. Blood welled up from the cut, and Patli gathered it in her hand. As if they were coated in oil, the drops rolled along her skin without sticking. She brought her cupped palm close to her lips and chanted. Then she smeared the blood along Kai's ribs.

The relief was immediate. Not all of the pain was gone, but Patli's blood magic—the same kind of magic that a different Quetzal had used to place a horrible curse on Cadoc—eased the ache.

Kai took a breath, and instead of the shallow wheezing she'd managed since Owain kicked her, she inhaled deeply with only a twinge. "Thank you. Again."

Patli nodded. The old woman wouldn't help her escape— Kai had already begged—but she had never been cruel. In another world, under different circumstances, Kai could have liked Patli.

Patli touched Kai's cheek. "I cannot save you, but as you did for the woman in the arena, I hope I've eased your suffer- ing. Take this." She pressed a capsule into Kai's hand. "Naga venom. It will ease your passage into sleep and prevent dreams. If it were my last night on Earth, I would take it."

Then the old woman was gone, taking light and hope with her. She reached across the bond. *Rhys?*

He answered with a sense of questioning.

Promise me something.

A sense of wariness. *What would you like me to promise?*

Don't let Owain win. I can't imagine— she swallowed. *He can't be allowed to have the whole mantle. The things he does already... The things he would do with more power... And people still follow him. People who should know better. Promise you won't make it easier for him just to save me.*

Silence. Then, *I swear it.*

I love you. She wouldn't tell him not to come or ask him if he was leaving. Rhys would do what he thought was best, like he always did.

I love you too.

Kai tipped the capsule into her mouth and swallowed. Patli had given her Naga venom before. It didn't last long—only a couple of hours—and temporary oblivion was the absolute best way Kai could think of to pass her time until either Rhys came for her, or death.

CHAPTER 9

RHYS

R hys soared through crystal air, suspended between snow
and stars. All was silent except for the rush of wind and
the leathery snap of wings. The cold was the greatest challenge.
He, Cadoc, and Morwenna were fine—the magic that allowed
them to manipulate heat also prevented them from feeling all
but the most extreme temperatures.

Juli and Ashem were a different story. Rhys had been able
to set up a spell that hovered around Ashem, warming the air.
He'd had to do it as a man—Draig weren't able to use their
magic in dragon form, only their breath weapons—so he hoped
it would hold. Juli had the most advanced arctic gear money
could buy, but winter here was no easy thing to survive, even
for dragons.

They flew across hundreds of miles of tundra and icy sea to
the island northeast of Greenland where Owain had made his
home. As they approached, Juli cast another barrier. It was a tricky
thing to do with multiple moving targets, but she managed. They
made it through two rings of sentries and landed outside one of the
less-used entrances into the underground stronghold. To Rhys,

Cadarnle looked like nothing more than a continuation of ice and snow, but Kavar had "shown" Juli where to go through their bond.

If there was a trap waiting for them here, it was already too late.

Juli slid from Ashem's back, and the dragons transformed. Human, they waded through the snow to the mouth of a cave cleverly hidden below a tumble of boulders. No one attacked. No nets fell from above. No magic halted them in their tracks.

Kavar was nowhere to be seen.

Morwenna clutched her sword. "Where is he?"

A derisive snort sounded from close by. Instinctively, Rhys called fire into his hands.

Kavar appeared to one side, no more than ten feet away. "He is under your nose. You Draig are the least subtle creatures on the planet."

Rhys was in no mood for posturing. "Are you here to help us or kill us, Kavar?"

"A bit of both, perhaps." Kavar shot Juli a furtive glance. She was watching him too.

Rhys glanced between them, then to Ashem, whose face was unreadable. He couldn't imagine how it was for Juli to be heartsworn to two people. She loved Ashem, but the magic compelled her and Kavar toward each other like magnets.

The feelings you have for Kai aren't real. They're lust and obsession and infatuation. Don't let the magic cloud your good sense.

Damn it. Why couldn't he get Morwenna's words out of his head?

"Stop," Ashem snarled.

Rhys looked up. Kavar had taken a step toward Juli.

Kavar's smile contorted. He was obviously straining to hold it in place. "You aren't my commander or my king, Ashem."

Ashem growled.

Juli said in a low but clear voice, "That's enough. Let's get Kai and finish this."

Kavar's stance relaxed. The tension between the two Azhdahā did not.

With one last silver-eyed glare at his brother, Kavar led them through the boulders to the entrance.

Ashem followed, then Juli and Cadoc. Rhys motioned to Morwenna, but she shook her head, gesturing for him to enter first. "I'll guard your back."

After stowing their bags in a crack in the boulders, Rhys and Morwenna slipped inside. The tunnel was a tight fit at first. The ceiling low and sides close. After a few paces, it opened into a wide, empty hall. Two unconscious guards lay just inside, one male and one female.

Rhys felt a grim satisfaction when he saw them. Kavar might still betray them, but this was a good sign.

Juli held up her hands, bringing them all to a halt. She closed her eyes, and Rhys guessed she was seeking any nearby minds.

Rhys had started to shift his weight from foot to foot when Juli opened her eyes. "There were a few people awake in this part of the stronghold. They're all sleeping now."

He suppressed a shiver. He didn't know how many minds Juli had just invaded, but from the stunned look on Kavar's face and the carefully blank expression on Ashem's, the power she used had been immense.

Kavar led them down several flights of stairs and through more halls. Rhys memorized what he could of their path, but wasn't confident he could find his way out on his own. Every now and then, Juli would have them pause as she ensured that everyone around them was asleep. After a while, Ashem bit off a curse and muttered that he would take the next minds they encountered.

"You have to be aware enough to fight," Juli said, sounding distracted.

"Why are we here, if not to lighten your burdens?" Kavar's voice dripped sarcasm.

He was right. This had been Juli's plan. Cadarnle was well guarded, but her power, with support from Ashem and Kavar, might be strong enough to let them walk the halls undetected long enough to save Kai and Seren.

Ashem scowled, and Kavar gave him a mocking smile in return. "I will take the next four minds we encounter. Ashem will take four as well. Few enough to defend ourselves, but perhaps it will lighten the load for our *lovely* Juliet."

Ashem bared his teeth, but didn't disagree.

They passed five more pairs of guards, some in front of doors, some patrolling the halls. Kavar made them pause at every intersection, checking thoroughly for anyone who might see them. He was also the one to make sure the guards they knocked out were completely asleep. Which made sense. If Owain suspected that Kavar had helped them, Rhys doubted that even a millennium-long friendship would save the Azhdahā's life.

Finally, when they were so deep beneath the earth that even Rhys could feel its weight looming overhead, Kavar stopped. Despite saying that he would only bespell as many people as he could handle, he and Ashem were both glassy-eyed with a fine sheen of sweat on their foreheads. "Her door is protected by two sets of guards who cannot be touched by Azhdahā magic. They wear a modified version of the stones you used to capture me." He shot a glare at Rhys.

Rhys glared back. His sense of Kai had grown until it was almost unbearable. *Mate. Heartsworn. Mine.* Close. So excruciatingly close. Sensing him, Kai stirred, her mind fighting off the last remnants of the drug she'd taken to sleep.

"Command them to leave," Rhys whispered to Kavar. If he didn't get to her *now* he was going to tear around the corner and murder anyone who stood in his way. He didn't care if it cost a river of blood. He clenched and unclenched his fists, feeling ants under his skin again.

Despite the strain on his face, Kavar snorted softly. "This is on you, puppet king. I got you inside. I've told you, I will not jeopardize my position with Owain."

Juli's voice was flat and distracted. "Take their charms. I can make them forget."

Ashem and Kavar stared at her. Ashem shook his head. "You're already stretched too thin. We're all almost at our breaking point."

Juli didn't look at them, her gaze fixed on some distant point. "I can make them forget," she repeated.

Kavar watched her for a long moment, then, without any warning, spun and strode into the hallway.

Rhys crouched low and peered around the corner. "Give me your amulets," Kavar barked.

The guards started. One raised his eyebrows. "It's the middle of the night. We're on duty. Why do you need them now?"

"There is a traitor." Kavar sounded shockingly like Ashem. "Have you forgotten what happened earlier today? You are guarding the most precious prisoner Owain has ever had, and he has commanded me to examine you. Do you think he cares about the time? Give me those stones. After I've looked inside your minds, I'll return them. Or I will kill you."

One by one, the guards gave up the onyx stones they had tied to their wrists.

Kavar pinched the charms between his fingers, disgust on

his face. As soon as the last of the four guards handed him her stone, they collapsed like birds shot from the sky.

Kavar twisted to stare straight at Juli. His mocking smile was gone. Ashem also glanced at Juli, then exchanged a look of mingled awe and concern with Kavar. He seemed to realize what he was doing, and schooled his face into a frown.

Rhys, Cadoc, and Morwenna darted around the corner. Ashem came more slowly, leading Juli by the hand. Rhys tried the heavy wooden door, but it was locked. He motioned for Kavar. His lip curled, the silver-eyed Azhdahā shot one more surreptitious glance at Juli before he pressed his palm against the door. It swung open. Rhys shouldered past Kavar and stepped inside.

Dim light shone in from the hall, but aside from that, the room was pitch black. He called a ball of golden fire, setting it just over his shoulder. It lit the room, casting a shimmering glow over a table, painted walls, a bed.

And Kai.

She lay stretched out on the mattress, pale and small, her face a white smudge beneath a spread of dark hair. He was next to her in an instant. He wanted to scoop her up, but held back. She'd been tortured for two weeks running. He'd felt her flinch away from the old Quetzal woman who healed her. He had to be cautious.

Fighting the overwhelming instinct to touch her, he took fistfuls of her blanket in shaking hands and gave her a small mental prod, whispering her name.

"Kai."

Her eyes shot open. As he'd thought she would, she shrank away and lifted her arms to cover her face. "No! Not again! Leave me alone!"

He noticed as she spoke the words that she slid a partial shield up between them, so smooth, so seemingly transparent that he might not have noticed. That he probably hadn't noticed. Several times.

She had been hiding the extent of her torture from him. How much?

"This is low, even for you." Her voice had taken on a harsh edge. Then it cracked and turned pleading. "Don't do this. Don't hurt me by looking like him."

Rhys would kill Owain, just to make sure he never saw that expression on Kai's face again.

CHAPTER 10
KAI

K ai, her brain muzzy from sleep, hid her face behind her hands so she wouldn't have to see him. This wasn't happening. Even Owain couldn't be so profoundly cruel.

"*Cariad*, it's me." His voice was that perfect, rich tenor she could only conjure in her dreams. She let her hands fall.

Rhys—Could it truly be him? Could there actually be an end to this hell?—dropped to his knees beside the bed. "I told you I wouldn't leave you. Let down your shields and let me prove it."

Kai dug her nails into her palms hard enough that a few of them punched through skin. If he wasn't here—if this wasn't Rhys...then Owain won. She would be well and truly broken.

But he knew her shields were up. Owain wouldn't have known that. She eased them down.

And there he was.

With a wordless cry, she threw herself forward, wrapping her arms around his neck. He lifted her from the bed as he stood, their minds intertwining, bodies slamming together, the contact exploding over skin, and sizzling through flesh and bone. Awareness of him surged through her like it hadn't since the moment they'd heartsworn.

His hands were on her face, in her hair, gripping her hips so he could press them closer still. Their lips collided, and he tasted so much sweeter than memory. To Kai, his thoughts were a muddle, cycling through how she was there. Alive. Warm. He actually had her in his arms. He'd been so afraid, so terribly afraid.

His fear raged through her like wildfire and met the morass of emotion churning through her head. It caught and blazed, scorching through her and charring the door that hid her horrors. Those horrors slammed against it from the other side, and she felt it give. Everything that had happened threatened to burst free in a choking, drowning tide.

She held on, fighting through it, running her fingers over the red stubble on his cheeks. Tears burned the backs of her eyes. She hid the near-broken girl she'd become. With him holding her, she could not escape the memory that she was supposed to have it together. Be a queen.

So she reassembled the door and put *everything* behind it. Fear, joy, immobilizing relief. She slid out of his arms and took a step back. When she spoke, her voice was steady. "You came."

Rhys closed the distance again and traced his thumb over her cheek. A furrow appeared between his brows. He scanned her up and down, searching for injury. His fingers, splayed over her back, ran over the indents between her ribs.

Only then did Kai realize how she must look. There was a mirror in the corner. She generally tried to avoid it, but she'd seen the reflection yesterday. Two weeks of torture-healing cycles and days of food deprivation had winnowed her down from athletic to fragile. Her eyes were sunken, hair lank— though she had bathed regularly. Heaven forbid she offend Owain's nose.

Heat prickled her cheeks. Maybe it was another twisted psychological aftereffect of the torture, but she wanted to apologize for not being the breezy, energetic woman she saw so clearly in his mind's eye.

"Don't." His arms tightened again and he kissed her, surrounding her with love. But hatred for Owain boiled just below the surface, frigid as liquid nitrogen, lining his peace with thorns.

A soft chuckle sounded behind Rhys. "Can you do that later? We still need to find Seren."

They ended the kiss, and Kai peered over Rhys's shoulder at Cadoc, his face cast in shadows from the ball of fire at his side. He grinned. "Good to see you, *brânwen*."

She grinned back. With Cadoc, smiling was as easy as ever. "It's good to see you too." She scanned the rest of the room. Ashem and Morwenna had taken up defensive posts next to the open door, keeping a lookout. Juli had come as well. And—

Kai recoiled at the sight of Kavar. He looked like a strategically tousled version of Ashem, with his shadow of a beard and shoulder-length black hair. Where Ashem was ramrod-straight and watchful, Kavar just leaned against the wall with his arms crossed, staring at Juli like a starving, waiting wolf.

"What is he doing here?"

"He let us in," Rhys murmured. "He brought us to you."

"Why...?" Kai frowned as her gaze fell on Juli. She didn't like her friend's vacant look. "Juli?"

Rhys cleared his throat. "She's keeping the dragons of Cadarnle asleep. Now that the heartswearing to Kavar has settled, she is...powerful."

"She is overwhelmed," Ashem said from close by the door. "We need to leave."

Rhys tried to shift them and Kai squeaked in pain. Startled, he loosened his hold, letting her slide to the ground. Kai winced. "Just bruises."

Cold hate burned through Rhys again. Kai flinched, narrowing their connection. She was barely hanging on to the pieces of herself—an emotional punch like that, even if it wasn't directed at her, was likely to send her over the edge.

Rhys went motionless. He inhaled. Then, slowly, he reached out.

He was so slow. So careful. Kai leaned into him again and gripped his forearms hard enough that the fine chains around her fingers dug into his skin. Too much emotion was overwhelming, but this—his arms around her, his solid frame towering over her, their minds tangled together—this was first time she'd felt safe in two weeks.

Except none of them were safe. Not until they got out of Cadarnle.

"Let's go, then," Rhys said, picking up on the thought.

He didn't have to ask her twice. Kai started for the door with the others, then remembered. "Wait."

They turned. Morwenna made an impatient noise.

Kai combed her hair away from the back of her neck with her fingers. Owain's device was still there. If she left the room, it would kill her. "This has to come out."

She didn't know what the scar looked like, but from Rhys's emotional reaction, it wasn't pretty.

He'd been "present" with her when Owain had sliced her skin and shoved the thing in. She'd questioned him after, but Rhys hadn't been sure what it was. Owain toyed with some aspects of magic that most sane dragons left alone.

Rhys hesitated, then unsheathed a short knife from his belt. His gaze went from the knife to Kai and back again. Worried, because taking the device out was going to hurt. If she connected him to the pain that was so close to shutting her down, would she be able to separate him from it?

Kai closed chained fingers over his hand. "You are the only one—" She faltered, her fingers tightening.

She wished it didn't have to hurt.

Rhys squeezed her fingers in return. "Cadoc."

The lanky bard gave him a questioning look. Rhys tilted his head toward Kai. "Hold her hands."

Cadoc raised his eyebrows, but moved in front of Kai without comment. A teasing smile lurked around his mouth. "The fair raven. We meet again." He had only one hand that worked, but it was almost large enough to swallow both of Kai's as she placed them on his palm.

Rhys sterilized the short blade by heating his fingers and running them slowly down the metal. He let it cool, then pulled Kai's hair farther out of the way, letting the strands run through his fingers.

Kai tensed. Thanks to Owain's torturers, she knew exactly how much being sliced open would hurt.

Rhys twined their minds tightly together and tensed to make the cut.

"So, Kai. How do you find Cadarnle? Not so hot, is it?" Cadoc grinned, wide and wicked.

She was so caught off guard by the awful joke and his "all hail my wit" expression that a bubble of laughter escaped her. She didn't noticed that Rhys had begun the cut until it was finished, blood spilling from a burning line down the back of her neck, just to the left of her spine.

Cadoc's hand tightened over hers when she jerked, and his voice gentled. "The first bit is done."

"The easy bit," Kai said through gritted teeth.

"Just keep your eyes on me. That's the easy part. I'm so handsome that my face overwhelms all perception of time."

Another little bubble of laughter. Then Rhys slid the dagger into the cut and levered one end of the device out as gently as he could. Careful as he was—and she could feel that he was trying—Kai couldn't hold in a quiet, high-pitched whimper of pain.

Rhys plucked the thing from her neck and tossed it onto the bed, a flat black rectangle that glimmered, wet with blood. "It's done."

Kai clung to Cadoc's hand. The cut still burned and she couldn't move her neck.

Ashem said, "Rhys. We *have* to move."

"I can only work so fast, Commander." Rhys reached into a small bag strapped to his thigh and pulled out cotton, disinfectant, and gauze. He cleaned and wrapped the wound as Cadoc kept up a steady stream of murmured nonsense.

Kai forced herself to breathe. To feel nothing. She was Wingless. It would heal soon enough.

When Rhys was finished, Kai released Cadoc. His fingers were white from the pressure of her grip. "Sorry."

He gave her a rueful smile and shook his fingers. "Who needs hands?"

Sorrow. Guilt. She still felt so much at fault for the way he'd lost use of his other hand. But there was no time for that—the longer they stayed in this room, the more vividly she could imagine Owain bursting in with his guards. More emotions to shove behind the door. More emptiness.

Rhys noticed. "Kai..."

She turned to face him. The pain in her neck was fading. Now that Rhys was here, she could think again. This couldn't just be a rescue.

This was an opportunity, and Rhys had to know it. Between Juli, Ashem, and Kavar they could move through Cadarnle unseen. *Rhys. What's your plan to kill Owain?*

Rhys's gaze flicked to Kavar, still staring at Juli like he was starving and she was a doe with a broken leg. It was off-putting.

She followed Rhys's thoughts. Killing Owain had not been part of the deal. Kavar would expose himself as a traitor before agreeing to it, and without him they'd never find their way through the maze that was Cadarnle.

We aren't. Not tonight.

Kai's eyes widened. "Are you kidding?" she mouthed. "We can't leave him alive. You're inside Cadarnle. You could end the war tonight, like you wanted." She shuddered. "Owain is warped. He's convinced that every sick thing he does is justified and he's so damned charismatic that he's got other people believing it too. You have to take him out."

Rhys glanced from Kavar back to her, obviously torn. *He let us in and led us to you. I swore to let Owain live. For tonight.*

Kai's nostrils flared. "There's honor and there's stupidity."

"Rhys." Cadoc's voice held an edge. "We've got to get Seren."

The words seemed to snap Kavar out of his reverie. His eyes narrowed. "The Seeress was not part of the deal."

Kai looked from Kavar to Rhys. Even if Seren hadn't been part of the deal, she'd have been part of the plan. Rhys would never leave his sister.

Cadoc's amethyst eyes luminesced. "She is now."

Kavar strode across the room, glaring at Rhys. "You get *her.*" He jabbed a finger at Kai. "Not the other one. Owain keeps the Seeress, or I wake the guards outside and you all die."

CHAPTER II

CADOC

C adoc shoved Kavar hard enough that the other man stumbled back. "Seren leaves with us, or I slide a knife between your ribs before you can squeak." Kavar was mad. As if Rhys would leave Seren behind. As if any of them would. Owain wouldn't kill her in revenge for Rhys taking Kai—not the invaluable Seeress—but he could still hurt her.

The biting fear that had threatened to eat him alive for two weeks was only natural concern for the Seeress, of course. Nothing more.

It couldn't be anything more.

"We should do it anyway," Morwenna said from beside the door, her eyes fixed on the hall outside. "We're here. We should kill him *and* Owain."

"She's right." Cadoc turned to Rhys, who regarded him with serious eyes. "We've got the chance. We can't let this war go on."

Rhys shook his head and opened his mouth to speak, but Kavar cut him off with a humorless laugh. "Of course. Though you'd have to kill me first. It shouldn't be too hard between all of you." His eyes fixed on Ashem. "Go ahead. It's your job."

Ashem frowned. Morwenna, however, turned from the hall and drew her sword. "If you insist."

"No." Ashem grabbed Morwenna's hand. "He's kept his promise. We will keep ours."

Without warning, Kavar collapsed. Shocked, Cadoc looked from his prone form to Juli, who still stared into the middle distance and swayed a little.

"He wouldn't have let us go," she said, her voice monotone and lifeless. "He wouldn't be persuaded. I know where she is. I—I can hold the minds he was holding for a few minutes."

Ashem did not look happy about that. Cadoc wondered how many minds she had under her control, and what the consequences would be if she took on one too many.

Stars grant they didn't find out.

Juli bent and pulled a flat, carved stone from Kavar's pocket. She held out her hand toward Rhys, gaze somewhere else entirely. "Unlock Kai's chains and follow me."

Rhys took the stone and pressed it to a matching indentation on each of Kai's cuffs and the collar around her neck. As soon as they were unlocked, Kai snatched them off and hurled them onto the bed next to the thing Rhys had pulled from her neck.

Rhys dropped the keystone onto Kavar's chest and took Kai's hand.

"The dragons of Cadarnle will wake soon. We've got to hurry." Juli glided from the room like a ghost, Ashem close behind.

The empty look in her eyes made Cadoc shiver. He made sure Rhys and Kai followed Ashem, then exchanged a glance with Morwenna and fell in behind.

Juli, with the golden lioness mask pushed up over her hair,

drifted through halls, descending stairs and turning corners until Cadoc was lost. She stumbled. Ashem caught her, but even from where he stood several feet away, Cadoc could tell that her hands shook. Sweat glistened on her face, and he caught Ashem's whisper. "You're doing too much, *jāné del-am*. Without Kavar—"

"I will do this." Her voice was still flat, but it had taken on an edge as hard as diamonds. Cadoc supposed he couldn't be surprised that the woman who bonded to Ashem would be one determined to do the impossible.

They descended tunnels and stairs until they had to be half a mile underground. Finally, they came to the end of a narrow hall, and Juli stopped and pointed to a door. "She's there. She's...sick."

The way she paused before the word *sick* made Cadoc grip the hilt of the dagger at his thigh.

"We don't have Kavar to unlock the door," Kai whispered.

"Ashem can do it," Juli said.

Cadoc glanced at the vee commander. "Will that work?" Ashem and Kavar were identical twins. It could be that whatever allowed Kavar to unlock the doors of Cadarnle would be fooled by the same genetics.

"There's one way to know." Ashem lifted one hand, the other clasping Juli's.

"Wait." Cadoc glanced down the eerily empty hall. There was no one else in sight, so he left Morwenna at the back and went to stand beside the door. Ashem and Rhys were so occupied with hovering over their mates that they hadn't even drawn their weapons. Cadoc slid his dagger from its sheath. "Might want to get yours out too, Chief."

Ashem's lips thinned and he let go of Juli's hand to draw his own dagger—short, broad and curved as opposed to the Draigs' long, needlelike blades. He eased Juli back and laid his hand against the door.

For a moment, nothing happened.

Then there was a *click*, and it swung open.

Cadoc pivoted around the corner. Instead of a room containing Seren, he found himself in a short hall, face-to-face with six fully conscious guards.

Cadoc swore and backed up a step, almost running into Rhys, who'd left Kai with Juli and drawn his daggers as well.

"Try not to kill them." Rhys sounded tired to his bones. "I've had enough death."

The guards charged. Cadoc leaned out of the way of the first one's blade and knocked him on the head. The guard fell back, stunned, and another took his place.

Fighting was never easy in cramped quarters. Cadoc took a slice right below his eye and kicked his attacker in the knee. Bone crunched. Cadoc grimaced. If he had to choose a least favorite part of hand-to-hand combat, it would be the sound of breaking bones.

Once they'd taken care of four of the guards, Morwenna squeezed in beside Rhys and Ashem. Seeing that their opponents were fully occupied, Cadoc darted past the fighting and through the archway that led to the spacious room beyond.

Where the rest of Cadarnle bordered on bitterly cold, this room held a damp heat. It amplified the cloyingly sweet smell someone had deployed to cover the stench of sickness. Cadoc had to swallow a gag as he took in his surroundings.

One wall was taken up by a huge fireplace filled with a roaring fire despite the early hour. The flickering light danced off gold-veined walls, which had been carved in bas-relief scenes of dragons in flight. One corner of the room was taken up by an enormous four-poster bed.

A scrawny old man cowered next to the bed. His gray hair

tufted around his ears, the same color as his nightshirt. "No, leave me alone! I only did what he told me to!"

Cadoc ignored him, strode to the bed and threw back the heavy golden curtains. The smell of sweat and sickness rolled out to greet him, but he hardly noticed.

"Seren." She lay on the bed with no veil, no gloves. Her red-gold hair was spread around her, but it was dull and lifeless. Her skin looked like wax.

For a horrifying moment, Cadoc thought she was dead. He leaned down to touch her wrist and check for a pulse, then caught himself.

He could not touch her.

Behind him, Ashem entered the room. The Azhdahā walked straight up to the cowering old man and touched a finger to his forehead. The man collapsed, asleep.

Ashem spared one bleak look for Seren before addressing Cadoc. "Juliet is losing her hold. If she slips, the backlash will damage her mind. We're going."

Rhys and Morwenna came in, and Cadoc saw Rhys's grin. "All alive." The smile faded as he caught sight of his sister. "Seren! Is she...?"

"I can't tell." Cadoc could barely get the words out. The world felt like it was falling in around him, folding into blackness piece by piece. His hands shook with the desire to touch her. To scoop her in his arms and cradle her against his chest and keep her fucking *safe*, because apparently no one else would.

But as an unheartsworn male, he was forbidden to make contact with Seren's skin. If he did, there was a risk she could heartswear to him. If a gold dragon became heartsworn, they lost the Sight.

Not ideal when there was only one gold dragon and they were in the midst of a war.

Rhys leaned over and picked up Seren's wrist. A pause, then, "She's alive. But her heartbeat is faint and erratic. We need to get her somewhere safe so we can stabilize her."

The world unfolded and Cadoc forced himself to move. Seren was alive. Everything would be all right. As long as she was alive, he could make it all right.

He helped Rhys use the heavy blankets from Seren's bed to wrap her in a cocoon, careful not to touch.

"Can you take her?" Rhys asked.

Pushing away his misgivings, Cadoc lifted Seren's limp body and cradled her to his chest like he'd imagined doing just a moment ago. Seren had never been a tiny woman—she was tall and strong and deliciously built. But now she was so light. Owain had only had her for two weeks, but damage had been done.

Even so, if Cadoc was honest with himself—something he generally tried to avoid—he savored her weight in his arms. Felt more at ease knowing he was the one who had her, because he knew exactly how much he'd give to protect her. Everything.

More fool him.

They filed back into the hall where Juli and Kai waited. Juli had turned nearly as gray and waxy as Seren, but straightened when she saw them. Ashem positioned himself in front with Juli. Cadoc walked just behind Ashem, carrying Seren. Behind him, Rhys put an arm around Kai's waist. Morwenna guarded the rear.

"Run," Ashem said through gritted teeth. "They're starting to stir." He swept Juli into his arms and, Cadoc assumed, getting his directions from Juli through their bond, dashed back the way they'd come.

Cadoc followed. They wound through corridors, climbing until his legs burned and even Seren's barely-there weight made it feel as if he'd tied boulders to his wrists and elbows.

Breath rasped in his lungs. Behind him, Kai stumbled, but picked herself up before Rhys could do what Ashem had done with Juli.

"I can't," Juli whispered as they neared the top. "There are so many. They're slippery. They want to wake up."

"Just a little farther, Jules," Kai panted.

Abruptly, Ashem stopped and swore, looking down at Juli. "Let them go. *Now.* Or both of us will have to deal with the consequences."

Juli let out a small sob. Nothing happened that Cadoc could see, but Ashem's face cleared. Then he started running again.

They burst out of the passage Kavar had brought them down, sprinting toward the two guards at the end of the tunnel, who, though Ashem had told Juli to let go, were still unconscious.

From down in the depths, Cadoc heard shouting.

CHAPTER 12

JULI

J uli panted, tears stinging her eyes. So many minds. She'd had them one moment, but when she'd let one go, they'd all slid through her fingers like water, taking her magic and energy with them. If Ashem wasn't already carrying her, she would've collapsed. She leaned against him, breathing in the anchoring scent of cardamom and mint.

Events in the tunnels were a blur. After she'd taken on more than a few dozen minds, she couldn't remember anything, and she was too tired to even lift her head and look around for Kai. *Please tell me we've got her.*

Yes. You succeeded. Ashem's thought was so fiercely triumphant that Juli mustered the energy to look around. Cold wind blasted her face. Above her were a thousand stars.

They'd made it out of Cadarnle.

But not away, Ashem said, responding to her thought. His hand was warm on her back. He addressed the others, everyone breathing hard from their race through the tunnels. "We need to transform, secure Juli, the Seeress, and Kai. Then we'll fly and see if we can outrun Owain's army."

Kai. Joy filled Juli. They'd gotten Kai. Ashem was there. Everything was going to be all right.

"She isn't running anywhere."

The cold voice froze Juli's blood. Kavar materialized out of the shadows of the boulders that concealed the entrance. Juli gaped at him. When had he woken? He must have thrown off her power a while ago to beat them up here.

Rhys and Kai were closest to him. In one untraceably fast motion, Kavar grabbed Kai's arm and jerked her against his chest, a dagger at her throat. Rhys made an inhuman noise and leaped forward, but Kavar pressed on the dagger and a dark droplet of blood welled from Kai's neck.

"Don't." Rhys held up his hands, sounded gutted. "Please. Kavar, please."

"No!" Juli gathered what little power remained to her and threw it at Kavar, aiming a spear of pain at his mind that would leave him writhing in the snow.

Nothing happened. She was too drained.

Kavar flashed his teeth at her, silver eyes cold as frozen night. "Sleepy, *delbar-am?*"

Rhys lunged, but Morwenna crashed into him, straining to hold him back. Rhys's eyes were feral. "Let her go!"

Kavar smiled. His gaze slid to Juli. He didn't need to speak. For this, she didn't even need their bond.

Unexpectedly, tears burned Juli's eyes. She had suspected this was coming—in fact, she had counted on it. But now that the time had come, she wished she'd been wrong. Ashem had been gone for weeks, and she'd only been reunited with him hours ago. She didn't want to leave him.

But her wants didn't matter. They could not waste this chance.

"Kavar." Juli stepped forward. Ashem caught her arm. She

caught his hand and squeezed. *Remember the plan. There's no other way to find out what's going on in Cadarnle.*

Despite her words and the fact that he'd agreed earlier, however reluctantly, the muscles of Ashem's jaw jumped. Then he moved. One second he was holding her hand. The next, too fast to see, he'd knocked Kai from Kavar's grip and sent her flying into the snow. Rhys lunged for Kai as Ashem grasped Kavar's chin in one hand, the top of his head in the other.

Ashem was going to snap his brother's neck. *I don't care what we talked about. I cannot let you go. Not so soon. Not with him.*

Juli stared, still dazed. Shouts echoed behind them, growing louder.

"If you're going to kill him, do it and be done," Rhys said, his voice like gravel as he lifted Kai from the snow. "This game between you two has gone on long enough."

Juli watched Ashem, half horrified, half relieved. The pain would be...great. She knew that. Unbearable. But after having both of them in her head for weeks, ripping her in two directions like dogs fighting over a bone, perhaps it would be better to have a rest. If she survived, her soul would be lesser. She knew enough about heartswearing to know that anything that took Kavar away, be it sundering or death, would slice away part of her as well.

But perhaps it would be best...

No. Not for Ashem. For all of their talk of hate, if Ashem killed his brother, he'd never forgive himself.

"Leave her with me. It's fair," Kavar said through gritted teeth, his knuckles white where he held Ashem's wrists. "You took more than you bargained for. Kai was paid for when Juliet released me from Eryri. The Seeress will cost you."

87

"She is not a bargaining chip." Ashem seemed intent on matching Rhys's earlier animalistic growl.

"Enough." Juli sent a mental prod at Ashem. *You don't want him dead.*

Ashem's muscles tensed. *I do.*

You don't. Slowly, Juli approached. She put a hand on the arm he had locked over Kavar's forehead. Slowly, she pushed it up and off. She was so tired.

With a face like a thunderhead, Ashem released Kavar and stepped away.

Kavar opened his mouth, and Juli held up a hand. "Don't you dare speak. I won't stop him from killing you next time."

Kavar's eyes narrowed and his nostrils flared, but he stayed silent.

Interesting. Insults rolled off Ashem—apparently that was not the case with Kavar. She'd known that they were different. She supposed over the next six months she would learn just how much.

With her magic, Juli imagined she'd make a formidable spy.

We can't miss this chance, she whispered into Ashem's mind, making sure all of her thoughts were fully shielded from Kavar. She was still working on that, shielding one—almost always Kavar—while letting the other in. Not easy, but she was getting better.

Fuck the chance. Ashem closed the distance between them, crushing her against him. He brought his mouth down, hard and hot, and kissed her with passion and fury that set her head spinning. Despite his words, it was a kiss goodbye.

Juli returned the kiss just as fervently. *I will still be with you.*

He encircled her mind with his, an embrace far more intimate than anything physical they could do here. *If he tries anything, run. I will find you and bring you home.*

That brought her to the second plan. One that had less to do with the war than her peace of mind. One that she hadn't run by either of them. "You should open your bond with Kavar."

Ashem let her go and stepped back. He and Kavar exchanged a glance. In unison, they said, "What?"

"There's no time to argue." Which was why she'd left it until now. "Ashem, you'll want to know how I'm doing, and you know I'm as likely to lie and tell you I'm not in trouble as tell the truth. Kavar..."

She really didn't have a reason Kavar might want to be connected to Ashem, but it didn't seem to matter. Ashem and Kavar were staring at each other as if for the first time in a thousand years.

"No prying," Ashem said. "No looking for military secrets."

Kavar's mouth fell open, as if he couldn't believe Ashem was considering it.

"We really do need to go, folks," Cadoc said, shifting Seren in his arms.

Kavar gazed at Juli, then Ashem. "Fine. Agreed." He clasped Ashem's wrist, and they shook hands. Juli knew the moment the old, unused path between their minds reconnected. There was an echo, like when she was a child and her parents had two landline phones. Once, during a phone call with Kai, Juli had gotten them both and held one up to each ear. Hearing Kai's voice in stereo had been disconcerting, and she'd hung up one of the phones after less than a minute.

She didn't have that option now.

Ashem and Kavar dropped each other's arms. Neither spoke. Juli wasn't sure either of them could. Kai moved to Juli's side and touched her shoulder tentatively. The caution in the movement was so un-Kai-like that Juli had to blink away the prick of tears again.

"I'm not leaving you." Kai glared at Kavar. "You can't stay with him. He tried to eat me. Twice."

The shouts from below were getting louder. Cadoc shifted Seren again. She moaned. "Rhys. Commander. Really. We need to go."

"Then go and transform," Ashem barked. He stayed where he was, but the others moved to clear spaces. Morwenna shifted first, and Cadoc, still human, laid Seren carefully in the snow to help the red dragon with her harness.

Juli would not cry. She would miss Ashem, but she'd still be able to talk to him. This would be the longest she'd been away from Kai since they were five. "We live thousands of years now. Six months is nothing."

Kai's grip tightened. "It's definitely something."

Juli pulled her into a hug. Rhys hovered nearby, something white in his hands. Kai's raven flying mask. Juli bit her lip for a second before she trusted herself to speak. "Take care of her. I'm counting on you."

Rhys took her hand. "I will never be able to repay what you've done tonight."

Juli squeezed his fingers behind Kai's back, still hugging her friend. "Survive. Make sure she does too."

Rhys handed Kai the mask, then backed away to transform. Cadoc lifted Seren's blanket-wrapped body from the snow and secured her awkwardly on Morwenna's back, the Seeress bundled like a saddlebag between Morwenna's wings at the base of her long, sinuous neck. Once Seren was tied on, Cadoc transformed, as well.

Finally, Kai let go. "If you really think you have to do this, be careful. This place..." She shivered, her voice dropping to a whisper. "Don't let him find you." She licked her lips and forced a smile. "I'll see you soon."

One last hard hug, and Kai was gone.

Ashem pulled Juli into his arms again, kissed her, all heat and power and desperation, and for an instant, she almost changed her mind.

Then Ashem let her go. He backed away and changed into the black dragon in a flash of darkness deeper than the night.

Doset doram, Ashem murmured into her mind. *I love you.*

Be safe, Juli replied, knowing he'd feel the undertone. She loved him too.

The dragons of Eryri took to the sky.

Shouts echoed up from the entrance they'd come through, close now. Juli watched her friends and her mate as the night swallowed them. She hugged herself. With only Ashem to hide four dragons, they'd have a hard time. But they would make it.

The shouts grew too loud to be ignored, and Juli turned away from the sky. "Come on," she said to Kavar. "You need to find Owain before he realizes you aren't where you're supposed to be."

Kavar was dazed, Juli could sense it. He couldn't believe she'd actually stayed. He'd known what he was doing at the time, making that deal—anger had made him want to hurt Ashem as badly as possible. That, compounded with the longing the heartswearing brought on, had driven him to do what he'd done. Now, however, he wasn't sure. "What about the four guards on Kai's room?"

Juli waved his words away. "I erased the memory of you taking their charms the second they were knocked out. They won't remember you interfered."

Despite the arctic frigidity of the air, Juli's eyelids were drooping of their own volition. Wherever Kavar was going to put her, it had better have a comfortable place to sleep.

Don't underestimate him. He agreed to this, but he's still Kavar, Ashem murmured. She cloaked herself in his reassuring presence. For a moment, she wished so hard that she'd gone with him that the pain was almost physical.

Kavar was looking at her like she'd grown a third head. He had expected Ashem to kill him. Instead, he had Juli, and he was closer to his brother than he had been in a thousand years.

It had been her biggest gamble of the night, hoping that there was a part of Kavar that was tired of war with his brother. She'd been right, as she tended to be. Now she was perfectly placed to find out everything she could about Owain's plans and feed them to Ashem.

Dangerous, yes, but she *was* heartsworn to one of his most trusted generals. Kavar would protect her whether he wanted to or not.

No dragon would ever let anything happen to his heartsworn.

CHAPTER 13
OWAIN

O wain woke when Kavar slammed through his door, the heavy wooden thing bouncing off the stone wall behind it. He sat up in bed and cursed, an odd, heavy feeling behind his eyes. "Ancients damn you, Kavar, what are you doing?"

Still in the previous day's clothes, Kavar looked as if he hadn't slept. "They're gone."

It didn't make sense at first, as if his friend had just spoken in a language Owain only partially knew. When Kavar's words sank in, Owain shot out of bed. "The Wingless?"

For once, the Azhdahā didn't smile. "Both." Owain stopped. His heart beat in his ears.

Both.

His scouts had sent a report late last night that Rhys had been taken by his Council and forcibly returned to Eryri. At first, Owain had been disinclined to believe it. But the reports kept coming in, citing Ashem's presence as well as Rhys's. At length, Owain had believed.

Besides, Rhys wasn't devious enough to come up with a plan that could fool Owain. He hadn't had the time.

"It cannot be true. How could he have done it?" Owain grabbed the clothing he'd laid out for the next day and started to dress. "When?"

Kavar's nostrils flared. "I don't know. They could be five minutes gone or over an hour. I've sent out two vees to search for them. They must have had something—some weapon—that forced anyone they came across to sleep."

Owain paused, studying Kavar. The man had been his general, his closest friend, for more than a millennium. Something about what he said was...off. "Was it Azhdahā magic?"

Kavar nodded slowly, as if remembering. Or perhaps thinking. "It could have been. My brother is heartsworn now. Rhys's magicians could have invented something that amplifies his power."

Envy seized Owain at the thought that Rhys's people might have been able to accomplish something he hadn't. He reached out to Jiang with his mind—she was sleeping elsewhere tonight, as she did from time to time—and jerked her awake.

What? she snapped, trying to hide how groggy she was.

Who do we have in Eryri?

He sensed her disgust that he'd woken her. Jiang was not generally an early riser. *No one placed high enough to do anything worth waking me.*

Owain dismissed his anger before he lost control. Losing control meant making decisions he would regret. *You were grooming someone.*

I was.

Rhys has taken his heartsworn. Whoever you've got, tell them to be ready for Rhys's return.

What? Jiang fumed for only a moment, then took control of herself with alacrity. Her ability to accept a situation and begin to search for solutions efficiently and quickly was one of the reasons he admired her. *I thought you didn't approve of my methods.*

He didn't. Poison—which Jiang had been suggesting for years—was a coward's way. But Rhys had escaped him one too many times. The war dragged on, and humans grew more numerous and advanced. He would end this, even if he had to gather all the dragons of Cadarnle and fly to Eryri himself.

Even if he had to sink to methods no dragon had stooped to in tens of thousands of years. *Contact your operative. Make sure he's ready.*

He will be.

Owain shoved past Kavar and into the hall, but paused halfway down the last set of stairs and narrowed his eyes. If Rhys had been so close, why had he left Owain alive?

That had been a massive mistake.

For the first time in a thousand years, Owain teetered on the brink of forcing Rhys into one final battle. Only the potentially catastrophic number of casualties stayed his hand. But Owain couldn't afford to lose face. Rhys would be punished for this.

Owain and Kavar descended the last of the stairs that separated his chambers from the door to the Seeress's room. He'd wanted her close. He'd taken every precaution he could, and somehow Rhys had been here, in his home, stealing his things in the night like a common human thief.

Owain threw open the door to the chambers that had once held his Seeress. The guards were scattered across the floor, just sitting up. Many of them were holding their heads or other wounds, groaning. Owain strode past them into the hot, firelit room.

The bed was empty.

His Seeress, gone. His chance to win the war, gone. All his

plans, blown away like powdered snow. Neither Kai nor Rhys would die today. Owain would not strike a blow for his people. He would not get rid of his infuriating cousin or—at long last—gain the full power of the mantle. The power he would have had if Ayen hadn't stolen the mantle that was rightfully Owain's and destroyed his life.

Ayen, whom he'd trusted. Who had set him up, encouraging him to explore the darkest avenues of magic, then reporting to his mother as soon as Owain went too far. Rhys knew what his father had done. How could he not? He might hide behind the lie that he wanted to protect dragons by keeping them away from humans, but he only wanted the power. Just like his father.

Red misted Owain's vision. He shouldn't have listened to Jiang. He should have killed the Wingless girl when he had the chance.

He spun and went back into the hall, where Kavar gaped at the unconscious guards. "All alive," the Azhdahā said. "Rhys left them alive."

There was awe in Kavar's voice. Admiration when he said Rhys's name. That would not do.

Owain drew the dagger at his waist and slit the first man's throat. He placed his hand on the head of the next and blasted it with all the power of ice and cold he could muster. The man fell dead.

Damn it. That had been a mistake. His magic would show. He'd have to have Kavar throw that man in the fire to make it look like he'd been burned.

Kavar stopped him with a hand on his arm. "What are you doing?"

Owain jerked free. He gutted the next one, slitting him from neck to navel where he lay on the ground. The man woke and screamed before he died. Owain didn't stop, only moved to the next one, then the next. Cold. Methodical.

Rhys could not be a hero. Owain's people hadn't responded well to his execution of the traitors who wanted to help the Wingless. They were too caught up in emotion to see that it had been a necessity. An example.

Still, the last thing they needed this morning was to hear a romantic story about how Rhys rescued his heartsworn *and* the Seeress right out from under Owain's snout without killing a single guard. That would sow discontent. He couldn't have an army that muttered behind his back.

"Don't you see, Kavar? Rhys came in and killed our people." Owain stabbed the next guard through the eye. "He came in the night and slaughtered us so he could take back his possessions. He knocked these guards unconscious, and then he murdered them in cold blood. These mates. Parents. Siblings."

Owain grabbed the last man by the hair, wrenching his head back to expose his neck. The man's eyes opened, then widened when he saw the dagger. "Majesty, no!"

The man had a name. Owain knew it, but decided not to think it. He sliced the guard's throat. Blood spurted. The guard gurgled, spasmed, and died. His work done, Owain wiped his dagger on his black pants and turned to Kavar. "Rhys must have cut the talisman from inside Kai's neck, or her remains would be splattered in the hall outside her rooms. I don't suppose they are."

Kavar was gripping a knife at his hip, staring at the dead guards. He cleared his throat. "No. She is not splattered in the hall."

Disappointing. "Find the talisman, and don't wipe off any bits of the Wingless that are clinging to it. Those are the parts I need. Bring it to my rooms, then take care of the mess. After that, call up six more vees and sweep the area for Rhys. If they're still close, I want them captured."

Without waiting for Kavar's response—the Azhdahā would obey, of course—Owain reached for Jiang's mind and prodded her awake again.

What?

The headdress you wore when Rhys swore you into his vee. Does it still have his blood? Part of the ceremony had involved Rhys smearing his blood across Jiang's cheeks, and plenty had gotten caught in the metal links of the headdress.

Hot excitement curled through Jiang's thoughts. *Of course. You told me to keep it.*

Bring it to me.

Rhys might have succeeded in rescuing Kai, but he wouldn't have her for long.

Owain stripped off his blood-soaked jacket and threw it into the fire in the Seeress's room. The old man in the corner was stirring. Owain thought about killing him too, but decided against it. Six was enough. No need for extravagance.

He stared into the flames, fascinated and repelled. He'd controlled fire once, but it was strange to him now. Deadly and alien. He touched his face, glad he'd had the Seeress heal his eye the first day she was in Cadarnle. Quetzals could heal, but Seren's power—which could regrow entire eyes and bring one back from the brink of death—was completely unique.

Perhaps he should wait, but the anger he'd been reining in was eating at him as surely as fire ate away his bloodstained clothes. Besides, he needed to wash off the gore on his skin.

Owain headed for his rooms. Kavar and Jiang would be there soon. He might not be ready to attack Eryri with all the might of Cadarnle, but he was going to allow himself a little revenge. It would cost the immediate advantage of attacking while Rhys was in too much pain to think, but his cousin would suffer longer this way.

Nothing would ever be right for Rhys again, not from this moment until his inevitable death.

Then again, perhaps he would handle sundering better than his father had.

Owain laughed.

CHAPTER 14

KAI

K ai watched the world pass below, arctic islands and frigid sea giving way to pine forests and the occasional glow of lights from a tiny town or lonely house.

She couldn't believe it. She was free.

But they'd left Juli behind.

She's intelligent and cunning. She'll do all right. Rhys's voice was gentle in her head. Soft. Comforting.

Kai tried to feel comforted. Maybe she could even forget. All the terror, pain, hopelessness. If the door stayed locked and she threw away the key, maybe none of it would come back.

She'd probably get the hang of feeling the good things again.

She lay against his scaled neck, wind whistling across the metal feathers of her white raven mask.

Behind it, she felt safe, like she might be able to be someone...not Kai. Someone who hadn't been tortured and nearly executed.

That got too close to unlocking the door, so she pushed the thoughts away, losing herself in the thrill of flying. Leaning over the side of Rhys's neck, she grinned at the stomach-dropping sensation of looking down. Emotions were all well and good, but she'd rather feel alive. Flying was a start. Once they got back to Eryri, she could climb again.

And there was Rhys. He could make her feel that thrill with his hands, his body. Yes. That would be exactly right for forgetting. *How long until we land?*

Rhys shuddered almost imperceptibly, sensing her need, his own rising up to answer. *We need to put distance between us and Cadarnle. And I want to fly far enough south that you can see the sun when it rises.*

The sun. She hadn't seen the sun for fourteen days. *Thank you.*

They flew on in silence, perhaps not as tightly intertwined as they could be, but comfortable enough.

Kai couldn't pinpoint the exact moment the pain started. It began as a pressure in her chest. Not much, just a little every time her heart beat.

Within a minute, the pressure grew into discomfort. Kai sat up and rubbed her heart. Rhys was having issues too. He raised one of his claws and brushed it against his breastbone like something beneath his scales itched.

The discomfort blossomed into an ache. Kai shifted, trying to relieve the feeling, but nothing she did seemed to make it go away.

Was she having a heart attack? Now? She tried to remember the signs. Wasn't her arm supposed to hurt? Or was that just for men?

Rhys. She reached out to him. Maybe she just needed to walk around a little. For some reason, sending him the thought was like shoving it through molasses. Like their connection was supposed to be liquid, but it was icing over, becoming brittle.

Breakable.

Kai?

She heard his thought as if from a distance. He hurt too. His chest. The pressure building like someone had stuck a balloon into his ribs and was blowing it up.

No. No, no, no. She might have been emotionally shut down, but she just needed space. Whatever this was, this separation, she didn't want it.

The pressure ratcheted up. Turned to pain. To agony. The night flickered. Or maybe not the night. Maybe she was the one winking in and out, emptiness threatening to sweep her away.

Rhys's wings missed a beat.

A great ripping, shredding, tearing sliced through Kai, like a vengeful angel had taken a fiery sword and cleaved her soul. She was bleeding. No, not bleeding. But something vital streamed from her. The things that were her and Rhys and *them* had been almost severed, their invisible insides streaming out into the air.

The forest rose up to meet them. On the horizon, a sliver of light. The sun.

Before its light could touch them, Rhys plummeted, the wind and Kai both shrieking. Kai thought she saw the strands that had bound her and Rhys together, like chains of golden light. Most had been severed, loose ends waving, unfixed.

Rhys!

K—

The last chain broke. And then...

Nothing.

KAI WOKE PROPPED against a splintered tree trunk. There was fire in her shoulder, and her chest felt as if someone had smashed through her ribs and ripped out her still-beating heart.

Kai clenched her jaw, willing her brain to stop buzzing, and tried to get her bearings.

She was in a pine forest, its dark needles stark against the pink-washed dawn sky. From the thoroughfare of downed trees, she guessed Rhys had crashed. She couldn't remember the impact, but either she'd jumped clear or the straps of the harness had snapped, because the row of broken trees continued past where she lay. Randomly, Kai wondered if some scientist would find the destruction and think a meteor had crashed. *Sorry, science. Just dragons.*

She sat up and gasped. It felt like her shoulder was dislocated. She knew the feeling. The same thing had happened the last time Rhys crashed. It hurt like a mother, but it was nothing compared to the pain lower in her chest.

Kai staggered to her feet, arm useless by her side, and bit back a yelp of pain. *Rhys?* Her voice echoed in her own head. Empty.

Alone.

No. Oh *no.*

She stumbled over a fallen branch and landed on her knees, bruising one on a stone that protruded from the ground. Her breath came sharp and fast. She couldn't quite get her bearings, like someone had cut off an ear and cut out one eye, so her ability to take in the world was half of what it had been.

She was half.

Kai pushed back to her feet, dead pine needles scattering. Months ago, when Rhys had come to her parents' home in Colorado to bring her to Eryri, he'd told her he'd come because Seren had a vision.

A white raven. Owain pulled out its heart and crushed it in his hand.

They'd thought it meant Owain would murder her. No. Seren had foreseen...this.

Owain crushing Kai's heart. Her heart.

"Rhys!" Kai staggered toward the end of the swath of destruction. There, a redheaded man lay face down in a churned mix of dead pine needles and snow. She searched desperately for him in her head, but he wasn't there.

Dread scooped out a hollow place in her middle. She skirted a fallen log and ran for him as best she could, leaping over splintered branches and lifting her feet high to keep them from the clutching, snatching roots of the overturned trees, every step jarring her shoulder.

He's dead. He's dead. He's dead.

The future loomed over her like a vast black tsunami, threatening to sweep her away. Thousands of years without Rhys. So long. So empty.

No, that was wrong. If Rhys was dead, there was no future.

The sun flashed off red-orange scales high above. The other dragons were circling, searching the dense forest for a place to land. They didn't matter. All that mattered was Rhys.

She reached his side and skidded on her knees into the snow, rocks shredding through her pants and slicing open her shin. Rhys had one arm pinned beneath him, one stretched forward, reaching. The side of his face was crosshatched with bloody cuts. His eyes were closed.

Kai touched his hair, afraid to take his pulse like she knew she should. Slowly, she slid the fingers of her working hand from his hair down to his back.

He inhaled.

"Rhys..." The door behind which she'd hidden all of her emotions was open, and everything was gushing out. All the times Owain's soldiers had hit her. Fried her. Burned her. Cut her. Tried to take *everything* from her. The world went dark around the edges. Blood rushed in her ears, deafening.

The pain. Holy shit, the pain in her chest blossomed anew,

spiking into something worse than the pain of what must be sundering. A word she'd heard the dragons use as a curse, and now she knew why. Another tear splashed onto the back of Rhys's shirt. She opened her mouth and panted, like she could breathe around the agony. A whimper escaped her throat.

Too fast. Too much. Close the door. Don't remember. Don't feel anything.

Rhys was alive. She needed to be calm. She needed to know if he was hurt.

He groaned and rolled onto his back. The eye Kai had been able to see was swollen shut. His other eye blinked open. He clutched his chest, his face contorting, and inhaled through his teeth. A few clipped Welsh words flew from his lips.

She couldn't understand them.

It took two eternal minutes for the pain to ebb. By the end, tears were streaming from the corners of Kai's eyes and she was rocking back and forth as best she could without jarring her shoulder. Like if she could just find the right position, the pain would ease. It didn't.

Finally, the agony released them. Not all the way, but enough for Kai to breathe.

"*Cariad?*" Rhys pushed himself up. Aside from his face and a few other cuts, he was in better condition than her. He curled a hand around the back of her neck, fingers rubbing soothing circles against her skin. "Are you all right?"

She reached for him with her mind—an action that had become as instinctive as breathing—but still, there was nothing. "I can't—you aren't—where are you?"

"I can't feel you either." He rubbed his chest. "It hurts like it did in the cave."

After he'd heartsworn to her, before she'd sworn to him.

It felt like someone had impaled her with a branding iron. "It felt like *this*? You lived with *this* to give me a choice?"

"And you wondered why I didn't tell you." He started to laugh, but it ended as a groan. "I forgot how bad it is. I think... I think we've been sundered."

The word called up emotions that were too big, too horrifying. Fast as she could, Kai shoved them behind the door. "Yes. I think so too."

Besides, it wasn't like it was forever. Or real.

He shifted, the weight of his arm coming down on her shoulder. "Ow!"

Rhys flinched like he'd been burned. "I'm sorry, I thought—I'm so used to being able to feel your pain—" He feathered his fingers over the wrongness of a bone popped out of joint. "I'm sorry," he whispered.

The sound of footsteps cut off Kai's assurance that it wasn't his fault. Ashem, Cadoc, and Morwenna came running through the fallen trees.

Ignoring them, Kai gripped Rhys's shirt. "Kiss me."

That's how heartswearing worked between dragons and humans. The dragon became sworn and kissed the human to complete the bond. They would kiss and their heartswearing would be fixed.

It *had* to be fixable.

She didn't need to ask him twice. Careful of her injury, he braced his hand on the back of her neck and brought their lips together in a desperate clash, hot against the cold, cold air. The kiss was hard and needy. When the first one didn't work, Rhys kissed her again, deeper. Harder.

Nothing.

"Stop that and tell me what happened." Ashem examined Rhys, then Kai.

Kai was only aware of his pat-down in a distant way. Caught in Rhys's fire-blue eyes, she touched his cheek. Everything behind them, lost to her forever.

He slid his hand over the back of hers and pressed it to his lips before he spoke. "We've been sundered."

"Sund—no! Are you certain?" Cadoc asked.

"How do you know?" Ashem's voice was considerably softer this time.

Kai curled her fingers in the hair at the nape of Rhys's neck. "We know."

A kiss hadn't worked. Maybe something more...intimate might? Automatically, she tried to send Rhys the thought. It didn't go through. She dropped her forehead to his shoulder, wincing when the movement jarred her arm, and squeezed her eyes shut. He was *right there*—but not there at all. The loss of him was like falling from the top of a rock wall. She expected to feel him—for the belay to kick in—but it didn't. She hurtled endlessly through space with nothing to break her fall and no mats to soften the blow when she landed.

Ashem heaved a sigh. "Let's bandage you up. Then we need to move. We're an hour from the cave where I planned to rest. Owain will have sent search parties, and we have no way of knowing where they are." Ashem helped Kai up, and Cadoc pulled Rhys to his feet.

"This is not going to feel good," Ashem said.

"What?" Kai asked.

He shoved her dislocated shoulder back into place.

Kai blacked out, but only for a second. When consciousness returned, Ashem was holding her steady.

"All right?" he asked.

Rhys was pale-knuckled and glaring at Ashem. "Warn her next time. Ancients, warn *me*."

Kai fought down the residual urge to vomit and the question that burned her lips. *Why? You can't feel it anymore.* Instead, she said in a high, unsteady voice, "I've had worse."

"Worse is yet to come." Ashem's face was set in grim lines.

"I was there when Ayen was sundered. The moment it happens is difficult to endure, but the magic ripples back, like aftershocks—only worse than the original pain. You two have a rough—" He shook his head. "I don't know how long it will be. A few days. A month. The rest of your lives. Ayen was dead before his stopped." He looked away. "You lived through the initial shock. You should survive the rest."

Kai swallowed, forbidding the tears pricking the inside corners of her eyes to fall. She'd thought she was done with torture. *I lived through that. I will live through this.*

She took Rhys's hand. Despite everything, she marveled at the realness of his palm, strong and callused. Most of her had thought she would never touch him again. "We will."

There was a brief argument over whether Rhys would ride or fly, but Ashem won. The others transformed, and Rhys and Kai climbed onto his back. Kai showed Rhys how to strap into the harness, then clipped herself in and wrapped her arms around his waist.

She pressed her face against his back, and he intertwined their fingers in his lap. She would not think about the next wave of pain or what would come with it. Possible insanity. Maybe death. And if they got through that, war. Because there was no way either she or Rhys would let Owain live after this. She didn't have to be connected to him to know that.

And if they got through war...what? Keep living together, sundered? She'd barely known Rhys five days before he'd heartsworn to her. Not much longer before she'd agreed to heartswear to him. They'd been separated or under extreme stress for their entire relationship. Not the most stable of beginnings. They'd never had time to find their rhythm as a normal couple. And now...

Kai breathed in Rhys's scent—wind and smoke and that nameless, masculine whatever-it-was.

That, more than anything else, told her this was real. She was here, with him.

Sundered.

Did he love her, or had it all been the magic? Did she truly love him?

Once, she'd thought bad things happened to other people. She would've assumed things would work out for the best. That they had to.

She knew better now.

Whatever the future held, she would face it when it came.

CHAPTER 15

JULI

Kavar burst through the door. Juli cut off her conversation with Ashem. Frantic, she jumped off the Roman-style couch, which had been made for reclining rather than sitting, and leaped for him, the chains around her wrists rattling.

That was the first snarl in her plan. Kavar had taken the manacles and collar from Kai's room and put them on her. For the moment, she was effectively useless.

But that wasn't why she wanted to scratch his eyes out.

"He sundered them!" The words were shrill. She'd told herself she would remain calm. Screaming and foot-stomping never solved anything. She hadn't realized the depth of her rage.

Kavar caught her clawed hands, dark curls tumbling over silver eyes. "Yes."

"How could you let him? You were supposed to help me save her, not throw her into more danger. You should have told us that this is what he planned! This wasn't our deal!"

Physically, at least, Kai was safe. Ashem had gotten Rhys

and Kai to the cave where they'd set up a rendezvous with Cadoc's rogues, who'd flown there with all their gear when the rest of the army left for Eryri. But that didn't mean Kai was out of danger.

Kavar's hands tightened around Juli's wrists until she hissed at the pain.

"I told you, I serve *him*. We may be heartsworn, but I am not your pet." He shoved Juli to one side. She stumbled and caught herself on the antique coffee table.

Kavar paced around the little sitting room, feet silent against the deep pile of the rugs scattered around the floor. For an unused suite of rooms far on the unpopulated outskirts of Cadarnle, these were certainly well furnished. "I didn't think he'd go through with it."

Juli's laugh was bitter. "Why not? He's done it before."

"Yes, when we were little more than boys. Before he was heartsworn. He couldn't have understood what he was doing then. I thought—"

Juli swiped her hand through the air. "Spare me. I've seen Kai's memories. Owain ordered a heartsworn pair to kill each other yesterday. What makes you think he'd have qualms about sundering?"

Kavar seemed to realize that he was pacing and stopped. Juli both saw and felt the moment when he pulled on his nonchalant persona. "I don't know."

Be careful, aziz-am, Ashem warned. *He is volatile. He always has been.*

It was hard to keep them from hearing each other in her mind, and even harder to keep Kavar from hearing her responses to Ashem while still appearing open to him, but she managed. *He's upset about the sundering*, Juli countered. *We can use this. If I can drive a wedge between Kavar and Owain, you could have your brother back.*

Anger curled in Ashem's thoughts. *Why? So you can have both of us? It was a mistake to open our connection. The only way this can end is with one of us killing the other.*

Imagine the advantage of having two Azhdahā on Rhys's side instead of one on each, canceling each other out.

What Ashem had said was also true—the part about having them both—but Juli would die before she'd admit it. She was so twined with each of them that their hatred of each other tore her apart. Who could blame her if she tried to stop them from killing each other?

Ashem, apparently. *That will never happen.*

Ashem, you are an adult. The magic makes this difficult, but you have a brain and agency. None of us chose this situation. I love you, not Kavar. I'm sorry that you don't like that I'm sworn to more than one person, but for now you'll have to be content. If we can get him away from Owain, that makes the white dragon that much weaker.

Silence. Then he let loose a string of curses. *They're having another wave of pain. I have to go.*

He withdrew, clouding their connection. Juli made a noise of disgust, but her hands shook, jingling her chains. She wondered if she could have stopped it, had she been with Kai at the time. Maybe shielded them somehow. Rhys and Owain were powerful, but the mantle was torn, and each of them only had half, if that. Ashem had told her once that the power of the healed mantle would be a question of multiplication, not addition. The same way her power had grown when she'd heartsworn to Kavar.

"What does the magnificent Ashem say?" Kavar sneered.

Juli gave him a cool look. Perhaps the magic of heartswearing and the aggression it engendered for anyone but themselves touching "their" mate did make it impossible for Ashem and Kavar to reconcile. That didn't mean she would put up with either of them acting like children. "Could you hear him?"

"No."

"Well then. It must not have been for your ears." Juli sat primly on the couch.

Kavar narrowed his eyes. "How does he abide you?"

Juli smiled. "If you don't want me here, I'll go. I'm sure he'll take back the six months if you don't want them."

"Don't be so sure. He *did* give you up. Must need a holiday."

Juli made an offended noise. Kavar smiled. It wasn't pleasant. "They're alive then. If Kai or the false king had died, you'd be trying to murder me with something other than your eyes."

Juli pressed her lips together. "Are you here for a reason?"

Something passed over Kavar's face. Fear? Worry? Empathy? "To see if I'd be searching for bodies or living beings. You've given me the answer."

Juli made sure her side of the connection to Ashem was shrouded just enough. Then she rose and stepped closer to Kavar, who stilled. "That's not why you came. You were upset."

Kavar scowled. It made him look like Ashem. "Why would I be upset? The son of the Usurper is sundered. Rhys is no longer heartsworn nor can he ever be again. That means he can't pass on the mantle because he can't have children. Owain has won."

Juli folded her arms so Kavar couldn't see her knuckles turn white. She'd forgotten about that—that only heartsworn dragons could reproduce. It was part of the reason they took heartswearing so seriously. Part of the reason dragons who chose not to heartswear—the Unsworn—were considered expendable.

How would Kai feel about never having children? It wasn't something they'd talked about much—they were young, after all. But Juli was fairly certain that a family had always been in Kai's vague plans for the future. "Rhys has a sister. If Deryn has children, Rhys's half of the mantle can pass to them. You haven't won anything."

Kavar shrugged. "If she lives long enough to heartswear."

Juli stepped forward again, close enough to prod a finger into Kavar's chest. "You didn't come here to find out if they were alive. You came here because being close to me comforts you. Because we're heartsworn. Because when Owain sundered Rhys and Kai, you imagined the same happening to us."

Kavar caught her hand and pulled her against his body. He was leaner than Ashem, and somehow harder, but not because he was more muscular—because the way he held her was less forgiving. He tilted her chin up with one hand and pressed a bruising kiss to her mouth. Juli struggled, but his grip was like stone and the kiss was...heated. Desperate. God, she'd never felt anything so desperate.

Against her will, Juli moaned.

If she was her own person, she would never be in danger from Kavar's dubious charms. But the magic—the part of her that was bound to him—wanted to let him carry on kissing her and see where it led.

Oh, no. None of that. She forced herself to picture Ashem's face. Remember his hands.

Juli bit Kavar. Hard.

Kavar grunted and released her. He wiped blood from his bottom lip with the back of his hand and smiled again. "Comfort indeed." He reached out and tenderly brushed a strand of blond hair behind Juli's ear.

She stiffened. "Clearly, someone failed to teach you boundaries. Let's start with this one: *don't touch me.*"

He leaned down, his lips brushing against her ear as he

whispered, "Be good while I'm gone, little viper." He pressed his lips to the side of her neck. Before she could jerk away, he straightened and mussed the hair he'd just smoothed. Then he was gone.

Juli shivered. She would be here only six months. She could ignore those treacherous feelings. They were only magic. Besides, she and Ashem had expected this. She allowed Kavar to think she was playing his game because it kept him occupied, distracted.

Juli settled on the couch and glanced around absently, waiting a few minutes to make sure he wasn't coming back. Kavar had surprised her. Sometime in the past few weeks, he'd prepared rooms for her. And he'd done a good job. Unlike Ashem's spartan quarters, the furniture was comfortable and the stone walls were covered in hangings depicting ancient gardens and dragons flying over a mountainous desert. Kavar had even provided her with cooling shelves—the dragon equivalent of a refrigerator—full of food. A small stack of books rested on a table next to the reclining couch, which was delicate and curving, with lion heads for armrests.

Juli narrowed her eyes. Apparently she and Ashem weren't the only ones who had been planning for her to stay after she'd rescued Kai. "Trading" for Seren had been an excuse.

She shrugged. They were both using each other. Very healthy way to start a relationship. Almost as healthy as moving in with your husband's brother, whom you were attracted to.

She shook off the final thought. Time to focus on the real reason she'd agreed to stay in Cadarnle. Juli leaned her head against the cushions that covered the couch's wooden frame and closed her eyes. She still hadn't recharged from rescuing Kai—even she didn't know how many minds she'd taken and held in sleep—but she didn't need much power to listen. Though the collar and cuffs had made it impossible.

Thank goodness for Kavar's arrogance.

Taking the key she'd lifted from his pocket when he'd kissed her, she pressed it to the indented areas on the collar, then the cuffs, then shucked the hateful things off so they clattered to the ground.

She closed her eyes and exhaled, releasing the locks on the layers of shields she'd learned to create, lifting one at a time until she touched the eddy and swirl of the nearest minds. Kavar had done well, putting her as far from the populated areas as he could manage. Even with all her shields flung open, she could only touch a few people as they whispered through nearby halls. The stone did nothing to dampen what she could hear, but distance did.

Luckily, Kavar hadn't gone that far yet.

With the heartswearing bond, Juli could only see what he chose to show her. With Azhdahā magic—a separate path into his head—she could see what she pleased. There was, however, the risk that Kavar would sense her if she dug too deeply. But at the moment he was speaking with someone. Another vee commander. And he was distracted.

—almost out. Can you ask Owain?

Ask him yourself, Kavar growled.

The unknown dragon tasted like fear. *He's not in any state for anyone but you or Jiang to speak with him at the moment.*

Resignation from Kavar. *If we're out of raw material, send the order to capture more humans. In fact, tell them to double or triple cordial production from now until further notice— quadruple it, if they can. Owain has sundered the false king and his Wingless mate. Whether he knows it yet or not, we're going to war.*

War? But...we've had no warning. It isn't easy to find descendants of the bloodlines, let alone kidnap anyone from

117

them and transport them all the way to the desert without raising suspicion.

Kavar was unsympathetic. *Jiang has a man in Eryri. I'll have him send you a list of their Wingless. Many of them are young. It will be easy enough to find their families.*

The other dragon chuckled. *I think we all know which Wingless's bloodline will be at the top of Owain's list.*

The room spun around Juli, and she clutched the couch for support.

The bloodline at the top of Owain's list. Kai's family. They were talking about Stephen and Leila Monahan, Liam and Colm. Juli pressed a hand to her mouth. Colm, Kai's oldest brother, had two young children. Would the dragons take them?

She ran to the door, trying to shave off some of the distance, and stretched her magic farther. Not into Kavar, who would know what was happening if she pushed any deeper, but the other dragon.

Searching through a mind wasn't easy. Each presented her with what it wanted more or less at random. But because the dragon was thinking about his conversation, it was easy enough for her to find the information she needed.

The dragons had identified about a hundred human families that carried heartswearing potential in their genes. The ability to become Wingless ran in human families. Uncommon, but not exceedingly rare.

She knew that. She and Kai were distantly related, which explained why both of them had heartsworn when the odds should have been abysmally low.

Her connection to the other dragon weakened as he moved farther away. With a growing sense of urgency, Juli dug for more information. At the same time, she planted a suggestion in the dragon's brain that he needed to stop, or at least slow down. Just for a moment.

He did. Juli felt him rub the nape of his neck, uncomfortable. She should be careful, but she *had* to know.

More knowledge drifted to the surface of her victim's mind. Wingless—humans who had been heartsworn—gained the same type of magic as their dragon mates and matched them exactly in amount of power. However, they also gained their own magic: the ability to give dragons or other Wingless a power boost. The boost nearly doubled the magic the recipient could use for a limited amount of time.

Potential Wingless—unheartsworn humans of those bloodlines—also had that power, but it stayed dormant unless unlocked by the touch of a compatible, unheartsworn dragon.

She sifted through another layer of thoughts and came across...horror. A flash of bloody flesh and bone, writhing bodies, echoing screams. Sickened, she backed away from that memory and turned it into a fact that she could catalog.

Owain, through several gruesome experiments, had found a way not only to awaken that dormant Wingless potential, but to bottle it and give it to his soldiers. This was the cordial Kavar had referred to.

Owain was making dragon steroids out of people.

She inhaled, trying to process it. Precious milliseconds ticked away. Deeper. She needed more. She needed to know how to stop them.

She sensed the dragon rubbing his temples. The pressure of her magic was giving him a headache. How sad.

She snatched at another cluster of thoughts, gritting her teeth at the strain of extending her still-exhausted magic so far.

To get to the dormant power, Owain had to kill the humans who held it, capturing it with magic as it drained from them with their blood.

The cordial-making facility was located...

The dragon walked out of range. If Juli believed in swearing, she would have cussed a blue streak that would make Ashem blush. She retreated to the couch to organize the knowledge she'd gained.

Owain was killing the families of Wingless to make dragons stronger. Kai's family, whom Juli loved like her own, and even Juli's boozy mother—whom she usually didn't care to think about—were at risk.

Juli closed down her Azhdahā powers and opened herself to Ashem. She explained what she'd heard, keeping her fears to herself. At first, Ashem was silent. Not even a curse. That was never a good sign.

When he did speak, his mental voice was filled with rage. *That cordial must be why they were so strong when they attacked us over the Bering Sea. Why Kavar was strong enough to resist questioning in Eryri. If they have enough for their entire army, we're all dead.*

Juli nodded despite the fact that he couldn't see her. *I thought the same. Now that we know, we can do something.*

You've done well.

I wish I'd heard more. We need to know where this is happening.

I think I might know where. The Taklamakan.

The Taklamakan. A vast desert in central Asia. For weeks, dead humans from all over the world had been turning up there with no clue why or how.

The Monahans, Ashem. Kai's family.

We have people watching the Monahans. Things in Colorado are quiet. His voice was carefully neutral, but she could feel the tense worry behind them.

Quiet? What does that mean? How do you know your people aren't already dead and Kai's family taken?

Ashem pushed a tendril of comfort toward her. *I...can't say for certain.*

So contact them!

There was silence from Ashem for a moment. Then, *They aren't answering.*

Ashem, find out what's going on. Now!

Resignation. He already thought it was too late. *I will.*

Stop sounding like you've given up. They're my family too!

I know. I'll find them. Ashem was silent for a moment. Then, *Rhys and Kai are settled, but we'll be stuck here for a few days. I'll make contact with others who might be able to get there in time.*

He withdrew.

Sick, Juli stood and paced. She thought about reaching out to Kavar and begging him to protect the Monahans, but she was afraid that if he knew how much she loved Kai's family he would only be more likely to hurt them.

He'd made it very clear whose side he was on.

CHAPTER 16
DERYN

Deryn curled her fingers around the arms of her heavy wooden chair and reminded herself that murder was never a good idea.

The Council—the lackadaisical, archaic bunch of lizards— would not respond well to being shouted at either. Rhys had proved that often enough, especially in the last few meetings before his departure. Deryn would not shout. Well, she'd try not to. Instead, she spoke softly, so the faint song of the waves outside the arching stone windows nearly drowned her out. So softly that her words never reached the high, mosaic-encircled ceiling of the Council chamber. Softly enough that the nineteen other people gathered around the doughnut-shaped mahogany table had to lean forward to hear.

"Gethin. I swear, if you bring up human casualties again, the next person to die will be you."

The wiry, brown-haired young man sat back, eyes wide in overwrought false surprise. "I was simply suggesting—"

"You were rehashing what my brother and your father have

discussed literally hundreds of times." Deryn's lip curled. "If you bring it up again, I'll have you thrown out."

Gethin gave a *tch* of disbelief. "You aren't the queen. You don't have the authority to throw out a member of the Council—"

"Aha." Deryn held up one finger, the morning sun flashing off her sapphire rings. "But *you* are not a member of this Council. Your father is. We've agreed to put up with you until Councilman Powell returns, but that doesn't mean you get to bring up issues that have been settled several times over. In any case, human casualties have nothing to do with the original issue, which was dispatching envoys to the rogues."

Several councilmembers snorted or made other uncomplimentary sounds.

Gethin the Buffoon, as Deryn had decided she would call him, opened his stupid mouth again. "But if the envoys didn't have to worry about hiding—"

Deryn ignored him, flashing a wry smile at the members of the Council who'd made angry noises. "All right, then. The final battle is coming. Owain's numbers are equal to—if not greater than—ours. If you don't want to go to the rogues, let's hear your ideas for ensuring we aren't all massacred."

She sat back and waited, scanning the dragons seated around the table. A salt breeze slithered in through the windows, reminding Deryn of how much she would rather be outside, flying. Or with her brother, freeing Kai. Fighting.

The distraction had worked. The army was on its way home. She hadn't heard from Rhys or anyone who had gone into Cadarnle since the small hours of the morning, though. They had better be on their way home, or she was going to murder someone. Gethin, most likely.

The silence that had filled the room was broken only by the

awkward clearing of a throat or the rustle of fabric. So. They didn't have any better ideas. What a surprise.

Deryn stifled the urge to sigh. Rhys was the diplomat of the family—well, truth be told, Rhys only did well as a diplomat until his temper got the better of him. Seren, now *there* was a diplomat—but either of them were a better choice than Deryn. She had zero patience for the asinine tedium that was government. She hated Owain, but she couldn't help but think that he'd been right never to have a Council. They moved slower than slugs, and there was no time.

She'd arrived back in Eryri nearly two weeks ago and only stayed because Rhys—the bastard—had used the mantle on her to prevent her from turning around and flying right back to him. Very carefully worded this time too. After Jiang had taken Kai "home" to Cadarnle instead of "home" to Eryri, he was completely paranoid.

Though maybe Deryn could understand why.

The silence dragged. Deryn let it, staring down any councilmember who dared meet her eyes, and tried to shake off the feeling that something with Rhys had gone horribly wrong. She wasn't the Seeress. She didn't get *feelings*. Hell, she tried not to have feelings about events that actually happened, let alone nebulous mights or maybes.

A chair scraped across the tiled floor. "I have a suggestion."

The eyes of the Council, Deryn included, turned to Athena, one of the Wingless representatives. The Wingless, the only non-clan body with representatives on the Council, usually didn't say much. Many of the dragons considered the inclusion of Wingless councilmembers a courtesy. But Athena and Sarangerel had recently been elected to the position— though Sarangerel was the oldest Wingless in Eryri—and they were shaking things up.

Deryn liked them.

Council Leader Kansoleh motioned to Athena with one slender umber hand, the golden scales of her headdress tinkling. "Speak."

Though nearly as dark as Kansoleh, Athena's cheeks were freckled, and her brown hair, instead of being cut close to her scalp, was a cloud of tight curls around her face. Charms and jewels dripped from a band around her head. Before she could even open her mouth, some of the anti-Wingless dragons were grumbling.

"We already know what she's going to say," interjected cold, beautiful Nerys, the Draig councilwoman. "You only just reprimanded Gethin for wasting time. Why are you going to let her?"

"Quiet," Deryn barked. Though everyone *did* know what Athena was going to say.

Athena returned the nod with a small, tense smile. "Highness, honored councilmembers, the answers are obvious. First, you should allow Princess Aderyn to send her envoys to the free dragons. Your prejudices are outdated and potentially fatal.

"Second"—Athena raised her voice over the outburst of muttering—"you must let the Wingless who wish it go into battle with their mates. You say you lack soldiers, but there are over a hundred Wingless in Eryri. Most of us are young. We love our mates, and we have come to love dragons. We'll fight hard, because if Owain wins, we lose. What can our place possibly be in a society headed by a king intent on killing humans? A hundred soldiers, or fifty, or even twenty-five, could make a difference that matters."

"They aren't my envoys," Deryn said mildly. "They're the king's envoys. But I agree that we should send them. And, as I've told you all before, I agree with Councilwoman Athena.

The Wingless are valuable assets. I've seen Kai—Queen Kai—in action. They should be allowed to fight."

"The Wingless exist so that we can continue as a species." Nerys tapped the table with a slender finger. "That's where their value lies: in the fact that even pairs with a male Wingless and female dragon can produce more offspring than a pair of dragons. We are tottering on the edge of extinction!"

"We are not your broodmares or stud stallions." Sarangerel looked down her nose at the other woman.

Deryn wasn't sure if the comment helped or not. After all, Sarangerel and her heartsworn had six children—*six*—when most dragon couples could produce only one or two. Deryn's own mother, Mair, had been Wingless and had three. Though Wingless hadn't been part of dragon history long, they had already done much to shore up the population's dwindling numbers.

"You forget that my own mate is Wingless," Nerys said, false affront written all over her. "I cannot *bear* the thought of taking him into battle. He'd be helpless as a hatchling!"

Deryn rolled her eyes. "That's because you can't bear to be near him in general. Just because Henry Harrow is useless in a fight doesn't mean the other Wingless would be. He's got other talents. And, I suspect, *other* talents."

Next to Deryn, Council Leader Leonidas cleared his throat. Across the table, Citlali, the only Quetzal in Eryri, smirked and drummed her nails on the table.

Nerys was not amused.

Deryn backpedaled. "Come, Nerys. If anything, Harrow should be used as an argument *for* the Wingless, not against them. They are capable." He might not like dragons in general, thanks to his awful treatment by Nerys, but her heartsworn played an essential part at keeping the dragons up-to-date with the impossibly fast changes in human technology and helping Ashem spy on the human world.

"Princess Aderyn is right," Citlali said.

Deryn winced at the use of her full name. Only her mother had called her by that name. Her mother, who had tried to kill Rhys, not realizing that the *only* thing she could have done to alienate her youngest daughter was harm the brother Deryn loved more than anyone else in the world.

Her mother, whom Owain had killed.

So maybe he'd gotten two things right.

The guilt of that thought made her grind her teeth. She should not be grateful for the death of her mother. She was just so *angry*.

Citlali continued, "Several of the councilmembers were present at the battle. We saw how Queen Kai flew, how capable she and King Rhys were together. Their partnership is flawless. We need more soldiers. I second the motion that the Wingless be allowed to fight."

Council Leader Kansoleh pressed her fingers to her lips. "Is there a third?"

The last Council leader, a Noodinoon named Shonke, raised his hand. "I will third."

Half of the Council, including Deryn, looked at him in surprise. The Noodinoon—the dragons of North America whose magic had to do with the weather—were notoriously neutral. If he supported the Wingless, it had to be because of Kai. Historically, dragons had kept Wingless out of the war because it seemed laughable for a human to fight giant flying beasts. The dragons had assumed the humans would be killed in moments.

Kai had proved that wrong. Wingless weren't humans, they were powerful magic users in their own right, and dragons had been denying themselves a valuable resource for far too long.

Shonke ignored the murmurs and looked placidly ahead, reminding Deryn of Seren at her most annoyingly mysterious.

"We will vote," Kansoleh said. "All in favor of allowing the Wingless to fight in the coming battles with their mates?"

Deryn and seven other dragons raised their hands, and she barely suppressed a grin. Eight. That was higher than the number had ever been. Thanks to recent events, Deryn wasn't sure of Rhys's vote, but if Kai and Ashem had been there—Ashem sat unwillingly on the Council as one of the two surviving members of Clan Azhdahā—they could have had half.

Of course, some members of the Council didn't want Kai to have a vote, or they wanted to kick one of the current Wingless councilmembers out and give Kai *their* vote, or they wanted to get rid of Kai entirely. Anything to strip her of as much power as they could.

Lizards.

"Motion denied," said Kansoleh gently.

Athena sat, but her expression said exactly what Deryn had felt.

So close. Next time.

A messenger scurried through the rows of slender columns that separated the Council chamber from the hall beyond. The room was open so the people could come and watch the meetings if they chose, which few did. The effect made the chamber feel airy, though, so Deryn liked it.

The messenger scurried to Gethin and handed him a slip of paper. Dragons tended to use gemstones for serious record keeping and longer messages, but paper was still the easiest way to pass a quick note.

"Council meetings are not to be disrupted," Council Leader Leonidas said, his thick salt-and-pepper mustache quivering slightly.

The messenger reddened, bowed, and scurried out. Gethin unfolded the note.

"What was so important that it could not wait until after the meeting?" Leonidas demanded. Deryn had to stop herself from rolling her eyes again. Gethin had a flair for the dramatic—like Cadoc, except not charming. He had probably asked that poor soul to deliver him a note so he could feel important.

But when Gethin looked up, his face was gray, his mouth slack. Deryn's stomach dropped.

Gethin cleared his throat. "It's from my father. He was contacted by Commander Ashem. King Rhys and his Wingless mate have been sundered."

Silence.

Deryn blinked. Once. Twice. Rhys and Kai...sundered?

Like Mother and Father.

She stood, pushing her chair back so hard it clattered to the floor. "You *lie*."

It couldn't be true. Not Rhys and Kai. Owain would have needed something from both of them to do it. He probably had plenty of Kai's blood and hair, but he couldn't have anything from Rhys. They couldn't be sundered. It could kill them. They could go mad.

Like Mother.

Gethin glared. "Princess Aderyn, I would not lie to the Council. And even if I would, I would not dare lie about this."

Maybe there was a hint of melodrama in his words, or maybe Deryn couldn't hear properly over the rushing in her ears. The world had gone blurry. All of her internal organs seemed to have disappeared.

"This—this meeting of the Council is adjourned." She sounded like someone was sitting on her chest. She couldn't breathe. "I must contact Commander Ashem."

She stumbled away from the table. The voices of councilmembers bounced and buzzed around her, echoing from the ceiling. She didn't care. Had to escape. Find a singstone. Call Ashem.

Someone moved from behind her chair. Strong, warm hands grasped her at wrist and waist. Evan. Steady and solid as always.

"I've got you, *annwyl*," he whispered.

Deryn leaned into him, letting his scent wash over her. They might not be heartsworn, but aside from Rhys, he was her best friend in the world. "This can't be happening," she whispered, glancing up and back.

He flashed her a smile, but his blond brows furrowed. He was worried. "We just need to get out of here, then we can figure it out."

Someone was in front of her, asking about Rhys. Deryn blinked and found herself staring at Shonke, the Noodinoon Council leader. He wanted to know if Deryn would update the Council when she found out what was going on.

"Yes, Council Leader," Deryn managed. "I'll send word once I've spoken to Ashem."

Evan led her out toward the widely spaced columns. Luckily, there wasn't much of an audience today. As they passed, Nerys's voice cut through general buzz. "Does this mean the Wingless isn't queen anymore?"

Did it? Deryn had no idea. None of this could be real.

She was almost to the safety of the columns when Gethin stopped her. Deryn shrugged out of Evan's grasp. "Move."

Gethin's face was a picture of solicitous concern. "Don't you want to see the note?" He held out the folded piece of paper in his hand.

Even looking at it made her feel sick. "No."

Gethin sighed and stuck the note in his pocket. "My father supports you, Princess Aderyn. He tells me there are many on the Council who do. Perhaps, now that your brother is sundered, you will consider that you must take his place as ruler of this people. You are our only path into the future."

Evan's hand was on her waist again, and his fingers tightened. If she became heartsworn, her relationship with Evan would—probably—end. Deryn had managed to avoid becoming heartsworn so far, but she was the right age, and it would likely happen soon. She and Evan had managed to keep their relationship light, both knowing it could never go anywhere. That didn't mean it had been easy, not falling in love with the boy who'd been with her since childhood.

"Even if they're sundered, Rhys is king and Kai is queen. That's how it will be. For as long as they live." She shouldered by Gethin, Evan on her heels.

"We'll pray to the Stars that they have long lives, then," Gethin called after her.

Deryn hunched her shoulders and walked faster, until Evan was almost jogging to keep up. At least she knew Rhys wasn't dead. If he had died, the mantle would have come to her, and she could have commanded every yammering, wind-for-brains fool in that meeting to shut their snouts and keep them shut.

Nothing's changed, she told herself as she and Evan made for her room so she could call Ashem.

Nothing's changed.

She was the warrior. Not the diplomat. Not the ruler.

Nothing's changed.

She made it to her rooms, found her singstone. It took five tries to get Ashem to answer. *What?* His voice was irritable.

Tell me it isn't true.

Deryn?

Tell me they aren't sundered, Ashem! And tell me you didn't tell Powell before you told me.

A pause. *They're sundered. I'm keeping them sedated for now, but we can't stay where we are for long. I told Powell because I couldn't get ahold of you. You didn't have your singstone.*

I've been busy! Deryn retorted.

Ashem's voice remained level. *While I have you, there's something else.*

Her stomach sank. *What?*

I've been trying to reach the dragons in charge of watching Kai's family. One of them finally got back to me. The Monahans were taken. The parents and one brother. The other wasn't home. He and his family are safe, I've tripled the guard on them. We're moving them as well. They believe their parents, brother, and Kai have been taken into some sort of witness protection program. But...

Ashem trailed off. He didn't have to continue. If Owain had Kai's family, there was no knowing whether they were dead or alive. That news, along with the sundering, might just break Kai and Rhys both.

Deryn sat hard on her bed, Evan beside her. Everything had changed.

Damn it, Ashem, you had better not let them die.

CHAPTER 17
SEREN

Seren woke to a scream. Her stomach knotted, and she squeezed her eyes shut, sure Owain had brought her to watch Kai being tortured again. He wanted to break her. He wanted her to stop fighting them when they forced her to take the drug that would plunge her into visions for days at a time.

"I'll take it," she whimpered. "Stop hurting her. Please!"

"My lady?" A voice, smooth and rich as cream. A voice that was definitely not her turtle-like caretaker.

Seren's eyes popped open.

A cold breeze raised goose bumps on her skin. No fabric canopy hung above her. No curtains cut her off from the rest of the room. Sunlight streamed through a few root-crossed holes and pooled on the ground. She was in a cave. Not a dragon cave. A wild, dirty, natural cave.

This was not Cadarnle.

A tall figure leaned against the opposite wall, broad-shouldered and narrow-hipped. Black hair tumbled over amethyst eyes, contrasting sharply with fair skin that was paler than it ought to be. His mouth—that gorgeous, musical mouth—was more serious than it ought to be, as well.

"Cadoc?" Seren touched her throbbing head with a shaking hand. Her thoughts felt like they were moving through syrup, sticky and slow. Her stomach was pinched between two sharp claws.

He crouched beside her. "The only and one."

"Oh." It was too good to be true. She had to be dreaming—but it was an accurate dream. She didn't know anyone else who'd say "only and one" instead of "one and only," as if switching it around made it some kind of poetry.

"I'm dreaming," she said. Stars knew she dreamed of Cadoc so often she could dream him well. In a dream she could admit to herself what she never could have awake.

She loved him. She had since she was a girl. And despite centuries of trying, she had never stopped.

Cadoc chuckled, but his smile was wrong, somehow. Empty. "A nightmare, maybe, waking up to me."

Seren wrinkled her nose. It wasn't right for him to look sad like that. If this were a dream, he wouldn't be over there. He would be next to her, kissing her. Those dreams were her favorite. Not that she knew what kissing felt like. Or holding hands. Or anything involving skin-to-skin contact with Cadoc.

Ancients, she was dizzy.

An agonized cry bounced from the walls, and Cadoc winced. "Of course, there are worse things happening at the moment than my face."

Seren would've made an incredulous sound if she'd had the energy. Cadoc's face—as he knew well enough—was breath-stealing. With a few days' growth of stubble shadowing his cheeks and jaw, the strong planes and fine angles of his face were thrown into even sharper relief. He was beautiful. Everything about him was perfect.

Except for his smile. It broke her heart.

True memories came back to her in fits and starts, but she still couldn't make things make sense. The last time she'd seen Cadoc, he'd been on the beach of an island in the Bering Sea, trying to kill Rhys. Cursed.

"Where are we?" Her voice was weak, whispery. She couldn't seem to make it stronger. Her whole body felt too heavy to move. Some dream this was.

"Safe." Cadoc settled back on his heels. "How much do you remember?"

"Remember...of what?"

"The last two weeks." Cadoc's voice was rough. "He had you for two weeks."

Another scream made her start. Seren became aware of the uneven floor digging into her back, of another swirl of cold breeze. She looked at Cadoc again and saw the white lines of scars that crisscrossed his left hand. His right arm—the one covered in carnelian scales arranged in a pattern like flames— was tucked into his jacket, his hand hidden. She reached out with her healing magic—a magic completely separate from the type that forced visions into her brain—and felt splintered bone and misshapen muscle.

She sat up, her stomach lurching and head spinning at the motion. Not a dream.

She was rescued.

Cadoc had saved her.

Someone cried out, the sound echoing through the cave as if the first cry had woken a chorus of tormented souls.

"You... How? Where are we?" She tried to push herself up, but collapsed back, shaking. So weak. "Who's hurt? Quickly, bring them to me. Is it Kai? Please tell me you saved her too."

"She lives, but..."

There was such pain in his voice that Seren almost reached

out to him. She'd thought she would never see him again, but there he was, his familiar combination of cedar and lemon oil faintly scenting the air.

"But what?" Seren stopped the reach before it was more than a twitch. She might be willing to admit to herself that she loved Cadoc, but he was far too loyal a friend and soldier to fall for her. At best, she was Rhys's little sister. At worst, she was a symbol. Something too sacred to think about as a woman.

She didn't want to be a symbol to Cadoc.

A cry echoed from deeper in the cave. Seren pushed forbidden feelings to the back of her mind. "Who is that? Bring them to me, Cadoc. Or me to them. Let me heal them."

Cadoc rubbed his face with his good hand. "It's Kai. And when it isn't Kai, it's Rhys."

As if his name had conjured him, Seren heard a groan. Rhys's voice. What had happened that they were both so severely injured? Panicked, Seren tried to stand, but fell. Cadoc started, but pulled himself up short of helping her. She wasn't wearing gloves or a veil. She caught sight of the items, folded and waiting on a low, flat stone.

No wonder he wouldn't come near.

She tried to sit up again. "Help me up. Let me heal them."

A muscle in Cadoc's jaw twitched. "Rhys and Kai have been sundered. There's nothing you can do."

Seren froze. It felt like someone had opened a trapdoor beneath her, and she was in free fall. "Sundered?"

Cadoc sat down again, brushing hair from his eyes. "Owain sundered them hours after we left Cadarnle. Rhys crashed. They seemed all right at first, but then..." He took an unsteady breath. "Some of the former rogues—Kephas, Rajani, and Tharah—they're here as well. But we're barely a day's flight from Cadarnle. We've been cowering here like rabbits in a hole for three days. Rhys and Kai are alive, but they... They aren't well. They keep getting hit by some sort of ripple effect of the sundering. Ashem has kept them unconscious through the worst of it, but he can't hold them forever, and it doesn't help them heal. We've seen Owain's scouts overhead four times. They'll find us if we don't move soon."

"*Three days?*" Seren squeaked.

A sad smile touched one corner of his mouth. "Ashem may have been helping you too. You were in a bad way from that poison." Cadoc let his head fall back onto the uneven cave wall. "Fuck. Owain hasn't killed either of them, but he's won."

"Don't say that." It couldn't be true. Her brother wasn't inches away from death or madness. His cause couldn't be all but lost. "There must be a way to fix it."

Cadoc shook his head. "No one has ever healed a sundered pair, my lady."

"There have only been a few sunderings in history." She gritted her teeth as her empty stomach cramped. "And every one that I've heard of was done by the choice of one or both partners. No one has ever *tried* to heal one before. There must be a way." She brightened a bit. "Maybe all it will take is a kiss. That's what sealed the heartswearing in the first place."

"They've tried."

Somewhere in the cave, Kai sobbed, raspy and raw. Seren cringed. "At least take me to her. If Rhys crashed while he was carrying her, she must have some injury I can heal."

Cadoc shook his head. "It's been three days. They may be sundered, but she's kept her powers, just like Mair did." He caught a glimpse of her face and added, "But I'll ask Ashem."

He returned a moment later with Ashem. The commander went down on one knee next to Seren. He touched her chin gently, tilting her head so he could look into her face.

Cadoc turned away.

Seren met Ashem's golden gaze. He had circles under his eyes. She wondered if he'd slept at all.

"Commander, I will heal my brother's injuries, as well as his mate's." It took a massive effort to keep her voice steady, but she managed.

"You aren't well."

Seren frowned. No one said no to a direct command from the Seeress. "I am well enough."

Ashem stood. "No. You are not."

Seren crossed her arms. The movement almost made her fall over on her side. "I am the Golden Lady of Eryri. I *demand* that you let me heal them."

Ashem raised an eyebrow. "All right, my lady," he said. "You can heal Kai."

"Good. Now—"

"If you can walk to her without assistance."

Seren bared her teeth. She didn't know Ashem well. The commander, it would seem, was insufferable.

She almost managed to stand before her shaking legs gave out. This time, however, Ashem caught her before she could land on her behind. He lowered her to the pile of blankets upon which she'd been sleeping, and Seren made a noise of frustration.

"Their superficial wounds are healed, and even you can't repair a sundering." Ashem's voice carried equal measures of exasperation and amusement, but his eyes were troubled.

Morwenna appeared in the doorway. "Ashem, Rhys needs you."

Ashem helped Seren reposition herself in the blankets. Seren tried one more time. "Please."

Ashem shook his head and was gone.

Cadoc toyed with an old stick he'd picked up off the

ground. "They'll survive, but you might not if you try to heal them while you're this weak. You're too precious to risk, my lady."

Seren wanted to snap at him. Worse, she wanted to cry. She wasn't more precious than anyone, and—stupidly—she wished he would use her name.

After a few minutes, Cadoc left as well. Morwenna stayed, offering Seren a dented metal bowl of thin broth. Too weak to even hold the bowl, Seren had to let Morwenna prop her up and feed her. She sucked down the broth greedily, however. It had been so long since she'd kept down food.

Was she precious? If she was, it wasn't because of herself, only her magic. Her visions had averted battles, and she had saved Rhys's life more than once—like the time she'd foreseen an assassination attempt. But there were so many times she hadn't foreseen things. So many lives she hadn't saved.

And the visions took so much.

Guiltily, she let her mind wander to Cadoc. To what life would be like if she wasn't the Seeress. She imagined dancing with him at one of the festivals. The Day of Light and Dark, perhaps, when the dragons celebrated the summer solstice in one hemisphere and the winter solstice in the other. And after, he would take her by the hand and tug her out of the room, the way she'd seen him do with the other girls. They might walk along the beach, his arm around her waist. Or they might... They might...

She finished the broth and Morwenna settled her back into her blankets. She would never dance with Cadoc. Never feel his hands or his breath or his kiss. Her calling was higher than that. She was the Seeress, a dragon born less than once in a generation. Born to the people, sworn to the people.

They needed her. She *wanted* to fulfill her duty.

Seren closed her eyes. She loved Cadoc, but she should have remembered that allowing herself to think of him—to wish for him—brought only pain.

CHAPTER 18

RHYS

R hys didn't remember the landing. Didn't remember sliding down from Ashem's back. As it had been when he'd been sworn to Kai and she'd run away, everything disappeared in a blaze of black fire so cold it burned. Time passed in fits and starts. He woke up once, realized he was in a cave. Kai was nowhere to be seen. He couldn't feel her in his mind.

Gone.

He lay on the ground on a blanket thrown over a pile of dried leaves. Morwenna sat against one wall, dozing, a fall of dark hair across her face.

Rhys scrambled off the makeshift bed. At least, he tried. But the blankets tangled around his feet and he was as graceless as a newborn lamb.

"Rhys!" Morwenna woke and she knelt by his side, a solicitous hand on his back. "Are you all right?"

"Kai." He ground the word through clenched teeth. The space where she was supposed to be had become ragged emptiness, half of himself torn away and lost.

Morwenna recoiled as if he'd raised a hand to her, but Rhys

couldn't bring himself to care. Black thoughts circled his head. Kai had been alive when they got to the cave.

Hadn't she?

Had her injuries killed her? Had the sundering?

He would return to Cadarnle this very instant and burn it and Owain until there was nothing left of either but ash.

Stars, don't let her be dead. Rhys gripped Morwenna by the shoulders. "Where is she?"

Morwenna flinched and shrugged away his hands. "In another chamber."

"Why would you keep her that far from me?" Rhys stood and staggered into the main tunnel of the cave. To his right, the entrance glowed with dim afternoon light. Pines whispered in a chill breeze, and the ground was a patchwork of white snow and dry brown needles.

A cry echoed to his left. He staggered toward it, away from the light. Morwenna appeared at his side and tried to slip under his arm, but Rhys refused her help, using the wall to push deeper into the cave.

He came upon another alcove. Seren lay on a pallet similar to the one he'd woken on, dozing fitfully. Cadoc stood against the wall, his arms folded tightly across his chest. On a pallet against the wall opposite Seren, Kai lay as still and pale as a porcelain doll.

For three long heartbeats, Rhys stared. *Dead. Dead. Dead.* He stumbled to Kai's side and sank to his knees.

Cadoc shifted and stretched. "She's alive. She had some broken bones and you kept thrashing. We thought it better to give her a little room."

Hands shaking, Rhys touched Kai's cheek. Warm. He found her hand, gripped it, and pressed it against his heart, trying to hide how his voice shook. "Has she healed?"

"Her bones have," Cadoc said. "It's been four days since

the crash. Ashem made sure they were set right and let nature take her course."

Rhys brushed Kai's hair back from her face and gazed down at her. Something was missing. The magnetic pull. The all-consuming *need* that characterized heartswearing. It was gone. When his skin brushed hers, there was no extra burst of energy. No wave of heat. For the first time since he'd known her, touching Kai felt like touching anyone else.

The feelings you have for Kai aren't real. They're lust and obsession and infatuation. Don't let the magic cloud your good sense.

No. He still loved her.

Of course he still loved her.

"All right?" Cadoc asked.

"Fine." Rhys drew Kai onto his lap. She was hardly more than skin stretched over fragile bones after her weeks with Owain, but her weight grounded him. He cradled her, waiting to feel something. Anything.

Was it just the magic?

Kai stirred, eyes flickering open. She fixed him with that fey green gaze.

"Ow." She put one hand to her chest. Then her eyes widened, and she grabbed Rhys by the shirt. "You're alive." She put a hand to her head and said, like a lost child, "But where are you?"

The reaction was so Kai, and the way she looked at him— like she needed him. Rhys let out his breath in a rush, emotion slamming into him like an unexpected gale-force wind.

Yes, he loved her.

"We've been sundered." He'd thought he was calm, but the words were rough and ragged. "Do you remember?"

Kai tightened the fist in Rhys's shirt. "Fix it."

The demand took Rhys by surprise. "What?"

"Fix it," she repeated. "Owain uses his half of the mantle to sunder people. You've got the other half. Put us back together."

Ancients knew he'd tried. Right after it happened, before the aftershocks started and Ashem must have sedated them. He hadn't told Kai, not wanting to get her hopes up.

That way he'd only shattered his own.

He shifted her so she could sit upright on her own, and brushed unruly midnight tendrils of hair from her eyes. His thumb lingered over her scattered freckles. "Imagine our bond as chains of glass. Owain smashed the place yours connect to mine. If I focus, I can sense the damage. I might even be able to piece the broken parts together. But even if I can, it will take power beyond what I can muster to fuse them together."

"Try." Her voice carried as much of a command as it had a moment before.

"Kai—"

"Please." Kai's voice was desperate now. Her fingers feathered through his hair. Sundered or not, to have her hands on him again was glorious.

Lust and infatuation...

"Wingless do have the ability to give a power boost to other magic users." Seren's voice made everyone in the room turn.

"Normal magic," Rhys said. "Not the mantle."

"You might as well try," Cadoc said.

Morwenna was silent.

Everyone's eyes were on him, but his gaze was locked with Kai's, and he spoke only to her. "I have to wait until morning to do the ritual again. Sunrise is the only time a mantle ritual can be done."

"No." Ashem set down the bowl of broth. "You're both weak. Wait until you're stronger."

"You get sundered and wait," Kai retorted. "You think Owain is going to sit back and relax?"

146

"Rhys has just suffered an intense amount of magical back-lash. If he does the ritual now, who knows what the consequences could be. Besides, I'm less concerned about Owain than getting you two to Eryri." Something in Ashem's voice was too careful. His face too still.

A foreboding unfurled dark wings inside Rhys. "Tell me what you know, Ashem."

The Azhdahā scowled.

"Ashem!"

Finally, he shrugged. "Juliet has been gathering information while you were unconscious. Kai is right. Owain is preparing for war." He hesitated. "And I know why we lost the last battle."

Rhys set Kai on her feet and stood. Neither of them was very steady. "Why?"

Ashem's scowl deepened as he launched into a recap of his conversation with Juli about Owain kidnapping people who had the potential to become Wingless and where he thought they were. Kai asked several questions throughout. When he was finished, she gave him a confused look.

"So...what does that have to do with us losing the battle? You never explained."

"I would get to it if you would stop interrupting," Ashem barked.

"Commander." Rhys couldn't help the warning in his tone.

But Kai only rolled her eyes. "You're going to be a barrel of laughs for the next six months, aren't you?"

Ashem growled.

Rhys gestured at him to continue, and he did so with ill grace. "As Seren pointed out, in addition to your Wingless powers, you can give a dragon or another Wingless a...power surge. That ability lies latent within you, even before you heartswear."

"So...in these families, even the unheartsworn have magic? Human magic?"

"Magic isn't what you see." Rhys skimmed his knuckles over the back of Kai's hand. "What dragons do—manipulate heat or read minds or cast illusions—we're all tapping into the same power. We just manifest it in different ways depending on our genetic makeup. That's why heartswearing between different clans was discouraged for so long. No one knew how dragons with the blood of two clans would manifest their powers. Like Griff. He has—had—" A pang of grief. He'd never get used to the fact that his friend was dead. "—the magic of an earth Draig, but he was half Bida as well. They're more or less telekinetic. He used that when he worked with stone or metal to produce finer work than any other earth Draig ever could."

Rhys cleared his throat, which seemed to be closing. "In any case, few dragons know how to touch pure magic. The Naga can do it when they craft magical objects, but only a little. Owain, it seems, has learned to siphon whole chunks of magic. He's always been...willing to experiment. So he's..."

Rhys looked to Ashem, who sighed. "He's taking potential Wingless, extracting the ability to give a boost in power, and bottling it for dragons. The process is fatal for the humans."

Kai shook her head, disbelief clear on her face. "That's insane. We have to stop him."

"We can't take Ser—the Lady Seeress to the Taklamakan," Cadoc protested. "And neither of you are fit to travel."

Rhys rubbed at the insistent pain in his chest. His father had fought Owain the same night he'd been sundered. Though Rhys's sundering had happened days ago, he was barely able to stand. No wonder the white dragon had been successful when he murdered Rhys's father.

Kai gripped his fingers. "What are we going to do?"

Rhys needed a moment to think. Blood of the fucking

Ancients, he was in the middle of a war. He'd just been sundered. Now this.

"Do we have to do anything?" Morwenna asked, her voice like cut glass. "Owain will come against us soon enough. The Seeress has had a vision of the final battle. If we win, Owain will be dead and his human harvesting operation will stop. If he wins, it won't matter. The humans will be doomed no matter what."

"Don't be so sure," Kai said through gritted teeth.

If Owain won, they would *all* be doomed no matter what. Rhys had been prepared to go into battle against him to get Kai back, but knowing about this potion changed things. He would not force his people into a hopeless fight.

But perhaps, if they could take down the facility Owain was using to manufacture the stuff, they could even the odds.

"We have to go after them," Ashem said, his voice heavy. "We believe they have Kai's parents and one of her brothers."

"They *what?*" Kai shrieked. She swayed against Rhys. With no heartswearing bond, he couldn't tell how tired she was or how much pain she was in. After weeks of constant awareness, of profound intimacy, it was as if he'd gone blind.

"We believe they're alive," Ashem said. "We're going to get them back."

"Yes we fucking are!" Kai shouted. "We're burning his whole goddamned operation to the ground!"

"Kai is right," Rhys said. "We need to take away Owain's ability to create this cordial. If we're going to face Owain in battle, the last thing I want is for him to have access to something that makes his soldiers stronger."

Everyone had an opinion about that. They all started talking at once, but Rhys wasn't listening. What was happening in the Taklamakan was important—vital, even. But first, he had to make sure Kai was all right. To comfort her. To get his bearings with her.

Ignoring the shouts of the others, he leaned down and murmured in Kai's ear. "Let them argue. Come with me. We need rest for what's ahead."

She tilted her head toward him and whispered, "Rhys, my family."

"We will recover, and we'll get them back."

"I want to kill Owain."

"Then he will be killed."

"I want to kill him *now*."

"I know, *cariad*."

Kai pressed against him, her fingers digging into his skin with an urgency that surprised him. "I can't do this."

"Then come with me. I just—I need to be alone with you. For a moment. Speak. Get our bearings."

"Only speak?" she asked.

"You just found out about your parents. We've been sundered."

Kai's voice was half sob when she said, "I need to feel connected to you."

He slid his hand up her back and let his fingers tangle in the ends of her silky hair. "Anything. I will do anything for you."

The rest of them were still arguing. Kai cut off whatever Cadoc was saying. "Ashem, Rhys and I need to talk. Alone. Is there somewhere we can go?"

That fooled exactly none of them. Cadoc's eyebrows rose. Seren raised her eyebrows. Red spots appeared high on Morwenna's cheeks. Ashem, of course, didn't change his expression at all. "The cave continues on about a hundred yards and opens into a grotto with a pool on one side. If you find you can't make it back, shout. Sound carries."

"Ashem!" Seren's expression was scandalized. "They've been through so much, how could you think—?"

"Thanks for the warning," Rhys said drily, cutting his sister off.

He scooped up Kai's blankets and pulled her away with him, heading deeper into the cave. It wasn't easy—the walls twisted and turned and came together without any semblance of reason, and neither of them were very steady.

Finally, they came to a place where the ground dropped about ten feet and opened into the cavern Ashem had talked about. Rhys jumped down. The impact sent him to his knees, and it took him a minute to get his legs back under him.

Kai followed, landing next to him in a crouch. She turned around and looked up at the wall, running her hands experimentally along the rock, longing on her face.

He moved behind her and lifted his hands to her shoulders, stroking down her arms. She leaned her head back against his chest.

"Kai..."

But she didn't want to talk. She turned to him and tugged his shirt up, her movements urgent. Glad enough to oblige, Rhys lifted his arms and pulled it the rest of the way off.

Kai brushed her fingers along his bare chest, tracing the scales of his indicium. Rhys didn't feel the cold, but his skin pebbled at her touch. He caught her hand, kissed her palm.

Kai pulled away and lifted her own shirt over her head, revealing the milky, taut skin of her stomach, the lean, inward curve of her waist, and the tattered white bra she'd probably been wearing when Owain took her.

Rhys's breath caught. At the sight of her, yes, but... "Kai. What have they done to you?"

He'd suspected when she'd raised that undetectable shield in Cadarnle that she'd hidden some of her torture from him.

He never imagined it had been this much.

Rhys sank to his knees, hands on her waist, so he could see better. White lines, all faded now, crosshatched her flesh. So many. And these were only the ones he could see—they didn't account for broken bones or internal damage. They wouldn't tell him how many times she'd been electrocuted or half drowned. He traced his fingers down her back, finding more.

"*Sêr yn yr wybren,*" he breathed. He tried to turn her around.

"Don't. If I— If you see, then I'll have to remember." Kai refused to budge. She bent and spoke against his lips, her hands sliding from his shoulders to his neck, then up to cup his face. "Help me forget."

He gripped her waist and lowered her, her body sliding against his, and the friction of skin against skin—the knowledge that he held her again—made him moan, soft and low.

They went slowly, just touching at first. Rhys hadn't realized that he'd wound himself up, that he'd become cold and inflexible and tight as a bunched spring. Not until she touched him, hands gliding over his skin.

It wasn't even sexual at first, just comforting. As if, though their minds were no longer intertwined, she knew exactly how to smooth her hands over his body to take away the worry. The stress.

They spread the discarded blankets on the water-smoothed stone floor and Rhys stilled her hands. It was his turn. Just touching, his hands traveled the length of her waist, the curve of her shoulder. Trying to smooth away the fear, the pain. Until she relaxed. Until he cupped her breast and she put a hand over his, encouraging him.

He lowered his head and kissed her shoulder. She let her head fall back, and Rhys took the invitation, kissing her exposed neck. He pulled down the straps of her bra, unhooked it, and let it fall. He filled his hands with her breasts.

Kai made a muffled sound of pleasure. She tugged at his clothes, pushing down the waistband of his pants, freeing him.

"Kai, we should go slowly."

She flashed a glare at him before going back to work. "Fuck slowly. I want to feel close to you."

She dropped to her knees, and before he could tell her to get up, she had wrapped her hand around his shaft and taken him in her mouth.

Now it was Rhys's head falling back. Rhys whispering, "Oh, *fuck*," as she swirled her tongue around the head, then relaxed her throat to take him deeper. She hummed and the vibrations just about undid him.

Automatically, he tried to sense what she was thinking. To see what she wanted him to do, how far she wanted him to go. But there was only emptiness.

Kai moaned again, sucking him, working her fist around his cock up and down as she knelt before him.

Rhys's control snapped. He buried his fingers in her hair and thrust into her mouth. Kai made a sound of pleasure, so he thrust again, losing himself in the bliss she offered him until he was close to losing himself.

He withdrew.

"Hey!" Kai reached for him again.

"No." He reached down and lifted her with one arm so that she was standing again. He cupped her sex and slipped a finger inside. Finding her slick and ready, he thrust another finger in, curving them forward.

Kai let out a cry at the sudden invasion, opening her legs so he could access her more easily. "God, yes. Rhys, don't stop."

Pleased to find her wet and ready just from having him in her mouth, Rhys pulled back his fingers and circled her wetness around her clit until Kai was clinging to him, standing on trembling legs.

"I wanted to be gentle," Rhys growled.

Kai opened her eyes. Her pupils were so large, they looked nearly black. "I don't want you to be gentle. I want to feel like I'm yours."

Another low growl rumbled from his chest. "You are mine."

"Show me. I want to see how desperate you are. Because I feel so fucking desperate, Rhys, and I don't want to feel that way alone. Trust me to tell you if you go too far."

"Desperate?" he whispered. He pushed her back down onto her knees. In the next second, she was bent over as he knelt behind her and plunged inside.

Kai let out a cry of shock and desire, arching her back and pressing her ass into him as he thrust. "You have no idea how desperate I am. How afraid I was. And now I have you again."

She was so wet, so tight, so good. Sounds of animal pleasure climbed up Rhys's throat as their bodies slapped together. As he let go of everything he'd been feeling for weeks. He twined his fingers in her hair and wrapped a hand around her waist, pulling her upright with her neck exposed. She cried out in pleasure again and writhed against him as he bit the place her neck and shoulder met hard enough to bruise, pinched and rolled her nipples, then slipped his hand between her legs.

"Come, Kai," he commanded, merciless in the pleasure he gave her. "Now."

She obeyed, her inner walls rippling around him as she screamed his name. He bit down on her shoulder, growling in satisfaction. "Good girl."

When she was done, he flipped her onto her back and pinned her hands over her head, then plunged inside her again, his mouth going to her nipples and sucking hard.

"Rhys... Ah!"

"Should I stop?" he asked against her skin.

Kai whimpered, her body relaxing, taking him deep. "N-no. Don't stop. I want you inside me. I want to be full of you."

"Good." Tension built at the base of his spine, his body begging for its own release at the feel of her beneath him. At how well she took him. At the way she wanted him.

Her second orgasm came fast and hard, and only then did Rhys give in to his own.

For a moment, he felt close to her again. For a moment, he felt okay, and he wondered if sex might have fixed the heartswearing after all.

Then the feeling faded, and he was still alone in his mind.

He lay next to Kai, pulled her close, and stroked her back.

"It didn't work," she whispered.

"No. I didn't really think it would."

She sniffled. When Rhys raised his head to look at her, she was blinking rapidly, but not crying. "Should we try again?"

He kissed her. After a few minutes, he was ready, and they did. This time they made love, slow and tender and desperate.

At the end, they were still broken.

When it was over, Kai curled into his side, her head on his shoulder. She sighed, and even though he wasn't in her mind, he thought he knew the depths of her sadness, her exhaustion.

The feelings you have for Kai aren't real. Wrong.

"*Dwi'n di garu di, fy ngariad,*" he said.

Kai lifted her head from his chest and kissed him. "I love you too." She hesitated, toyed with the blanket. "Rhys, what will this change?"

He stroked her back, feeling the scars again. Once, he'd been self-conscious about the marks on his own skin. Now she had more than him, and yet remained flawless. "Nothing."

Kai shook her head and sat up, hugging her knees, but for some reason, the distance between them felt larger than it was.

"The dragons didn't want me before. Now that we're sundered, we'll be lucky if I can stay in Eryri without backlash."

Rhys wrapped his hands around her biceps and pulled her down again. It had been better. While they were making love, he swore he could almost feel her. Almost pretend that they were whole. He wanted that again. "If they try to make you leave, they will have to find another king."

Kai's expression turned fierce. "If they try, I'll gut them. As long as Deryn heartswears and has a kid, the mantle can go to her or the kid someday. It would be stupid of them to get rid of you. You're sort of like an insurance policy."

"That's cold comfort."

Kai looked away. "Sorry. It's all I've got."

The silence grew until it was awkward. He didn't want awkward, he wanted connection. So he kissed her again.

She seemed eager enough, so they made love one more time. After a while, they pulled the second blanket over themselves and fell asleep. Rhys woke briefly when golden light shimmered behind his eyelids. When he opened them, he saw Cadoc standing above them in the tunnel mouth. He set down a golden bowl and dagger—items needed for the flamecalling ritual. When he saw Rhys awake, he waved and said, "Just checking," then left again.

Hours later, Rhys woke to Kai sitting up and stretching beside him. He wasn't sure what time it was, but Ashem would probably come looking for them soon. Wordlessly, Rhys prepared and lit a fire out of the kindling Cadoc had supplied, then he and Kai performed their flamecalling ritual together. She hadn't had much chance to use magic in captivity, but it never hurt for one's internal well of power to be full, especially as vulnerable as they were in that moment. It was another small moment of connection. Of comfort.

When they were finished, Rhys finally spoke. "*Cariad*."

"Hmm?"

Rhys toyed with one frayed corner of the blanket beneath them. "I want to end the war, and I want to do it by luring Owain to Eryri."

Kai stared at him for a long moment. Then, "Yes."

He lifted his gaze to her in disbelief. "Yes? Not 'you're an idiot' or 'you don't have the right to endanger your people'?"

Kai shook her head. "You'll be on your home turf. We can set traps, plan. Control the situation."

The words washed over him with terrible truth. It had been his idea, and he'd thought of the traps, of knowing the terrain.

Rhys found himself arguing against his own idea. "But I'll be inviting Owain to our home. If we lose, where will we go?"

Kai spoke through gritted teeth. "We will not lose. We have to do this, Rhys. Owain can't be allowed."

He waited for her to say, "to win" or something like it, but she didn't.

"All right. I'll call Deryn, talk to Ashem. This issue with humans in the Taklamakan—with your family—I think we can use it to force Owain's hand."

She took a breath. "Rhys, I'm going to free them. I know you probably can't go—that you need to get back to Eryri, but..." She shrugged. "Owain has hit me where it hurts hundreds of times. I think it's fair that I get a chance to hit back."

Rhys closed his eyes and tried to breathe. Even without being in her head, he'd known this was coming. The thought of her in danger again made the muscles on the back of his neck tense until he could feel a headache building and tied his stomach in knots.

Ancients, he'd just gotten her back. They'd barely survived a sundering. He knew they'd been down this road once before, but he'd been careless. He'd thought they were both immortal.

They weren't.

He chose his words with care. "We'll go take a look. After that, we'll have to see where things stand."

He didn't want to fight with her, so he wouldn't stop her from going to the Taklamakan. If her parents *were* there, she had every right to go. But if things went the way he wanted, when he and the others freed the humans and destroyed the facility, Kai would be at least ten miles away.

When they walked back into the main area of the cave, they found Ashem, Cadoc, Morwenna, and the rogues gathered together around a smokeless, fuel-less fire. Cadoc held a battered metal bowl in his good hand, and Rhys could feel the subtle buzz of fire magic surrounding it. It smelled a lot like food, and only then did Rhys realize he was ravenous.

"What's that?" Kai asked Cadoc, leaning toward the bowl. Apparently she was more than a little hungry herself.

Cadoc tasted the steaming liquid. "Broth for Seren. If you two are hungry, there's some elk."

"I'll get it." The male Derkin rogue, Kephas, stood and left the circle.

Rajani, the Naga rogue, scooted over to make room for Rhys and Kai in the circle. They sat, and Rhys leaned over to speak to Ashem. "Do you have your singstone?"

"Yes."

"Call Deryn. I need her to speak with the Lung, Noodinoon, and Mo'o councilmembers."

"Why?" Cadoc asked.

Rhys put a hand into the flames, letting them trickle through his fingers. "They're about to have second thoughts about supporting me, and they're going to contact Owain and tell him so."

"They are, are they?" Ashem considered him, and Rhys nodded.

"Yes. Let Owain believe my rule has been destabilized. That way, when we destroy his potion and pretend to steal some—just after stealing Seren and Kai from the heart of Cadarnle itself, of course—he'll have no choice but to attack Eryri directly. Inside a month, I predict. He never could stand to lose face."

"What?" Ashem asked, voice flat.

Rhys pressed on. "I want ideas for traps. When his army comes for us, I want to subdue as many of his people as we can. I don't want them dead, just unable to fight."

Dead silence met his words. Then Ashem gave a humorless laugh. "You want to anger him enough that he'll attack us? Then draw him to Eryri? Our home?"

"Yes. Where we will be prepared to meet him."

More silence. They all looked at each other. Kai took Rhys's hand. Then Ashem laughed again. "Damn you, Rhys. I think that might work."

Kai stood. "Enough talk. It's time to free my parents, my brother, and whatever other humans Owain is torturing."

Ashem looked to Rhys. Rhys had hoped for time to convince Kai that she didn't need to go to the desert, but he'd known he wouldn't be able to do it. He locked eyes with Ashem. "How soon can we leave?"

Ashem considered. "One hour."

Rhys nodded. "Then let's move."

Owain had sundered his heartswearing, but Rhys was not his father. If Owain had thought that everything he'd done in the past weeks would make Rhys an easier target, he'd been mistaken. He'd finally pushed Rhys beyond his breaking point.

It was time to end the war.

CHAPTER 19
CADOC

"You want me to *what?*"

Cadoc stared at Rhys, a slow dread rising from somewhere around his stomach and overtaking his brain.

Rhys sighed. Around them, the others busied themselves preparing to leave. "I'm promoting you, boyo. Congratulations. You're the new primary bodyguard for the Lady Seeress of Eryri."

"Why?" Cadoc reached for a joke, but seemed to have lost them all. The curse was gone, though only the Ancients knew why. They had Kai and Seren back. He was with his family— most of them. That should have fixed him, but he couldn't seem to stop being broken.

Rhys's gaze went somewhere distant. "We can't take Seren on the raid, and I don't control the vees who guard her in Eryri, or the Lady Protector—the Council does. I can't replace them, and they aren't doing their job."

Fuck. There had to be a way out of this. It was far and away the worst idea Rhys had ever had, and he'd had some bad ones. "Which job?"

Rhys lifted a brow. Despite his apparent ease, Cadoc could see the strain around his eyes, in his movements, which weren't quite abrupt enough to call jerky, but it was a near thing. Sundering was taking a heavy toll.

"The one where they keep her from running off and disappearing for months on end. I need someone in that position I can trust."

Cadoc held up his crushed right hand. "You trust this? You're making a mistake, Rhys. I'm useless." He let his hand drop.

Or maybe that was *why* Rhys had chosen him. Rhys, Ashem, and Morwenna were flying into a potential battle. Rhys had chosen him—weakened but still more or less capable—for the safer job.

Cadoc could hear the stiffness in his own voice. "Ashem would be a better choice. She'll listen to him. She won't to me."

Rhys shook his head. "Ashem can travel without being seen. I need him."

"What about his connection to Kavar? You aren't afraid that will give things away?" Cadoc tucked his bad hand into his jacket.

Rhys's mouth twisted. "I think Ashem knows how to keep his secrets."

"What about Morwenna?"

"Morwenna...doesn't get along with your rogues. I need them to go with Seren too."

Cadoc suppressed a sigh. Morwenna. If the vee was family, she was the rampaging, bossy eldest sister no one wanted to cross. An annoyed Morwenna made life hell for everyone.

Cadoc pressed his lips together and shrugged gracelessly. "Fine. If you need me, I'll do it. I'm sure Rajani and the others won't mind."

The rogues were the only thing that had made life in the

tiny cave bearable. Rhys and Kai had been unconscious. Seren was off limits. Ashem and Morwenna were constantly brooding. Despite that, Rajani told stories every night, illustrated by Tharah's illusions. Kephas, young and bored, needed someone to spar with—even if that someone only had one hand.

Rhys relaxed. "Thank you." He rubbed his chest.

Cadoc pushed his own apprehension to the back of his mind. "You all right?"

Rhys dropped his hand. "It's like being part of an incomplete bond again. It *hurts*. It fades a little when we're close, but it doesn't go away."

"That's something."

Rhys shook his head. "I don't know. Not being heartsworn to her... It's different. Like I used to be able to see all of her, but now I can't. She doesn't mind being...ah...physical, but it's like we can't fully connect."

Cadoc rubbed his lump of a hand. "Seren is a healer. Is there some way she might be able to heal your heartswearing?"

Rhys frowned. "The heartswearing isn't a living thing."

"Relationships grow, change, breathe, die. They seem alive enough to me."

"Figuratively. Not literally." Rhys pinched the bridge of his nose. "It would be worth a try, I suppose. When she's feeling better. I'd—" He exhaled. "In some ways it's freeing, being separate. Kai has always treasured her freedom. The longer this goes on, the more I worry she won't want to be bonded to me."

"Don't be a scalebrain." Cadoc changed the subject. "What about Tharah, Kephas, and Rajani? They've stuck with us. I don't want the Council to do anything stupid once we're back because they used to be rogues."

"If they want to stay in Eryri, I'll assign them a vee when I get back."

Good. They'd hoped for that. "*Diolch.*"

Rhys looked out of the mouth of the cave. The sun was rising. "How soon can you be ready?"

Cadoc forced himself to grin. "As soon as our eminent Golden Lady is."

Rhys gave him a smile just as forced and clapped a hand on Cadoc's shoulder. "Take this." Rhys placed an egg-shaped sunstone in Cadoc's palm. "Ask Seren if she'll look at it again once she's rested. She was always better at interpretations."

Cadoc curled his fingers around the stone and slipped it into a pocket. "I'll tell her we're leaving."

Rhys followed the left fork in the cave and Cadoc went right, toward the exit. He found Seren sitting in the sun at the cave's mouth, alone. Green forest shaded the world beyond the cave, but she sat in profile in a pool of light. The sun kissed the soft lines of her face and brought much-needed pink and gold to her pale cheeks. She had a tatty gray blanket wrapped around her shoulders, clutched closed with one hand at her chest. Her red-gold hair had been washed. Now it dried, loose and draping her body in rich, thick waves.

He pulled up short, heart aching at the sight of her. Beauty and grace made flesh.

She leaned over a broken shard of mirror surrounded on all sides by shards of quartz crystal, humming low in her throat.

Her lightcalling ritual. He hadn't seen this in years. Like transformation between human and dragon forms, Seren's visions required no ritual. But her other abilities, like healing, did.

Like a swarm of fireflies, fractals of light danced off the mirror and crystals, sparking the air around her in a beautiful, delicate swarm. She lifted one pale hand to the center of the swarm, palm down, then slowly turned it over. The dancing lights leaped into her skin, which glowed as it absorbed each little piece. She smiled, and her humming turned to low singing in words he couldn't make out. She opened her eyes, which luminesced, the gold scales around them shimmering.

When Cadoc pictured pure magic, this—Seren's ritual in all its complexity and beauty—always came to mind.

She finished and looked up at him with eyes the color of a tropical sea. More pink suffused her cheeks. "Oh. Yes, *awenydd?*"

"I..." He cleared his throat. "Something. I came here for something."

"I see. Come sit in the sun with me a moment and maybe you'll remember. It's so lovely to be warm after being so long in Cadarnle." And then, curse the Stars, she smiled, and the thoughts that had been on the tip of his tongue fled. He couldn't remember why he'd come to find her, except to stare at her and admire her and love her from a distance from now until the end of his days.

What had Rhys gotten him into?

CHAPTER 20

JULI

J uli slipped through the halls of Cadarnle, invisible to the
minds of the dragons around her. She trailed her fingers
over its veins of gold and ice. The ice should've crumbled
the stone, she knew, and wondered why it hadn't. She thought
of human roads, buckling and cracking from the continual
cycles of heat and cold. The things dragon magic could do for
the human world... Roads, of course, being the least of it. Magic
could improve many, many lives.

Juli had been haunting the corridors of Cadarnle like a
ghost for nearly a week. She'd hidden the stolen key in her
room and was careful to wear the cuffs and collar any time she
wasn't out exploring—not as easy as it sounded when the halls
grew unexpectedly crowded or when one of the emotion-
sensing Lung walked by. Aside from Kavar, they were her only
concern.

Thankfully, emotional control was one of her fortes. The
events of the past few months had been trying, but she was
determined to return to the person she had once been: intelligent, efficient, and self-sufficient.

A child ran down the hall toward her and paused, the girl's little mouth falling open. With a chagrined frown, Juli strengthened the magical barrier that allowed her to pass through the halls unseen. She reached out to the girl's mind and gently folded other thoughts around the memory of a disappearing woman, burying the memory so deep that it would only be found in dreams.

Be more careful, Ashem murmured in her head.

Juli started. *I'm always careful. Now go away so I can listen.*

Kavar almost walked in on your ritual this morning.

Juli let out a quiet huff of breath. *But he didn't. I sensed him in time and still finished before he arrived.*

Ashem's response was the mental equivalent of a grunt. Then his tone turned more serious. *I thought you should know —Rhys and Kai want to sabotage Owain's operation in the Taklamakan. Rhys thinks he can use that and a few other things to prod Owain into attacking Eryri in a few weeks, give or take. We've sent word for Deryn to start laying traps and preparing the people. Except...*

Except what?

I've told Kai that Owain has her parents.

Oh. Terror and worry welled up like blood from a wound. But Juli couldn't let herself think about the Monahans. Emotion, panic included, was like scent to the Lung. That was why she'd spent her time wondering about veins of ice and what dragon magic could do for humans instead of worrying about her chosen family. The best help she could be to anyone from her current position was to do what she had come here to do and not get caught.

Ashem sent comfort through their bond. *We're flying to the Taklamakan now, and we'll be there inside a week. I'm only concerned that this won't be enough, even with the other things Rhys has planned.*

Juli's lips thinned. From what she'd gleaned from Kavar—who was heavily shielding his thoughts from both of them despite his and Ashem's still-open bond—Owain was on edge as it was. It probably wouldn't be hard to push him off the cliff. *If I get close to him, I can plant some suggestions.*

Never mind that a battle like that put Ashem, Kai, and everyone in Eryri in horrible danger.

...and Kavar.

Juli pushed away the thought. She had to focus on the task at hand. *Will that work?*

I don't know. I wouldn't be surprised to find that he wears an onyx bracelet. If you have the chance, do it. But be subtle, aziz-am. Owain is paranoid. Jiang will be in his mind as well, watching him like an eagle. At the very least, I'll need to know if what we're doing is working, and when he starts preparing for the battle.

I can do that, she said. *I'll start now. Be safe.*

And you.

He withdrew.

Despite Kavar trying to keep her out of his head, she knew that he had returned from yet another sweep of the tundra empty-handed. Part of her felt a little guilty, knowing that Rhys and the others had left the area two days ago when he was still out there searching in the cold and dark. But only the very smallest part. It would be a risk, sneaking around Owain with Kavar present, but she had a good hiding spot.

She frowned as she moved through the halls and down several sets of stairs, gently pulling her location from passing dragons' heads as she went, heading for Owain's rooms.

Most of the dragons whose minds she skimmed knew nothing of import. Not surprising. Even Rhys and his Council weren't overly forthcoming with the dragons who called Eryri home. But at least they attempted some sort of transparency with open Council meetings and places around Eryri where the dragons could read about what the Council had been doing.

There was nothing like that here. Owain had done away with the tradition of having a Council. Juli suspected that was why some of Rhys's more hostile followers stuck with him: it was their only chance at power. Owain ruled by himself, with his law enforced by Kavar's vee. But even the vees weren't traditional. In Eryri, dragons were placed in groups when they were children and raised together, learning, working, training, and fighting. By the time they came of age and went to battle for the first time, they were a seamless team. There could be some shuffling if dragons chose to join their mate's vee when they became heartsworn, and there were more elite vees like the Ironscales that pulled the best fighters. But vees, like families, were a fundamental and deeply important part of dragon life. They could remain unchanged for centuries.

In Cadarnle, Owain had broken up the traditional vee system. Instead of being raised in vee groups with only a dozen or so dragons and a focus on cooperation, the young were raised in large, highly competitive classes. Once they became adults, they were organized according to skill. The more elite the warrior, the higher their rank under Owain. He had broken up all the old vees—the dragons who had been adults when he came to power—and done the same thing, forcing them to compete and ranking them by skill on the battlefield. The most elite warriors became part of Kavar's vee. Unlike Ashem, whose vee had held ten dragons at its largest, Kavar commanded about two dozen.

Once, she'd snuck to the surface to watch Kavar and his dragons train. Their skill was astonishing. In a clinical way, Juli wondered if it might be more efficient for Rhys to do the same.

But though Owain had forged several highly effective blades out of the elite vees, he left the weaker ones vulnerable. And few of them cared for each other or protected each other the way Eryri dragons did. Perhaps loving each other gave them an edge, like the Sacred Band of Thebes, a military group comprised of one hundred and fifty committed romantic couples—three hundred—that had been an unstoppable force in the Mediterranean in the fourth century BCE.

Juli's thoughts continued to wander as she cut through the bustling cavern with its huge central amphitheater, keeping to the walls and out of the way of traffic. Balls of white lightning floated in the air, providing light that reflected from the icy ceiling. She suppressed a pang of longing for the sunlit beaches and salty air of Eryri. Sighing with relief to be out of the crowds —it was always harder to hold up a barrier against so many— she reentered the halls on the other side.

She flattened herself against a wall to avoid being run down by a galumphing pack of juveniles. Muttering, she reentered the narrower tunnels that wound through residential areas. The closer she got to Owain's rooms, the emptier the halls were —and the more aware she became of Kavar.

Juli sighed. He was with Owain. She'd have to make sure she hid herself *very* well.

Composing herself, Juli settled across the hall from Owain's room. Cadarnle was dotted here and there with statuary and fountains. This statue, which would be visible to Owain every time he opened his door, was her favorite. It towered over her, a white dragon carved of marble with such skill that she could almost feel the wind that lifted its wings or hear the whistle of air over its scales. It rose into the sky of the artist's imagination, magnificently framed in the alcove by tapestries in jewel tones that draped all three of the surrounding walls. Juli squeezed in behind the statue and settled in the corner where two of the tapestries came together. There was just enough space in the corner for her to slip behind the hangings and sit with her legs drawn tightly to her chest. She pulled the fur-lined blanket she'd brought from her room over her shoulders.

She'd just sat down when Owain flung open the door, shouting. Juli jumped and peered through the small crack between tapestries. To her surprise, a dozen other dragons filed out of the room. She wasn't sure, but she thought they were all vee commanders. The one Owain was shouting at just happened to be Kavar.

"He's sundered. I *handed* him to you, and you still couldn't find him? It's been a week. Ashem will have smuggled him back to Eryri by now, no matter how bad his condition."

Kavar's reply was muted, but Owain's response wasn't. "Your brother is the reason you're here, Kavar. If Ashem is so clever, maybe I should employ him."

Kavar didn't respond to that, except for a surge of rage Juli could feel. On instinct, she reached out to soothe the anger. Kavar's head snapped toward the alcove. He searched for a moment, then his eyes settled on the crack between tapestries.

Oh, no.

He didn't speak to her, but she felt his rage darken. By the time Owain dismissed him fifteen minutes later, Kavar was a roiling sea of anger. Unable to go after her in front of Owain, Jiang, and the other vee commanders, he forced their connection open with shocking strength. *Get back to the room or I'll tell Owain you're there.*

Juli pressed her lips together and shut down the connection. Kavar might be able to see through the barrier that kept her invisible to the other dragons, but it wasn't like he could grab her and drag her out of the corner. Ridiculous man. If she was discovered, he'd only expose himself as her heartsworn and suffer terribly when Owain killed her.

Not waiting for her to emerge, Kavar stalked away with the other vee commanders. Then Owain and Jiang started down the hall in the opposite direction.

Curious, Juli slipped from her hiding spot and followed them. This could be her last chance to find anything out for a while. Kavar would put the cuffs back on after this...unless he couldn't find her. She wondered if she might be able to find another set of abandoned rooms. Perhaps steal food.

She padded after Owain, careful to keep her distance. Jiang, who had stood next to Owain throughout the lecture he'd given Kavar, glided at his side in a body-hugging red gown heavily embroidered with gold.

"You should get rid of him," Jiang snapped. "I don't trust him."

"He didn't give you up in Eryri." Owain's voice was mild now, his thoughts like a calm, dark lake.

He wasn't wearing an onyx charm. He thought Ashem was long gone and didn't think of her at all. Wingless were generally beneath his notice, unless that Wingless happened to be Kai.

Subtly as she could, Juli peered beneath the surface. He had been angry at Kavar, but Kavar had been punished. Justice served, he could let the anger go. Jiang, however, was getting on his nerves. The woman didn't care about anything but her own power.

Juli switched focus. Jiang was frustrated as well, and plotting out ways she could show Owain that Kavar was a traitor. *How did he get out of Eryri? He was supposed to be there to take the blame for the poisoning. I'll have to—*

A hand gripped Juli's arm and yanked her back against a hard chest, another hand going over her mouth.

If you make a sound, we are both dead. Kavar.

Juli thrashed and bit his hand, trying desperately to hear the end of Jiang's thought. But she'd lost the thread and couldn't focus with Kavar dragging her back the way they'd come. Trying to catch Jiang's thoughts again was like trying to catch mist in her hands.

Kavar half carried her, silently kicking and clawing, all the way to her rooms and closed the door behind them. It was a good thing he could also cast a barrier that made eyes slide away from him, because he would've looked like an idiot wrestling with air.

"How did you get out?" He thrust a finger toward the manacles and collar she'd abandoned on the low table. "How did you get those off?"

Juli shrugged, wary. She might be magically stronger than him, but physically she wouldn't stand a chance. There was nowhere to run here. No one to help her. Kavar was the closest thing to an ally she had. If he turned on her, she was alone.

"Don't shrug at me." He stalked toward her. Juli stood her ground, but that only made him angrier. Kavar grabbed her shoulders and shook. "Do you know what will happen to you if you get caught? What will happen to me?"

Juli tried to pull away, but he squeezed until she writhed in pain. She stomped on his instep, but she was only wearing socks—it was easier to sneak around without making noise that way—and Kavar was wearing heavy boots.

"Why do you think I agreed to stay with you, Kavar? Out of the goodness of my heart? Because Ashem couldn't have wiped the floor with you?"

Something dangerous flashed in Kavar's eyes. He shoved, and Juli fell hard onto the low couch. "So much for holding up your end of the deal." He bared his teeth. "I shouldn't have expected you to have integrity, Wingless." He spat the word like an insult.

Juli resisted the urge to rub her bruised arms and stood. "You're one to talk about integrity."

"When have I ever broken my word? I let Kai go." Kavar gestured wildly. "I have you here, Ashem's heartsworn, and I haven't said a thing to Owain."

Juli snorted. "I'm also your heartsworn, and it's in your best interest to keep me safe. Let's call a spade a spade, Kavar. I'm here because you want to hurt Ashem. You're hoping I'll sleep with you. As if I haven't made it abundantly clear you repulse me."

She told herself that last part wasn't a lie.

Kavar grabbed her so fast she couldn't react. He snaked one arm around her waist, the other grabbing a fistful of her hair and yanking her head back. Juli squeaked and struggled.

He only held her tighter.

His face inches from hers, he pushed his way into her mind, flooding her with a hot rush of lust—his, not hers—that made her weak in the knees. Despite the fact that it made her sick, she couldn't stop her own body from responding.

He nuzzled her cheek and whispered in her ear, "Oh, Juliet. If I wanted you, I would take you."

Oh...my...

A flash of queasy unease passed through Kavar, bringing Juli back to her senses. He might threaten these things, but even he couldn't stoop so low as to actually go through with it.

Let me go. She sent a spear of pain lancing through Kavar's mind. He winced and stumbled back. When he straightened, Juli wound up and slapped him full across the face.

Kavar lunged at her, silver eyes alight and livid, but Juli skipped out of the way and he tripped over the coffee table, sprawling onto the floor.

Ashem—who had become aware of the altercation as soon as Kavar grabbed her—was shouting something into her mind. From the intensity, he meant it for Kavar and she was just getting the spillover. But she'd spent twenty-one years defending herself. She didn't need to depend on a knight in shining armor just because one was willing.

Juli leaned over Kavar's prone body. Speaking through her teeth, she said, "If you touch me like that again, you will *never* wake up."

She turned and marched away. Ashem was in a state, so she assured him that she was all right, and no, he could not come get her, because Rhys needed him. When she went to fill one of the ceramic mugs in the basin that served as a kitchen sink, she realized her hand was shaking. Steadying her mug with her second hand, she turned to regard Kavar over the rim.

He pulled himself off the floor. His cheekbone had hit the corner of the table, and he was bleeding. She expected rage. Instead, he was quiet. Not contrite, not from the way he was clenching and unclenching his fists, but...uncertain?

Kavar had always seemed smug and cocky. But for all his show, he lacked the conceited surety that everything he did was right. A surety Ashem had in abundance.

Curious, Juli slipped into Kavar's mind, just a little bit.

He was worried. Not just that Owain would find out that Kavar had brought Ashem's heartsworn into Cadarnle, but that she might be caught. Hurt. He was torn between wanting her and hating her. He knew how precious she was to Ashem, and that, combined with their own heartswearing bond, made him want to protect her—which he also hated.

He *did* still care for Ashem.

Shocked, Juli pulled back before he could catch her there.

Kavar snatched the cuffs from the table. "Put these on.

You're here to keep me from climbing the walls, not to spy for my brother."

It was degrading, standing there while he clasped the manacles around her wrists and the collar around her neck, but she did it. Fighting wouldn't do her any good. When he finished, Juli took a cloth and wet it in the water from her cup. Kavar stepped back as she approached, but he came up against the counter and had nowhere to go.

Silently—and while ignoring Ashem's mutterings—she pressed the cloth to his cut. Kavar swallowed, and Juli could feel him wavering between hate and want.

That was fine. Good, even. She could use that. After today, she would have to.

After a moment, he shoved her hand away, then tossed the room until he found where she'd hidden the key, in the stone container that held flour. Turning it over in his hand, he glared at her, then stalked from the rooms without a word.

You're going to be the death of me, Juliet King, Ashem murmured.

Juli sagged. She knew how much Ashem hated when she let Kavar close or took risks, and she'd done both in the past hour. *We have to make the most of this chance, love. If he's conflicted, that means we could win him over. Can you imagine what the three of us could do together?*

Ashem said nothing, but from what Juli could sense, it was as if Ashem felt about Kavar the way Kavar felt about her. He missed his brother, but hated missing him. He felt betrayed by their past, the way Kavar had chosen Owain over him.

Probably the same way Kavar felt betrayed by Ashem choosing Rhys.

Juli tried to imagine suddenly finding herself on opposite sides of a war with Kai. How painful it would be.

Love could so quickly turn to hate. Maybe she was crazy...

Or maybe she could help the brothers turn it back.

CHAPTER 21

CADOC

C adoc watched Seren from across the fire as she laid gentle fingers on Tharah's face.

Bare fingers.

Kephas had whacked the Wonambi woman a good one while they were sparring after dinner, and she had a goose egg on her temple. She said it was nothing, but Seren insisted on healing it.

She still wore the fur-lined dress Owain had provided her. The veil was over her face as well, so her hands were the only bit of skin he could see. Cadoc found his gaze sliding over them. Small and square palms, nimble fingers, round nails short to keep them from catching on her gloves.

Ancients, he wanted those hands on him.

Stop. This road leads nowhere but ruin.

A slight tremor ran through Seren's fingers as soft golden light gleamed between them. The goose egg shrank, but Cadoc watched the women in concern. Seren still hadn't recovered—Rajani had to carry her when they flew, and going carefully meant they were taking twice the time they should to get home.

Seren stood, her skirt falling in graceful folds around her, and accepted her gloves gingerly from Kephas.

Cadoc glared. The Derkin man had taken to following her around like a forlorn pup. If he wasn't careful, Cadoc was going to have to remind him—forcefully—about the sacred nature of the Seeress.

Seren spoke, voice sweet and serene. "Thank you, Kephas." She glanced around at the other rogues huddled by the fire they'd made in an abandoned human building. They'd stopped for the night outside a rural town in the southwestern United States.

"Anyone else?" Seren asked.

Kephas and Rajani shook their heads. Kephas, of course, was a fool. Even if he'd been at death's door, Seren couldn't have healed him. Cadoc tucked his maimed hand deeper into his pocket, and his good hand toyed with the hilt of the long dagger strapped to his hip.

She couldn't heal either of them.

Something hard and cool brushed his broken fingers. Seren's pearl on its gold chain. He'd found it after Owain took her. He'd forgotten he was carrying it around.

"Sing us a song tonight, *awenydd*," Rajani said from her place by the fire.

Sunder it, she *knew* he didn't want to sing.

"Come," the scarlet-eyed woman coaxed. "You're going home. Surely there's a song for that."

Cadoc tried to beg off, but she wouldn't let him. He sighed. "All right."

He chose a song about homecoming. Partway through he lost the heart of it. The music was flat to his ears, the words empty. From the way the others smiled and clapped or stomped their feet, they didn't hear anything wrong with it. That was something, he supposed.

You're going home.

Could a man go home if he wasn't the same man who had left? Would it be home, changed as it was? Griffith was gone, Ffion pregnant, and Rhys and Ashem sworn. And now Rhys and Kai sundered. Nothing would be the same.

He hoped the others were safe.

The song ended, and Cadoc convinced Rajani to tell a story instead of giving in to a request for another tune. He absently counted the dragons in the old abandoned living room, blinked, then counted again.

He swore. Seren was gone.

A smear on the dusty floor from the trailing skirt of her dress led Cadoc to the back door, which sat slightly ajar. Cadoc yanked it open and nearly ran straight into her. She started to topple back, and he caught her by the sleeve with his good hand.

"Damn it, Seren. What are you doing out here?" He pulled to keep her upright. She overbalanced and crashed into him, her arms going around his neck, soft body coming full against his. The scent of sandalwood, roses, and *her* stampeded his brain into mush. He remembered what her lips looked like without the veil. Full, pink, luscious—

He swallowed and waited for her to regain her feet, battling for all he was worth not to let his mind wander. Not to remember that he'd held her like this once before.

Once, when they were young, and he'd thought there might be a way.

Then she'd had a vision that saved Rhys's life. That moment had thrown everything into perspective. She was the Seeress, and her visions were necessary. He was no one—an idiot bard whose only use was to make others laugh.

He'd walked away and never looked back.

Liar. You look back every lonely night.

"What are you doing out here?" he repeated, voice sharper than he intended.

"Getting air." She matched him tone for tone.

Cadoc willed his irritation away. "Rhys asked me to protect you. I can't do that if you wander off."

"Thank you for your concern." Seren pulled her arm from his grasp and lifted her chin. "But I assure you, I had no intention of running away."

Cadoc squinted. There were wet spots on the veil below Seren's chin, as if water had dripped onto it. He looked up, but there was no rain. Had she been crying?

He didn't get to ask. Seren swept past him into the entryway of the abandoned house. He followed and caught up to her before she rejoined the others. "I told him you wouldn't want this. Me for a bodyguard."

Seren didn't turn. "I can understand the need for it on the road, but once we get to Eryri I won't need anyone. I have Iolani and the vees assigned by the Council to watch my rooms." Her voice was prim beneath the veil. "Besides, I'm sure you'd rather be with Rhys."

Cadoc's smile was bitter. "I'm afraid there isn't much use for a one-handed warrior in the King's Vee."

Seren made a sound of disgust and resignation, but when she spoke again, her voice was softer. "You are still a warrior."

Her words struck something in him that felt like hope. Acceptance. Life *as he was*, not as his stubborn pride wished him to be. He deflected the thoughts with humor. "It could be worse, my lady. He could have assigned Ashem."

Seren's laugh was surprised. "Stars forbid."

She leaned against a wall outside the living room. Cadoc could see the others beyond the empty doorway, listening raptly to Rajani's story. Her tales had that effect.

Seren said, "I keep wishing I was different. That I hadn't

been so stupid. That I could have been a soldier, like Deryn. Maybe I wouldn't have gotten captured in the first place."

Cadoc settled against the opposite wall and kept his voice low. "If Owain had wanted to take Deryn that day, he could have."

She paused. In the shadows of her veil, he thought he caught a smile. "Do you not wish me different , Cadoc ap Brychan?"

Cadoc knew he should go into the well-lit room with the others, away from her. But he kept remembering their last trip to Eryri. Remembering before. For all he'd pushed her away outside, he craved time alone with her, and this—with several feet of space between them—was safe enough. Seren's presence comforted him. When he was with her, it was easy to believe the world wasn't all bad. Easy to believe he could still find his way, even if his path wasn't one he'd expected.

"No, my lady. I do not."

She tilted her head down, as if looking at her hands. "I wish you would call me Seren. You do. Sometimes."

He was trying to break the habit. "It wouldn't be right."

Seren gave a dismissive flick of her hand, and Cadoc's mouth twisted in a wry smile. If only he didn't *like* her so much, he might be able to stay away better.

He fished her necklace from his pocket. "Here."

Seren's eyes brightened and she took it. "You found it?"

"I went to enough trouble to fetch that pearl for you out of the sea." He'd well-nigh drowned. "I wouldn't want you to lose it. The chain is broken." He'd been tying it—with much trouble —around his wrist.

"That's easy enough to fix. Thank you."

"Lady Seren!" Tharah called from inside the room. "You said you'd finish telling me the story of what happened on the island!"

Cadoc—who'd made sure he was visible to the others through the doorway—glanced at Seren. He wasn't ready for their time to end. "The lady may not want to talk about how she was captured."

Seren shrugged and went into the room, turning her veiled head to look at Cadoc over her shoulder. "Why not? It's only a story of my own incompetence."

She said it so cheerfully that the former rogues smiled. Seren settled next to Tharah on the couch, firelight shimmering off the veil. "Where did we leave off? That's right. Mair had drugged Princess Aderyn and me and locked us in a room. I was dead asleep, but sometimes I get...premonitions, a feeling like something is about to happen. They always wake me and this one was no different. Only, I couldn't wake Deryn. I used my healing magic to purge the drugs from her system. She broke us out of the room and we ran outside. Cadoc was still cursed and attacking Rhys—"

"We remember that part," Kephas said.

"Of course." Backlit by the fire, he could see the shadow of Seren's lips curve beneath the fabric. "Deryn told me to stop Mair, so I ran to her and begged her not to kill Rhys—Deryn never would've forgiven her, you see. She's never wanted to be queen.

"Mother wouldn't listen. She struck me." Seren's fingers rose to the side of her face. "Her rings sliced my cheek." A self-deprecating laugh. "I suppose I can say I've been injured in battle at least once. It did bleed quite a bit."

Cadoc's anger flared at the thought of Seren being hurt, and by her own mother. No one deserved that, least of all someone as kind and good as the Seeress.

Then his mind caught on something she'd said.

Her rings sliced my cheek... It did bleed quite a bit.

Oblivious to his thoughts, Seren continued. "Mair

commanded Penelope and the others to force-feed me the vial of potion I wore that would bring on a vision. The next thing I knew, I was in Cadarnle. As you can see, it isn't exactly a heroic tale. I was taken captive because I was silly and weak."

"You woke Princess Aderyn," Kephas said. The others chimed in as well, insisting she'd been strong.

Cadoc was only half listening. That day was a jumble of memories, but one stood above the rest. There had been nothing. Red mist. And then warmth melted the ice of the curse. He'd been out of his mind, then he'd come back to himself. Cursed, and then not. There hadn't been time to question it that day, and hardly any since.

Her rings... It did bleed...

Throat dry, heart pounding, Cadoc stared at Seren.

An image flashed through his head of Mair removing a sharp-edged ruby ring from a silver keeping box—a box that blocked magic. She'd hidden the ring inside to make Cadoc believe the curse was broken, so she could get him close to Rhys again.

Ashem had suggested Mair's death broke the curse, but Cadoc had come to himself before then.

The curse is bound in pain, in coming apart and destruction. To untether a binding that dark, you need light. Creation and love. You need the blood of your parents, your children, or the blood of your heartsworn.

Cadoc inhaled, everything in him rejecting the realization that, heedless, crashed into him, upending everything. *No.*

But there it was, laid out in front of him at last. Seren bled on that ring. Seren's blood had undone the curse. She wasn't his parent or child.

He clutched his bad hand in his lap. Luck may not have been fond of him, but surely even she wouldn't be that cruel.

"Are you all right?"

Cadoc jumped. Rajani stood in front of him. The others were laying out blankets, getting ready for bed. He wasn't sure how much time had passed.

"Well enough." His gaze darted to Seren. Maybe a stronger man could have lived with the mystery, but he had to know. He had to be sure. "Lady Seren, if I could speak to you about...ah... our travel plans for tomorrow?"

"Of course." She followed him back out to the tiny porch where he'd nearly knocked her down. Cadoc scratched the back of his neck. "Lady, I was wondering. You said Mair's rings cut you?"

"I did." Her tone was unreadable. He wished she didn't wear that cursed veil. She probably thought he was crazier than humans on a hunt.

"Do you remember which of Mair's rings it was?"

Seren's head tilted, and she was silent for a moment. "It had to be either the ruby or the moonstone. Weren't they the ones that looked like contorted porcupines? Why?"

His throat constricted.

Seren was his heartsworn. Or would be, if they ever touched.

He couldn't feel his feet under him. His body had gone numb. Cadoc put his good hand against the closed door, holding himself up. "Just curious. She—she wore so many."

Right in front of him. All those times he'd been so careful not to touch her, but he could have his future. His hand. A family.

He could have *Seren*.

It would take no more than the whisper of skin against skin.

She tilted her head. "What does this have to do with travel?"

"Nothing. About tomorrow..." *Get ahold of yourself, boyo. Don't think now. Think later.*

186

His brain refused to comply. Seren was his heartsworn, or his potential heartsworn, and she was the Seeress. If he touched her—if she became his heartsworn in truth—she would lose the Sight and the advantage it gave Rhys.

Cadoc remembered Rhys's eyes, glowing like twin stars the night Cadoc had kissed Kai. That night and every night since, Cadoc had sworn that he wouldn't make a mess of things again.

"What about tomorrow? Are you all right?" She sounded concerned.

His breathing was harsh in his ears. "Just a dizzy spell. It will pass."

Seren raised her hands as if to touch his face. "You don't look well."

Cadoc backed away.

"Cadoc?"

He straightened. "I am well, I promise. I just wanted to say that you should rest. I want to make it to the waystation tomorrow. It will be a long flight."

Seren hesitated. "You wanted me to come out here so you could tell me to get some rest?"

Cadoc nodded. For the first time in his life, his words were gone.

"All right. Well...thank you. I will."

"Good night, my lady."

"Good night, Cadoc." She went inside, leaving him alone.

Cadoc sank onto the step, his head in his good hand, eyes squeezed shut. Seren.

Kind. Beautiful. Strong. Forbidden.

Hardening himself against his feelings, Cadoc straightened. It didn't matter what he'd found out. It didn't matter what he wanted. He would not make a mess, and he would not hurt her.

He had to keep her safe, even if that meant protecting her from himself.

As for Seren, if she knew, she might— What? Pity him? Avoid him? Or—the thought brought both hope and horror to his mind—want him. If she asked to be with him, despite it all...

He'd wanted her for so long. Denying himself was one thing, but if Seren asked him, he would say yes.

That meant that she could never, ever know.

CHAPTER 22
KAI

K ai climbed onto Rhys's back as the sun began to set. They flew west through the mountains until they crossed the final peaks into the desert basin, only stopping twice when sundering pains ripped through Rhys and Kai. Tane and two of the Ironscales went ahead to scout. Kai waited for their return with Rhys and Ashem, huddling between sand dunes a few miles outside where Ashem said the city was located. Morwenna was there as well, a slender red-black dragon curled in the sand a little ways away, studiously ignoring Kai and Rhys. That suited Kai just fine.

Rhys lay on the ground, absorbing the last of the sun's heat from the sand, his tail impatiently flicking dust into the air. Kai lounged in the crook of his elbow, letting sand trickle through her hand and over his scales as she sang quietly to herself.

She leaned back against Rhys's blood-red scales. "Remember, before the battle over the Bering Sea, I asked if you were afraid and you said no?"

Rhys arched his neck so he could look down at her. *Yes.*

"You want to hear something strange?"

Always.

She ran her fingers through the sand. "I don't think I am either. Some of the worst things that could happen to me have happened. I survived."

She should have been afraid, she knew. Pre-dragon Kai would have been afraid. Post-dragon Kai was ready to reclaim her family and grind Owain's plans into the dust. If she died... Well, death was just nothing, wasn't it? It wasn't worse than torture and sundering.

Rhys blew a short, sharp burst of hot air, sending loose tendrils of hair streaming back over her shoulder. He tried to hide it, but she knew he was upset that she wouldn't stay out of the fight.

"Come on, Rhys." Kai tried to keep her tone conversational. "Griffith never tried to stop Ffion from taking part in a fight. Not even when he knew she was pregnant."

Rhys brought his head down and gave her a gentle nudge with his nose. *Amusing that you think you know the content of their marital conversations better than I.*

She cocked a brow. "So he did try to keep her from fighting?"

Rhys was quiet a beat too long. *Ffion has been a soldier for a thousand years.*

"Uh-huh. So you never heard him argue with her either."

That doesn't mean it never happened.

"True." But Kai had known Ffion for months now, and the vee told stories of Griffith. Kai was confident he wouldn't have presumed to make decisions for Ffion.

A shadow blotted out the stars. Rhys leaped to his feet, scooping Kai below him so he was between her and the newcomer, but it was only Tane and his scouts. The Mo'o's wings fluttered like lionfish frills as he landed with his scouts on either side of him. One was a large bronze-scaled Bida, the other a small, hawklike Noodinoon with feathered wings.

Kai hadn't spoken to them much, but she knew the Noodinoon woman was named Isi and the Bida man was named Thabo. Noodinoon were weather-controlling dragons indigenous to North America. As dragons, they came in a variety of colors that reminded Kai of a great purple and blue storm rolling in over a red desert. The Bida were the largest of the dragons, a study in the marriage of elegance and power. Their bodies were covered in palm-sized metallic scales that ranged from gold to bronze to a deep, shimmering black. Two twisting horns arched back from their triangular heads. Their magic was the manipulation of kinetic energy. Which, according to Ffion, made their powers among the most versatile of all the clans. Kai hadn't lived among dragons long enough to see their power in action, but hoped to soon.

Kai scooted out from under Rhys's scaly red belly as Tane began his report to Ashem.

So far, all is quiet. The city is laid out like a circle. It's about eight miles in diameter. You can't see it from here, but you will once we go through the barrier.

"Barrier?" Kai interrupted. "Is Kavar here?"

Tane shook his huge head, frills waving as if he were underwater. *The Ancients had their own ways of hiding things. Kohu te Moana has a barrier, as well. It's more modern, so not as strong. Dragons and Wingless can see through it, but humans cannot.*

"What's Kohu te Moana?" Kai asked.

Tane glanced at Rhys, as if he was surprised Kai didn't know. *It's the name of the archipelago where the Mo'o offered sanctuary to the king when his home was destroyed.*

"Eryri?" Kai asked.

Rhys blinked his enormous blue eyes. *Eryri is only the*

name of the mountain in which we live—the Mo'o were gracious enough to let us call it that when we got there. The island is Wailele. The archipelago is Kohu te Moana. I should have said so before. My apologies, Tane.

Tane nodded, and Kai filed the information away. It was an effective reminder of how little she knew about dragons. "So dragons have other ways of making barriers. Kavar isn't here."

Not Kavar, but there are sentries. Tane looked over his shoulder toward the invisible city and told them what he knew. Each sentry flew patrol over approximately a mile of land around the border of the city. In addition, the sentries visually checked in with each other each time they circled around. They didn't go quickly—there would be about ten minutes between each check-in. If one sentry didn't see the other when they made their rounds, they would roar. If the missing sentry didn't answer using a certain kind of roar within thirty seconds, the original dragon would sound the alarm. Half the dragons that guarded the perimeter would immediately head straight for the place where the cordial is made. The other half would tighten their circle, moving in to cover the inner part of the city.

"How do you know all that?" Kai asked.

We've been watching. They do drills. Ashem's voice carried an overtone of "duh" that made Kai narrow her eyes.

"You do drills," she muttered.

Ashem snorted, sending up a shower of sand. *Of course I do.*

Kai ducked the sandy wave of air and rolled her eyes, wishing Juli was there. "So, that's what we're up against. What's the plan?"

The others gathered around as Rhys spoke. Even Morwenna left off kicking sand or whatever she was doing to stand nearby, tail flicking impatiently. He had to stop once, rubbing his chest. But thankfully the pains seemed to be bearable for both him and Kai that day.

Their routes cover a mile, Rhys said. *They may notice dragons, but probably not much smaller humans. We'll transform and sneak past them on the ground.*

"How many dragons are in the middle?" Kai asked.

Our scouts only counted ten guarding the facility itself, which lies directly at the heart of the city. With his head, Tane indicated what looked to Kai like empty desert.

"Only ten? Wow. Owain was really counting on the fact that you'd never find out about this, wasn't he?" she asked Rhys.

Both of us are working with extremely finite resources, Rhys said. *We can only do as much as we can do.*

Tane continued. *There are too few of us to fight them, but with only ten, Ashem may be able to overwhelm enough of them to give us the upper hand. We also have some devices loaded with Naga venom. They're made of glass. When they break, the venom will vaporize into a cloud that should put anyone who inhales it to sleep.*

Kai frowned. "Where did we get those?"

Dragons from Eryri brought them when we thought we were going to besiege Cadarnle, Rhys said. *They're experimental. Untested. But if they work, it will be a perfect way to remove enemies from the battlefield without killing them. Once the way is clear, we'll destroy the artifacts used to manufacture the cordial and free any living humans we find.*

Like her parents. Her stomach tightened, and Kai looked around at the dragons. "Well? What are you waiting for? Let's go."

The dragons all became human and huddled close to Ashem. He cast a barrier around them, though Kai couldn't sense any difference. The entrance to the city was marked by a tree on a pile of rocky, solid ground. It stood like an island among the shifting sands. Sands that were finding their way into every nook and cranny of Kai's clothing, hair, and eyes.

She took Rhys's hand as they walked, but didn't make eye contact. She didn't want to see the "I wish you'd stayed behind but I can't say anything because I don't want you to hate me" look in his eyes again.

Kai saw the sentry first, a shadow flying low, wide figure eights through the sky to the east, making its way toward them. Then the air shimmered, distracting her. Magic poured over her like a cold shower. This was the barrier. Between one blink and the next, they were through.

The dusty desert fell away to reveal the magnificent remains of a vast ruined city that glowed in the light of the stars. The stone the ancient dragons had used was like nothing Kai had ever seen, shining with a cool, pale light. Like someone had captured the full moon and carved it into buildings and streets.

Inside, the air was heavy with age and emptiness. Tumbled towers and fallen columns engraved with intricate geometric patterns were scattered among half-toppled conical buildings. In some places, entire walls had fallen away, leaving empty rooms open to sand and sky.

No one spoke as they crept beneath the sentry flying overhead and in between the buildings.

Kai had visited a few cities in her life. Denver, Chicago, L.A., Seattle—but she'd never seen buildings like this. Dragon-sized skyscrapers. She gaped and didn't feel bad about it—Rhys was gaping too. Maybe he'd never seen a city built by his own people before. Kai tried to imagine seeing Denver or Chicago for the first time. Or, more accurately, the ruins of Denver or Chicago after humans had lost the ability to create anything but villages.

"We've lost so much," he murmured. "They call me a king,

but what do I rule? Ruin and remnants. Nothing compared to what we were."

Kai squeezed his hand. "That's why they need you, Rhys. If Owain has his way, there will be no more dragons at all."

The roads were laid out in curves that flowed back and forth, wide enough for several dragons to walk side by side. Once they'd gone about a mile in, Ashem motioned them into one of the few buildings still standing. They walked through a stone archway and entered a space large enough for at least twenty dragons to mingle comfortably.

"In our human forms, it will take an hour of walking to reach our destination. We want to strike quickly, with no chance for them to raise alarms." Ashem glanced out of one of the enormous windows at the moon. "We'll transform, fly low through the city, then turn back into humans when we reach our destination."

"Where are we going?" Kai whispered. "Where are they holding people?"

Thabo answered in a voice as smooth as Cadoc's, though several notes lower and flavored with an accent from West Africa. "The city was set up to channel magic into its center, to a tower where they performed their greatest magics. That's where we will find Owain's people."

Thabo folded into a crouch and picked up a broken bit of white stone. It was almost translucent, like white smoke made solid, and it shone against the darkness of his hands.

Kai crouched beside him. "Is it marble?"

Thabo shrugged. "Perhaps. The Ancients had ways beyond what dragons today can dream. For all we know, they magicked it into being without a second thought."

Isi picked up her own bit of stone. She was younger than any of the other dragons Kai had seen, hardly more than their equivalent of a teenager. "If ancient dragons were so powerful, why aren't they still around?"

Thabo gave her a flat look. "What is that human phrase? The bigger they are, the harder they fall."

Thabo chafed his arms. The temperature had plummeted with the sunset, which didn't bother Kai as much as the fact that it was so dry it sucked the moisture right out of her mouth.

Rhys broke off his conference with Ashem and Tane and approached them. "Thabo, Isi, would you stay with her?"

He was going to try to keep her out of the action after all. But she *needed* this. Already, she could feel the thrill in her blood pushing away the emptiness. She advanced on Rhys, thrusting a finger at his chest. "I don't want babysitters."

His face was impassive, but he grasped her wrist and pressed her hand against his heart. "I told you that you could fight. I didn't say I was going to leave you unprotected."

Beneath her palm, his heartbeat was steady and strong. It was almost enough to make her waver. But that wasn't going to happen. "We're saving *my* family, Rhys. Wherever they are, I am going."

"I know, *cariad*. But not only are you the Queen of Dragons, you are the very breath in my lungs. If you want to fight, you will fight. But *I* will take precautions to ensure you see the sun rise."

The tenderness in his eyes and subdued desperation in his voice reached deep into her chest, sparking the emotion she was trying to keep suppressed as if he'd touched her with a live wire.

Then a sundering pain hit. She gasped. Rhys's face went pale, and he took her into his arms, rubbing her back until it passed.

He might have held her longer, but being close to him was

too much. She stepped away, and the dragons transformed. Rhys slid into his harness. Since she might have to jump off at a moment's notice, Kai climbed up between his wings and held on to the straps instead of clipping herself to him. Rhys leaped into the air, keeping low as he soared after Ashem through the wide lanes between buildings. The others glided silently behind.

The city flowed around them, clusters of broken towers stacked like massive Jenga blocks, their magnificent white stones scattered and buried in dust-pale sand. The Ancients seemed to have preferred open buildings. Most of them were like cakes—layers stacked on top of each other separated by stone columns. They towered overhead, dwarfing the sixty- to eighty-foot dragons the way human skyscrapers dwarfed people. Scattered among the wreckage were huge shards that looked like shattered gemstones, darkly glittering in every color Kai could name.

It hit her then that she wasn't just flying toward death; she was flying toward Owain's dragons. Fear shot through her, turning her blood to ribbons of ice. What if they didn't kill her? What if they took her back to that cold, opulent room with its drain on the floor and its chains?

She shook herself as Rhys set down behind a ruined wall. *Shut out the fear. Don't let it touch you. Don't let anything touch you.*

They settled outside a huge, clear space. At its center was the largest building they'd seen yet. A mind-bendingly tall construction that twisted toward the sky in elegant, ever-narrowing spirals of carved stone.

That's it, Rhys said.

Instead of shining white, it emanated a dull pewter glow. There was a thirty-yard circle of open sand around the base of the tower. Kai couldn't see any dragons peering out of its many arching windows, but that didn't mean the dragons couldn't see them.

Shifting back and forth much more will leave us too exhausted to fight, Tane said.

I don't see that there's much of a choice, Commander, Rhys replied. *A diversion to pull the guards' attention away could bring every dragon in this place down on us.*

What about something normal for the desert? Isi asked.

All of the dragons looked at her, and she crouched a little lower. She had to be good, Kai knew, to be in the Ironscales. At the moment, though, she looked like a nervous teenager. Even if she was a dragon.

A sandstorm? Ashem asked.

Isi nodded, nervously readjusting her storm-colored wings.

Tane shook his head. *One Noodinoon alone couldn't do it. She would need to link with at least one other.*

"Me." Kai stepped forward. "That's what Wingless magic is, right? I'm like extra batteries or nitrous or something."

Rhys sputtered, *No,* at the same time Ashem said, *That might work.*

We were just sundered, Rhys protested. *She needs to save her strength for the fight.*

Kai touched his hand. "If this works, the fight will be easier. We might as well try. How does it work?"

Nothing but shuffling feet and swishing tails.

Kai swept her gaze over all four of them. "You won't tell me, or you never cared enough about the Wingless to ask?"

None of them met her eyes. Kai guessed it was the second, or else Rhys would be giving her a defiant look.

It's instinctive, Ashem grumbled. *You should just know.*

Kai shook her head and brushed sand from her clothes. "Wow. All right. I guess we'll experiment."

Rhys's claws sank into the sand, but he didn't argue further.

Isi transformed back into her human body. She had an athletic build, like Kai, with warm terra cotta skin and gray-brown eyes that were both direct and curious. Also like Kai, she had black hair. Isi's, however, was thicker and smoother, and she wore it pulled half back in a topknot. She and Kai settled on the ground cross-legged in front of each other. Isi held out her hands, and Kai put her palms over the other woman's.

"Noodinoon link to do larger magic," Isi said. "I'll attempt a link with you, and we'll see if that works."

Kai nodded and braced herself. But when a tendril of power wrapped around her, it was far gentler than she expected. Her first instinct was to push it off. Instead, she leaned into it until something inside her *clicked*, like it was snapping into place. Magic rose up in her. Not the familiar maelstrom of the fire, but something...purer.

Something like possibility.

It flowed out of her through the tendril, which Kai could tell connected her to Isi. The Noodinoon opened her eyes wide and gasped, a tremor running through her body. "I have never linked with Wingless before. There is so much magic here."

The incessant breeze that had been swirling at their feet picked up, blowing sand the way Kai had seen snow blow across roads during windy winter nights. It rose, snatching at Kai's clothes and tugging the hair that had escaped her braid. It took a few minutes, but far in the distance—only visible because of the soft glow of the buildings—dust began to billow up off the ground like rising smoke. The smoke grew, forming a cloud that wasn't near large enough to encompass the dragon city. It would, however, be plenty large enough to cover their entrance into the tower.

Kai pulled off the scarf she'd wound over her hair to protect it during the flight and looped it over her mouth and nose instead. The dust cloud had grown into a black wall that swallowed the glow of the city as it advanced, rolling toward them like a tsunami of darkness.

Isi smiled at Kai. "It's begun, and that's the hardest part. I need to move around to work. I'll maintain the link as long as I need it, but you should stand near Rhys before the storm reaches us."

She released Kai and they both stood. Kai walked over to Rhys and positioned herself between his front legs just as the sandstorm hit them. A thousand particles stung her skin. But instead of being buried, she just felt gritty.

"This is not nearly as dramatic as they make it seem in the movies," Kai said. The air smelled dry and dusty and the wind sighed in her ears, sounding remarkably like waves crashing against shore. "I thought I'd have to fight not to be blown away."

Does that disappoint you? Rhys asked.

Kai laughed without humor. "No. Everything else is dramatic enough."

A few minutes later, however, she found out that the movies had gotten something else wrong. She might not be half buried in sand and unable to breathe, but everything was very, very dark. Yes, it was night, but the whole desert had been lit by the moon and the ambient radiance of the city. Now she couldn't make out her hand an inch from her face. Though she was standing right beneath Rhys, she might have been alone in the world. At one point he shuddered above her. She unconsciously rubbed his scaled leg as he had her back.

Ashem said one day the pains would pass. Kai wasn't sure if she believed him.

A strand of terror twined around her like a strangling vine. She shot her arms out to either side. She banged her fingers against the hard muscles of Rhys's legs, scraping the skin off a couple of her knuckles. Kai swore, but didn't take her hands off Rhys. She just needed to know he was there.

All right? His voice was gentle.

"Yeah." Her response was quiet, but he would hear.

Power drained out of Kai and into the Noodinoon, and Kai could feel the magic leeching both of their strength as they fed the storm. Then Isi severed their connection, and the backlash smashed into Kai. A wave of exhaustion hit her so hard that she dropped to one knee.

Kai? Concern edged Rhys's voice.

"I'm fine." She wasn't. She was reeling, drunk with exhaustion like she hadn't slept in days.

How long will the storm last? Ashem asked.

Isi answered mentally, meaning she had transformed back into a dragon. *The wind will pull more wind behind it. I only had to get it started. Though I tried not to make it so big that it would feed on itself and make our escape impossible.*

Kai had no idea where either of them were. Since they used dragon thought-speech instead of audible speech, she had no way of placing them. She kept one hand on Rhys's scaled leg, stepping over his claws and hauling herself onto his elbow by feel. She forced weary muscles to keep pulling her up until she could fling herself across his broad spine. With a groan, she threw one leg over and smacked him on the scaled flank with a hand—the signal that she was ready to go.

Ready, Rhys said. The others said the same.

How will we know we're headed in the right direction? Morwenna asked from somewhere in the darkness. Kai had nearly forgotten she was there.

Thabo. Kai wasn't sure, but she thought Tane had said that.

She readjusted the scarf over her face and closed her eyes, leaning down close to Rhys. The storm was worse up on his back, and dust kept getting in her eyes.

"How?" she asked as loud as she dared.

His magic has to do with the energy of motion kinetic force.

If it's moving, he can manipulate it, Rhys said. *And he can sense where it stops. He'll be able to sense where the building blocks the sand.*

Too tired to reply, she gave him a couple more firm pats the way she'd seen people give horses so he'd know she had heard. He huffed, and it was somehow a longsuffering sound. So much so that Kai almost laughed.

They started forward, and Kai was grateful beyond measure that she didn't have to do anything but hang on. The space between the central tower and the fallen wall behind which they'd crouched wasn't huge, but the crossing, done in pitch-blackness with no way to orient herself, made Kai dizzy.

Or maybe that was an aftereffect of sharing her power with Isi.

Rhys's gait changed and his claws clicked on a surface more solid than shifting sand. At the same time, the sound of the wind disappeared. This was dragon magic she was familiar with. Instead of using glass or something solid to keep the elements out, they constructed semipermeable walls of air.

In the silence, Kai became aware that someone was fighting. Rhys tensed, his body curling protectively around her. Then there was the sound of breaking glass. Almost as soon as Kai became aware of the noise, the fight ceased. For a second that stretched an eternity, there was nothing in the darkness but silence.

It worked, Tane said. *This one is sleeping.*

That is a great relief, Ashem replied.

Light, please, cariad, Rhys said.

Kai reached for the fire swirling inside her and pinched off a thin strand, forming a tiny fireball in her palm. She closed her fingers loosely about it, dampening the light, which streamed in golden beams between her fingers. After so much darkness, even that small light was nearly blinding.

Two dragons lay prone across the room. Next to them, Thabo and Morwenna shook themselves off. Morwenna turned to lick a long, shallow wound down her scaled side.

All right? Ashem asked.

Fine. Morwenna's voice had a snap to it, but that was nothing new.

Then let's get what we came for, Ashem said. *Kai, you, Thabo, and Isi will guard these two and watch for others.*

Kai was stupidly wiped out from helping Isi. If she could just sit for ten or fifteen minutes, maybe the creeping exhaustion sucking at her limbs and pushing down her eyelids would go away. Still, she narrowed her eyes at Rhys. "This is not what we talked about."

Rhys wouldn't meet her eyes, but Ashem growled. *You don't answer to the king here, soldier. You answer to the commander of your vee.*

Damn it! This was not something Kai had foreseen. She knew Ashem gave orders during battle, but it hadn't occurred to her that he would be the one in charge during the actual mission. In military encounters, even Rhys usually obeyed his commands without question.

Kai gritted her teeth, knowing that any argument would only endanger the more experienced warriors around her. "Okay."

When she didn't argue, Rhys's expression changed from cautious to concerned. He leaned in close, his warm breath washing over her. He smelled like smoke and reptile. *You're pale. Are you all right?*

A crooked smile found its way onto her face and she pushed his nose away. She kept her voice low, so only he could hear. "Fine. I just need a rest. And I'm not an idiot. Ashem knows what he's doing. Don't tell him I said so."

Rhys nudged her with his nose, like a monster-sized horse

sniffing for an apple, and Kai let out a surprised laugh that she stifled with a hand.

Knock it off, Ashem barked. *Let's move.*

Kai let her fingers trail over Rhys's long, scaled nose as he pulled away, and a shocking burst of tenderness for him swept through her.

"Be safe," she whispered.

And you.

The cloud of dust outside was clearing. Weak starlight filtered in shafts through high arched windows and holes in the walls. As the ambient light grew brighter, Kai saw that the floor was covered in a thin layer of sand. A sweeping, dragon-sized stone ramp on the far side of the room spiraled to the blackness above. Rhys, Ashem, Morwenna, and Tane climbed it cautiously, then disappeared from sight.

That left her with Thabo and Isi. Perhaps to be companionable, they both shifted to human, though neither of them tried to speak to her.

Kai sat down on the sand to wait. Mistake. As soon as she relaxed even a little, the rest of her exhaustion tried to flatten her. She leaned forward and rubbed her grainy, dusty hands across her forehead. To keep herself awake, she started heaping the sand into little piles, and thoughts crept in that she'd firmly locked away.

Her parents were here. Liam was here. They could be hurt. They could be dead.

Relax. She needed to hold it together until the guards were taken care of. Then she could find them.

She couldn't think about how long it had been since they spoke to her. Or Juli. How she'd gone missing from their lives not just once when she'd first met dragons, not twice when she'd gone to Eryri with Rhys, but *three times*, as her parentally required weekly phone calls had stopped once she'd been kidnapped by Owain. They probably thought she was dead. *Again.*

Sand shifted beneath Kai's hands. Too tired for surprise, she watched it funnel away into a sinuous, inch-wide crack. Curious, she swept a wide swath of sand to one side with her arm, not quite baring the stone floor. The movement caused sand to run down into several more cracks. They made a pretty pattern, though the larger design was still obscured by sand and time.

She briefly wondered how a floor with a bunch of holes in it could support the weight of dragons, then poked her finger into the first crack. No ground beneath that she could feel. Nothing but smooth stone sides and air. She got down on her knees and pressed her ear to the ground.

Below, someone sobbed.

Adrenaline surged through her, momentarily obliterating her lethargy. The humans. They weren't above, they were below. She jumped to her feet and pointed at the ground. "How do we get down there?"

Isi shrugged. So did Thabo.

Kai struggled to her feet. "We're going to find out. Look for an opening. There has to be something."

She expected an argument, but—perhaps annoyed at being left behind to babysit—both dragons jumped at the chance to do something. They split up, combing the dark room. After a minute, Thabo called out. He'd located a dark recess in the far wall. No wide staircase led down into the forbidding blackness —it was nothing but a hole. A chute of some kind, maybe. Or a ventilation shaft.

Kai peered into it. A single, weak beam of moonlight shone from some unseen opening, illuminating a patch of sand at the bottom. No ladder, no other doors, only this chute.

But she had definitely heard someone crying.

Kai motioned Isi and Thabo away from the shaft. The humans below could be alone, but knowing Owain as she now did, Kai doubted the paranoid dictator would leave something so precious unguarded. Especially if he'd gotten his frosty claws in her parents and brother.

Guards would not stop her. Not now. If there were dragons in the dark, she refused to fear them. She was not who she had been.

Gesturing Isi and Thabo close, Kai explained her plan. After some fine-tuning with their input, they walked back to the chute.

Kai looked inside. Blackness. Owain had left her without light so many times that she had almost forgotten she could make her own. The memory sent anger surging through her, and with anger, heat. Power.

She met Thabo's eyes. He nodded. She jumped.

Her fall slowed, like she was sinking through water instead of air. Kai squeezed her eyes shut and turned her face to the side. She raised her hands, palms facing each other, and called the flames, pooling magic between her palms, shoving more and more into the tiny space until it raged and bucked. Fire snapped into being, bright as a flashbang. Kai was nearly dazzled, even with her eyes closed.

Somewhere in front of her, a dragon snarled. So there was a guard down here. No one screamed, though. Had she really heard the sobbing?

No time to think. Her feet hit sand. She let the light rage for another few seconds before she dropped the pressure-cooked magic. It exploded like a mini supernova, sending Kai staggering. She dropped her arm and called forth a much dimmer ball of golden fire, flinging it to the ceiling so that it would illuminate the room.

Isi landed next to her, whipping sand away from them in a

scourging wall of wind. The dragon—there was only one—had just lifted his blinking eyes, only to have them filled with sand. He curled on the far side of a room half as large as the one above, the stained-glass pattern of a Wonambi clear on his scales.

The Wonambi opened wide jaws as Thabo hit the sand, but the elegant man raised his hands like he was expecting someone to pass him a ball. The roar that came from the dragon's mouth was no louder than a cat's meow—Thabo had muffled the movement of the air that would have carried the sound.

Kai, panting and exhausted, sprinted to the dragon, forcing her overextended muscles to obey. Thanks to all her practice with Rhys, she managed to clamber onto the Wonambi's back, then high onto its swinging, spiked neck, and wedge herself just behind its head.

The dragon bucked and raised its claws to tear her away, but Kai pressed her palms against the dragon's neck and let heat flare. "Don't move, or I'll melt your head right off your neck."

Apparently unimpressed, the dragon thrashed its head from side to side to dislodge her. Kai had to wrap one of her hands around a neck spike, but she poured more fire into the other. Blessedly, this dragon wasn't a fire Draig. If he had been, they'd be screwed.

The dragon thrashed harder with the heat. Kai repeated her threat three more times before he finally stilled. She lifted her hand. The scales were discolored and warped, the skin beneath bubbling with blisters. "Lie down," she commanded.

The dragon growled, and Kai put her hand against his neck. The Wonambi lowered himself to the ground, resting his chin on the sand.

Kai was so tired. It took every ounce of her self-control not to collapse in a heap. *Not done here yet. Almost. Then rest.* She took a breath. "Good. Now change to human."

She had to burn him again before he listened. She jumped clear as the magic of his transformation took him. Once human, the man tried to run, but Isi tackled him to the ground and Thabo took out one of the few Naga venom bombs they'd been left with.

"Sorry," he said. Then he smashed the glass right next to the man's face. Isi jumped up, and she and Kai scurried back, out of the range of the sleeping gas.

The man went dead still. Isi checked for a pulse. "Success," she declared. "He lives."

With the dragon knocked out, Kai could finally look around the room. Almost identical to the room above, except that a wall of stone divided it in half. The wall had an arching dragon-sized door that looked from the tracks in the sand like it might slide open rather than swinging.

The prisoners. Her family. She strode over and pulled it open, walking it to one side as it slid easily, silently, even though it had to be eons old.

Nearly laughing, Kai stepped inside. She didn't even have time to call up a new fireball before she was attacked again.

CHAPTER 23

KAI

The attack came out of nowhere. One second all was darkness, then a heavy, hot body smashed Kai's face into the sand.

The stench of unwashed, sweaty man assaulted her. Her attacker leaned forward, a knee on Kai's back, threatening to crush her ribs. A shard of something razor-sharp pressed into her neck, breaking the skin. Blood dripped down her neck. Fetid breath washed over her as the man leaned to her face and whispered in heavily accented English, "Let's see you heal from a slit throat."

The knife pressed harder into Kai's neck. She stiffened, her hands heating.

Then he was gone, his weight flying from her back. There was a wicked *thud*, and Kai coughed and gasped, pressing a hand to her bloodied throat. Kai tried to call the little ball of fire, but adrenaline made the magic hard to control.

Knives and cutting and bleeding and pain. Pain, and no escape.

"Are you all right?" Thabo's voice brought her gasping to the present.

Isi took Kai's arm and pulled her up. Kai grasped Isi's hand, and Isi squeezed her fingers, giving Kai an encouraging smile. Kai kept her gaze on those stormy eyes, her focus on Isi's hands —supporting, not imprisoning. "She's all right." The other woman dropped her voice. "You will be all right. Come back to us."

Thabo's voice filtered through Kai's panic. "I forget how fragile they are." There was the sound of footsteps in the sand. "He's alive."

Finally coming back to herself, Kai released Isi with a whisper of thanks. She reached for her fire, summoning her control. This time she succeeded, producing a small, dim ball of golden light that hovered at her shoulder.

The light revealed Isi and Thabo, then the crumpled form of the man. Kai brushed sand from her pants and shook it from her hair, spitting grit. Because of her efforts, it took her a moment to hear the rustling and terrified breathing behind her.

Isi whispered, "I don't think they know we're here to save them."

"Shine your light over there, Majesty." Thabo indicated the darkened corner.

Kai complied, feeding more fire into the globe. It grew in size and brightness, and Kai gave it a gentle push with her mind, sending it toward the ceiling.

Scrabbling and quiet cries of fear melted into frozen silence as light reached the far wall. A small knot of people appeared. Some stared defiantly, some huddled with their arms over their heads, trying to hide. She scanned the crowd for her parents, but the people were too close together and coated in dust to tell one individual from anyone else.

One of them, a woman with a swollen lip and a sheet of knotted brown-black hair, spat in their direction. "*Monstruo*," she hissed. "*Bestia!*" Then she rattled off a long string of angry words in what Kai suspected was Spanish or Portuguese. Or Italian. Maybe.

It hadn't even crossed her mind that the people she was aiming to rescue would think they were the enemy. Or that she wouldn't be able to explain what was going on.

Clearing her throat, Kai addressed the huddle of twenty or so people. "I'm looking for Stephen, Leila, and Liam Monahan."

Silence. Her heart lifted a little. Maybe her parents weren't here. They never had been. Then she sank back into fear. Maybe they had been, but now they were dead.

"Do any of you speak English?" When they got out of this, she was going to have to have Rhys start teaching her a couple of languages. Thabo and Isi probably spoke quite a few, but Kai was still shaken from the flashback to her torture. Still needed to be in control.

From the back of the crowd came an ancient-looking woman with white hair piled into a dusty bun on top of her head. "I do."

Kai scanned the crowd for her parents one more time. "Great. Okay. Do you know the Monahans? Are they here? Were they ever here?"

The woman regarded Kai warily. "Why? Are you going to kill them as a family? I thought you were keeping them alive for some kind of show."

Kai swallowed hard at the implications of those words. "No. I'm going to set them—all of you—free."

"Dragons lie!" someone shouted from the back. The voice was familiar. Male. Liam?

Kai edged around the small crowd. "I'm not a dragon."

Several people made a noise of derision. The old woman said, "If you aren't a dragon, how are you controlling fire?"

Her accent, Kai realized, was the same as Rhys's, though far more pronounced. The woman had to be Welsh. "It's hard to explain. There isn't much time."

"How do we know you're human?" someone else called.

Kai yanked up her left sleeve, revealing the colorless scales of her indicium. "I'm not human. I'm Wingless. Now give me my family."

A gasp sounded from the back of the room. "It is her. Stephen, it's her. She's real this time! Kai?" Her stomach dropped. The crowd parted, revealing...

"Oh, thank God." The words tore from Kai as her mother ran forward and flung herself onto Kai, weeping. Her father and Liam followed.

Kai patted her mother's back as her father and brother embraced her on either side. "Colm wasn't taken? He and the kids are really safe?"

"No. They didn't get him," Liam said, as if that was a triumph. "He and Marissa were at her parents' place in Grand Junction last I heard. We haven't seen them here."

"Okay," Kai said, dazed. She thought she'd been prepared for this. Her parents. Dragons. Knowing about each other. It would take time to process. "But you guys are here."

"So this is your family?" Thabo asked.

"We found them?" Isi smiled broadly. "I knew we would!"

"Yes. We found them." Kai turned to her father. "How did you get taken? Ashem lost contact with the dragons he assigned to watch you."

"Ashem?" Her father blinked, apparently at a loss for words.

"They were watching us?" her mother cried.

"As far as we saw, they swooped out of the sky and grabbed us," Liam answered. He seemed to be handling things better than either of their parents. "We were on a hike. It was a normal day, and then BOOM! Dragons." He paused, regarding her with sudden wariness. "How are *you* here, Kai the Fly? Why are you with dragons?"

"I'm with the good guys, and we're here to get you out. Let's save the rest." She would have time to explain later, when she'd also had more time to *feel* something about this. Anything. Or maybe anything would be too much, and she still wanted to feel nothing.

Kai was strongly starting to suspect she was going to need therapy.

Just then, another pain ripped through her. She staggered. Liam grabbed her and held her upright. "Kai? What's wrong?"

"Nothing," she gasped. She waited for the pain to end, then straightened. "I'm fine."

The old Welsh woman spoke up again, not as hostile as before but thankfully cutting off any more awkward questions from Kai's family. "How do we know this isn't some elaborate trick to get us to come quietly?"

Kai jerked her head toward Isi and Thabo. "These two can turn into sixty-foot monsters. Do you think they need you to come quietly?"

There was a murmur at that.

"Kai?" Rhys's voice startled Kai out of her family hug. He was in the other room, and he sounded angrier than she'd heard him since Morwenna dragged her in front of the Council.

This was going to be fun. "In here!"

Rhys strode in through the door, face thunderous. When he saw her, it only got worse. "I didn't know where you were. I thought someone had come and taken you again. I—"

He broke off, staring at her family. His eyes darted to Kai, then back to her parents. He visibly composed himself and stuck his hand out to Kai's father. "Mr. Monahan. It's good to see you again."

CHAPTER 24

RHYS

R hys ran his eyes down Kai's body, checking for damage, resisting the urge to grab her and pull her close. It would have been awkward, since Leila Monahan was still holding on. He ran a hand through his hair and forced himself to let go of the blind panic. She was here. She was fine.

Just because he couldn't sense her didn't mean she was dead.

Kai tilted her head. "I found the humans."

Rhys took in twenty or so humans in the corner, watching him like they expected the dragons to turn on them any second. "I see." He'd come down to tell her that they hadn't found the prisoners, but they had found Owain's stash of cordial.

And the artifacts.

Rhys pushed the gruesome scene out of his mind. He'd have to deal with it again soon enough.

"Are all the guards taken care of?" Kai asked.

"They are," Rhys said. "Ashem and the Naga venom are working wonders."

"Let's get these guys upstairs, then." Kai gently extricated herself from her mother's embrace, but didn't pull away when Leila took her hand.

It wasn't easy—a few of the humans had to be threatened. One man had to be carried. Thankfully, most of them seemed to believe that Kai was going to help them.

Rhys led the way to the chute he'd come down. He'd only found it because dim golden light had shone through the opening.

"Where did you find a ladder?" Kai asked, motioning to the rope ladder that dangled from the floor above.

"Upstairs." It had been in the same room where he'd found the cordial, and he'd picked it up because if it was there, he figured they'd have a reason to use it. Rhys suspected the humans' captors had only lowered it when it was time to change guards.

He led the way up, using the burn of the climb to refocus his mind. The Naga venom was experimental. He wasn't sure exactly how long it would last. They had to get out as soon as possible.

Kai started to climb after him. Halfway up, she hooked one arm through the rungs, panting.

"Kai?"

"I'm fine."

She didn't sound fine. She sounded wheezy and breathless. Rhys climbed the rest of the way up. Kai was still in the same spot, still panting.

Not fine.

He hauled the ladder the rest of the way to the top and grabbed her arms, pulling her off. She landed on top of him and he let himself fall back, the ladder tumbling down the chute once again.

Kai groaned and let her head fall onto his chest. "I am so tired."

Rhys ran his hands up and down her back in silence. They had to get up, move, finish what they'd come to do. For a moment, though, she was here, and he just wanted to be.

People rose out of the chute, both by ladder and by drifting out of the top and arching gracefully over onto the sandy floor. That had to be Thabo's work, his magic lifting those too weak to climb.

When Kai's father, mother, and brother clambered up out of the hole, he nudged Kai and they stood.

"So," Liam said. "What are you doing with Ashem's friend?"

An old woman levitated above the edge. Kai caught her arm and helped the lady over the side. The woman caught sight of Rhys and said in Welsh, "I see you, *Y Ddraig Goch.*"

Rhys stared at her. The woman gave him a canny look and went off to shush the people in the huddle.

Kai leaned over to clasp a tired-looking Thabo by the forearm and pull him from the empty shaft. "Um, yeah. Mom, Dad, Liam... You remember Rhys."

Rhys had expected the Monahans to be here, but he was having trouble reconciling the sight of them with reality. That they were here at all was Owain's fault. Anger surged hot inside Rhys. In recent weeks, Owain had rained blow after blow down on Rhys's head. Every time he blocked one punch, another caught him in the jaw. A man could only take so much, and now each blow that landed only served to enrage.

But he couldn't let that show—not the fury, not the strain of being at war, not the pain of the sundering—not in front of Kai's family.

So he inclined his head. "*Nos dda.*"

Her family only looked at him. Rhys sighed. "We will explain, but there are things we must do first."

"Let's do it, then," Kai said. "You found what you were looking for? The cordial that makes dragons stronger?"

"Yes." Rhys saw the awful images in his mind's eye again. "Ashem is...preparing it. Tane and Morwenna are on one of the middle floors. We found a vault filled with cordial. They're emptying it. When it's clear, we'll drag Owain's people inside and lock them in."

"And what will you do with us?" the old Welsh woman asked.

"Once we're finished upstairs, we'll take you out of this place." Rhys didn't say that they'd be taking all of the humans to Eryri. He didn't have the numbers to return them all to their homes yet. "It won't be long. Kai?"

Kai couldn't convince her parents to stay behind with Isi and the rest of the humans, so all of the Monahans accompanied Rhys and Thabo on the grueling walk up the spiral ramp that led to the top of the tower. There, they found Ashem, still in his dragon form, just completing his grisly task. The air was hot and itchy with the sizzle of too much magic.

Rhys turned Kai toward the main room, however, hoping to protect her from the sight as long as possible.

Only a handful of slender columns supported the roof, and the open walls offered a breathtaking view of the city and the crystalline desert night beyond. The room, though it was the smallest in the tower, was large enough to hold thirty dragons.

Ten identical human-size draconic runes—the symbol for power—were inlaid in a circle in the center of the semitranslucent stone floor, each harsh stroke depicted in hundreds of shards of purest, pale-yellow citrine.

The stones were hard to see, however, because of the puddle of black *something* congealing around them. Broken chains littered each rune. Kai paled at the sight, but in Rhys's opinion, it was the scent that made the scene truly horrific. The metallic, rotten smell of slow death.

Kai turned to Rhys, but her eyes focused beyond him. Beyond her family, who stood behind him. She'd found Ashem.

The black dragon had some kind of tarp. With delicate claws, he laid it over the line of ten bodies in one corner—one for each of the citrine runes. Rhys wanted to tell her to look away, but she'd made it abundantly clear that he wasn't allowed to protect her from everything.

But Ancients, he wished he could.

They're ready, Ashem said.

Kai pressed her hands to her mouth and Leila Monahan took her husband's hand. Even her brother looked pale and sick.

"They're dead?" Kai asked. Her voice was flat, distant. Her mother tore her gaze from the dead long enough to peer at Kai in concern.

"Yes." Realization washed over Rhys as he watched the Monahans react to the humans he'd found chained to the runes. Those people—some of them, at least—had to be related to Wingless in Eryri or Cadarnle.

That made them his people. His responsibility. He'd come here to take Owain's weapon away. Now, he wanted justice. Owain's debt was mounting, and it could only be paid in blood.

"Let me see them," Kai said.

Rhys nodded in resignation. He'd known she would ask. "Come."

Kai took his proffered hand.

"Sweetheart." Her father sounded horrified.

She turned to look at him, and there was a calm dignity to the motion. "Did you know their names?" she asked.

Liam straightened. "I do. Some of them didn't want to tell... Didn't think we'd live long enough for it to matter. But

I kept asking. I just... If I was going to die, I wanted to keep my name. And I didn't think anyone else should go... forgotten."

"Tell me." Kai released Rhys's hand and took Liam's instead. Together, the dark-haired brother and sister walked to the bodies and made Ashem uncover them, staring at every empty, drained face. Liam pointed them out, naming them. Rhys watched her lips move as she memorized. When she had finished, she motioned for Ashem to cover them again.

We need to destroy the runes, Ashem said.

Rhys examined the stones set into the floor. "Can you claw them out?"

Ashem dragged his claws across the stones. They didn't leave so much as a scratch.

"There." Kai pointed. One of the columns that held up the roof had crumbled, leaving large chunks of rock scattered across the floor. "Smash them with those."

Rhys and Thabo went down a few floors and found a windowless room where the light of their transformations wouldn't give them away. They came back up and grabbed huge stones, joining Ashem in smashing the boulders down on the runes, scattering broken citrine over the white floor like bloodied drops of amber in snow.

Rhys worked until his shoulders burned and his back ached, but it felt good to hit something. To focus some of the anger that built and built with nowhere to go. As they made their way around the circle, the hot, prickly feeling of magic in the air lessened and died.

When it was over, he stood next to Kai. She stared at the broken gems, her lip curling. "They look like Jolly Ranchers. Bits of broken candy rolled around in blood. Delicious. Enjoy, Owain." She kicked bloody citrine out of her way.

When they were finished, Ashem and Thabo headed down

the ramp. Rhys and Kai made to follow, but Kai's mother stopped them.

She indicated the bodies. "We can't just leave them here."

Everyone was so exhausted that Rhys's first instinct was to refuse, but that would solve nothing. Rhys called Ashem and Thabo back. Together, the dragons carried the bodies all the way down the ramp and into the city. There were only ten. With the three of them, that made one trip. They buried the bodies in the sand, sheltered by the walls of one of the fallen buildings, marking their grave with a circle of stones.

When they'd finished, he turned to Kai. *We'll come back after we've finished with Owain. Perhaps we can return them to their families.*

Her face was blank. He'd expected more of a reaction when she'd seen the bodies, but Kai hadn't so much as gasped or said anything beyond her comment about candy.

Before he'd freed her from Owain, he'd worried that there wouldn't be any of the girl he loved left. She was there, but maybe not all of her had survived.

Heaviness settled over him. The night was a success, but between ten dead humans and Kai's coldness, it didn't feel like one.

As they crossed the threshold back into the tower, someone screamed.

Tane and Morwenna had been watching the guards, all asleep thanks to Naga venom. But the first two—the ones they'd encountered as they entered—had woken up. One fought Morwenna and Tane. The other was making short work of the human prisoners. Already, three lay dead on the floor.

He reached for the mantle but felt only a vast dearth of power where it should have been. He still hadn't managed the ritual, too weak from his sundering to risk it.

It was Kai who staggered forward and dealt the death blow.

She called a ball of intensely hot fire into her hand and squeezed her fist closed around it, putting all that heat under pressure. Then, almost too fast for Rhys to see, she flung the ball of fire with preternatural speed. Her aim was true. The superheated ball shot right through the dragon's chest and out the other side, and he fell. Ashem made quick work of the one harassing Morwenna, but unlike his companion, he was snoring. Ashem was able to put him to sleep, and that meant he would live.

The fighting stopped, but the damage had been done. Of the twenty humans they'd rescued, five lay dead, including the old Welsh woman who had called him *Y Ddraig Goch*.

As the others arrived and began cleaning up the mess, Rhys kicked one of the bottles of cordial. It shattered, sending viscous black liquid spattering over the wall. Tane and Morwenna had emptied the vault already, so once the guards were inside, Rhys slammed the door and locked it.

Knowing the guards were captive didn't improve his mood. He'd failed to protect his people. Again.

He turned to the stacks and stacks of crates in front of him, each filled to the brim with glass bottles the size of his palm. Rhys didn't know how many bottles one human life could fill, but he suspected it had taken hundreds of deaths to create this.

So much power, Morwenna said in wonder.

So much death, Rhys growled. She at least had the decency to look chagrined.

They buried the murdered humans with the others. Then dragon and human alike carried as many crates as they could down the ramp and just outside, into the shadow of the building. Ashem smashed each and every one with his spiked tail, and their black liquid drained into the sand.

Let Owain see everything he'd worked for draining away.

When there were about fifty bottles left, Rhys called a halt to the destruction. Morwenna had found another tarp in a storage room. She cut it into six sections, one for each dragon, and they filled their bundles with the remaining bottles of cordial.

He would not keep it. In fact, he was going to drop it into the sea. Now no dragon had cordial, nor would they profit off of human death again.

But when Owain saw the cordial gone, he would *think* Rhys had taken it, and that was exactly what Rhys wanted.

Rhys's mind went numb as they repeated the process of entering the city, except in reverse. Loaded with human passengers and bundles of cordial, the dragons glided to the outskirts of the city, where they unloaded and the utterly exhausted dragons became human one more time. Huddling as close to Ashem and his barrier as they could, they staggered out of the city and into the desert, undetected by the sentries.

Owain would not know Rhys and his people had been here until they were partway back to Eryri.

Dawn began to lighten the eastern horizon as the bone-weary group stumbled away from the ancient city. They found an outcropping of rock that would hide their final shift from the eyes of the now-distant sentries. Ashem wanted the dragons to shift immediately, but Rhys overruled him and called for a much-needed two hours of rest. Though they were out of the sentries' immediate range, he couldn't help but listen for their warning cries the entire time.

Thank the Ancients, those cries didn't come.

At the end of those two hours, the dragons transformed and took to the skies again, each one loaded with human passengers and carrying a bag of cordial.

In all his life, Rhys had never been so tired. *We did it,* he whispered.

But of course, it had cost them lives.

Kai, who had given up the safety of her harness to her mother, sat farther up his neck than he was used to. She lay down against his spine, one arm looped around a spike. He couldn't see her, but he imagined she sighed.

The first step in his plan was complete. They would dump the cursed cordial into the sea and then reach Eryri in a week, weather permitting. If everything happened as it should, Deryn and the others would be busy preparing the archipelago for battle. He'd have to tell her about the success of the Naga venom.

After that, all that was left was to convince Owain to go to war.

CHAPTER 25

KAI

The overladen dragons picked up even more baggage when they retrieved their travel gear from the camp as they left the Taklamakan Desert. They traveled through the remainder of the night and on until dawn, then set down in the mountains a hundred or so miles from where they'd spent the previous day.

Of course, the only reason Kai had the faintest idea of where they were on the globe was because Isi kept her filled in on their frequent breaks. Dragons, Isi said, had an instinctive sense of navigation like birds or butterflies, but more refined.

Rhys busied himself with camp setup and tense discussions with Tane and Ashem about what they should do with the humans, which left Kai alone to explain things to her parents.

A lot of things.

Once she couldn't find any more excuses to stay away, Kai went to the tent she shared with Rhys and ducked inside. Her parents sat on the thin pad Rhys and Kai used as a mattress. Liam sat in a camp chair. The dragons' designs were so efficient and their dragon bodies so large that carrying around human-sized camping equipment wasn't really an issue.

Unless, of course, they were also carrying several humans and heavy tarp-bags of that disgusting cordial.

"So...hey." Kai sat on the ground, her hands on her knees. "I guess you guys have a lot of questions."

Dad raised his eyebrows. "I'm pretty sure I've been dreaming for the past couple of weeks, but why don't you go ahead and start at the beginning?"

So she did. She told them how, when they thought she was lost in the mountains for days, she'd actually been taken by dragons. Not in a bad way—she'd helped the good-guy dragons and in turn they'd taken her with them when they were attacked by bad-guy dragons, effectively saving her life.

She told them the truth about the night Rhys had showed up in Colorado, worried because his sister had seen a vision—yes, a vision—that Kai would be kidnapped by Owain. Mentioning Owain led her off on a tangent, because then she had to explain the war and the mantle, though she did *not* tell them that Rhys was one of the warring kings. She could only expect them to take in so much at once.

"But why you?" Mom asked when Kai started winding down. "Why us?"

Kai grimaced. "So, you know how I was in that cave the first time I went missing?"

Nods.

"Dragons have this thing where they bond to one person for life. Usually it happens with other dragons, but I guess some human families carry a sort of predisposition for it...and we belong to one of them. Rhys bonded to me. And Ashem is bonded to Juli. That's also why I can do magic with fire. Because that's what kind of magic Rhys has."

"What kind of magic does Ashem have?" Liam asked. "And where *is* Juli?"

At the same time, her mother squeaked, "You are dating a *dragon?*"

Kai rubbed her temples. Equating dating to heartswearing. Hilarious. "It's a little more permanent than dating."

Or was it, now that they were sundered? Would Rhys's people decide they didn't want her anywhere near power and just toss her out?

In a very Dad-like tone, her father said, "Permanent how?"

Kai leveled her father with a look. "I am in my mid-twenties. I've spent the last few months going through hell, and for the most part, Rhys and I have gone through it together. Whatever he and I have, I don't need parental approval or consent." She paused as her parents stared at her, dumbfounded, then added, "Though I do hope you like him."

Her father grumbled something inaudible, but Kai didn't press the issue. It wasn't her parents' fault that she'd grown from listless dropout to Queen of Dragons—if she still was—in the span of months. She was different, and they hadn't had time to get to know her yet. Hell, she hadn't had time to get to know herself.

"So," her mother said, obviously trying to hide the delight in her voice, "You and the handsome Welsh redhead are married?"

Kai sighed, then nodded. "Yes, Mom. Rhys and I are married."

Liam gave a hoot of laughter. "Rhys married *you?* Why?"

Kai glared at him. "He didn't have a choice. Neither of us did."

"He must not have," her brother said, still smirking.

Kai leaned over, palmed his face, and shoved him. "Get bent, dickwad."

He grabbed her hand and jerked her toward him, then got her in a headlock and gave her a noogie. It devolved into a wrestling match, but now that Kai was Wingless, she was stronger. She pinned him in moments. He grinned up at her. "Damn. Find a dragon for me."

Kai rolled her eyes and let him up.

"So, you're bonded with Rhys?" her father asked. "And there's no chance you could just come home?"

Kai tilted her head, considering it. "Well..."

A few months ago, all Kai had wanted was a way to escape her heartswearing. Without it, she supposed she could be—as some might phrase it—free.

But being with Rhys didn't make her less free. She chose him. He was good, and good for her, and she hoped she could be good for him.

Aside from that, there was the war. Before the dragons, she'd drifted through life without purpose. She had purpose now, and a belief in both Rhys's cause and her place in it that would not allow her to walk away.

As if her thoughts had summoned him, Rhys entered the tent and came to sit next to Kai on the ground. He braced a hand just behind her, and she leaned against his arm. He inclined his head toward the Monahans. "How are you?"

Kai's mother beamed at him and didn't speak. Her dad scowled and pushed up his glasses. Apparently they hadn't moved on from the idea of "married" as quickly as Kai had thought.

"We're fine, considering the circumstances." Liam's tone was businesslike and respectful, which surprised Kai. She'd expected him to razz Rhys about their relationship. "Honestly, it sounds like you all are caught up in some intense shit."

A surprised but genuinely amused smile played around one

corner of Rhys's mouth. "Intense shit? That's one way to put it."

Liam grinned at Rhys's dry tone. Oh, god. They were going to be friends.

Before Kai could internalize the pure little-sister horror of Liam befriending her significant other, Isi poked her head into the tent. "Hello! Sorry, some of the humans are demanding an audience with the king."

"One of these warring kings is here?" her father asked. Isi looked from Rhys to Dad in confusion.

Damn it.

In unison, Kai's family swung their heads toward her. She lifted her hands helplessly. "I may have glossed over some things."

"Rhys." Dad's tone held warning, as if Rhys had better not *dare* to be royalty. "Are you one of the dragon kings?"

"I am," Rhys replied.

"Which one?" Mom asked. "The one who wants to eat people or the one who doesn't?"

"I do not want to eat people," Rhys said.

"Unless you count Kai's—ow!" Liam ducked, rubbing the spot where his mother had flicked him on the back of the head.

Rhys looked less amused by this.

"Oh, come on, Kai the Fly," her brother said, looking from Kai to Rhys and back again. "The dragons? Okay. I've seen that. You can set shit on fire with your eyeballs now? Cool. But please don't tell me that makes you some kind of queen."

Rhys's arm tightened around her, and Kai reminded herself that this stupid brother had kept her from falling off Rhys's back more than once during the grueling escape from the Taklamakan.

"It does," Rhys said. His voice was quiet, but it resonated

through the tent. "Kai Kiera Monahan, Queen of the Dragons of Eryri."

Finally, even Liam's smile dropped. After a heavy silence, he said, "That explains the kidnapping. Kai is tangled up in this, and therefore, so are we. None of us can go back." He swallowed. "Someone is going to have to tell Colm. His family is in danger too. His kids."

"We'll see to it," Rhys said. "What happened to you won't be allowed to happen again."

After that, they all fell quiet.

It was going to be a long flight back to Eryri.

CHAPTER 26

JULI

Juli spent hours trying to free herself from the cuffs—not only because it was difficult, but because dragon locks weren't like human ones. They were activated by magic, so there was no way to physically manipulate them. She wanted to give up, but couldn't shake Jiang's thoughts about poison in Eryri.

There were only a few people in Eryri important enough to poison, and to one degree or another, Juli loved every single one of them. Rhys was the most likely candidate, but since he and Kai ate together, anything that got to him would probably kill Kai as well. Now that they were on their way back, her time was limited. She had to find out who Jiang's contact was.

She couldn't give everything up for Kai only to have her die anyway.

Two days after the incident with Owain, Kavar cooled off enough to come visit her again. He paced around and snapped at her, but they both felt the relief of being physically close.

It only took the edge off for Juli, however. The longer she was with Kavar, the more she wanted Ashem. Not only in the normal "I miss you" way, which was bad enough, but in the biting, hollowed-out way of the heartswearing. Even spending time deep within their mental connection was little comfort for either of them. They needed to be together.

But when she was with Ashem, she would still *need* Kavar. If Kai's behavior when she'd been away from Rhys for nearly two months was any indication, soon her emotions would be completely unmanageable.

Juli watched Kavar pace and wondered whether she was doomed to a nearly immortal life only to become a starving wraith—insatiably craving something her heart would never want.

It would drive her insane.

Desperate, Juli told Kavar what she'd heard in Jiang's mind—that he was supposed to be in Eryri to take the fall for poison.

"You lie," he said. "Poison is a coward's way—a human way. If dragons poisoned each other's food, Owain would've killed Rhys a thousand years ago."

"You think so?" Juli opened their connection and shoved the memory into his mind.

His eyes widened, then he spat Jiang's name. "Owain can't possibly know about this. He let Rhys capture me so Jiang would have credibility, but he would not have condoned my execution."

That was the end of that day's visit.

Juli sank back onto the couch, scratching at her chained fingers. She felt bad for Kavar. Bad enough that she wished she didn't have to push. But her need to get free was more important than his hurt feelings. If she could find out who was supposed to deliver the poison and who their target was, Ashem could stop it from happening.

She needed the key. To get it, she would have to distract Kavar. So she decided to seduce him. Just a little.

Ashem was not on board, but there were lives at stake. Besides, Juli was sure she could do it.

She'd gleaned the most important thing she could about Kavar: he was jealous. Growing up in Ashem's shadow had been difficult. Ashem, cantankerous as he was, had been the golden son...at least in Kavar's memories.

Firstborn, best at everything, beloved. Ashem was the day, bright and blazing, and Kavar had been the night. Younger brother, adequate instead of gifted—in his own mind, that was. Kavar wanted to be great on his own, without Ashem looming over him. He craved recognition. Appreciation.

That, more than anything else, was the reason he'd followed Owain. Juli shared her thoughts with Ashem.

He was not less loved. If anything, our mother loved him more. He sounded exhausted. He had plenty of reason. At the moment, he was flying somewhere over the Pacific loaded down with several humans and too much gear.

Juli didn't have brothers or sisters, wasn't sure who her father was, and didn't care for her mother. However, she'd been part of Kai's family long enough to recognize the sullen tone of sibling rivalry. And besides, she'd seen both their memories. *Don't be an idiot,* joon-am. *Your parents loved you the same. Besides, the truth is less important than how Kavar felt. How you felt.*

I don't have feelings, Ashem said, voice dripping with distaste.

Juli sighed. *You are ridiculous. I love you.*

Her love for Ashem, however, didn't negate her need to get close to Kavar. She had to find the key.

Kavar came again the next day. Since he apparently couldn't help dropping an innuendo every few sentences—and since his main goal was still to cuckold his brother—Juli didn't have much work to do. She let him fluster her. Flatter her. The first time she let herself blush, he became wickedly smug. The first time she let him come close without jerking away, he was out-and-out delighted.

The fact that Kavar truly thought she could be so easily manipulated made it more frustrating for her than anything else. He was so focused on "taking" her from Ashem that he didn't notice she was leading him around by the nose.

It wasn't even a little bit challenging.

On the third day, while Ashem sheltered from a storm on a tiny island with Kai and the rest of their group, Juli drew Kavar into conversation about his past.

She shivered, drawing her ever-present fur blanket closer around her. "How long did it take you to adjust to this cold? I don't know if I can ever get used to it, and Colorado winters were bad."

Kavar frowned at her. He'd brought fresh food, which was good, because her stock had been running low. She sat close to him as they ate. Juli had never been next to him for so long without him grabbing her. He smelled distractingly enticing— clean and masculine.

"I'm not used to it."

Juli tucked a piece of hair behind her ear and tilted her head. Today. She was going to get the key today. She didn't *want* to seduce Kavar. It made her feel sick, remembering what her last semi-voluntary kiss had done to Ashem. But she had to get out of this room, out of these cuffs, or her whole time here would be wasted. People might die.

She just prayed she wouldn't have to do more than kiss.

Juli gave in a little more to her bond with Kavar, allowing the longing from their heartswearing to float to the top of her mind. If he was listening, that's what he would pick up first. "You miss...the heat?"

He flicked a glance at her, then went back to his food, so

casual that she knew he'd heard the innuendo. "The heat. The food. The people. The gardens. The groves. But it doesn't matter. It's been more than a thousand years. The home I knew is gone."

Juli rubbed a finger along her lips, as if thinking. She'd allowed Kavar to pour her a cup of wine. She sipped it for courage, but every once in a while when he wasn't looking, she dumped it into the thick dark wool of the blanket puddled around her feet. When she wasn't looking, he refilled her cup. Kavar was working her almost as hard as she was working him.

Kavar watched her touch her lips like a starving dog might watch a steak. "Are you curious about Ashem's childhood?"

"And yours," Juli replied smoothly. "What did you do for fun?"

Kavar's eyes went distant. "Explored. Our clan had a stronghold in the mountains. We had a game, a tally of who had found the most caves." He smiled. It shocked Juli, not because he was smiling—Kavar smirked as much as Ashem scowled—but because it was a genuine smile. "I was winning."

"How many caves did you find?" Juli stood, slipped her feet out from under the wine-soaked blanket, and took her dishes into the kitchen. She loved Ashem. Kavar's smile would not get past the defenses around her heart.

"Twenty-five." Kavar followed her. Coming to stand by her side, he placed his own dishes in the stone basin that served as a sink.

Juli leaned one hip on the basin, facing him. "Impressive."

Kavar shrugged. "It was the one thing I was better at than my brother."

She quirked an eyebrow, seeing the obvious opening. *I will not enjoy this. I will not enjoy this.*

She swallowed. "I doubt it was the only thing."

Kavar's eyes widened. He leaned back, then seemed to

realize he had retreated and stood his ground instead. "What are you doing?"

She resented his tone. As if he wasn't trying to get her drunk and seduce her too.

At the same time, a pit of panic formed in her chest. If he saw through her, this would never work. So she kept her voice easy. "I told you, I'm interested in learning."

Once she got the cuffs off, she'd be able to use her magic to put him to sleep. That was all she needed, just to get close enough, distract him long enough, to fish the key out of his pocket like she had the first day. She smiled lazily, letting her eyelids droop as if the wine was getting to her.

Kavar's narrowed-eyed suspicion turned to a smirk, and Juli's disgust almost overwhelmed her ability to act. He was insufferable.

Kavar leaned in and trailed a finger down her arm. "I'm more than willing to...educate. But I don't know that my brother would approve."

Juli smiled wistfully, but her brain was whirring. She'd have to goad him into it. She let her normally crisp words run together just a little. "I didn't realize you needed Ashem's approval to take what is rightfully yours."

A shadow of anger passed over Kavar's face. "You're the one who's supposed to love him."

Anger on Ashem's behalf? Fascinating.

Juli shrugged, loosening her body. The few sips of wine helped. "There's love and there's...love." Idiotic. No one had ever said something so blatantly asinine in their lives.

She relaxed into the heartswearing more than ever, letting go of her reservations and broadcasting the longing. She shut down her connection to Ashem even further, so he couldn't tell more than that she was alive. He was busy dealing with the humans, in any case. Juli expected word of the cordial's destruction to reach Cadarnle anytime.

Besides, he didn't need to worry about this.

"Ashem isn't here, Kavar." She hooked her finger beneath the edge of his jacket and ran it up his chest. "You are."

She stepped into him. Kavar watched her, mesmerized. His voice, so smooth a second ago, was choked. "I told him you would be faithless."

Juli smiled lazily. "I'm heartsworn to you too."

His lip curled, but he didn't stop staring at her mouth. He was hungry for her, Juli could feel it. And heaven help her if part of her—the traitorous part—wasn't starving, as well.

But now that she was offering herself to him, Kavar had apparently decided to have doubts. "I don't need Ashem's leftovers."

Juli's anger sparked and her tipsy act slipped. "I'm nobody's leftovers. I am myself. Who I've been with has no bearing on what I'm worth."

Kavar stepped closer, so their bodies brushed. It was as if he'd tried to get her drunk, but despite himself, wanted her sober. "You're up to something."

"Oh, you can count on it." If she was honest with herself, Kavar had surprised her. He was ruthless, but loyal. A good friend and a better solider—like Ashem. But his moods changed like the wind. And unlike Ashem, whose silences were filled with thought, sometimes Kavar could just be quiet.

Sometimes a woman needed quiet.

Kavar was not evil. He just had a different cause.

She jumped when he kissed her. For the first time, he wasn't mocking or bruising or desperate. He was soft, exploratory, curious, playful. Kissing him like this—a real kiss— was also a bit like having a bucket of ice water dumped over her head. Or an electric shock. Or both at the same time.

Her treacherous mind took off running down forbidden paths. What if she had sworn to Kavar first? Would she love him instead?

Was love so arbitrary?

She was so surprised by the kiss that she almost forgot to slip her hand the rest of the way inside Kavar's jacket and pull out the key. She told herself that she should stop there, that she'd gotten what she wanted. Instead, she let him carry on. Just for a minute.

What she wouldn't do to get rid of the part of her that craved him.

Finally, she broke off, pretending to yawn. She smiled at him sleepily, though her heart was thudding in her chest. "Thanks for the food. And the wine." She ran her thumb across his stubbled bronze cheek, and the gesture wasn't empty. She might not love Kavar the way she loved Ashem, but—despite everything—she couldn't help caring for him.

That didn't mean she felt guilty about her deception. After all, it had been a mutual seduction. She stepped to the side, and Kavar let her go. "When will you come again?"

He seemed dazed. Then he came back to himself, pressing his full lips together in something that didn't quite have the heart to be his normal smirk. "Tomorrow."

Juli nodded. With a little more verbal wrangling, she got Kavar to leave and pulled the key from her pocket.

Time to get back to work.

JULI SLIPPED OUT of her rooms early the next morning. She moved through the halls, invisible once more, and settled in her spot behind the tapestries. Preparing for a long—and hopefully fruitful—day, Juli leaned her head back against the wall and searched for Owain's mind. When she found him, he wasn't alone. He was with Jiang, and they were—

Juli backed out of their minds like she'd stuck her hand in a fire. No, thank you.

Putting *that* scene out of her mind, she scanned for Kavar instead. He was training with his vee. Good. That would keep him more than occupied. This time, he wasn't going to catch her until it was too late.

The only other minds she sensed within Owain's large complex of rooms were a handful of guards close to the door. She skimmed, but none of them were thinking about anything useful. One wanted a nap, the other had missed breakfast, things like that.

Twenty minutes passed, and only a few low-level soldiers walked down the hall. They didn't know anything useful either. The only thing Juli had been able to find out since taking her cuffs off the night before was the news about Rhys and Kai's raid had finally hit Cadarnle. Owain had been waiting for enough cordial for his whole army. Now he had none, and Rhys and Kai were getting stronger by the day. Things were looking up.

Juliet. Ashem's voice in her mind was soft as a feather falling. Homesickness for him rose up, threatening to overwhelm her. *I miss you.*

He enfolded her in something like a mental hug. They wound around each other, knotting her insides tighter and tighter until she was sure she would crack and shatter.

I miss you too. She expressed it as a feeling more than words. Pure, heartbroken longing. *Where are you?*

Nearly to Eryri. The storm yesterday only grounded us for an hour.

She smiled. *Good. I'm glad you're safe.*

He hesitated. *I don't want this anymore. I want you home. Have you found out more about the poison?*

Juli pulled up her knees and wrapped her arms around them. *Not yet. I stole the key again and got my chains off, so that's what I'm doing now.*

Distress. Ashem might say he had no feelings, but just because he refused to talk about them didn't mean they were nonexistent. *Be careful,* nooré cheshm-am.

His love surrounded her like a cocoon, warm and safe. Juli returned the feeling, tears pricking the back of her eyes. She *wanted* to go home and be with Ashem, away from this cold and darkness. Away from Kavar, so pitiable and so tempting. Even if love was arbitrary or magic-driven, she had chosen Ashem.

Romantics could deny it until the cows came home, but love *was* choice. It was commitment despite temptation. It was forgiveness, even when forgiving hurt. *Have you spoken to Kavar at all? He says your connection is still open.*

A grumble. That was a no, then. Juli sighed. Some wounds were too old to heal easily, but at least they hadn't completely closed each other out.

She was just about to check in on Owain and Jiang again—heaven help her—when the door to their rooms opened. Startled, Juli peered through the crack between tapestries.

Jiang exited the room, Owain and four guards behind her. She was looking straight at Juli.

Thought fled, replaced with terror. *Ashem—*

Before Juli could even think about moving, Jiang strode over and ripped away the wall hanging.

Juli pulled a barrier over herself, but it was too late.

Jiang slapped Juli across the cheek so hard that Juli tasted blood and saw stars. She was so shocked that someone would actually hit her that she dropped the barrier she'd just erected.

Jiang's rosebud lips curled in triumph. She addressed Owain over her shoulder. "Can you see her now?"

Owain's eyes narrowed. "I can."

Juliet! Ashem's exhaustion had turned to panic.

"Bring her," Jiang said, moving out of the way.

Juli scrabbled at her power. She could drop Owain and Jiang in an instant. She urged their minds to sleep...

But nothing happened. Jiang sneered and held up her hand. A black leather cord with an onyx pendant was tied around her wrist.

"You think when I sensed someone hiding here I didn't take precautions? As if anyone but an Azhdahā would dare enter Cadarnle and spy directly outside the king's chambers."

Panicking, Juli tried to edge around the statue that took up most of the alcove, but she was trapped. The guards grabbed her and hauled her out of the corner. She tried to resist, but her socks slid across the smooth stone. One of them smashed a fist into the side of her head, and her vision exploded into stars. It loosened her tight control over her bond with Kavar, and suddenly he was there, too.

Juli, what—damn you!

"This is the female bonded to Ashem?" Owain put two stone-cold fingers under Juli's chin, tilting her face up so she had to look into his eyes.

Jiang was practically purring. "Yes. Her name is Juliet King. She is Wingless."

Owain's fingers tightened painfully on Juli's chin, growing cold enough to burn. For a long moment, she was caught in the ice of Owain's gaze. A wave of dizziness swept over her—not because Owain had some kind of special magic.

Because she knew she was going to die.

The guards dragged her into Owain's rooms. Juli had an impression of a two-story foyer worthy of a palace, a long black-

and-white hall, a lavishly furnished but coldly colored sitting room, and then they were in an office. A black desk took up most of the room, cluttered with papers and glass orbs that projected holograph-like images from record stones into the air above.

The guards forced Juli into a huge black chair. She didn't try to run—she didn't have a chance. Owain rummaged through the chaos of his desk.

Jiang paced. "That must mean her mate is here too. We can use her to catch him."

Owain pulled a singstone out of the mess and jammed it over his ear. His eyes went distant for a long minute, then he yanked the singstone off and tossed it on his desk. "Kavar is on his way. He'll find out what she knows."

Owain's eyes darkened and he glared at Juli. "You have had the misfortune of catching me in a very bad mood." He sighed. "At least I'll be able to repay Kavar for the business in Eryri. He's been wanting to kill his brother for years."

Kavar. Owain was calling Kavar here to question her.

What would Kavar do?

"H-How did you know I was there?" Juli hated the way her voice shook. If she was going to die, she didn't want to sound weak.

Jiang patted her on the cheek, and Juli had to resist the urge to bite her. "Emotion. About five minutes ago you started practically screaming at me."

Juli closed her eyes. She'd been stupid. So very, very stupid.

Ashem had gone silent. He was there, though, offering her strength that was tinged only a little with his own gut-numbing fear. *We won't let anything happen to you, Juliet.*

Juli could sense Kavar storming toward her in a wordless rage. For the first time, she wondered if he would help her at all. *We'll see about that.*

She found her voice, though her throat was dry as cotton. "Ashem isn't here. He's in Eryri."

Owain's lip curled. "As if he would leave you here alone." He came around the desk and grabbed a handful of Juli's hair, tipping her head back so far that her neck and scalp both began to burn. "Tell the truth, and things will go easier for you."

"I—" She swallowed convulsively, and her voice was so soft it was almost inaudible. "I am telling the truth."

Owain bared his teeth. He let her go and gestured at one of the guards. "Fine. We won't wait." The guard, a burly man with a green indicium, took Juli's hand in his and snapped her little finger. Juli screamed. In her mind, Ashem's cool and Kavar's rage dissipated. Their emotions surged, overwhelming her. Everything became a jumble.

Owain had taken up a casual position leaning against his desk. His face was devoid of compassion. "Tell me where your heartsworn is."

Juli tried to speak through the sobs that were clawing up her throat. "He's in Eryri." Owain nodded at the man who still held Juli's hand. Juli braced herself.

"Where is your heartsworn?" Owain asked again.

Kavar burst through the door so hard that it bounced off the wall. "Stop! Don't harm her."

From the look on Jiang's face, Christmas had just arrived.

CHAPTER 27

KAVAR

K avar stood in the doorway, panting.

I know you have no love for me, but damn you, Kavar, don't let him hurt her!

Kavar had never heard Ashem so desperate. Somehow, it wasn't as sweet as he'd thought it would be.

Owain smiled, obviously pleased. "Do you know who this is?"

Kavar gave a tight nod. The pain on Juli's face made him see red. He balled his hands into fists. He could not lose control. There could still be a way out of this.

"I want to know where your brother is. Then you can kill them both." Owain obviously thought he was giving Kavar some kind of gift.

"I—" Shit. He had no idea what he could say that wouldn't end in both their deaths.

Except, perhaps, the truth. Which did he value more—Owain's trust, or Juli's life? Owain's trust, or Ashem's happiness?

Kavar thought about lying, saying that he'd captured her

when Rhys freed Kai and kept her for his own pleasure. But Owain always saw through his lies. If Kavar had captured someone so important, and with such potentially dangerous magic, he would have told Owain. Things wouldn't go better for any of them if he lied.

Juli looked up at him with pain-clouded eyes. Even through the privacy of their bond, she didn't beg.

Kavar exhaled. "She is my heartsworn as well."

Owain looked at Kavar as if he'd just grown two heads, but he didn't miss a beat. "Explain."

Kavar glared at Jiang, waiting for her to leave. For Owain to dismiss the guards.

Neither of those things happened. Once upon a time, Owain would've kept this between them. Obviously that time had passed.

So Kavar told a room full of people about the time Juli had come with Ashem during an interrogation when he was a prisoner in Eryri. Ashem had hit him, and Juli had helped him clean up. Thinking that perhaps he could spin it, Kavar also told them how Juli had set him free. Skipping the part where he'd promised he'd free Kai in exchange for Juli's company six months out of each year. He made it sound like Juli had betrayed Ashem and come with him—like he'd asked her to—that she'd been in Cadarnle ever since, as *his* mate. On their side.

Owain, his face dangerously blank, demanded to see the room. Kavar took him there. Owain dug around, and Kavar folded his arms and leaned against the open door, waiting for Owain to be finished. When his king had done a thorough check of the quarters, he came to Kavar with the collar and cuffs that Juli had slipped.

With a lurch, Kavar realized that's why she'd seduced him last night. She'd stolen the key. Again.

He was about to die for the woman who loved his brother. Worse, the woman his brother loved. He rolled his eyes upward as if he could see the Stars, cursing them.

"I have just lost our most important asset to a raid, and I come back to find that you are sleeping with your brother's mate? A *Wingless*?" Owain made a face like someone had just tried to feed him feces. "Identical twins heartswearing to the same mate. I've read of such a thing before. I thought it was a myth."

Owain's face darkened. "Is she the one who let my cousin's soldiers in to take back the girl and the Seeress? Is she the reason Rhys's Ironscales and a *Wingless* found out what we were doing in the Taklamakan and ended my chances to finish this war as bloodlessly as possible?"

"I—uh—" Sunder it. He hadn't foreseen this. Of course Owain would think Juli was the traitor. His king was not merciful.

Ashem, who had been "listening" silently, barked something about saving Juli. Kavar snapped at him to shut up. "No. She's been with me. However the son of the Usurper got in, it wasn't because of us."

Kavar wondered if he had a huge sign on his forehead that flashed: *Liar, liar, liar.*

"Why didn't you tell me she was here?!" Owain screamed, a vein standing out on his neck.

Kavar flinched. In all the time he'd followed the white dragon, he'd never seen Owain lose control like this. "I thought you would kill her."

"I *am* going to kill her! I don't know what tricks she's played on you, but she's a spy. She has cost me centuries of research and potentially hundreds of dragons' lives. We'll have to rebuild before we can go to war against the humans. I can't allow her to live."

Shit, shit, shit. Bloody, bloody shit. "You're right, I've betrayed you. I understand that you need to make an example." Kavar took a breath. "But we are leaving for Eryri in days. If you kill her, I'll be useless to you for weeks."

"Ashem would be useless as well, and that will even the odds." Despite his words, the angry light in Owain's eyes dimmed. He stood there, silent, weighing his options. If Kavar knew him—and he did—Owain was trying to step back from his emotions and see the problem from every angle.

Finally, Owain said, "You can share a cell until I decide what to do with you."

Sunder me.

It struck him then that he could ask Owain to sunder him. Except that would also mean he couldn't take part in the battle. Even if he wanted to cut himself free of Juli and Ashem, he wasn't ready to face the pain of it.

He wasn't ready to face the loneliness.

Though Stars knew Juliet King was going to drive him to that point sooner or later.

Kavar followed Owain and his guards without complaint, trooping through Cadarnle. They retrieved Juli from Owain's rooms and marched on. The few people who were out and about early in the morning scattered when they saw Owain and his guards. After a few minutes, they reached the lowest level of tunnels. Owain's dungeon.

They tossed Kavar and Juli inside one of the cells. He groaned at the familiarity of it. Like Rhys's cells in Eryri, they were lined in iron that kept him from using his magic on anyone outside. Unlike Rhys's cells, they lacked chains in the walls, meaning at least he could move around freely.

Also unlike Rhys's cells, there was no light, and it was cold enough to chill him to the bone. At least he wasn't alone.

Juli cried softly in the corner. Anger flared in Kavar at her weakness. *She* had gotten him into this. He stalked toward her.

"You seduced me so you could get the key. I told you not to wander. I told you this would happen."

Her voice was hard. "Why do you think I'm here, Kavar? Out of the goodness of my heart? I agreed to stay with you so I could spy on Owain. Why else do you think Ashem would let you anywhere near me without killing you? Why else would *I*?"

Her words shouldn't have been a shock. Damn him, he'd caught her spying once already. He'd been so wrapped up in her and the reopened bond with Ashem that he'd let himself be blinded. They didn't care about him. They were using him.

Juli sniffed. He could imagine her over there, curled around her broken finger and crying. "Anyway," she said, "you told me he would kill us both. We're alive. That means there's hope."

"There is no hope." Kavar ran his hands along the wall until he found her corner, then crouched and groped for her in the dark. Soft hair, damp face, shoulders, arms, hand.

He found her broken finger, discovered that it was merely dislocated, and popped it back into place without warning her. He ignored her yelp of pain and went to the opposite corner, black hatred growing inside him.

There is hope, Ashem said into his mind, stubbornly present. *I'll get you out.*

You're talking to the wrong person, brother. Your woman is over there.

Ashem's mental voice was dry. *I mean both of you.*

Kavar snorted.

You will not get us out. Juli's voice had a strange echo. Since Kavar was open to her and Ashem, her words came to him from both. *We'll figure this out. You concentrate on keeping Rhys and Kai safe. We can take care of ourselves.*

Kavar didn't speak, only listened as the two of them comforted each other. Forgotten again.

To Kavar's surprise, Juli succeeded in convincing Ashem not to come—at least not at the moment and not with all of Eryri at his back. She claimed Owain wouldn't hurt her much because she was Kavar's heartsworn.

Kavar rolled his eyes. Whatever friendship he'd had with Owain was over. Kavar hadn't wanted to admit that it had been crumbling for a while—ever since he'd found out his "friend" had condoned Jiang's betrayal, leading to his capture by Rhys.

When he was young, Owain was the only person who'd seen Kavar as the dragon he could be instead of as Ashem's brother. In recent years, Owain had changed. Slowly, but the boy who'd been an idealist, who'd wanted to set things right for himself and his mother's memory, had become a power-hungry man with a twisted sense of justice and sacrifice.

Still, for a thousand years, he'd been all Kavar had.

Kavar picked at a spot of ice on the floor. Soon, he and Juli would have to huddle together for warmth. He smiled.

Ashem would hate that.

CHAPTER 28

KAI

E ryri appeared on the horizon on a day when the wind whipped the sea into foaming whitecaps and high clouds scuttled across the sky in bunches like raw cotton. Kai clung to Rhys's back, exhausted and aching and terrified for Juli. Ashem had told them of her capture the day before. He'd wanted to take off after her, but even he couldn't make another trip that long so soon.

And apparently Juli believed—even though she and Kavar were sharing a cell—that they would be safe enough for the time being. She'd overheard that Jiang was sending poison to Eryri. Kai wondered if she'd misheard. Poison wasn't a very dragon-like way to kill. According to Rhys, it violated some unwritten moral rule. When a dragon killed, it was only ethical to do it in person.

The sight of the archipelago scattered like white-ringed emeralds on the velvety blue sea lodged a lump in her throat.

Home.

More than fear or pain or darkness, the all-encompassing relief at being in this place, safe with Rhys and her family, sent

Kai's control spiraling out of her grasp. She shuddered and let out a helpless sob. It had been an entire month since she'd been home.

No, please no. Not yet. They'd flown near enough to the central island that she could see the crowd of toy-sized dragons waiting for her. She couldn't land in the middle of them sobbing like a lunatic.

They already thought she was unstable by virtue of being born human. She couldn't give them any more excuses to encourage Rhys to find a new queen.

Kai slammed the door on her emotions one more time. She was so weary. For the first time, she thought she would rather cry than keep it all inside.

"You okay, Kai?" Liam shouted about the wind.

Her brother had been riding behind her, his arms around her waist, for most of the trip. Though Kai had thought it would be weird to have her family in Eryri, her brother's presence was a comfort. Her parents might not have been accepting of every-thing—the dragons, the fact that their daughter was basically married to a stranger—but they were doing okay.

"Just glad to be home," she called back.

Still, she was relieved Rhys had promised to give the Mona-hans their own suite of rooms. Sharing would be too much togetherness. Most of the humans would be placed on a less populous southern island until Rhys could talk to the Council about what to do with them, but Kai's family would be housed in one of the empty apartments off the rotunda where the vee lived.

She thought she could deal with that.

Kai rubbed her chest and gritted her teeth against the pain of the sundering, which spiked and waned so randomly that she couldn't get used to it. Another sharp pang hit, and she inhaled through her teeth.

She twisted in the harness to look behind her. Ashem and the others followed them closely. All of the dragons were worn almost to breaking, heavily loaded as they were. To make the trip in anything like normal time, they'd ditched most of their camping gear.

Thankfully, Rhys had also ordered them to empty, then drop their bottles of cordial over the sea as soon as they were over deep water. The bottles sank into the blue, leaving no evidence to show they'd been destroyed instead of stolen. If things went according to plan, Owain would believe Rhys had taken the nasty stuff back to Eryri.

To help give the lie wings, Rhys had called Deryn, and she'd started a rumor that Rhys was bringing the cordial back. That he was planning to use it against Owain.

Even if Rhys didn't "plan" to use it as a weapon, Kai thought Owain would do almost anything to get his hands on it. After all, they'd destroyed his ability to make more any time soon. If Owain wanted human juice for his war, he'd have to come to Eryri.

They circled around and made a pit stop on the second southernmost island, leaving Tane, Isi, and Thabo in charge of the dozen humans who'd survived the desert and weren't related to Kai. Then Rhys, Kai, Ashem, and Morwenna—along with Kai's family—got back into the air and headed for the central island. This time, Kai rode Rhys alone. Ashem carried her parents. Liam rode Morwenna.

As tired as everyone was, they couldn't go directly to their rooms. Instead, they headed for the valley cradled between two long ridges that extended out from the base of the mountain. The valley held a massive circle of standing stones that sat between the ridges, as if it were cradled in the island's arms. A lake stood just beyond the circle. Several dozen dragons and some Wingless waited for them there, including Deryn and what looked to be the entire Council.

Deryn greeted them first, swooping upward on azure wings, her slender body nearly the same color as the ocean and her head and horns draped with elaborate platinum chains that dripped in sapphires and diamonds. She and Rhys circled each other in a way that felt ceremonial, but their greeting definitely was not.

You wind-for-brains idiot. I can't believe you pulled it off! Welcome home. Deryn gave Rhys a dragon smile, showing silvery teeth.

I see the mountain still stands. Thank the Ancients. Rhys's voice was dry, but Kai knew him well enough to hear the amusement beneath.

Deryn snorted, and a puff of steam curled from her nostrils. *As if I could make a bigger mess of things than you've done, with your Wingless mate and your insane plans.*

They landed, the dragons below clearing the way so the king and his sister could spread their wings and bow low to each other. Ashem and Morwenna landed somewhere behind them.

King Rhys, Queen Kai, Deryn said with immense gravity now that they were on the ground. *We have eagerly anticipated your homecoming. Your people are grateful that you have returned.*

Rhys replied with equal gravity. *Princess Aderyn, we thank you for your service. We are grateful to be home.*

Rhys and Deryn straightened, and Deryn backed away so that some of the Council could approach Rhys. As Deryn and most of the councilmembers were still in dragon form, he retained his as well.

Not wanting to be an ant among lizards, Kai stayed on Rhys's back. He was just on the larger side of average for a

Draig, and that made him bigger than most of the dragons there except for a few of his own clan and the Bida.

One of the Bida, Council Leader Kansoleh, bowed her horned head to Rhys. Like Deryn, she was crowned in an elaborate headdress, but hers was gold and rubies and other glittering stones Kai had no name for. *Majesty. Welcome home. We grieved when we received word that you'd been sundered, but we are glad that you've brought your...mate...home successfully.*

Kai frowned at the hesitation.

Rhys dipped his head. *Diolch, Council Leader Kansoleh.*

Powell—the Draig councilman—stood next to Kansoleh with a dragon who could have been his much younger twin. A son, maybe? Powell flicked his moss-green wings. *How can you have brought humans to the islands? It is against our laws.*

Rhys's wings rustled in response. *I had no other option. They will be given rooms on the far island, guarded, and sent home at the first possible opportunity. And if the words collateral damage come out of your mouth, Councilman, I swear, I—*

Rhys cut himself short. Sounding like a parent repeating instructions to a particularly dense child, he growled, *Leave the humans alone.* Rhys's tail lashed, audibly scraping stone. *You should recall better than I that there used to be humans in the court of Eryri frequently.*

Used to be. Powell scoffed. *They are not the same as they were. They can't be trusted.*

Behind Kai, Leila Monahan made an indignant noise.

Powell's eyes darted toward them. The young dragon at his side hadn't stopped glaring at Kai and her family since they'd landed.

Kai gritted her teeth. The first time she'd come to Eryri, she'd been a secret. Now she was a sham. She wasn't even Rhys's heartsworn anymore. For a minute, she felt like the past four months hadn't happened. That she was still a mostly irresponsible law school dropout who had no idea what she was doing. Who was so afraid of screwing up that doing nothing seemed like a better idea than trying.

Then she shook herself. She'd been a huge part of taking down Owain's supersoldier manufacturing plant. She'd been tortured. She had survived. Fought. Saved people. She *deserved* to be here.

As soon as she opened her mouth to say something, however, Powell began to speak again. *Majesty, I would like to convene an emergency meeting of the Council. I demand the reconsideration of...certain decisions.*

Kai's eyes narrowed. Before she'd been kidnapped by Owain, Powell had suggested locking her away as a sort of broodmare, suggesting Rhys would be happier if he chose a queen and companion from among the dragons. If he suggested that again after everything she'd been through, she was going to wait until he was human and punch him in the face.

Rhys vibrated, and it took Kai a minute to realize he was growling. *You're always one step ahead of me, aren't you, Powell? The Council will meet tomorrow, and not a second before.*

That was a relief. Though one night of rest wasn't going to cut it. Not when it came to dealing with the Council.

Powell looked like he wanted to protest, but Deryn pushed past him. *Let's allow their Majesties to retire and rest.*

Thank you, Rhys said, his gratitude genuine this time. Kai smiled. She and Deryn had had a rocky beginning, but more and more, she was coming to appreciate her sister-in-law.

There was no more debate after that. Rhys took off, Kai still on his back, and Ashem and Morwenna followed with their human passengers.

They landed on the ledge outside Rhys's rooms, and Kai inhaled the smell of stone and water and dragon that *was* this place. Kai slid from Rhys's back, stumbling when she hit the ground.

It had been a long few weeks.

A small—relatively speaking—silver dragon rose from the shadowed tunnel mouth. *Rhys! Kai! You're back.*

Kai grinned despite herself. "Ffion. God, I missed you!"

Ffion headbutted Kai gently, and Kai wrapped her arms around Ffion's delicate head, which was about as long as Kai was tall. *I'm so glad you're safe.*

Kai and Ffion retreated up the tunnel that led into Rhys's rooms while her family dismounted and Rhys, Morwenna, and Ashem changed. She leaned on Ffion as she walked, drinking in the sight of the worked stone covered in stylized dragons. Beyond the short tunnel, she could just make out the sound of the waterfall and see the vivid green of the plants that bloomed inside Rhys's rooms.

Already, it was beginning to feel like everything she'd gone through since leaving had been a bad dream.

"Oh my word," Leila Monahan gasped as Kai's family caught up to them. "This place is gorgeous!"

Kai managed a low laugh. "Yeah, and this is just a tunnel. Wait until you see an actual room." Kai introduced her parents to Ffion, explaining the situation as quickly as she could. She was *home*. She'd been stuck in a torture chamber or fighting or in a cave or on a dragon's back for a month, and all she wanted was to shower, sleep next to Rhys, and forget.

"Where's Cadoc?" Rhys asked, coming into the tunnel with Ashem and Morwenna close behind. Rhys. Home. Kai wanted to melt into him, but he looked so tired she thought she might knock him over.

He's with Lady Seren. Ffion's voice was troubled. *He's not the same as he was...before.*

"What happened to Cadoc would change anyone,"

Morwenna said softly. "He'll recover and be an idiot again. One day."

I don't know. Ffion blinked gray eyes the size of dinner plates. *I suppose time will tell.*

"Come," Ashem said to the Monahans. "I'm going to my rooms, and I'll show you where you'll be staying." He looked out to the sky. The sun was barely to its zenith. "We'll meet back here at sundown to discuss what comes next and prepare for the Council meeting. I don't know how the Council found out you were sundered, Rhys, but Powell is going to make trouble."

Kai groaned. "You think?"

Ashem didn't respond, only gave her a long, level look before turning to Ffion. "Are you all right to stay here for a while?"

Of course. I've been trading off with the members of the Ironscales who returned to Eryri. I've only just started my watch.

"Good." Ashem gestured for Kai's family to follow him, and Kai assured her parents three times that she would be all right before they walked out of sight.

As Morwenna went to follow, Rhys said, "Keep an eye on Ashem. Make sure he doesn't leave to go after Juli. Having your heartsworn captured by Owain can keep anyone from thinking straight."

Morwenna nodded and went out.

"How are you?" Rhys asked Ffion.

She rustled her wings. *Lonely. Though it will be better now that you're all back. Cadoc has been trying, but he has his own ghosts.*

Rhys furrowed his brows. "His hand?"

Ffion tilted her head. *His hand, I think, is the least of it. But he won't speak to me of anything serious except*

Griffith. She sighed. *Still, it's been a comfort to have him home.*

"I'm glad he's here." Rhys's gaze flicked to Ffion's belly. Even as a dragon, it was beginning to swell with her pregnancy. "If you need a break, we can call a member of the Ironscales."

Kai wondered how that worked, then assumed that whatever magic allowed Ffion to change back and forth must work on the baby. Then she wondered if the baby went back and forth from being a human baby to an egg. After all, dragons were reptiles. And with dragons having such an extraordinary life span, how long would Ffion be pregnant?

Strange.

Then, with a serious downturn in her mood, she realized that the length of a dragon pregnancy wasn't something she would ever have to worry about.

Ffion chuffed. *I thought I was Kai's bodyguard.*

Rhys reached for Kai's hand and intertwined their fingers. "You are. I know you want to keep busy, but don't push yourself. Tell me when it becomes too much for you, and we can figure something out."

All right.

They said goodnight, and Rhys pulled Kai the rest of the way into the cave.

The waterfalls sang in the atrium, ruffling the still waters that surrounded the mossy island exactly as they had a month ago. It was like no time had passed at all—like the bad things had been imaginary.

They crossed the arching stone bridge that connected the entrance tunnel to the central island, then climbed the staircase that swept from the island to the second floor of Rhys's suite of rooms.

Kai inhaled, breathing in the scent of stone and water, then let out a long, slow breath.

Peace.

There was no torture here. No rushing wind or harness straps that dug into her middle. No camp full of other people. No battles. No complaining humans or odd looks from her parents.

Tears pricked the backs of her eyes, and she had to stop at the top of the stairs and tug her hand from Rhys's to dash them away.

As if he could still read her mind, he gathered her close, and Kai found words spilling from her lips without any help from her brain. "I can't believe we made it home. I can't believe what we did in the desert turned out all right."

His arms tightened. "It's not all right. Not yet."

"I need it to be. Just for a minute."

He stroked her hair. "Of course. For this moment, everything is fine."

She leaned against him, letting his warmth seep into her, and they let the silence drag on.

Then Rhys swept her off her feet, and Kai let out a yelp. As a Wingless, she'd become stronger, but his strength was astonishing. It never stopped surprising her that she'd ended up with him. Kind, intelligent, responsible, gorgeous.

He carried her into his bedroom—their bedroom—and Kai finally had the shower she'd been craving for weeks. Not that Owain hadn't kept her clean—he was a fan of hygiene—but that had mostly been wiping herself down with a washcloth and a basin of water while trying not to freeze.

This was so much better.

Being with Rhys made everything better.

They showered quickly and crawled into bed. For the first time, Kai didn't feel like she had to seek pleasure from him to escape what had happened to her. Here, they could just *be*.

They wrapped themselves in each other. It was time. She

knew it was time to talk. But exhaustion crept up on her, and before she could find the words, she was asleep.

"KAI! It's all right. Wake up."

Kai writhed in the sweat-soaked sheets. Someone had her, was pinning her, trying to keep her still. She kicked and screamed, her throat raw. Captured. Trapped. Everything, darkness.

A ball of golden light burst into being above her, beautiful and bright. She squinted and closed her eyes against it, turning her face into the solid warmth of whatever had her pinned.

"*Cariad*, it's me."

"Rhys." His name came out a sob. She swallowed and stilled, her heartbeat slowing, her body shaking. She turned her entire body toward him, clinging. His arms came around her, fierce and tight. She tried to say his name again, but couldn't form the word. Every emotion that she'd locked behind the door was out, and she was paralyzed.

He slid his fingers into her hair, pressing her closer, his breathing uneven. Gently, he stroked her hair, murmuring words in Welsh that Kai could no longer understand. As the adrenaline of the nightmare faded, the shakes set in. Her teeth chattered. No matter what she did, she couldn't get her body to still. Through a clenched jaw, she spoke. "I dreamed I was— I dreamed he—"

"Shh, beloved. You're here. We're home. You're safe." He didn't loosen his grip, and she realized he was shaking as well. That his words were as much for himself as they were for her. For the first time since being tortured and sundered, she didn't want to be numb.

"I'm afraid to sleep," she whispered against his chest. "I'm still afraid you're a dream."

He leaned his forehead against hers. "I should have kept you with me. Ancients, I can't wrap my mind around you. I need this to be real."

"I'll stay real if you do." She squeezed, her arms tight around him. "You couldn't have known."

He shook his head, his skin brushing against hers. Abruptly, the ball of fire went out. "I made a mistake. Such an enormous mistake."

His voice was thick and choked. He inhaled sharply. Something small and wet plopped onto Kai's cheek.

"Rhys?"

He didn't answer.

"Rhys...are you crying?"

He tucked her head beneath his chin, holding her tighter than ever—so tight it almost hurt. He didn't speak, but took another sharp breath. The golden light went out, plunging them into gray shadow.

Gently, Kai pulled away from him far enough to put a hand to his cheek. It was wet. He turned his face away.

Shocked, Kai scooted up on her pillow and wrapped her arms around his neck, cradling his head to her chest. She wished, as hard and sharp as diamonds, that she knew what he was thinking. That she could offer the comfort of her mind as he had when she was Owain's prisoner.

They were both so very broken.

He curled around her, tangling their legs together. Disoriented, Kai looked around, trying to figure out what time of day it was. Her eyes fell on a narrow beam of afternoon sun that blazed between the window curtains.

She stroked Rhys's hair and kissed the top of his head. "It wasn't your fault, *cariad*. Owain and Jiang are the only ones to blame." Her cheeks heated at the endearment. She hadn't meant to say it, it had just slipped out. "You've never done anything but try to keep people from being hurt."

His breathing eased and his arms loosened, but he shifted, fitting their bodies closer still, not letting go. "That seems to be how I've made my greatest mistakes."

Kai snorted. "Yes, well, perfect is boring."

"Thank the Stars you are alive." Softly, he drew her down until she was caught in his starfire-blue eyes, until their hips pressed together. He kissed her forehead, her nose, then her lips. Kai found that her breathing was unsteady for a new reason. Despite everything, despite the terror of her nightmare and the pain in her chest and the thunderstorm of emotion she was realizing she wouldn't be able to hide from or escape, need rolled over her. Not just for physical closeness—they'd managed that. She wanted to *feel* him again.

"I miss you," she whispered. She kissed him again, deeper. "We could be together forever, and I would still miss you. Close like this isn't close enough."

His smile was sad. "I miss you too. But after almost losing you completely, I'll take what I can get." Rhys tilted her head, taking her mouth so fiercely and tenderly Kai thought her heart would break.

"I love you," Rhys broke the kiss long enough to say. "*Tan o fy enaid, fflam o fy nghalon.* Sworn or unsworn, I belong to you. I belong with you."

He'd said those words to her before, after they'd made love for the first time. *Fire of my soul. Flame of my heart.*

"And I belong with you." The door to her emotions finally flung wide, Kai brought her mouth back to his, and then there were no more words.

CHAPTER 29
SEREN

Seren watched Cadoc pace beyond the golden filigree bubble that cut her off from the world. "If you would've agreed to go down and meet them, you wouldn't be worrying right now."

Cadoc glanced at her, then went back to pacing, his booted feet loud against the gold-and-white mosaic tiles of her cavernous audience chamber.

A salt-scented breeze blew through the mostly open wall to her left. Enough afternoon sunlight spilled into the room that flowers and trees grew in abundance around its edges, though none as large as the great tree that grew at the room's center, its branches still only halfway to the ceiling. Birds called to each other and a waterfall sang down into a pool, which fed into a stream that wound through the room. Cadoc happened to walk by at just the right time, and Seren caught his faint scent—cedar and lemon oil. Glad for the veil, she closed her eyes and breathed it in.

"Too many people," he muttered, changing directions to stalk the other way.

"What are you worried about? Kai?" Seren tried to take a teasing tone, but her words sounded forced. She loved Kai, but couldn't help but remember that kissing Kai was the reason Cadoc had gone through so many horrible things.

Cadoc's pacing didn't slow. "Of course I'm worried about Kai. And Rhys. They've been to Hades and back. You aren't?"

Seren's brow furrowed. When they were younger, Cadoc had never been this irritable. Something was truly bothering him. "They're home now. They'll be all right."

"Home," Cadoc said derisively, "and planning to invite Owain over for tea."

Seren reached up and smoothed her thumb across the fat golden pearl that hung from her necklace. A pearl he'd given her centuries ago. Silence fell between them until Seren couldn't stand it. "Cadoc, what is bothering you? Is it Kai and Rhys?"

She never could've asked if Iolani was there, but her Protector was off visiting her grandchildren for the day, leaving her alone with Cadoc—and the entire vee that guarded the room and hall outside.

Cadoc blinked and stared. "What?"

Seren toyed with the lace edge of her golden veil. "You can talk to me. Truly. I know what it's like to be able to look, but not touch."

Cadoc gave a sudden, sharp laugh. "You think I'm mooning over Kai?" He shook his head. "I asked for that one, didn't I?" He sighed heavily. "Lady, I was a fool. I like Kai very much. As a friend. And not because Rhys would scale me like a fish if I touched her, but because..." He shrugged. "That's how I feel."

Relieved that Cadoc didn't harbor lingering feelings for her brother's heartsworn, Seren tried to lighten the mood again, teasing him. "Kai's embrace isn't the one you long for?"

He gave her the strangest look. "No. It isn't."

Seren swallowed, pinned by that amethyst gaze. Suddenly she very much wanted to know. "Oh? Then whose embrace do you long for, Cadoc ap Brychan? Who did you dream of on those lonely nights when you were cursed and wandering?"

The question felt dangerous. Forbidden. She didn't know what she imagined he would answer.

For a long time, he didn't. He studied the tiles. Finally, he spoke. "I just wanted to come home."

Seren didn't have anything pithy to say to that, so she remained silent and studied him as intently as he did the ground.

This wasn't the first time Rhys had assigned Cadoc to be her guard. Though perhaps the last time he'd been more like a spy. They'd been juveniles still, and Iolani had just brought her to Eryri after centuries in hiding. Rhys had been curious, but the Council watched him like eagles. As the Seeress, she wasn't supposed to have a family, so the Council had done all they could to prevent her from forming a relationship with Rhys and Deryn.

So Rhys sent Cadoc instead.

Cadoc being Cadoc, he hadn't exactly been subtle about his mission. He'd ended up hanging about the audience chamber for hours every day. Finally, Seren had begun to talk to him, and he'd begun to play for her. To sing.

She loved to sing with Cadoc.

After months of harmless flirtation, they'd agreed to meet one night. He knew how she hated the visions. He'd said he would take her away—a childish dream, two juveniles thinking they could escape their responsibilities. Before they could go through with it, Seren had had another vision. She'd foreseen an assassin killing Rhys.

That vision had saved Rhys's life.

Cadoc stopped coming after that. Then he'd come of age, and life in the vee—protecting Rhys and Deryn—had become more demanding. They'd hardly spoken since. Until two months ago, when Seren walked into a hospital lobby and found him there, waiting for her.

"*S'mae*, Rhys. *Brânwen*."

Cadoc's voice jolted Seren from her reverie. Kai and Rhys had come through the gate entrance to the audience chamber, which Cadoc had closed only a few minutes ago to send the last petitioners of the day on their way.

Cadoc shooed a guard and pulled the gate closed with his left hand, his right tucked securely into a pocket. The door snagged, and Rhys grasped the metal and helped. Cadoc's grin took on a wry twist, but he didn't say anything, only hugged Rhys in the back-smacking way men had. He and Rhys spoke in low voices for a moment, then Cadoc led both her brother and Kai across the mosaic floor.

Perhaps he still was more of a spy than a true guard.

Cadoc bowed low. "Lady Seren, Seeress of Eryri. I present Rhys ap Ayen ap Thân, King of Dragons, and Kai Monahan, Queen of Dragons."

"I don't know if we can call me that anymore," Kai muttered.

Seren stood, her trailing golden skirts rustling. The jeweled charms sewn in rows dangling from the skirt made a tinkling music. She waved a hand at Cadoc. "I know my own blood, you scalebrain."

For some reason, Cadoc paled.

To cover her confusion at his reaction, Seren pressed her fingers to a hidden latch on one side of the golden bubble that surrounded her dais. It opened a cleverly hidden door. One section of the intricate golden vines swung outward, and she escaped the cage-like structure, opening her arms and hugging first Rhys, then Kai. "I'm glad you made it home. Are you ready to try to heal the sundering?"

Seren had been thinking about Cadoc's suggestion since the last time she saw Rhys and Kai. The more she thought about it, the more she hoped it would work. Perhaps there was something in Rhys and Kai that had been physically damaged. If so, she could fix it.

Rhys looked sheepish. "We came to see you too. Not only to ask a favor."

"Nonsense." Seren picked up their bare hands in her gloved ones and squeezed. "It isn't a favor, it's a necessity. Are you ready?"

"Are you?" Kai asked. "It's hard to tell anything about you with that veil on. Are you sure you're well enough?"

"I feel quite recovered." Seren and pulled off her gloves, tucking them into the belt of woven silver and gold wire at her waist. "What about you, Kai?"

Kai's sea-green eyes widened. "Me?"

"Yes. I thought, if you had the energy, you might help me."

"Of course. Whatever you need. I think I even know what I'm doing now."

At Seren's questioning look, Rhys told the story of the raid, and how Kai had helped the Noodinoon Isi create a dust storm.

"Excellent. I hope we can be just as successful." Seren took Rhys's and Kai's hands, one in each of hers. She closed her eyes and let her awareness sink into their bodies, scanning them for anything bruised or broken. Her healing power was strong, but her range was limited. She could only work the magic when she made skin-to-skin contact.

Which was why she couldn't heal Cadoc. If she touched him and they became heartsworn—Ancients, she could dream

—it would mean she could no longer see visions. Visions saved lives...sometimes.

With her power, Seren confirmed that there was nothing wrong with either of them except old scars and exhaustion. In Kai, a few of her injuries from her time with Owain hadn't healed quite right. Seren knew she'd probably need every bit of her magic to heal the sundering, if indeed she could, but she couldn't resist putting those few things right.

Kai inhaled sharply, but said nothing.

Not finding anything else to fix, she sank deeper, to the level of the mind. She couldn't read thoughts, only sense if something wasn't working like it was supposed to. Seren had limited power to repair damage on this plane, but again, nothing seemed to be wrong. She pushed deeper still.

Beyond the physical body and the mind lay the soul. She'd only gone so far a handful of times. Perhaps the gold dragons of old had known how to deal with the intricacies they found there, but she did not, and she'd had no gold dragon to teach her. Only Iolani and record stones of lore so old even they had been damaged by time.

Aha. There *were* problems here. Nothing Seren could see, per se, but...it was as if there were dozens of golden strands floating in a void, like a spiderweb someone had carelessly walked through. Once, they'd connected Rhys and Kai. Now they floated, broken, unable to reconnect.

Seren nudged at the strands. But even though they looked like threads of fine silk, they were too heavy to move far. Undeterred, Seren grasped one of Rhys's ends and one of Kai's and dragged them together.

Nothing happened.

Seren poured healing power into that broken space, willing the edges to meld. Still nothing.

"I'd like to borrow your power, if I could, Kai." Seren heard her own voice as if from a distance.

"Go for it," Kai said.

Seren had used Wingless help in difficult healings before. "Picture opening your mind to me the way you do with Rhys. I will essentially take what you're offering."

As if a sun blazed just below the horizon, Seren sensed a sudden source of power lurking beyond sight. She opened herself to it and became a conduit of raw magic, her body taking it in and converting into energy that healed.

She poured that power into the broken threads, willing them together and trying to reforge the bond between them. When they didn't respond, she siphoned more of Kai's power. Then more. Still, the chains resisted. Seren gritted her teeth. She *would* do this. She would help her brother.

"Enough." Rhys's voice.

Seren's eyes popped open and she let go of the bits of magic she'd been holding. A tingling buzzed through the air, then was gone. Seren blinked.

Kai was white as a sheet and leaning against Rhys. Seren put a hand over her mouth. "I'm so sorry. I didn't realize how much I was taking."

"It's okay." Kai smiled wanly. "I wanted you to try. Who knew it would take more energy to do that than make a dust storm?"

Seren folded her hands into her sleeves and squeezed her wrists. She'd failed. "It's like there are strands that used to bind you, but they've been broken. I was thinking of them like silk, but now I wonder if they're more like metal. They need to be heated and forged back together. But all that magic didn't even leave a mark, and I was only trying to fix the first of a dozen breaks. Maybe two dozen. I'm sorry."

"It's all right." Rhys smiled at her, but Seren could see that he was disappointed. "We knew it probably wouldn't work."

Seren wasn't ready to give up. "There must be a way, Rhys. I think the mantle could do it, but I don't know if the half you have would work. It might need to be the whole thing. Still, you should try it, once you've rested."

"Lady Seeress?"

Seren turned. A woman at the gate was calling her name.

Cadoc made his way toward the door. "Lady Seren isn't seeing any more supplicants this evening."

"I can see her, bard," the woman said in a flat voice. "I think she can speak for herself."

Amusement tinged Seren's discouragement at her failure. She knew that voice. Athena, one of the Wingless who sat on the Council. "Let her in, Cadoc."

Cadoc muttered something, but opened the gate on the far side of the audience chamber.

The woman entered, following Cadoc across the room. As she approached, she dipped her head at Rhys and Kai in a perfunctory way.

Athena was a composed woman of average height with sepia skin and tightly coiled hair that floated like a cloud around her pretty oval face. Seren inclined her head. "Councilwoman Athena. How may I serve?"

The woman returned the gesture, the metal disks of earrings clinking with the movement. She sent a sideways glance toward Rhys. "Conveniently, I'd like to speak to both you and the king. During the emergency Council meeting tomorrow, I have a feeling Wingless will feature heavily in what is said. My people have asked that I put forth a measure that will allow Wingless—all Wingless who choose—to ride into battle with their mates the way the queen has ridden with the king."

It was not a new measure. "I already support you, Council-woman. You know that."

Rhys, to Seren's surprise, didn't speak. Kai frowned at him.

Athena fixed him with a piercing gaze. "Majesty?"

Rhys shifted. "I'll think on it."

Kai turned on him with her own withering look. "What do you mean, you'll think on it? Of course we're going to support them."

Rhys's expression hardened. "You were taken from me and tortured. That wouldn't have happened if I'd left you here. I won't stop you, but that doesn't mean the rest of the Wingless should fight as well."

Kai's mouth formed an O. Then she drew in a breath, and Seren thought it was rather like watching a thunderstorm form before her eyes.

"Oh, *hell* no, *Your Majesty*. You are going to support the Wingless."

Rhys appeared unmoved. "Perhaps we should speak of this in private."

Kai raised her eyebrows. "No. This is a fine place to speak. They're people, Rhys. They have just as much right to decide how to spend their lives as the dragons do. I was *essential* on the raid. You couldn't have done it without me. There might be fights you can't win without them."

"Kai, we'll talk about this later." Rhys's voice grated.

"No."

"Yes." The word came out harsh enough to surprise Seren. Kai pressed her lips together, her cheeks flaming, her eyes narrowed.

There was no way Rhys had heard the end of that, but it was not a good idea for Rhys and Kai to fight in such a public place. Seren made her voice serene. "Councilwoman, you can understand why the king might be hesitant. Perhaps it's a good idea for all of us to sleep on your question. You've met the queen?"

Again, Athena inclined her head in that perfunctory way. "I recognize her."

Kai was staring hungrily at Athena. "Are you... Sorry, but your accent. Are you American? I've met some of the other Wingless. I thought Juli and I were the only ones from the States. And I wasn't aware that there were other Wingless who wanted to fight."

Athena raised an eloquent eyebrow. "I am. And why would you be aware? It's not like you've come to us and asked."

Kai stepped back, apparently disconcerted by the vehemence in the woman's tone.

"Councilwoman," Rhys said, his voice warning.

"No. Let her talk." Kai turned back to Athena. "Was I supposed to?"

Athena crossed her arms and looked at Kai like she was the biggest fool she'd come across that day. "You're the first Wingless in memory to have any kind of power. By all accounts even Mair was kept on a short leash by Ayen. What do you think? We are your people, and we need you."

Kai's eyes widened, a spark lighting in them Seren recognized. It was the look of a person who'd found a cause. "I'm... I'm sorry. I should have known. I should have thought. Should have acted before you had to ask me to. When and where?"

Rhys sighed.

Athena pursed her lips, expression skeptical. "Tomorrow afternoon."

"All right." Kai smoothed her hands down her sides. "Where?"

Athena laughed a little. "I'll send someone for you." Her gaze jumped back to Rhys, and this time Athena bowed, pressing the fingers of her left hand to her forehead. "Majesty. I do hope you'll consider. She's right. We *have* the right to choose. You are just preventing us from exercising it."

Seren silently agreed.

Rhys bowed in return, but he didn't look happy. Seren exchanged a few pleasantries with Athena, then Cadoc showed the councilwoman out.

Rhys watched Athena go. "I think we'd better get back to our rooms."

Kai looked worse than she had when she'd come in. Seren felt guilty about that. She really should have been more careful with Kai's power.

"Wait." Cadoc looked to Rhys. "Before you go, I need to speak with you. Alone."

Rhys followed him toward the open wall that overlooked the sea, the two of them speaking too quietly for Seren to overhear.

"He is not okay," Kai said, watching Cadoc, who still had his broken right hand inside his jacket. "He looks like Napoleon. Which would be funny if it weren't so terrible. And my fault." She rubbed her face. "I don't know what I'm doing here. I don't have a job. I don't have a purpose. I'm not even heartsworn to Rhys anymore. I can't tell if people expect me to be a queen or to sit in a corner. Juli's been captured. Deryn apparently has everyone flying around the archipelago, laying traps. And now my parents are here, and I'm afraid if I spend too much time with them, I'm going to regress into who they think I am."

Seren felt a wry smile come to her face, though Kai wouldn't be able to see it. "Expectation is an odd thing. Sometimes people expect both too much and not enough of us, and we get crushed in the emptiness between."

Kai rubbed her thumbs over her fingertips, her face thoughtful. "I guess we have to grow to fill it, then. I want to do

275

that. I want to be enough for Rhys, and for whatever the people here need of me. I've seen Owain close up, and whatever happens, he can't be allowed to control the dragons."

"No, he can't." Seren watched Cadoc, thinking of what Kai had said. She'd spent her entire life trying to grow large enough to fill the emptiness, but no matter how much she tried, she couldn't quite make herself big enough.

She hoped it worked for Kai. As for herself, Seren didn't know if she could stretch much further.

CHAPTER 30

CADOC

C adoc's fingers itched with inactivity. He stood with Rhys, as he had a hundred times, watching the sun lower itself into the ocean. With no instrument to hand, it felt like he was only half there. Like the sun shouldn't be able to sink unless he could play it down.

That's a grandiose thought if you've ever had one, wind-for-brains. The world will literally stop turning because you can't pluck a few strings at sunset.

"Cadoc, what's going on?"

Cadoc drew a deep breath. For once, he wasn't sure what to say. So he dove right in. "I can't be Seren's bodyguard."

Rhys's brow furrowed. "I don't trust anyone else."

Cadoc nearly laughed. "I'm the last man you should trust."

"What do you mean?" The question came out sharp.

"Fuck me. Rhys, she's my heartsworn. Or she would be, if I touched her."

Rhys sat back, his mouth turning up a bit. It wasn't the reaction Cadoc had expected. "Why would you think Seren is your heartsworn?"

So Cadoc related Seren's story of Mair's dissolving ring and the conclusions he'd drawn.

Rhys ran a hand through his hair and smoothed it down again. "Perhaps she didn't see what she thought she did."

Cadoc took a calming breath. Of course Rhys didn't believe him. Cadoc hardly believed himself. "It happened at the exact moment the curse broke. Mair showed me that ring. There is no other explanation. If I touch Seren, she'll be sworn, and you'll lose your Seeress."

"I need Seren protected, and I don't have anyone else. I need you to do this."

This was not going as well as Cadoc had hoped. "Until when?"

"Indefinitely. Just… Ancients, just stay away from her."

Cadoc flinched. "That's what I'm trying to do."

Rhys pinched the bridge of his nose. "Sorry. Listen, she may be one of the people you could swear to, Cadoc, but there's no reason to believe she's the only one."

Cadoc snorted. "And when, in all the fragments of history we have, have you ever heard of there being more than one option for a person's heartsworn? Identical twins being the exception."

Rhys shifted. "Never. But we've never known two dragons could heartswear to each other before they actually touched, either. It could be entirely possible that you'll swear to someone else. Perhaps you should go out a little more. Try. Then you wouldn't have to worry about accidentally heartswearing to Seren."

The thought of heartswearing had always appealed to Cadoc. Suddenly, it made him ill.

Rhys wasn't finished. "Perhaps Seren didn't dissolve the blood charm because she's meant to be sworn to you. She's the only one of her kind—a healer. Her blood could have some kind of special ability to break curses. In a way, breaking the curse was a healing. There could be no more to it than that."

"I didn't— I— Perhaps." The thought gutted him. He'd only "known" that Seren was his for a few days, but somehow it had already become one of the foundational truths of his life, inevitable. She was his heartsworn. He was meant to be with her. There was no one else.

Rhys frowned. "That's good news. Why do you look like someone cut off your tail while you were sleeping?"

Cadoc shook himself, then forced a grin. "Just remembering I haven't eaten dinner yet."

"Do that." Rhys hesitated. "Leave her inside on her dais and keep yourself on the outside. We can get this sorted when things settle down."

"All right." Cadoc looked at his feet, then back at Rhys's face. "Just... Just remember, if I do anything...stupid, know it's because I'm too stupid to see a way out."

Rhys's frown deepened. "Cadoc. I've got enough going on. Do not do anything stupid."

Cadoc didn't respond as Rhys walked back to Kai.

He didn't make promises he couldn't keep.

CHAPTER 31
RHYS

R hys was not looking forward to meeting with the Council.

He rose, leaving Kai and his warm bed to stand on the ledge and watch the sun rise. To his surprise, Ffion was there. She wore her human body instead of that of the dragon. Her face was as pale and unreadable as carved marble.

"Have you left this ledge since you've been back in Eryri?"

She gave him a look. "I feel useful here. Don't worry, I trade off shifts with the Ironscales so I can eat and sleep. Would you rather I went back to moping in my rooms?"

Rhys raised his hands defensively. "No." After a pause he asked, "How are you?"

She looked to the sea. "Alive."

Rhys crossed his arms, watching the sky lighten bit by bit. "I've never hated Owain before. Maybe I should have, but I never did. Iain, Griffith, Cadoc's hand, Kai... I swear Owain will pay."

Her face softened, her lower lip wobbled. "I want you to win this war, but answering death with more death is not the way to peace. Once you've won, we have to become one people again. There are so few of us. When that happens, if I see Demba, I have to walk by. If we reunite only to take vengeance on those who killed our loved ones, there will be no dragons left."

He hadn't thought about it like that. When Rhys thought of the war, it mostly involved ending the threat to himself and the people he loved. Not having to watch his back, or fight. But if he won this war, he would be king of all the dragons—even the ones who had been trying to kill him nearly half his life.

Tears dropped from Ffion's eyes, and she put a hand over her stomach. "Vengeance is not what Griffith would have wanted. More than any of us, I think, he wanted peace. When you win, that will be your hardest job. You'll have to heal us. You and Kai. Our people used to be such a fire, Rhys. We lit the world. But we've become embers—scattered, dying coals. We can burn bright again, but not as we are. You must unite us."

The truth of her words sank into his bones. "If every dragon were as gracious as you," he whispered, "that might not sound like the most impossible thing I've ever heard."

They watched the rest of the sunrise in silence.

After a while, Kai shuffled out to join them. She was wrapped in a thin blanket and soft with sleep. "Are you ready for today?"

Rhys smoothed her mussed hair from her forehead, his heart swelling a little when she leaned into his palm. He wanted to kiss her and make her breakfast, to spend the day talking to his friends, reading and falling asleep with Kai on the couch. Maybe—in his dream world—they could take a walk along the edge of the lagoon, and he could show her the tide pools.

Instead, he had to plan a war.

Kai didn't ask what he knew she wanted to—whether or not

he would support the Wingless. Rhys wasn't sure himself. It was one thing to allow Kai to ride with him. She was queen, after all. If he told the Wingless they could do what they wanted, their mates—not to mention the rest of the dragons—could mutiny.

As always, it came down to a choice between what was easy and what was right.

He went to the kitchen, leaving Kai on the ledge with Ffion, and made breakfast for them all. Afterward, he and Kai got ready for the meeting.

Easy or right?

Could a decision be right if it cost him the support of his people? He'd lost a large group of soldiers once, when it had come out that he'd sworn to a Wingless. He couldn't afford to lose anyone else.

"I've been thinking," Kai said as he buttoned the back of her dress. "You know those rogue friends of Cadoc's? Maybe you should send them to their clans with some kind of offer. You lost a bunch of soldiers over me. You should try to get some back."

Apparently he wasn't the only one remembering the past. Rhys considered. He hadn't assigned Tharah, Kephas, or Rajani a vee yet. The idea had merit. "If they're willing, I wouldn't say no. We can bring it up at the meeting."

He finished the last button. Kai turned to him and grabbed his hands. "Thank you."

He smiled. "It's not difficult to button a dress."

"No, I mean for listening." She sighed. "I tried to explain some of this to my mom. She didn't really get it. Dragons and Wingless. I'm not sure if she and Dad have internalized that it's real."

Rhys ran his fingers over her raven-colored hair. She didn't do it in the complicated updos most dragon women preferred.

Instead, she'd brushed it out, long and silky, and wore one of the circlets she'd been gifted at their pledging. "That's understandable."

"I think Liam gets it," Kai said. Then she grimaced. "While we were on our way back here, I noticed he keeps following Morwenna around. I'm debating whether or not to tell him she's your ex and completely terrible."

Rhys flinched, but didn't speak. Conversations about Morwenna were thunderstorms—only idiots flew into them on purpose. She wasn't terrible, she was grieving. But that angry side of her was all Kai had seen. Perhaps with time, the two of them could reconcile.

They walked down to the Council meeting together, passing a much larger crowd than normal. They took their seats at the round table and sat next to Deryn as Council Leader Leonidas brought the meeting to order.

It didn't take long for things to get ugly. As she'd said she would, Athena put forth her suggestion that the Wingless be allowed to go to war. Seren, who had attended specifically to support Athena's measure, formally agreed with her.

The Council proceeded to argue about it for the next hour. Finally, no decision reached, Council Leader Kansoleh decreed that they would revisit the issue at the next meeting. Rhys waited, frustrated with every last one of them. He needed updates on their preparations for Owain's still-uncertain attack, not a squabble over the Wingless.

Then Powell got personal. "Majesty, rumor has it that you and..." he gestured vaguely at Kai, "are sundered."

Rhys clenched his teeth, willing himself not to lose control. "If we are, Councilman, it's hardly relevant."

"I disagree," said the Derkin councilwoman. "No offense to our potential queen, but if you were sworn you'd know her

284

thoughts, which would allow you to guard against betrayal. I know that would put my mind at ease."

Kai shifted next to him. He could see her tightening and loosening her fists beneath the table, her knuckles going white then returning to normal, white, then normal.

"Easing your mind isn't the queen's burden," Deryn said from her place next to Rhys.

"I trust Kai implicitly," Rhys said, shooting his sister a grateful glance. He'd seen so little of her lately, he really needed to make time, and soon. "Sworn or not, nothing has changed. I will not put her aside for another." Before any of them could respond, Rhys said, "I'm sending envoys to the rogues."

There was general uproar.

"Majesty, the rogues cannot be trusted," Powell said through gritted teeth.

"Who do you trust, Powell?" Rhys asked, throwing his hands into the air in frustration. "Not the rogues. Not the Wingless. Certainly not the humans."

When Kai spoke, her voice was quiet but carrying. "It seems, if left to Councilman Powell, the dragons of Eryri are to be completely without allies." She tapped her fingers restlessly on the table, frowning at no one in particular. "Is that what you want, Powell? To weaken the dragons of Eryri with your paranoia and fearmongering?"

A ringing silence followed this statement as all eyes turned to Powell. The bulldog-like councilman of Clan Draig turned red, his cheeks wobbling with suppressed anger. "I—I would never seek to weaken my own people!"

"Then you may want to consider trusting someone who is— and I know this is radical—different from you," Kai said.

This, again, was met with silence. But in the silence, Rhys

could hear consideration. He could see some of the dragons looking at Kai with curiosity instead disdain.

"Who do you propose to send, Majesty?" asked Leonidas, seated across from him.

Rhys crossed his arms over his chest. "Several free dragons abandoned Mair and followed Kinsman Cadoc after our battle in the Bering Sea. Since then, they've proven their loyalty more than once. I want to send them back to their clans and have them gather as many followers as they can. Kephas will go to the free dragons of Clan Derkin, Rajani to Clan Naga, Tharah to Clan Wonambi. For those clans not named, I will accept suggestions from the Council."

In the end, they decided that this was a good idea. Powell's face was priceless.

They decided on delegates, and then Rhys finally got his updates on the traps around the archipelago. After nearly four hours of sitting in hard wooden chairs, the Council leaders called the meeting to a close.

Rhys stood. Kai did as well, and put a hand on his arm. Voices rose behind him in a tide as they left the room through the wall of columns and headed for the top of the mountain. As soon as they left the Council chamber, Rhys was inundated with questions by the crowd outside.

He stopped and spoke to as many of them as he could. After another hour, however, he was ready to be finished. Out of the corner of his eye, Rhys saw the dragon in charge of the juveniles approaching. Powell had cornered him again, and the Wonambi councilwoman was standing nearby, clearly waiting to speak with him.

Rhys squared his shoulders, ready to deal with the next crisis. Then Kai stepped smoothly between him and the juveniles' caretaker. She'd been speaking to Athena, but shot the councilwoman an apologetic smile as she addressed the dragon in charge of juveniles in low tones. A moment later, the dragon nodded, turned, and left. Kai went back to her whispered conversation with Athena.

She had been right when she'd said she was essential. Rhys was only now starting to appreciate how much he had needed a partner. Both in battle and in politics.

Kai was right. She was capable. She deserved a chance to fight.

Perhaps the other Wingless deserved that too.

CHAPTER 32

KAI

K ai paced silently next to Rhys as they made their way from the Council chamber to their own rooms. He seemed troubled, which troubled her. She put a hand on his arm and smiled up at him.

"What are you thinking?"

Rhys sighed, placing a hand over hers and squeezing her fingers. "Powell. And his son, Gethin. I pushed so many things on the Council this morning. Something is sure to circle around and bite me. I wish Seren's visions were more explicit. If we had some warning, we might prepare."

Kai tilted her head. "What did she see last time?"

Rhys told her about the vision: his father speaking to him, the mountain coming back together, dragons drowning in the sea. To Kai, nothing sounded like it might have to do with the Council. The scene with Rhys and his father stuck in her head, though. "Is he going to come back from the dead too?" she asked, her voice dry.

Rhys's laugh was entirely without humor. "Stars, I hope not. We've enough contenders for the mantle without him."

Kai tapped her lips, turning the images over in her mind. "Speaking to him. What do you think that means? Is there a way you could do something that is symbolic of speaking to him, like, did he leave any of those record stones you use?"

Rhys shrugged. "Yes. And I've been wanting to go through old records of him, but I don't know how it will help. None of those were made for me. None of them 'speak' to me."

"Literally, no. But metaphorically I think it counts." A memory struck Kai. One of Rhys reading an ancient-looking book in the cave complex where they'd hidden when she first met the dragons. "Don't you have his journal? Or did you lose it when we had to collapse that ancient dragon palace in the Rockies?"

Rhys stopped walking. "I have it. Ashem got it out before the cave was destroyed." Then he shook his head. "But I've read it all. I don't know what else it could have to show me."

Kai shrugged. "It wouldn't hurt to look, right? Now that you know you're looking for something."

"No, it wouldn't. You're right." Rhys strode forward with new purpose. They entered their rooms and went upstairs. Rhys pushed open the door to their bedroom and went to his bedside table, where he picked up the ancient book Kai recognized as his father's journal. He ran his fingers over the embossed diamond shapes that ran across the top of the cover. "Will you read it with me? I've been over it hundreds of times. Fresh eyes would help."

Kai took the ancient tome—which was insanely well-preserved—and opened to the first page. Her mouth twisted. "This is not English. It's not even my alphabet."

"The script is a form of draconic writing adapted for *Hen Gymraeg*. Old Welsh."

It looked like chicken scratches. "I want to help, but we aren't heartsworn anymore. I don't have you autotranslating in my head. How are we going to do this? I mean, even I know translation is tricky. It's never direct, there are different connotations I might not pick up on due to time period and culture, and you've read this so much that you've already decided what your father means, so that's going to affect how you translate."

"I didn't say it would be easy or interesting," Rhys said. "I'll have to give you every possible translation for each word."

Kai frowned. It *didn't* sound easy or particularly interesting, but she wanted to help. She handed the journal back to Rhys. His fingers slipped, and the ancient book fell to the ground, landing on one corner. The brittle old cover cracked, and a few pages separated from the binding and scattered onto the mosaic floor.

Rhys swore and knelt.

"Shit!" Kai carefully picked up a few brittle old pages, her finger brushing something hard. She picked up the hard thing, which turned out to be a tiny gemstone.

Rhys lifted the book. The old hide or whatever the cover was made from sported a long crack, bending in the center where it should have been straight. The crack went right through two of the embossed diamond shapes.

"I found this." Kai handed Rhys the tiny stone.

"It was a decorative stone in the cover. It must have come loose." Frowning, Rhys took it and fit it back into the cover. It slipped out, and he swore some more. "Maybe someone can fix it. It's time it was re-bound anyway."

But Kai's eyes were caught on the small stone. "Rhys. Is that not a record stone?"

He glanced down at it. "No, it's..." His eyes widened. "Blood of the Ancients. *Is* it a record stone? It's so small. Nothing like what we usually use."

"How do we find out?" Excitement welled within Kai. Literally moments ago, they were discussing speaking with his father, his journal. Now here they were, potentially holding words from Rhys's father that he had never heard before.

Kai picked up the broken journal. Ignoring Rhys's noise of protest, she bent the cover and poked at the embossed diamond shapes. The rest of them were hollow. "It's just that one."

"You're right." Rhys looked back at the gem, wonder and excitement written across his face. "We need a glass. There's one in the library."

Rhys took off. Kai followed him down the stairs and into the atrium, lit with the greenish light of sun filtering through leaves. Waterfalls sang into the pool, but there was no time to enjoy the peace of this place today.

Rhys made for his library and burst through the door. He walked right through the main room, which was packed to bursting with bookshelves, and headed up a small flight of three stairs. This room, Kai had only seen once. It was filled with airtight glass display cases, illuminated manuscripts, and scrolls so old they looked like they would turn to dust at a touch.

Rhys retrieved a glass from a small stack in the corner and set it on one of the long, low tables that held open books. He dropped the diamond in the glass. Instead of falling to the bottom, it hovered in the center. Rhys brushed his fingers across the sphere.

A single pure note shivered into the air, lingering. Then the image of a man from the chest up appeared above the glass like a hologram of a Roman bust.

Kai stared. The man could have been Rhys. Older, his hair a few shades lighter... Kai inhaled sharply. She was looking at the infamous Ayen.

He looked over his shoulder, panting and clutching his chest with one hand, in obvious pain. As he spoke, Rhys translated his words into English. "Rhys. I'm making this record to hide it in my journal. If I die, Dumos has agreed to deliver it."

The man paused, his expression contorting, and Kai found herself gripping her shirt over her heart in empathy. The pain of the sundering had faded to bearable, but it was still there.

"There are things I was supposed to tell you. If I survive tonight, I will. But Owain is coming, and I don't know where that woman is, but she's dead or we're sundered—"

He broke off as a roar ripped through the air, so real that Kai fought the urge to duck. Ayen twisted, as if he could see something they couldn't, then bared his teeth in a feral snarl.

His words tumbled over each other in an effort to get out fast enough. "The necklace I gave you last week. Seren had a vision—I don't think she knows what it means, she's just a child —but I saw... Ancients, I don't have time for the details. The vision led me to believe that you were to have that pendant, or our people—all of our people—will fall. Keep hold of it, son. Because if I die tonight, you're going to need it."

Ayen took a breath. "The Sunrise Dragon never went missing. After some disgruntled idiot tried to steal it and assassinate your grandfather, he had it reforged and spread a rumor that it was lost. That necklace is the Sunrise Dragon."

The image kept talking, but Rhys froze. Kai didn't blame him. Her own head spun. She let go of Rhys's hand and sank into a hard wooden chair.

Rhys's necklace was the Sunrise Dragon. The necklace she'd had for months. The necklace Owain had taken.

There was another roar. Ayen snarled. His image disappeared.

That was all the record held. Silence fell over the room for several long heartbeats.

"Kai." Rhys's voice was rough. "Please tell me you have it."

She closed her eyes, unable to meet Rhys's pleading gaze. "No. He took it from me."

Owain had the necklace. Owain was heartsworn, and they

were sundered. They were inviting Owain to Eryri for a war, and he was going to massacre them.

Tears burned behind Kai's eyes, caught in her throat. "I'm sorry, Rhys. I'm so, so sorry. I begged him to let me keep it. It's my fault."

"It is *not* your fault." Rhys sounded strained and distant. He leaned against the table. "What did he do with it?"

Kai dropped her head, swiping at the tears. In reality, nothing she could have done would've stopped Owain from taking what he wanted. But maybe she could have hidden it. Or maybe if she hadn't made it so obvious that the necklace was important to her, he wouldn't have taken it. "He gave it to Jiang. She wears it."

"I had it," Rhys said. "All those years, I was wearing the sundering thing around my neck."

"You could have ended the war."

"No."

Kai frowned. "I... I thought that's why you were looking for it. Why it was a big deal that you find it instead of Owain."

Rhys raised his hand and jerked it to the left. The image of his father reappeared and moved like a tape rewinding, stopped, then spoke again. Rhys translated the part he hadn't before:

"Reforging changed the artifact's power. I suspect when my sister passed the mantle to me, it tore. It's never been as strong as it was supposed to be. I think Owain has a piece of it. If you're going to take what belongs to you, son, you and Owain must both touch the necklace at the same time. *You* must hold it, and then have him touch it. The Sunrise Dragon is activated by blood, need, and will. The mantle *wants* to repair itself. Touch Owain with that necklace dipped in your blood, and it will come to you.

"Along with that, receiving the full mantle through the

Sunrise Dragon instead of killing the other person will multiply your natural magic. You will become vastly more powerful. They added that, I think, to discourage murder." Ayen made a face. "And the last thing, once the Sunrise Dragon is used, its power will be depleted for years. For that time, it will be no more than a necklace. So get it right."

Another roar. Ayen snarled. "I can wait no longer. If I die, Rhys ap Ayen, avenge me." The image flickered out again.

Kai wished she was connected to Rhys. His face was as hard and blank as a stone mask. She didn't know what to do. Wasn't sure what he needed her to say. He'd been in her head. They'd dealt with horrible things together. But this was different, somehow. This was his family. It was the war he'd fought since childhood.

For the first time, Kai felt Rhys's age.

She went to stand beside him where he stared blankly at the image of his father. "It's not your fault for not knowing. Why would he leave a message inside the cover of a book like that? How the hell were you *ever* supposed to find it?"

"He sent it with Dumos, like he said he would. But that night... That night was chaos. Before Dumos could find us, he died. He gave the journal to one of his vee-mates. That dragon brought it to me instead. I would bet that my father told Dumos where the message was hidden—they were inseparable—but Dumos died before he could pass that on."

Kai looked down at her hands. "So...what does this mean? For us?"

Finally, he glanced at her. "You and me?"

"No. *Us*. The Eryri dragons."

His lips twisted in a grimace. "It means I have no choice but to end the war in fire and blood. Owain and I have spent all this time thinking the Sunrise Dragon would solve our problems, but it's useless. I'm as likely to get close enough to Owain to kill him as I am to steal that necklace off Jiang and touch him with it. More likely, in fact."

Kai hugged herself, a shiver slithering down her spine. She had a flash of denial, like she shouldn't be here. She shouldn't be standing with a king, talking about a violent conflict that could potentially kill one or both of them.

It passed as quickly as it came. The girl who could pretend that she wasn't part of this war—the girl who hadn't wanted to be part of it—had died in Cadarnle. For the good of dragons and humans alike, Owain could not be allowed to be king.

In part, it was her responsibility to see that he never was.

Tentatively, she rubbed Rhys's back. "As long as we're still standing when it's over, I don't care how we beat him."

He put an arm around her shoulders and pulled her in close. "We'd better tell Ashem. If Juli hadn't been discovered, I'd ask her to steal the necklace back. I suppose the best we can do now is hope Owain doesn't find out what he has."

CHAPTER 33
DERYN

"Poor fools." Deryn followed the Unsworn through the sky with her eyes, shading them from the sun with one hand. Down the white beach, waves crashed. Seabirds screeched and wheeled overhead, as if mocking the dragons above.

Rhys shot her a look. "You aren't even the least bit tempted to become Unsworn for Evan?"

Deryn snorted. "No. And it's not just because you had to go and get sundered and now I *have* to heartswear."

She heaved a sigh. *Thank you for that, brother dear.* Of course, it wasn't like she could've become Unsworn for Evan before. All other dragons had that right, but not a dragon with royal blood. Mantle blood.

Besides, she liked Evan—loved him, even—but deep as her affection went, she'd always known what she was destined to do. That made it easier. Sometimes.

Rhys dropped his gaze from the drilling Unsworn. The four mismatched vees of dragons were never quite as in sync as the others. They didn't have a lifetime of training together. Yet because they'd chosen not to heartswear, they were thrown into the most dangerous situations. Considered expendable.

Deryn squinted at them again. No matter how Rhys tried to spread out the deadliest assignments, the Council always managed to send the Unsworn in first. Chances were, only one in ten of those dragons would survive the coming battle.

If Owain ever decided to show up.

"Anyway. The halls in Eryri aren't overcrowded, but they're getting close, and dragons are getting snappish. They don't like that we've made them move to the mountain instead of spreading out over the archipelago or wherever else they've been making their homes. The people aren't used to you issuing arbitrary commands, and they don't like it."

"They'd like it less if they ran into the traps," Rhys muttered, sounding sullen. "The commands aren't arbitrary."

Deryn elbowed him. "Well, they don't know that, do they? Anyway, it's not like the traps will kill them." She was particularly proud of her idea to use Naga venom—the poison that caused sleep rather than death—to booby-trap the islands around Eryri.

She glanced up and caught sight of the Unsworn again. Depressing. If Rhys wanted to sit out here on the beach and watch them prepare for death, that was fine. She'd had enough of it. "I'm going to find Evan."

They said goodbye, and Deryn clapped him on the back and walked down the beach. The Unsworn practiced at the farthest end of the island, while normal vees filled the skies closer to the mountain. She spoke briefly with the few dragons she passed on the ground, gleefully telling them to see Rhys if they had a problem. Now that he was home, she planned to thoroughly unburden herself.

Except when he needed her, of course.

Deryn could have changed and flown directly to her

rooms. Instead, she decided to check on the state of the dragons in the lower levels of Eryri. Usually, the mountain was close to empty. Now they'd forced most of the dragons to temporarily move in. The cover story was that Rhys was having earth Draig renovate most of the caves on the outer islands. The truth was that the Ironscales, a precious few trusted members of the Council, and the King's Vee were preparing them for invasion.

It irritated Deryn to no end that the preparation had to be a secret, but they still hadn't found the mole Jiang left in Eryri. Owain could *not* know they were luring him here on purpose. He needed to think attacking was his idea—he'd never fly into something he knew was a trap.

Finding everything more or less peaceful among the displaced dragons, Deryn climbed the road that spiraled up the hollow inside of the mountain, dodging crowds in a way she'd only ever done during festivals. There were so many voices, she couldn't hear the waterfalls that trickled down around the edges of the shaft. Even the sunlight, bounced by mirrors to provide natural lighting, seemed dimmer.

Ancients grant Owain took the bait soon so everyone could go home.

She took a shortcut, crossing one of the thin bridges that spanned the open center of the cavern instead of going all the way around, where the road wound past shops and various entertainments. She passed the guards at the topmost level of the shaft, offering the Wonambi on guard her hand so that he could verify she wasn't someone else casting an illusion. Then she climbed a wide set of stairs into the top of the mountain.

She skipped the level that held the offices of councilmembers and Ashem's nest of information gatherers, heading to another staircase that would take her to the summit where the royal family and its vee had their quarters.

When she saw what waited for her there, she almost turned around.

Gethin. He leaned casually against the wall, as if he had every right to be there.

"What do you want?" Deryn asked. She didn't care that her voice was sullen. Gethin was the last person she wanted to see anywhere, ever.

Gethin gave her a sickly grin he probably thought was charming. He held a dark glass bottle toward her. "My father, Draig Councilman Powell, has charged me with delivering this to the king as a sign of his friendship in these troubled times. Now that their majesties are back, I thought you could take me to them, and we could drink to their health. All of our sympathies go out to them at this trying time."

"You're not seeing Rhys or Kai. Jump off a ledge." Deryn turned to continue up the stairs.

Dragons had been dumping gifts on Rhys and Kai since their return two days ago. Not because they supported Rhys, necessarily, but because even dragons who didn't approve of Rhys were horrified by what had happened to him.

Rhys and Kai were sporting some grisly scars, both figurative and literal. Knowing they were sundered and trying to talk to them was like speaking to a person with a bone sticking out of their arm. Some people—idiots—found being sundered grotesque. They couldn't see past the fact that it made *them* uncomfortable. Which was stupid, since they weren't the ones dealing with it.

Inconveniently for the Council and several other morons in Eryri, Rhys and Kai refused to retire quietly to a place where no one had to look at them.

"Princess Aderyn!" Gethin grabbed Deryn's arm, turning her back around.

She wrenched her arm from his grasp and gripped the

collar of his coat, slamming him against the wall. She was not a small woman, and he let out a satisfying grunt. She leaned in, teeth bared. "Remember to whom you speak, Gethin ap Powell. Do not *ever* lay hands on me."

"Apologies," he gasped, thrusting the bottle out in front of him like a shield. "I only wish to bestow a gift, as other families have done. Surely the king is not too high to accept our humble offering?"

Deryn glanced down at the bottle, which contained mead. No surprise there, Powell had sent her half a dozen bottles of mead while Rhys was away. But this one was from her favorite brewer. "Another bottle of mead. How creative. This one is for Rhys, I assume?"

"And his mate. I would dearly love to present it to them. My father wanted them to know—"

"That he stands with them. I heard." Deryn huffed out a breath. She was tempted to keep the mead for herself—Rhys had never truly appreciated good mead—but Powell was such a pain in the ass. Rhys probably needed to receive the gesture, even if there was nothing behind it and the councilman had already made this exact gesture several times. "You're not going to see him. But I'll give it to him."

Gethin's eyes widened. "You'll deliver it yourself?"

"I will."

"Thank you!"

He scrambled away. Deryn watched him go for a moment, then put him out of her mind. She rounded the corner, breezed past the guards, pausing barely long enough for the illusion check, and climbed the stairs. She passed through the vee's rotunda and went up another flight of steps to Rhys's door. He wasn't there, but Kai should be. She'd stayed behind from checking on the traps and the Unsworn because tonight she had a meeting with the Wingless.

301

As Deryn had expected, Kai answered her knock. Deryn handed her the bottle. "You look nice."

Kai glanced down at her queenly robes, a pleated and column-like dress the color of red wine, held up with a jeweled halter around her neck, covered in gold embroidery, and dripping with gems. The deep purple-red looked well against her pale skin and dark hair. Kai blushed. "I'm not used to wearing a small fortune every time I get dressed."

Deryn made a *psh* sound and waved a dismissive hand at her own clothes—diaphanous draped pants and a fitted top of sapphire silk glittering with diamonds and moonstones, and embroidered with thread of silver. "Do you think dragons would respect you if you didn't wear a small hoard everywhere you go? No. So enjoy it. Don't just wear it like a queen, my friend. Wear it like the Queen of Dragons."

Kai's smile grew, and she pulled her shoulders back. She really did wear the clothes well, when she wasn't overthinking it. "Thanks. I'll remember that. What's this?" She lifted the bottle.

"A gift from Powell. I almost kept it, but make sure you tell Rhys it's from him. That's an excellent bottle of mead."

Kai hesitated. "Should we check it? Juli said Jiang mentioned poison."

Deryn grimaced. There was no way Powell would poison a bottle of mead, and if they cracked the seal before it was ready to drink, they'd ruin it. "I checked. It's fine."

Relief washed over Kai's face. "Great! I'll make sure he gets it."

"Thanks." Deryn smiled at Kai. She wasn't normally a smiler, but she felt bad for the Wingless. Kai had been through almost as much in four months as any of them had been through in a thousand years, and she hadn't broken. She was a good match for Rhys. "He should be back in a bit."

Kai's expression softened. "Good. Do you want to come in?"

Deryn was not a romantic, but warmth enveloped her chest at the look on Kai's face. Things had been rocky, but despite being sundered, she was still head over heels for Rhys, and him for her. As long as Rhys was happy, Deryn was as well.

Suddenly, she wanted to find Evan. He should be guarding the ledge outside her room. "No, I have to go. Enjoy the mead."

They said goodbye, and Deryn descended the staircase. She hoped, when she heartswore, she could find what Rhys and Kai had.

CHAPTER 34

KAI

K ai put the mead on the shelf in the kitchen, glad for something to do. Of course, it didn't take more than a second. Then she was back to waiting for whoever Athena was going to send to get her, moving restlessly through empty rooms.

Finally, a knock sounded on the door. Henry Harrow stood outside. He pushed his floppy hair out of his face and grinned at her. "Evening, Majesty. You look magnificent."

One corner of Kai's mouth ticked up. In addition to the dress, she'd braided her hair and pulled it over one shoulder, and had made sure to wear as much of the jewelry that had been gifted to her since her return as she reasonably could. Gifts that were apparently supposed to say something like, "Congrats! You're alive!"

Dragons weren't like humans. They wouldn't see the massive amounts of precious gems and gold as showing off. Rather, they'd see it as a token of appreciation that Kai was enjoying the gifts they'd sent, and word would go around about whose gifts she'd worn and whose she hadn't. So she tried to specifically wear things given by those who might be on the fence about her. Their gifts, and those given by the Wingless.

Move and countermove. She hated having to be so constantly calculating, but wouldn't give it up for one second. Not if something she did could help Rhys.

So instead of nervously fidgeting with her dress, Kai smiled. "Thank you, Harrow. Should we go?"

Harrow shook his head, smiling crookedly. "I'm a little early."

"Oh. Come and have a drink or something, then." Kai led the way to the kitchen. Her hand hovered over the mead for a moment, then she changed her mind. Instead she grabbed some glass goblets from a cabinet and some fresh juice from the cooling shelves. She wasn't used to the taste of mead. And besides, it was a gift from Powell to Rhys, so he should be the one to drink it.

The juice was sweet, rich, and thick. Definitely not like what she was used to back home. Still, it was obviously the real thing, and she liked it.

She poured the yellow-orange liquid into the goblets then turned, startled to find Harrow standing close behind her. She smiled and handed him a drink, then stepped around him to the broad granite slab that served as a kitchen island. "So. What can I expect at this—gathering? It's not really a meeting, is it?"

He set his glass next to hers, once again standing closer than strictly necessary. He grinned down at her, leaning his elbows on the counter and bending his head down like they were coconspirators. "No, no. It's more like a Wingless social club. Have to stay sane, you know, living with dragons. There will be complaining about spouses, reminiscing about home. Campaigning to be allowed to go to war. The usual things."

Kai sighed. Home. For her, "home" was mostly a complication that had followed her here. She'd spent most of the afternoon with her family. It was nice having them to visit, but she was pretty sure everyone involved was eager for them to return to Colorado.

"Harrow!"

Kai jumped. So did Henry. She leaned back so she could see around him and smiled. "Rhys. Deryn said you'd be back soon."

Henry stepped away from her, but slowly, a smile curving one side of his mouth. "Evening, Majesty."

Rhys looked back and forth between them. "What are you doing here, Harrow?"

Henry gestured to Kai. "I'm here to take Queen Kai down to a meeting with the Wingless."

Rhys's frown deepened. "I thought Athena was going to take her."

"I volunteered."

"Rhys," Kai said, a warning in her voice. "He was early. We had juice. In the kitchen."

Rhys grunted, still glaring. Not at her, not even once. Only at Harrow.

Sighing, Kai led the way to the door, making sure to stop and press a kiss to Rhys's cheek on the way out. "It's just a meeting," she murmured.

He grabbed her and planted a possessive kiss on her mouth. Kai melted into it, parting her lips for a possessive sweep of his tongue, a nip of her bottom lip, but pushed away when his hands wandered down toward her ass and up into her hair. Keeping her voice light, she said, "You're going to mess up my hair."

Rhys cast a mistrustful look at Harrow. "Would you like me to come with you?"

Kai gave him a wry smile. "No dragons allowed. I'll see you in a few hours."

Rhys hesitated, then nodded, and Kai followed Harrow out the door.

They walked down through the abnormally crowded mountain, stopping frequently so people could greet Kai. It threw her off, but she was learning—slowly—just to greet them back. Rarely, someone would come up to her with a problem, but she referred them to Rhys or the Council. She wasn't sure of her position here, sundered as she was, so she tried to be diplomatic.

They descended until they came to the wide lake at the very bottom. As far as Kai knew, this was the largest cavern in Eryri. After she and Rhys had their pledging, every dragon on the islands had gathered here to celebrate.

There were tunnel entrances all around the lake. Henry chose the southernmost tunnel, which led into a spacious cavern with lights on the ceiling and a gorgeous blue-and-white mosaic floor. An open space in the ceiling allowed dying sunlight into the room. Right below the opening, a pool teemed with aquatic plants and the iridescent shapes of darting fish. Long tables lined the sides of the room, filled with food. More tables, circular ones, had been set up around the little pool. There were about a hundred people present, Kai thought. A hundred Wingless.

And they had all gone silent, watching her.

"May I present Her Majesty, Kai Kiera Monahan, Queen of Dragons and Lady of the Haven Lagoon." Henry swept Kai a grand bow, and everyone in the room followed suit to varying degrees. If she was going to estimate, Kai would have said the room held about three-quarters women, the rest men. Kai spotted Athena in one corner. The dark woman didn't bow, but she did raise one eyebrow and give a nod.

Henry took her arm, placing one hand over hers. "Don't be overwhelmed. They're just as afraid of you as you are of them."

"Afraid?"

Henry tugged on her arm, grinning. "Let's meet your people."

First, he introduced her to an old woman with skin the color and wrinkled texture of a walnut, her long, white-streaked black hair caught back in braids and studded with jewels. The woman nodded graciously but didn't speak, leaving Henry to make the introductions.

"My queen, this is Sarangerel. She is the eldest Wingless in residence at Eryri."

Instead of inclining her head, Kai bowed low at the waist. "Councilwoman Sarangerel. I am honored to meet a woman of your great wisdom."

"Ha! Great age, you mean. Well. You are correct. I am wise."

Kai didn't doubt it. The woman looked to be sixty or seventy, but adjusting for dragon years, that meant she could be six or seven thousand years old. She regarded Kai with disconcertingly clear eyes. "It's good to see you taking an interest in your people."

Kai tried to smile. "I've been neglectful. I'm trying to correct my behavior."

Sarangerel gave a low chuckle. "Indeed."

Henry left to find food. Unsure of what to do, Kai sat in the chair next to Sarangerel.

"So," the ancient Wingless asked, her voice creaky and high. "I'm curious. Has being sundered changed your relationship with the king?"

Kai blinked. "Yes. How could it not? Everything from the beginning of our relationship has been such a whirlwind. When we were heartsworn, that worked. But now..."

"You aren't sure if you love him?" Sarangerel finished.

Kai frowned. "Actually, no." She had wondered that at first, but her fears had eased since she'd been in Eryri. She did love Rhys...but at the same time, she wondered if love was enough to make a relationship work. "But it's still not the same."

Sarangerel made a noise of agreement, as if that made perfect sense. "It wouldn't be, would it? You had a taste of the dragon way of doing things—which, in my opinion, is the easy way. Now you've got to go back to the mundane human way of making relationships last. Working at it. That doesn't make your relationship less valid."

Kai gave her a humorless smile. She'd said pretty much the same thing to Ffion, once. *Family and love don't need magic to make them real. Or permanent. Or binding.* "The dragons don't see it that way."

Sarangerel's eyes flashed. "Dragons lack common sense. Being mythical goes to their heads."

Kai laughed and looked around the room at the flower-bright silks and flashing jewelry of the Wingless and realized she was comfortable there.

So much had changed.

When Kai had first learned about the war, about Rhys, she'd kicked and screamed and resisted everything. But it wasn't as if she'd known what she wanted to do with her life before dragons. She had never been like Juli, who had everything planned out thirty years in advance. She'd been drifting. Like she was waiting, unsure what she wanted.

Now she knew: to stop Owain from going to war with humans. And she wanted Rhys. If that meant work, she was willing to do it.

Henry came back with a currylike dish of tender meat swimming in an orange-red sauce next to a bed of fragrant yellow rice studded with spices. It was utterly delicious. They talked to Sarangerel a little longer, then he took her arm and introduced her around. Sarangerel was the only Wingless of such immense age in Eryri, apparently, though Henry told her there were a handful more among the rogues. The next oldest Wingless were about the equivalent of forty-year-old humans—still exceedingly old. Some came from Egypt, or ancient Mesopotamia, but many were from nomadic tribes that had wandered the world.

Dragons had only recently gathered into one place—well, recent relative to the life span of a dragon—and the nationalities of the Wingless seemed to be representative of the numbers of each clan who had joined Rhys in Eryri. The majority were Asian or Pacific Islander and heartsworn to the members of the Lung, Naga, or Mo'o clans, along with a number of Europeans sworn to Draig, and Wingless from Africa sworn to Bida. One of which was Thabo's mate, Lindiwe. Kai was surprised—Thabo hadn't mentioned being heartsworn to a Wingless when they were in the Taklamakan. He seemed like a private person, but Lindiwe spoke of him with such love, it made even more sense that he would volunteer to go on a mission to save Wingless families.

Kai had wondered if there were any more Wingless from the United States, but aside from her, Juli, and Athena, the rest of the Wingless from North America were from precolonial indigenous American nations. Most of the Wingless were youngish as well, the bump in numbers seeming to coincide with the human population boom of a few of hundred years ago. Even more, it seemed, had been sworn in the past fifty years. Perhaps, with humans growing so numerous in the last few decades, it was harder and harder for the dragons to avoid coming into contact with them.

After a few hours, Kai yawned, and Henry offered to take her back up. He chatted at her as they climbed, and Kai let his words wash over her. When they reached the top, Henry paused outside her door. It felt bizarrely like a date.

Even more so when he leaned down to kiss her.

Kai put a hand on Henry's chest and gave him a quelling look. "Do you know what Rhys did to the last man I kissed who wasn't him?"

"You aren't sworn—he won't know." Henry slurred a little. Kai hadn't realized he'd been drinking.

Kai pushed him gently away. "You're funny, Harrow, and wildly intelligent. And I'm pretty sure you're nice, but if you try to kiss me again, I'll set your hair on fire."

"Damn it. I'm sorry. I just *hate* Nerys so much." His face was so comically dejected that Kai had to press a hand to her mouth to stifle a laugh.

Shaking her head, Kai pressed her palm to the door, unlocking it, then slipped inside and smiled at him. What had Deryn said about Nerys and Harrow? *I think they have a lot of hate sex.*

Kai sighed. "Go home, Harrow. You're drunk. Thanks for taking me to the meeting."

"You're welcome, Your Majesty. Another time." He sighed morosely and headed down the stairs.

Rhys came out of the kitchen, as if he'd been waiting for her. He was barefoot, his shirt untucked and his hair mussed.

He was perfect.

"How was it?" he asked.

"Good. I like Sarangerel." Kai wrapped her arms around his waist. He put his around her shoulders, and they stood like that for a long time.

Finally, he spoke. "Are you hungry? It's late, but I made something."

She tipped her head back and smiled at him. His face had become so familiar, but she never got tired of studying it. Contentment settled over her. A long-haul kind of feeling, like she could hold him forever and never get bored.

"Yeah. I'd like that." Maybe that's what love was. On top of all the work and drama and try/fail. Not the flash and burn of lust or the heady feeling of being romanced. Just contentment.

From the way he was looking at her, Kai thought Rhys probably felt the same, which made everything that much sweeter.

CHAPTER 35
KAVAR

Kavar knew Juli and Ashem were keeping something from him. Now that he was connected to both of them in some sort of malignant triangle, he sensed the moment Ashem told Juli something they were both trying to conceal.

He'd been stuck in this cell with her. He'd kept Owain from hurting her—mostly. His own people had put chains and a collar on him. He had lost *everything*.

They were still keeping secrets. Fuck that.

After a few days, Owain took him from the cell, leaving Juli behind.

"Where's Jiang?" Kavar asked as he sat in a hard chair in Owain's office. "She keeps coming by to gloat. She's missing an opportunity."

He hated Jiang, but he didn't mind that during her visits she dropped details here and there. Like the fact that there was poison, and that he was supposed to take the fall. Though how on earth he was supposed to have given Rhys mead, he had no idea. The whole thing only made Kavar more determined to reclaim his place as Owain's right hand—Jiang talked too freely and was a fool made foolish plans.

Owain grimaced. "She's organizing the army's departure. She doesn't need to be here for this."

"I see." The journey to Eryri was long. Owain had begun sending vees a week ago, just before he'd imprisoned Kavar. Each traveled a slightly different route, never gathering in one place. Doing everything they could to avoid human attention. If the humans found out about them too early, it would ruin the surprise.

Ashem and Juli weren't the only ones with secrets.

Kavar wouldn't know, himself, if one or two of the loyal members of his vee hadn't slipped him information when they brought food. They'd also informed him that Rhys had not only destroyed the majority of the cordial cache in the Taklamakan —he'd taken the rest for himself. That had been the scale that tipped the balance for Owain. That, and finding out from their source in Eryri that both the Wonambi and Lung clans intended to break off from Rhys entirely.

There was no better time to go to war.

Owain braced his chin on his folded hands, elbows resting on his ebony desk. "I don't know what to do with you, Kavar. I know what it's like to be sworn. You do things you would never consider, were you in your right mind. I simply cannot trust you."

Betrayal bitter on his tongue, Kavar spat, "In a thousand years, have I not adequately proven myself?" He had stayed with Owain through everything. Fought for him. Killed for him. He'd even tried to kill Ashem—his own brother and the last remaining member of his clan. And he'd almost succeeded more than once.

You were my family. You were my brother. I told you the truth when I could have lied. Does no one anywhere trust me?

Owain's lips thinned. "I can't take any risks."

"Let me prove it to you." The words came up like bile. He should have been beyond this. He *was* beyond this. He had commanded Owain's most elite soldiers for years. Would have laid down his life for his king. Then again, he had always known that no one dragon was more important than the cause.

But if he didn't have Owain, he had no one.

Ashem. Juli.

He didn't have them. They had each other.

The words tumbled from his mouth before he could think better of them. "Let me interrogate her."

Owain lifted his brows. "You would question your own heartsworn?"

"Why not?" After all, Ashem had questioned him. His brother wasn't the only one who could do his job.

Kavar closed off the part of him that wanted to keep Ashem's trust, now that he sort of had it again. Shut down the part of him that said even though he still supported Owain and his cause, what he was about to do was wrong.

Owain nodded slowly. "If that's what you want."

Two guards joined Owain to march Kavar back to the cell —Demba and a Draig Kavar didn't know. He shielded his emotions from Juli, whom he could feel dozing in a corner of the cold cell, and banished the memory of the past week curled up against her, both of them struggling to stay warm. He concealed his thoughts from Ashem, who was busy preparing for the battle in Eryri.

He hadn't told Juli or his brother about the poisoned mead.

Vaguely, Kavar wondered if he should have, but shrugged it off. After all, he'd nearly killed Rhys twice himself. Just because he'd helped Kai escape and gotten cuddly with Juli didn't mean he had switched sides. Dragons had to retake their place as the dominant species. Ultimately, Rhys *would* have to die.

Kavar's newly reopened connection to Ashem would have to be severed, in any case. There was no way he could live with Ashem in his head and do what came next.

OWAIN SWUNG their cell door open with a *bang*. Juli sat up from her doze, coming fully awake in less than a second. She regarded Owain with a wary gaze.

Then her eyes fell on Kavar, and he felt as if he'd swallowed a tangle of thorns.

Owain looked from Juli to Kavar, as if he expected some kind of trick. Kavar only shrugged and let a smile play around the corner of his mouth. Owain would expect that. He wouldn't want to see that Kavar was uncertain, or any hint that he did not want to do what he was about to do.

Wordlessly, Owain handed Kavar a bottle of cordial—twice the highest dose Kavar had ever taken. No fewer than three Azhdahā-blocking onyx charms were tied to Owain's wrist. Kavar took the bottle in his manacled hands.

Owain gestured, and Demba stalked into the room. As large as he was, Demba moved like a tiger. The Draig Kavar didn't know came into the room as well. Each was weighed down with onyx charms. Owain took a keystone from his pocket.

"What's going on?" Juli had shrunk as far as she could into the corner, frowning at the men. That frown covered so much fear.

Kavar clamped down on the connection as much as he could. He had to numb himself. Couldn't afford to feel anything from her. Anything for her.

She struggled against him, tried to reopen the connection. Her voice rose an octave. "Kavar?"

Ashem barged into his mind. *What do you think you're doing,* barâdar?

The word nearly stopped Kavar short. Ashem hadn't called him brother—not like that—in nearly ten centuries.

Kavar steeled himself. It didn't matter. Ashem hadn't been his family—not his true family—for just as long. Owain was his brother. Demba. The dragons of Cadarnle, who had agreed to do everything they could to wipe away the human plague staining the earth.

Just because he didn't hate Juliet King like he should did not mean humans deserved to live.

With a wrench, Kavar sealed shut his connection to Ashem. Staggeringly adrift and dizzy, he held up his chained hands to Owain.

He had to retake his place here. He had nothing else.

Owain pressed the keystone into the locks on Kavar's manacles, then the collar around his neck.

Juli rose to her full height. "I demand to know what is going on."

Owain ignored her, leaning to speak low in Kavar ear. "If you do this, you're free."

Kavar could not look at Juli. He kept his voice just as low. "And the girl?"

Owain shook his head. "She's connected to Ashem. I can't let her live. Not when killing her will cripple Rhys's deadliest asset."

That was not the answer Kavar wanted to hear. "As I've said, you'd take me out of the fight as well. Do you really want to do that before you go to war?"

Owain considered. "I want you by my side, but I don't want to face your brother. When this is done, you go. Tomorrow morning at the latest. Draw him out. Get rid of him once and for all."

"Rid of him?" Kavar echoed.

Owain nodded. "If you can kill Ashem before I'm ready to attack Eryri, you may keep the woman. In the meantime, I want her sedated and locked away."

You may keep the woman. Convenient. Simple. Ashem dead, Juli his. His place in Cadarnle assured.

Everything he wanted. "You have to move her someplace warmer," Kavar pressed.

"Of course," Owain said.

Juli's blue eyes swung from Kavar to Owain. "What are you doing, Kavar?" Her voice was low. Threatening. As if she was in any position for that.

Owain jerked his head, and another guard came in.

Juli tried to run, but the cell was small. The guard caught her and shoved her onto a low wooden chair he'd brought.

"Tell me what's happening!" The command was gone from Juli's voice. It trembled. He couldn't care. He would not.

He smiled. "You're hiding information from me, *delbar-am.*"

Her white skin went even paler. Kavar hadn't known that was possible. Instead of showing weakness, however, she clenched her jaw and narrowed her eyes. "Well, it isn't good for couples to share *everything*, is it, darling?"

He allowed himself a small chuckle at her scathing tone, wishing desperately that Owain and the others would leave. "Tell me what Rhys told Ashem yesterday. Whatever it was he told you that you two hid from me."

"I don't know what you're talking about." Her voice was dead, but fear glittered in her eyes.

"You know what I mean. Rhys summoned Ashem, all in a flutter, but as soon as they started to speak, Ashem shuttered my connection with him. I don't think he closed down on you. I think you know exactly what Rhys told him."

Juli lifted her chin. "You can't break me, Kavar. You aren't strong enough."

Even with their bond so tightly shut they were almost cut off, he sensed her meaning. He wasn't strong enough, because Juli was potentially the most powerful magic user alive. He wasn't strong enough, because she didn't think he was capable of hurting his own heartsworn.

She didn't know him at all.

Kavar thumbed off the lid of the cordial and lifted the finger-sized vial to his mouth, downing the disgusting stuff in one quick shot.

Power surged, magic sweeping over him like a cold wind. Goose bumps rose on his flesh. He was surprised that lightning didn't crackle over his skin. "Tell me what you know, Juliet King."

"You just drank the stuff made from the dead, didn't you?" Her lip curled. "That is disgusting."

Clenching his teeth, Kavar sent a spear of pain through her mind. She winced, but didn't make a sound.

Ancients, she was strong. But even Juliet King, freak Wingless, wouldn't be enough to match him when this much power sang through his veins.

He reached into her mind, but she blocked him. He tried to find a different way in. The exercise felt good, like his magic had been confined to a little box for too long and now he could finally stretch. He was going to find the thing Juli was hiding from him, give it to Owain, and be free of this fucking cell. This woman and his brother were not what he wanted. They would never be enough.

He'd cut Ashem cleanly from his life before. He could do it again.

Finally, he found a crack in her shield. Balling his power into a mental sledgehammer, Kavar slammed into her mind. Juli gritted her teeth. Kavar set upon her defenses again. This time, she grunted. Through their heartsworn connection, he felt pure heat lance from her brow to the back of her head.

When he broke her, it was going to hurt.

He smashed the hammer into her mental shield again and again, Juli first going pale, then gray. Finally, the wall broke. She let out a keening shriek, and Kavar sank to his knees before her. She was in agony.

Stay conscious, you. His hands gripped her knees and his mind grappled with hers, forcing her to live through the pain, forbidding her entrance into the softness of oblivion. If she had just told him, if she hadn't fought him so hard, he wouldn't have had to do this.

Memories flashed before him. With the ease of long practice, he skimmed through them, locating the one he wanted.

Ashem. The memory was all tied up in Ashem, and he had to fight through images of his brother to find the one he wanted. Ashem smiling. Laughing. Pledging to Juli. Kavar saw the moment they became heartsworn. Saw the moment she discovered dragons lived when a black beast snatched her out of the air as she tried to dive into a frozen river to save Kai.

Her love for Ashem—and his brother's for this woman—burned through him. Overwhelming. All-encompassing. Juli was nearly senseless from his invasion, but she felt Kavar falter at that love.

She gathered herself and threw more at him. Her love for Kai, and for Kai's family. Even her growing attachment to him —not love like she had for Ashem, but affection.

That was Juli. She did things she hated herself for. Things everyone might hate her for, but her reasons always went back to love.

Kavar pulled from the sucking tide of emotion, calling on all the strength the cordial had given him to shove it away.

The memory of Ashem's secret. It had to be here. It was recent. Just yesterday. He'd gone too deep, and he needed to free himself from her, back away from her.

He hauled himself to the surface of her mind. And there, though she'd tried to hide it, was the memory he sought. Kavar grasped it and dove in.

Ashem's voice, tense in her mind. Juliet, have you seen Jiang wear Rhys's necklace? The golden one with the sun on the pendant?

Sensing his urgency, Juli dimmed her connection to Kavar. She never takes it off.

That pendant is the Sunrise Dragon.

Juli gasped, taking the meaning of the words from Ashem's mind, closing Kavar out even more.

What do we do?

Take it from her. At any cost short of your own life.

Her emotions whirling, Juli agreed, though she had no idea how she'd do it from a cell. Ashem hesitated, then said, He is treating you well?

He's imprisoned with me, Ashem. We're both snapping at each other like starving dogs on short leashes. But he's keeping me warm.

A grunt from his brother. Then, What I said before, about both of us being in Eryri... Try to bring him home.

A mental nod from Juliet. I will.

Kavar exited Juli's mind so quickly that their connection snapped, stinging. Her eyes rolled back into her head. The dragon holding her in the chair let go, and she slumped to the side. Kavar caught her before she could hit the floor, then laid her on the ground and stood, turning to face Owain.

He'd done it. The worst was over.

Had Ashem been serious about bringing Kavar to Eryri? After all this time, were they ready to make peace?

No. It was a trick. Had to be.

Kavar smiled at Owain. "That necklace, the one you took from Rhys's mate?"

"Yes?"

The smile grew. "It's the Sunrise Dragon."

Owain grinned and grasped Kavar by the arm, his eyes going distant. He was summoning Jiang. His eyes refocused. "If that is true, you're fully reinstated to your position."

Yes. This was what he wanted. He had his place back.

"You will be able to take the mantle from here," the Draig said. "We can call in the vees."

"No. I have records from my great-grandfather. Fragments my mother left. I will have to get close enough to touch Rhys. However, if I gain the mantle in this way, the Sunrise Dragon will multiply my power tenfold. When we go to war with the humans, I will be unstoppable."

Kavar lifted Juli from the floor. Owain, caught up in his victory, wouldn't remember to move her to a room where she wouldn't freeze to death.

The war still wasn't over. But now, instead of killing Rhys, Owain only had to get close enough to touch, and the mantle would be his. Not only the mantle, but the extra power of the Sunrise Dragon.

He would be invincible.

Kavar thought of Juli. Her pain. How he'd violated her in one of the most intimate ways. Guilt dug cold fingers into his gut.

Victory shouldn't feel so empty.

CHAPTER 36

RHYS

R hys adjusted the plate on the table once, then again, waiting for Kai to come back from yet another meeting with the Wingless—the second in as many days. He had yet to declare public support for them, and despite the contentment they had found in each other lately, this morning she had not been pleased. Add that to the news Ashem had brought—that Kavar had attacked Juli, and Owain knew about the Sunrise Dragon—and perhaps it was no wonder that today both of them were on edge.

But just as he couldn't force her to sit out of the fight, she couldn't expect him to make political decisions—decisions that would deeply affect hundreds of lives—because of their personal relationship.

Every time he thought they were safe, something else came between them. The stress of being sundered from her made him irritable. It had been weeks, and he *still* felt like he was missing one of his limbs. But irritability meant that he ended up driving her away, which made him even angrier.

Time to break the cycle.

He pulled a bottle of mead off the shelf and laid out the dinner he'd made, refusing to allow himself to fuss. It was only dinner. Only him and Kai.

He'd just poured the mead when someone knocked on the door. When he opened it, Deryn swept in like a hurricane.

"Damn it, Rhys, Powell and Citlali got into it again and they need someone to mediate. You're home. You do it." She inhaled, and her eyes popped open wide. "What is *that*? It smells amazing. I hope you made enough." She darted into the kitchen, barely glanced at the table, then opened the pot that had been cooking over the coals for hours and pulled out a shred of pork. She dropped it into her mouth. "Damn, that's good. Evan can't cook. I'm moving in with you."

He trudged after her, willing himself to remain calm. Despite her breezy behavior, there were dark circles under her eyes. But he needed tonight. "I know I'm asking too much, but can you handle it? Aderyn. Stop eating that."

She gave him the side-eye and moved to the table, where she picked up the glass he'd poured for Kai. She inhaled appreciatively and swirled the amber liquid. "I'm tired, Rhys. You're not the only one who has someone to go home to, you know. I don't want to be out doing your job at all hours of the day and night."

"Evan is with you when you're out," Rhys said, annoyed that she was right. He would have pointed out that Evan and Deryn weren't heartsworn and the fate of the world didn't rest on their relationship, but he and Kai weren't sworn anymore either. The fate of the world *did* rest on Deryn. More, even, than it did on him.

She put the glass down and sighed, running her hands over her hair. Somehow, she did it without mussing any of the intricate updo. "Fine. I'll go—"

The door opened and Kai came in. Rhys straightened and

just stopped himself from running a hand through his hair the way Deryn had. Something about seeing Kai made him feel like a juvenile at his first festival—eager to dance, but afraid of tripping over his own feet.

Kai smiled awkwardly. "Hey." She looked like she was about to say more, then she saw Deryn. "Oh. Hey, Deryn. How's it going?"

"You two. Get it together. I'm having this." Deryn picked up the cup she'd discarded and tossed back her head, draining the mead in several long swallows.

Rhys let out an annoyed huff. "Aderyn—"

He didn't get further than that.

Deryn's body stiffened. She moved to set the cup back on the table, but only made it halfway. It fell to the tiled floor, shattering. Deryn crumpled into a puddle of azure skirts, her body convulsing.

Shocked, Rhys went to his knees, pulling her onto his lap. "Deryn!" He tried to hold her, but she writhed, her body arching and out of control. Then, just as suddenly, she collapsed.

Utterly still.

"Deryn!"

Kai was white, one hand reached toward Deryn like she would help her up. "Oh my God. Oh my God. Deryn!"

Rhys's head spun. He couldn't breathe. Everything felt surreal, as if he'd sped up and the world around him had slowed.

He turned her over, afraid of what he would see.

Deryn's eyes were open wide enough to show whites all around her turquoise irises, as if she'd been surprised. The skin around her mouth had turned purple. Her lips were black.

"No." He pushed a stray braid from her forehead, but he

327

knew she wouldn't respond. He recognized the signs of Azhdahā venom when he saw them. "Deryn?"

There, and then gone.

His sister was dead.

She was dead.

His eyes fell on the broken remains of the glass, then the bottle of mead, still on the table.

Posion. Juli warned them about poison, and they'd been testing every bit of food and drink that came into his rooms. How had they missed this?

Strong, small hands gripped his shoulder. Kai said something, but he couldn't hear. Couldn't see anything except Deryn, and the surprise on her face. Glass crunched as Kai took off, leaving their rooms.

Rhys touched Deryn's hand. It was warm, but her fingertips were black. Her eyes stared at nothing, and her body sprawled across the floor, lifeless.

This wasn't happening. Couldn't be true. Any second now, she would move. Any second she'd blink and laugh and tell him he was a wind-for-brains fool. He'd fallen for her prank. Any second.

Any second.

Ancients, any second now.

Please.

He was still kneeling on the floor when Kai came back with Ashem. Ffion and Morwenna arrived. Then Evan.

Evan made a noise like a wounded animal and dropped to her other side. Only Ashem's barked warning stopped him from slicing his knees and palms on the broken glass of the goblet when he leaned forward to press one hand to her cheek.

"No!" He let out a torrent of words in Welsh, anguish clear in every one. "Stars, how? *How?*"

Ashem knelt next to Rhys and took Deryn's hand, folding

her fingers gently into his. When he spoke, his voice was rough. "The venom goes to the brain first. She wouldn't have been aware..." He swallowed. "She didn't suffer."

Kai caught Rhys as he sank back, her arms warm around his neck, her whispered words of sorrow flowing over and around him. Vaguely, he registered that Ffion was clearing away the broken glass, and then that she and Morwenna were kneeling at Deryn's side as well.

Ffion joined the circle then, and Evan clutched her, sobbing. Her face was streaked with silent tears too. Morwenna sat, staring, her expression dry-eyed and vacant. As if, like Rhys had, she expected Deryn to jump up and laugh.

But she wasn't coming back.

He clutched Kai's arms. All his life, he'd been treading dark water, and Deryn was one of the few things that kept him afloat. Without her, he would drown.

Cadoc and Seren arrived. Ashem must have called them, able to speak into their minds. Seren cried out when she saw her sister, gloved hands catching at Cadoc's wrist. Then she was beside Rhys, touching Deryn's cooling forehead, weeping as she spoke. "I didn't see this. Why didn't I see it?"

There wasn't much more room around Deryn's body, but Cadoc managed, sinking to the floor at her head between Seren and Ffion. He put his hand to his mouth, his face crumpling. Tears welled in his eyes, and he kissed his fingers and reached down to close Deryn's eyes. "Dance with the Stars, little sister. May the wind carry you well."

There was silence then, except for the tears.

After a long moment, Cadoc stroked Deryn's hair and began to sing *"Pais Dinogad,"* an ancient lullaby. Seren joined him, their voices weaving a tapestry of sound that separated them from the rest of the world, pulling them out of time. It was mostly nonsense, a song from mother to son, describing his father's hunting prowess.

"Ni ddihangai'r un oni bai'n nerthol ei adenydd," they sang. *And none could escape, but those with mighty wings.*

Rhys touched Deryn's cheek. Images flashed through his mind. Deryn sparring. Laughing. Her boots on his desk, her face when she called him a scalebrain and a fool. Her life filled a place in his heart. Now that place was shockingly torn and empty.

He wasn't sure how long they stayed by her cooling body, keeping watch. One by one they stood, until only Rhys knelt on the floor.

When Owain had taken Kai and Seren, there had been things to do. Plans to make. Hope of getting them back. But this... He couldn't plan for this. Couldn't fight it. Couldn't change it.

He touched her blackened lips. If one of them died, it was supposed to be him.

Owain's people wouldn't know he'd stooped to this. If there was a crime worse than heartswearing to a Wingless, poisoning might just be it.

Owain had stolen his sister just like he'd stolen Rhys's heartswearing.

Rhys leaned back against Kai, and her touch dulled the edge of his grief just enough for him to stand, still cradling Deryn's body. In death, she was limp and loose in a way that belied the taut grace she'd had in life.

Ashem put a hand on his shoulder. "Let me lay her upstairs. There are arrangements to make." Rhys swallowed. He didn't want to let Deryn go. To let her go was to accept that she was gone, that her soul wouldn't find its way back.

He had never left her behind if he could help it. He couldn't leave her now.

As if reading Rhys's mind, Cadoc said, "It's all right, boyo. You aren't leaving her behind. She's—" his voice caught, "She's gone on ahead. We've got to carry on until we meet her there."

This time, when Ashem tried to take Deryn from his arms, Rhys let him. When her weight disappeared, he felt unanchored. Out of control. He was drowning, adrift.

Then Kai was there, wrapping her arms around his waist and holding tight. He caught her up as if she was the anchor he'd been missing. She was so small compared to Deryn, so light. He buried his face in her shoulder and let the tears come. She didn't move, didn't speak, just stood, her hands rubbing his back in slow circles, her tears falling onto his shoulder.

Rhys didn't know how much later it was when he regained control. Ashem was seated at the kitchen table with both the bottle of mead and the glass Rhys had poured for himself.

Fresh horror struck him.

He had poured that broken glass for Kai.

If he hadn't lost Deryn, he would have lost Kai. Again. Completely and forever. His sister or the woman he loved.

Ashem poured Rhys's mead into the bottle without spilling a drop, then took the glass and wrapped it in a towel. "Who cleaned up the broken glass?"

"I covered my hand with a cloth and threw it all down the garbage chute," Ffion said. "It's probably already been incinerated."

"Good." Ashem took them all in, his golden eyes shadowed. Then he sat hard on the kitchen chair, the poisoned bottle in front of him. "She's gone. I can't believe she's gone. Kavar and Juliet, and now..." He covered his face with his hands.

"We... We must tell the Council. Allow them to announce it to the people," Ffion said, her birdlike voice quavering. "Owain will be on his way once he hears about this. This battle we've planned..." Her voice broke. "It's still coming."

"We should increase the guard on Rhys." Morwenna rubbed her hands together over and over, knuckles white. "Without Deryn, he's the only thing standing between Owain and victory."

"Standing between him and victory?" Rhys laughed, his voice harsh. "I stand between Owain and *nothing*. I am sundered. He's *won*."

Silence met his words. At last, Kai took in a shaking breath. "What happens if you both die, and there is no heir? Would it pass to some distant cousin?"

"It has passed between the clans before. But always on purpose," Ffion said. "With magic and ceremony."

"What if the dragons who are supposed to hold it die?" Kai asked. "Would it just...disappear?"

More silence. In all honesty, Rhys didn't know. There was so much about their own magic they no longer knew.

"Does it matter?" Rhys grated. "Deryn is dead. I cannot father heirs." Then, more quietly, "He won."

"He did not win," Kai snapped, coming to stand in front of him. She lifted her chin and held Rhys with her fey green gaze as if that alone could keep him from falling forever into an abyss of grief. "So what if you can't have children? As long as you're alive, he can't start a war with humans. As long as you live, there is *hope*."

"And what of the future?" Rhys asked, desperate. "What of the time after, when both of us are dead?"

She took his hands in hers and brought them to her lips, kissing his knuckles. "Rhys. I don't have all the answers right now. But you can't give up."

Rhys took one breath, then another, tears threatening again. "But Deryn is dead, *cariad*. My baby sister is dead."

"I know, love," Kai said, tears streaming down her face, her voice a fierce whisper. "And we will mourn her, and we will celebrate her. And then we will avenge her."

Slowly, as if his body was only now remembering how to move, Rhys nodded. "Yes. We will avenge her."

"Where did you get that mead?" Ashem asked.

"Powell," Kai said when Rhys had no answer. "A gesture of goodwill. He gave it to Deryn, and she gave it to me, and I put it on the shelf." Her eyes widened. "I asked her if we should test it and she said she already had."

Ffion gasped. "Damn it, Deryn. You and your mead. She got so many bottles from Powell while you were gone. She drank some of them. She would have assumed this one was safe. She probably didn't want to ruin it by opening it."

"Rhys..." Kai whispered. "I should have—"

"Don't you dare say this is your fault," Rhys growled. *Damn it, Deryn*, he thought, echoing Ffion. Deryn had always been bold and brash and never cautious enough. But it wasn't her fault, either. The fault was Owain's, and the traitor's who worked for him.

Powell. Rhys would wrench open the man's jaw and force-feed him the rest of the mead himself.

Before Rhys could move, Ashem caught him by the shoulder. "I will handle Powell. You call a meeting of the Council and start the arrangements for her—her funeral."

Rhys ripped free of Ashem's hand, but he didn't try to head to the door. If he saw Powell right now, nothing would stop him from murdering the man. But he could not. Not until they were certain their suspicions were correct.

Rhys didn't care if he was sundered and Owain had won. He didn't care about the mantle. Or about saving humans. Or the responsibilities of being king.

Owain had come for his family for the last time.

He was going to kill the white dragon. Even if it meant dying himself.

CHAPTER 37
KAVAR

K avar couldn't go through with it.

He paced his rooms, far closer to the center of Cadarnle than the one in which he'd stashed Juli. Owain hadn't allowed him to take her back there. Instead, she'd been moved to Kai's old cell and drugged out of her mind. On top of the manacles and collar, Owain wanted to make sure she didn't have the chance to spy. Kavar's instructions were to leave her and fly to Eryri and kill Ashem.

But he couldn't.

Kavar paced back across the room. Owain had been vacillating about the attack on Eryri. Though he'd been sending vees out in waves for days, positioning them close enough to attack at a word, he hadn't gone himself. As always, the number of casualties the battle would cause held him back.

Which was why Kavar hadn't left on his assignment to kill Ashem. He'd needed time to think, and he'd gotten it.

Though he'd only been reconnected to his brother for a couple of weeks, Kavar missed Ashem's presence in his head. Ashem had tried to reopen the connection more than once.

Kavar had allowed it, but only for a moment. Only long enough to tell him that his precious Juliet wasn't slated for immediate execution.

Kavar growled and spun when he reached a wall again. He'd bargained for six months. He'd *earned* six months, and Juli had to go and ruin it by getting caught. There was no point to her even being in Cadarnle now. He couldn't be close to her. Couldn't even use her to rile Ashem.

And he didn't trust Owain.

The white dragon promised many things, but as soon as it no longer coincided with "the greater good," Owain would break his promise. If Kavar left Juli in Cadarnle, chances were she'd be dead before he'd been gone a week. He'd been an idiot to think of Owain as a friend. To crave belonging in the eyes of a man who forced him to prove himself over and over again. That wasn't friendship. It wasn't love. He was being used. Owain had always been using him, and he'd been too stupid to see it.

He was finished.

Fuck it. He was going to have to take Juliet King back to Eryri.

Not that she meant anything to him. She'd freed him once, likely saving him from execution. He was returning the favor.

Kavar's vee—under Demba's command—had left already. Owain had made up some excuse about giving Kavar more flexibility to deal with Ashem, but it wasn't about that. Owain still didn't trust him. He wanted to keep Kavar from commanding the handful of dragons who might have been loyal to him over Owain.

In the end, it was good. It meant someone else was guarding Juli. Which meant he wouldn't have to kill any of his comrades.

Decision reached, Kavar strode along the side corridors of

Cadarnle, a barrier hiding him from prying eyes. He peered around the corner at the guards at Juli's door. Each wore a black stone strapped to one wrist.

Good thing he'd had the foresight to replace the polished onyx charms in Owain's office with useless obsidian.

Kavar sent the guards to sleep with a thought, and they collapsed in a heap. He relieved the captain of her keystone and pressed his palm to the door.

It swung open. Instead of on the bed, Juli lay on the floor inside, mostly unconscious. The room was frigid. Kavar slipped his arms under her back and picked her up. She was disturbingly cold.

He strode into the hall, and light fell across her face. Her lips were purple. Damn Owain. The white dragon probably wouldn't have bothered to kill her himself; he'd have let her die of exposure and claim it was an accident.

Kavar carried her back to his rooms, where he stoked the fire, then laid her on the rug before the fireplace. He packed, throwing things haphazardly into a bag.

The cold was one thing he wouldn't miss about Cadarnle. In fact, going rogue—which he planned to do after he returned Juli to Ashem—had many positives. He'd make it clear to Ashem that once he was settled—preferably somewhere in the mountains of their homeland—he would still expect his six months per year. Especially after sticking his neck out like this.

Twenty minutes passed. Juli didn't stir—whatever drugs Owain had given her were still in her system—but she did warm up. Kavar dressed her in his spare winter gear and wrapped her in a blanket. He coiled an extra harness over his shoulder and around his torso. He'd stolen it shortly after his return from Eryri.

Perhaps, even then, he'd known it would come to this.

Casting a barrier around them both, he lifted Juli and left

Cadarnle the way she had entered—the little-used entrance that led to a cluster of boulders against the hill. It was dark, though the sun would've been well up farther south. Carrying Juli, his bag, and the harness, he hiked half a mile through rocky hills, until he was sure he was too far away for anyone to see him transform.

Juli woke up when he was nearly there, probably thanks to the biting, arctic wind. She struggled and squirmed until he half dropped her, half set her on her feet.

"Ow! Kavar! What is going on?" Groggy she might be, but her tone was as frigid as the slicing wind.

He scowled. "I'm taking you home."

The expression of speechless shock on her face was by far the most satisfying thing he'd seen in a long, long time.

CHAPTER 38
CADOC

The morning after Deryn's death, Cadoc walked into Seren's audience chamber. He'd been with Rhys, making arrangements, and had figured Iolani could be trusted to keep Seren where she was supposed to be for a couple of hours.

When he saw the Lady Protector on the padded bench inside the golden filigree dome and Seren's chair empty, he almost snarled.

Containing his anger, he bowed to Iolani, though perhaps not as long and low as he should have. "Lady Protector, where is the Seeress?"

Iolani raised her eyebrows, but she didn't take her eyes from the string of tiny white shells and gold-dipped amethyst crystals she was stringing, then knotting in intricate loops. Her head was tilted, as if she was listening to the storm that had blown in. It raged outside, tinging everything in the audience chamber a restless purple. The Mo'o and the Noodinoon were always half in a trance during gales like this—the song of storm and sea was too loud not to listen, he supposed.

Iolani sighed like the crashing of waves. "She is mourning her sister and unwell. Take the day off, *awenydd*."

Cadoc closed his eyes and exhaled. "Lady Protector, last time you told the Council that the Seeress wasn't well she disappeared for three months and I found her in a human city several thousand miles away."

Iolani shrugged. "You found her in a hospital, did you not? As I said, unwell."

"May I see her?" Cadoc asked through clenched teeth. He might be her bodyguard, but that didn't give him unrestricted access to her private rooms.

"*A'ole.* Go, go. Take the day off and chase a woman. Drink away your grief. Leave my girl alone."

In his frustration, Cadoc seriously considered it. He hadn't so much as flirted with a woman since Kai in the cave, and Ancients knew he needed a release.

His thoughts shamed him. Deryn was dead, and numbing the pain for a moment or two wouldn't bring her back.

Ignoring Iolani, he walked past the delicate golden dome— Seren's cage, as he'd taken to calling it in his mind—and made for the half-hidden door at the back that led to her private rooms.

He just needed to make sure she was there.

"Hey! *Pupule!* Get back here!" Iolani stood from the bench and came after him. Cadoc lengthened his stride, hurrying down a short hall and into Seren's rooms.

She wasn't in any of them.

"*Kapu, makaainana!*" Iolani snapped as she finally caught up with him. "I told you to go."

Cadoc spun toward the Protector. "Where is she?"

Iolani made a *pfft* noise and went back to knotting the string of shells and stones she'd carried with her. Not because she didn't care, Cadoc knew. But because she wanted to make it clear that she didn't have to listen to him.

Fury flashed in Cadoc, but he reined it in. Shouting at Iolani would only make her less likely to speak. "Please, Lady Protector. If she's out in the storm—"

Iolani glared at him through narrowed eyes. "Are you crazy? She just needed a day to herself. One day." Iolani sighed again, and this time it was a sigh of defeat. "She's in Deryn's rooms, mourning."

Deryn's name sent a pang of grief through Cadoc. Stars, he wished he could trust Iolani. If that was truly where Seren had gone, he didn't want to intrude. Iolani, however, was more concerned with Seren's happiness than her safety, and damn him if he wasn't going to make absolutely sure that Seren hadn't run away.

Cadoc transformed in the enormous audience chamber and flew from one of the wide openings into the buffeting winds and rain of the storm. Sticking close to the mountain, he made the short trip around the peak to the ledge outside Deryn's chambers, where he landed and shifted back into a man. Though he was only a dozen steps from the archway and the spell that blocked rain and wind, he was soaked by the time he stepped inside.

He walked up the winding passageway. Unlike Seren's and Rhys's rooms, Deryn's contained no central cavern with a pool of water. Instead, a stream ran through a long hall that twisted down through the mountain, full of mysterious doors and wide, airy rooms that opened unexpectedly around corners.

Deryn's scent lingered; water lilies and fresh breezes. The grief returned, and Cadoc had to stop for a moment to compose himself. *Stars, why? You already had Iain and Griffith—why did you have to take Deryn?*

He'd never had sisters by blood, and Ffion was more like a

mother than a sibling, but Deryn had been as much his baby sister as she was Rhys's. Griff and Iain had been his brothers.

His family was dying all around him.

Cadoc followed the hall and its stream downward. He found Seren in her sister's bedroom, the last door at the bottom of the hall. She curled on Deryn's bed, weeping. She'd cast her veil to the floor, and her gold-edged white skirts spread across the azure of Deryn's coverlet.

Cadoc stopped inside the door, feeling like the worst kind of fool. Of *course* she was still in the mountain. And here he was, intruding. He clenched his good hand into a fist. If he left quietly, she would never know he'd been there.

Seren sat up and pushed red-gold hair away from her face, blotchy with crying. Her cheeks, already pink, flushed darker. "Cadoc?"

"Forgive me." Cadoc took a step back. "I had to make sure you were here."

Seren sniffed and swung her legs over the side of the bed. Her feet were bare, and she clutched Deryn's pillow like a lost child. Fine gold scales rimmed her upper and lower lids. The red around them only emphasized their bright turquoise, so like Deryn's.

She wasn't wearing the veil.

Damn him, she was grieving, and he was staring. He turned to go.

"Wait."

He stopped. Seren might not have the mantle, but he couldn't disobey.

"Please don't leave," she said in a small voice.

Cadoc didn't turn around. "We can't be alone."

"We were alone when you brought me back from Chicago."

He made his voice hard. "That was a mission."

Silence stretched for five heartbeats, then ten. He turned.

She had the pillow on her lap, her body slumped around it. Her fingers squeezed rumpled fistfuls of the fabric of Deryn's coverlet.

Seeing her grief magnified his and thickened the air until it stuck to his lungs.

She spoke, her voice barely more than a whisper. "I've lost my parents. I've lost my sister. All I have left is Rhys, and I'm not even supposed to have him. The Seeress is born to the people and sworn to the people." Her face crumpled. "I'm so lonely, *awenydd*."

Her voice broke, compelling him to move toward her. He couldn't bear her pain on top of everything else. "The people love you."

She nodded, her face empty.

Another step. A few inches closer. "You have Iolani. But sunder me if she doesn't think it's her job to protect you from your own bodyguard."

One corner of Seren's mouth tilted up.

Closer, until he was standing next to Deryn's bed. "No matter what tradition says, Rhys loves you. So do Ffion, Evan, Morwenna. Even Ashem. They love you as a sister, my lady, not as a Seeress. You are not alone."

"We're lucky, aren't we? We've built a family of friends as strong as any family of blood. A family of love." Her wobbly smile faded. "That doesn't make me miss Deryn any less."

Cadoc sat on the edge of the bed. Before he could stop her, Seren leaned into his side, twining her gloved fingers with his.

Alarmed, he started to pull away, but she tilted her head up. Filtered light from the cloud-covered sky fell across her face, muting the redness. She was a creature of round highlight and soft shadow. Beautiful, ethereal, alive.

Red-gold hair tumbled around her face in messy waves. Her skin, though pale, had a golden cast nearly washed out by the stormy light. Her lips were full and lush, their color like sweet summer peaches in a pool of cream.

Cadoc became suddenly, keenly aware of how long it had been since he'd been with a woman. And why, for years, he'd hidden his sorrows by chasing so many. Seren was a ghost in his heart, haunting it so completely that no one else could abide there long.

"What of you, Cadoc?" The movement of her lips mesmerized. "Do you also love me?"

Stars, yes. He loved Seren. He'd loved her for hundreds of years. She was supposed to be his heartsworn.

Kiss her. Pretend it was an accident. Pretend you only meant to comfort. Have your family. Take your future.

Her gaze fell to his lips, her eyes half closed. She pressed against him. One gloved hand came to his cheek, and he leaned into her touch.

"Cadoc."

His name on her lips nearly broke him. They were *meant* for each other.

No one will know you did it on purpose.

Her scent twined around him, earthy and dark and intoxicating. If he leaned down an inch, he could taste her. As often as she'd let him for the rest of their long, long lives.

He had lost music, but if they were heartsworn, she could heal him. He had lost his family, but she could be the beginning of a new one. He could have everything.

Rhys would forgive him.

Rhys. The war.

Cadoc jerked away and stood. He could not deprive the dragons of their Seeress.

Sick, he backed up, forcing an easy grin to his face. As if it weren't the most difficult thing he'd ever done—as if he didn't know it would hurt her and he would hate himself for it—he said, "Of course I love you, my lady. As a sister. As a friend. You're everything to our people."

Seren flinched, then stood and gathered her veil off the floor. She pulled it over her head, gracefully draping the fabric so that it trailed behind her. Without a word, she glided to a table against the wall and picked up a jeweled pin that was made to look like a cloud of gray diamonds raining drops of sapphire. It had been one of Deryn's favorites.

Seren pinned it to her dress beneath the veil and turned to Cadoc. "Kinsman, I'm ready to return to the audience chamber."

Her formality was a dagger of ice, but he was glad for it. Instead of going out into the storm, they left Deryn's rooms and went through the rotunda that housed the apartments of the rest of the vee. They saw no one, and thank the Ancients Ashem was nowhere around, because Cadoc's thoughts were so outside of his control that he couldn't have hidden them from the Azhdahā if he'd tried.

He trailed behind her all the way to her airy chamber with its golden cage, unspeaking. He opened the golden door and she glided inside. Iolani stood to embrace Seren. Like a queen, like a goddess, she ascended the stairs to sit upon her golden throne.

Cadoc watched, then strode from the room, turning only at the door, where he was out of sight, to sag against the wall.

That moment of weakness in Deryn's room had shaken him. He was no hero. Eventually, he would lose the will to fight his feelings, and the cost of his failure would fall on every single dragon on Earth—and perhaps on the humans as well.

Rhys was right, though. They knew little about heartswearing. It could be that there was another woman out there, dragon or human, who could bond with him. If that happened, he could still have everything. Once he was heartsworn, Seren could heal him. He could have a family.

The thought of having those things with someone else made him sick at heart.

When he had been cursed, he'd thought all he needed was to come home. He'd been fine before. Happy, even. Breaking the curse, however, had shattered his veneer of contentment, revealing the emptiness beneath.

Perhaps, for him, emptiness was all there would ever be.

CHAPTER 39

OWAIN

Jiang burst into Owain's office. "The poison worked. The princess is dead. The false king is sundered and weak. We have to strike *now*."

Owain sat up. "Aderyn is dead? Not Rhys?"

Jiang waved him off. "Rhys is sundered. Don't you see? This is better. No matter what they do, Rhys cannot pass on the mantle. We've *won*. All we have to do is claim it."

He watched Jiang pace, impatience radiating from her. "We've been hearing rumors for months that Rhys's hold on the Council is slipping. If we strike hard enough, put the few vials of cordial we have left to strategic use, we might be able to take Eryri with a minimum loss of life."

Owain considered. "No matter how we go about it, many will die."

It could be dangerous. Or it could be perfect.

Tempting. So tempting.

Especially if Rhys had the missing fifty bottles of cordial. He'd be too ethical to use it, Owain knew. Which was stupid. They ate deer and cow and other animals. Consuming a product made of humans was no different. Those bottles—aside from the precious few that had been in Cadarnle—were all he had. He couldn't replicate the artifact used to make it—the one Rhys had destroyed in the city of the Ancients. That knowledge was lost. But Owain had delved into deep magic before. Deeper than any dragon since time immemorial. If he had enough cordial, he might be able to work backward with his own notes, his own knowledge.

He would need more when he went to war against the humans.

Owain considered his options, wondering what Kavar would say. The Azhdahā had taken off a few hours before—presumably to kill Ashem—and Owain missed his counsel. Lately he'd been the only thing that balanced Jiang.

Owain ran his knuckles back and forth across his jaw. Rhys could get weaker. His people could continue to turn on him and abandon him until all Owain had to do was walk in and take his power. Or, given time, Rhys could solidify his position.

Word among the rogues was that he had approached them looking for alliances, offering them positions of power. The rogues' numbers equaled Rhys's and Owain's followers combined. If even a handful of the larger rogue families answered, Rhys's people would outnumber his.

He couldn't allow that.

Jiang continued to pace. "It's time to end this. Our soldiers are in position. You keep talking about the war to come, but you can't fight that battle until you win this one. So win."

Owain stroked the rhombus-shaped golden pendant at his neck, which he'd taken back from Jiang. After all these years, he had the Sunrise Dragon. Despite knowing it wouldn't work, he'd tried every way he knew how to activate the thing with no success. Perhaps if he'd had any of Rhys's blood left, he could have done it. But he'd used it all in the sundering.

He'd never thought he would regret doing that.

Owain frowned. He could attempt another assassination, but he'd tried that before. More than once. Aside from that, he was tired of waiting. Scheming. It was time to try something new.

His queen was right. It was time to end this. He gave her a short nod. "Go. Tell the vee commanders to prepare for war."

CHAPTER 40

KAI

K ai stood by Rhys's side on the westernmost edge of the island, feet in the night-black waves as the dragons sent Deryn to the Stars. She had only died the night before, but they had already wrapped her body, and now Evan—also a water Draig—and an honor guard of Mo'o laid her to rest by taking her body to a burial ground far out in a sunlit part of the sea. Every dragon on the island and many who were stationed within a day or two came to say goodbye. They kept silent watch in rows along the water as the stars rose, their reflections cold in the rippling ocean. Then Cadoc sang again. It was the first time he'd agreed to perform in public since returning to Eryri.

After, Seren spoke. She talked about Deryn, her life, her bravery. She spoke about how Deryn had welcomed Kai as a sister, which made several of the dragons turn to look. Kai kept her gaze stoically ahead. It was terrible that even here, Seren and Rhys had to be aware of politics. They never got to rest. And now, neither did Kai.

When Seren finished, silence fell once again over the

crowd, only to be broken a moment later by shouting. Kai turned with Rhys. Up the beach, beyond the dragons, a man sprinted toward them. From the voice, it was Henry Harrow.

"Majesty!" The Wingless man shoved his way through the crowd and dodged through the legs of those who'd attended as dragons. "Majesty!"

Some of the dragons growled. Murmurs went up about Wingless and lack of respect, but no one stopped him. Harrow stumbled as he reached Rhys and Kai, but Rhys caught him by the shoulders. "Careful."

Kai glimpsed Harrow's face by the moonlight and inhaled sharply. "What happened?"

"Owain." Harrow panted so hard he could hardly speak. "Owain is coming. I sent the Unsworn out to do a sweep. His soldiers are already here. I mean, not here. Close. Ready to attack. He'll be here in days."

There was uproar at that. But to Kai, the sound was distant. She looked up at Rhys, and he looked down at her, and it was as if they were a bubble of calm in the center of a storm.

"It worked," she whispered.

"It did." He intertwined his fingers in hers, gripping hard as he looked out at the chaos in the crowd. "It's time to tell the dragons of Eryri they're going to war."

A war they might even win, thanks to Deryn's preparations around Eryri.

Rhys gripped Kai's hand in his as he moved up the beach to a wide, flat boulder that stood knee-high in the sand. Kai tried to pull back when he stepped atop the stone, thinking it might be better for the dragons to hear the news without seeing her, but Rhys would not let go.

He bent, his lips brushing her ear as he pulled her upward. "My queen does not hide in the shadows. Let them see you."

So she followed, standing beside him as he raised both

hands above his head, simply waiting until the dragons fell into utter silence.

"My friends. You heard correctly. Owain is on his way to attack Eryri."

Chaos erupted once again. Dragons roared. Some Wingless screamed. Rhys raised his hands and waited for quiet. "You've wondered why we asked you to move into the mountain and leave the outer islands. This is why. The Council, Clan leaders, Seeress, and I have orchestrated the coming battle. We've been preparing for weeks."

More cries of outrage, many directed at the Council. At least, Kai thought, they weren't just mad at Rhys this time.

"It's frightening." Rhys raised his voice above the crowd again. "But we are in control of this situation. All of those too old and too young to fight will be evacuated. All of the islands except this one have been filled with traps that Princess Aderyn helped oversee and prepare. Plans are in place. When Owain's forces land, we will capture them with minimum danger to them or to ourselves."

This did not appease the people. Kai curled her hands into fists, her fingernails biting into her palm. "Be *silent!* Listen to your king!"

At her voice, there was silence once again. For a moment, anyway. Then there were a few discontented murmurs that she would dare.

Rhys once again took Kai's hand in his, in full view where all the dragons could see. Then he spoke again, his voice so quiet that they had to remain still to hear. "You know my sister died, but we haven't told you how. She was poisoned. She drank mead sent by Owain, planted by a traitor. It was meant for me..." His voice cut off, but he took a breath and pushed on. "But she drank it, and now she's dead in my place."

Little gasps of surprise and grunts of disapproval rippled around the assembled dragons.

Rhys continued. "It was a coward's tactic. I could return the favor, but I refuse for the exact reason we stand here, mourning my sister. That mead was a gift from a councilmember I thought I could trust, despite our differences. He is in the cells now, awaiting questioning. I could let this make me paranoid. I could ask one of you to become my food taster. I could decide to disband the Council and rule all of you alone, as Owain does."

He let that sink in for a moment, and Kai saw fear dawn on some of the faces in the crowd.

"But I won't," Rhys said, his voice rising again. "I refuse to retaliate against Owain and kill him dishonorably, the way he murdered Deryn. I refuse to fear, to suspect my friends, and I most especially refuse to take away your power. I will not to give in to the temptation to see the world only as I want to see it, or to ignore or belittle dissenting voices!

"The end of this war could be at hand, but victory will not come without a cost. A cost that most of us are already far too familiar with."

His voice broke again, and Kai squeezed his hand.

"Eryri is our home. It is our place of strength. Owain broke the Eryri of my father's time. I don't believe he can break us. My sister was a warrior, a counselor and a friend—as strong as the mountain that is our home. With her death, Owain has sealed his own. We cannot allow the man who murdered our princess to become king!"

A wave of sound met this. At first, Kai thought it might be jeering. But it wasn't. Quite the opposite. The dragons of Eryri *had* loved Deryn, and like Rhys, they were enraged at her death.

When they stilled, Rhys spoke again in a quiet, carrying

voice. "A wise friend told me recently that we have become embers, scattered and dying. If we cannot come together, our future is lost. We must unite. In cause. In memory of those who have passed. In hope for the future. Deryn told me once that birth gave me the mantle, but the people give me power. She was right. You are the power of Eryri. When Owain comes, do not let him take it from you!"

Another cheer went up from the crowd. For the first time since Kai had been in Eryri, everyone seemed to agree.

But this meant it was real. Owain was coming. Rhys's army was still depleted, and the white dragon's soldiers would outnumber them.

If only the dragons would allow the Wingless to fight, they would have a chance.

But that meant both Rhys and the Council would have to be convinced.

CHAPTER 41

SEREN

Seren pretended there was not a headache throbbing at her temples as she sat on her dais with late afternoon sun setting her golden filigree dome ablaze. Not that the day had been particularly hard. Most dragons—perhaps remembering, for once, that Deryn was her sister—had stayed away. The ones who had come were mostly seeking a blessing for the battle to come. Not that Seren had the power to bless—she was no deity. Normally, a day like today would have been wonderful.

But worry and grief meant she hadn't slept, and forced inactivity meant she couldn't help but brood on that same worry and grief until it had snowballed into something far larger and more soul-crushing than she had ever dealt with before. It was all she could do to keep her breathing under control. To maintain the veneer of serenity for those who did come to see her, though they were few and far between.

Seren resolved for the thousandth time not to look at Cadoc. She had a gift for him, but wasn't sure if she should give it. Since he'd come upon her in Deryn's rooms, he'd been differ-

357

ent. Distant. He refused to make eye contact and answered all of her attempts at conversation with monosyllabic muttering.

He wasn't muttering at the moment. Nearly half an hour ago, he'd been joined by a pretty Lung girl. He seemed more than happy to talk with her. Flirt with her. Smile when she reached up to brush some imaginary speck from his shirt.

Seren was beginning to understand why Rhys sporadically set things on fire when he was in his feelings about Kai.

"Lady Seeress?"

Seren snapped her attention back, remembering that, at this particular moment, there *was* someone in front of her. She could not let herself wallow. She was the Seeress. "I'm sorry. Please, continue."

The man, an earth Draig Seren knew she'd seen ready to follow Ceri on the awful day the former councilwoman took over a hundred dragons and flew off to Ancients knew where, ducked his head. "It's my mate. She's Wingless, and she's saying she wants to come to battle with me the way the king took his mate to battle. But we all know how that ended. It isn't right, my lady. It isn't good or helpful to allow the Wingless to ride to battle. What if she dies?"

Seren kept to the low, even, nearly singsong tone she'd developed over the centuries. Always serene. "Dragons who are heartsworn to dragons risk their mates."

"Yes, but the Wingless—they might as well be human. Too small and weak. It's like allowing a rabbit to ride a wolf into a battle between packs. The rabbit is only going to die. Maybe get eaten..."

Seren snorted. "Why do you bring this to me, brother? Wingless are forbidden in battle by decree of the Council. Queen Kai is the exception."

He made a sour face. "Is she queen?"

"She is in this room." Seren's voice was dangerously sharp, and the man—who put Seren in mind of a mouse with his hunch and his chittering voice—flinched. She took a breath and smiled. "Please, continue."

Looking less certain, he did. "She's changing things. Mair might have brought us war, but she never tried to change our traditions. I want my mate to swear that she won't try to ride into battle with me, even if the Council allows it. I want you to bind her to her promise."

Seren stilled, allowing her rage to roll over and around her like waves against a stone. She could not be moved. She would not publicly chastise this man. All dragons had the right to seek her help as they would.

But it was her choice whether or not to do what they asked. She smiled and tucked her hands into her sleeves, intertwining her fingers and clenching them together. Beneath the gold fabric, she knew, her knuckles had gone white. "I don't think binding your mate to this promise would be wise. If you're afraid for her, speak with her. I will not take her agency."

She turned to Cadoc. "I believe I'm finished with audiences this evening."

The man pressed his lips into a thin line. "My lady—"

"Cadoc," Seren said imperiously.

In a blink, Cadoc was there, his left hand resting casually on the man's shoulder. "*Prynhawn da*, my friend. Time to go."

"But—"

Cadoc's easy smile didn't slip, but the man flinched away from him abruptly. Grumbling, he bowed to Seren. "Your light illuminates."

Seren dipped her head.

Cadoc sauntered toward the gate with the man, the Lung woman trailing after him. When he reached the pair of guards who stood at the outer door, he spoke to them. Then he addressed the few dragons still waiting to speak to her, dispersing them. He moved to reenter the audience chamber, but the girl caught his arm. He turned back toward her, leaning down, smiling.

Seren moved toward the golden lattice. The girl tilted her head up and put a hand on Cadoc's cheek. Before Seren could process what was happening, she'd pulled down Cadoc's head and was kissing him. *Kissing* him. Right there, in the hall outside the audience chamber.

Cadoc didn't wrap his arm around the girl, but neither did he break off the kiss. They lingered, and after a moment, he straightened and brushed a knuckle over her lips. She said something, and he laughed softly. She stood on tiptoes, pressed another quick kiss to his lips, and was gone.

Iolani sighed from her plush chair to one side of the dais. "You're bending the gold, *kaikamahine.*"

Seren started. Her fingers were wrapped around the delicate golden wires, which were indeed bending under the pressure. She released them and stepped back. There were red lines indented in her skin.

"You are not for him, Seren," Iolani said, her voice infinitely gentle. "Cadoc ap Brychan is who he is—loving all women, but never one."

Seren closed her hands into fists, hiding the lines, and pressed both fists to her chest. As if that would stop the ache caused by Iolani's words. "The way he looked at me when he found me in Deryn's rooms... I swear, *makuahine,* he wanted *me.*"

Iolani gave Seren a pitying look. "A man wanting your body in his bed is not the same as a man wanting *you,* my love. Come, we'll have dinner. You haven't eaten in two days."

Seren hardly heard. She watched Cadoc come back into the room, the guards locking the gate behind him.

"You are not meant for him," Iolani repeated softly.

Seren bit her bottom lip and willed the burn of tears away. She was meant for no one.

Iolani pushed herself up from her chair as Cadoc approached. "Come. We are going to eat. I will make certain you do, this time. Your sister would not wish you to waste away. Not when you're still recovering from your captivity."

Seren fished a keystone out of her pocket, then unlocked the gate and left the golden cage. She let Iolani precede her. Cadoc stood nearby, and Seren hesitated. "I'll be there in a moment."

"Seren..." Iolani gave her a warning look.

"I'll be there," Seren said, a slight plea in her voice. "Please?"

Iolani sighed heavily and walked off, muttering in Hawaiian about the idiocy of young girls around handsome men.

"Someday I'll have to learn that language," Cadoc said.

Seren folded her hands into her sleeves, uncertain why she had wanted this now that Iolani was gone. "Perhaps your friend will teach you."

Cadoc gave her an odd look. "I don't think she speaks any of the Mo'o languages."

Seren shrugged. "Well, you're the one who's...*intimate* with her. I'm sure you would know."

"Intimate?" Cadoc's voice was half confusion, half amusement. "You've lost me."

"I saw you, just now."

He rubbed his jaw, smiling ruefully, and shrugged. "Nothing but a kiss between friends. It's been a difficult few days."

Seren hesitated, then said, "Wait here." While Cadoc watched, a bemused look on his face, she returned to her seat on the dais and retrieved two items she'd left there. One—a long, thin box—she handed to him. The other she held behind her back.

"What's this?" Cadoc asked when she handed him the box.

"Just open it."

He did. Inside, a finely crafted wooden flute. His eyes went wide when he saw the contents. For a moment that felt like it stretched into years, he said nothing.

Seren cleared her throat. "It's a tabor pipe. It's meant to be played—"

"One-handed," he finished.

She nodded, her hands tightening on the gift still behind her back. When he still didn't say anything, she thrust it forward as well. It was a small, round drum. "Here's the tabor. Um. I thought you could still play it, even with your hand..."

She swallowed as he looked up at her. There were so many emotions moving across his expressive face, she couldn't pick out any specific one. Then he smiled, slow and beautiful.

"I could play these. You're right."

Relief that he seemed to like her gifts made her laugh, a breathless sound. "See, Cadoc? You aren't condemned to a life without music. You must simply learn to make it differently."

He looked down at the box with the flute, and the drum still in her hands. "Thank you, Seren. What would become of me without"—he cleared his throat—"without a friend like you."

A friend.

He is not for you. Seren nodded, but his words turned the sweet moment bitter. She would never heartswear to Cadoc. She'd never heartswear to anyone. But maybe she didn't have to. The Lung girl he'd kissed was his friend. She was his friend too. And the odds of them being heartsworn were so infinitesimal. Surely, he wouldn't begrudge her something as simple as a kiss. Nothing but a kiss between friends. And—perhaps—he could hold her for a while. The way he used to.

She wanted so badly to be held. For him to help shrink the looming emotions that threatened to swallow her whole.

Seren took the instruments gently from his hand and set them to one side.

"What are you doing?" His words were wary.

Instead of answering, she reached up and pulled the veil from her head. It slid to the floor in a tinkling, sparkling wave. She sighed in relief and smoothed mussed red-gold hair from her face.

Cadoc's eyes widened. The sun caught in his amethyst irises. He was so, so beautiful.

"Seren, what are you doing?"

Seren stepped forward. She tried on a smile she hoped might look seductive. She had no idea if it worked. "You are my friend, are you not? You just said so."

Cadoc licked his lips. "Uh..."

She shrugged, feigning nonchalance. "Well, there's nothing to a little kiss between friends, is there? I can't heartswear. That doesn't mean I want to live untouched. Unloved." He had almost kissed her in Deryn's rooms. She knew he had.

"I—" He stepped away. The metal of the dome clinked as Cadoc's back came against it.

Seren took another step toward him. They were only a few inches apart now. The air sparked with a heat that made her forget herself. Her fear. Her duty. Her sadness. She could be bold. Determined. Like the Lung girl had been.

Cadoc's breathing had changed, going shallow. His beautiful eyes went dark and clouded, and he wrapped his good hand around her arm, gold fabric bunching beneath his fingers, apparently frozen between pulling her close and pushing her away.

He did want her.

She closed her eyes and stood on tiptoe, tilting her face up, waiting.

Cadoc's hand tightened painfully. "Put that veil on." His voice was rough and cold. "You're the Seeress. Act like it."

Seren stumbled back, eyes flying open. His rejection was a knife, sharp and merciless. "You kissed that girl! You kissed Kai, for Scales' sake, and Rhys was heartsworn to her! Why won't you kiss me?"

The muscles along Cadoc's jaw jumped at the mention of Kai. "I was an idiot when I kissed Kai. And yes, I kissed Mari. I've kissed hundreds of women. But you aren't a woman, Seren. You can't—" He stopped, as if he couldn't breathe. For a moment, his face was a mask of stark agony. "You can't *be* a woman. Not to me."

If he'd hit her, he could not have hurt her more.

Not a woman.

Not a woman.

What was she if she couldn't be a woman to even this man?

She gasped at the pain of it, and when the words came, she didn't mean them to, but she couldn't play at friendship anymore. "I am a woman. And I love you, Cadoc ap Brychan. I am sick to death of watching you kiss other women while I sit in a cage."

Cadoc went very still, and only then did it hit Seren what she'd said. What she'd confessed. She put a hand to her mouth and wondered if she should run. But Cadoc was staring at her. His breathing had gone strange and ragged.

"You... You love me?"

Seren flushed. But she couldn't swallow the words again, so with all the hope and bravery she could muster, she said, "Yes."

"Yes. You love me." His voice was a mix of wonder and despair. He laughed, but there was no humor in it. "This can't be happening."

Seren flinched. His words were a razor to her heart. She felt it open, start to bleed. She pulled on the veil and fled.

CHAPTER 42
CADOC

S eren loved him.

Seren was his heartsworn.

Seren was begging him to kiss her.

She *loved* him.

Fuck him sideways, Seren was the *Seeress*. He could *never* have her.

But he couldn't let her run away.

She'd backed him up to the golden cage. She'd been so confident. So damn sexy when she asked for that kiss. But now her face crumpled. She picked up the veil and ran.

"Wait!" Cadoc chased her to the door that led into her rooms. She hadn't quite reached it when he grabbed her by one veil-draped shoulder and spun her around. He knew what this meant for him. What he'd have to do after this. But he couldn't —wasn't brave enough—to walk that path without knowing what this felt like first. Even if that knowledge would torture him for the rest of eternity.

"Cadoc?" Her eyes were wide beneath the veil as he backed her against the stone wall. The greenery around the edges of the room was lush, all trees and vines and little flowering shrubs. In this corner, they hid the entrance to Seren's room. They'd hide this from anyone passing by as well.

He pressed her back slowly, their bodies coming together as her back hit the wall and he leaned in, savoring every point of contact, every instant. Every sensation.

The veil, like her gloves, was made of lace. He might have worried about skin touching skin through the tiny holes in the fabric, but like the windows of Eryri, they'd been magicked so nothing but air could pass through.

This was the closest he would ever get. He took both her hands in his good one, intertwining their fingers, and pinned them gently to the wall over her head.

"Cadoc..." Her voice was breathless now, but not with fear. She arched into him, and he bit back a curse at the feel of her, the sheer pleasure of touching her like this, at the way her eyes were wide and wanting. He moved his other hand behind her, pressing against her back to bring her closer, then slid a knee between her thighs to pull her closer still. She made a quiet sound, like a gasp, and tugged one gloved hand free to touch his neck, his jaw, his cheek. Her gold-rimmed, sea-colored eyes were clouded with desire.

Thank the Stars he was a glutton for punishment, because he would never stop yearning for this.

He leaned down and kissed her, the thinnest barrier of gossamer between their lips. She melted against him, and he reveled in her softness, in the sweetness of her scent. He moved his hand up her back, and she shifted closer. Her teeth closed over his bottom lip through the fabric, and his breath caught, then he was the one melting.

Seren. Compassionate, stubborn, duty-bound, endlessly kind. Her curves were perfect under his hands, supple and exquisite. But the veil denied him the heat of her skin, the satin of her lips. He groaned, wanting. He released her hand, twining both of his arms around her waist while hers came around his neck. He wanted to deepen the kiss, to explore her, to actually taste. But he could not. The veil would not allow it.

And then it became too much. He could never touch her, not truly. Even if he could become heartsworn, it would be to someone else. Not Seren. He didn't want a life like that—stuck with someone he couldn't love. Neither did his potential mate deserve it.

Alone. For the rest of his long, long life.

Though with what he had planned, it probably wouldn't be so long after all.

He broke off the kiss. From beneath the veil, she looked at him with half-closed turquoise eyes. Stars give him strength for what he was about to do.

"Seren—" He couldn't think with her molded to him, but he couldn't bring himself to pull back. Not yet. One more heartbeat, one more, one more. Stars, let time stop. Let the mountain fall on top of him. Let this never end. "There's something you should know."

"What?" Her voice was dazed. The damp fabric over her lips was sheer, revealing how full they were. How pink. He couldn't help it. He kissed her again. His hand went to the back of her neck, cupping the back of her head, fingers threading in her glorious, soft hair.

She gasped, and he almost lost control. He broke off, breathing hard. Breathing her in. Because he would never be this close again. "That night, on the trip back from Cadarnle. You told the rogues the story of what happened to you during the battle. How Owain captured you."

She nodded, her eyes coming back into focus.

"You said Mair hit you. One of her rings cut your cheek and you bled."

"Yes." The word was no more than a whisper.

Cadoc dropped his voice lower, nuzzling her nose, pressing his lips to her covered cheek, her forehead. He would die happy here and now if only he could touch her skin. "That ring was my blood charm. You broke my curse."

"Me?" Seren nuzzled him back. It took a moment for her to follow what he was saying. "But only family could do that. Or... or... Oh, Scales. Oh, Stars. Cadoc?"

One more kiss, slowly. Savoring her. Memorizing what her body felt like against his.

"My heartsworn," he whispered at last. "You are my heartsworn."

Before she could react, Cadoc sank to his knees, grasping her hands in his good one. He couldn't let go completely. Not yet.

Not long ago, he had pitied the Unsworn. He couldn't understand what would drive a person to that life. Being Unsworn wasn't inescapable—Seren's magic couldn't make a dragon impervious to heartswearing, only bind them to their promises to put the lives of sworn dragons ahead of theirs.

He understood now. Sometimes, life was just too hard. Not because he was physically broken. As she had wisely pointed out, he could still have music if he stopped whining and went out and found it.

But he could never have her, and that was too much to bear.

Seren had straightened from the wall, her body tense. She tugged on Cadoc's hand, trying to get him to rise.

She knew what he was about to do. He could tell from the fear in her voice when she said, "Cadoc, why are you on your knees?"

Choking on the ritual words, he spoke. "Golden Lady, I wish to declare myself Unsworn."

Her eyes went wide. She tried again to pull him up, harder this time. "No! I will not let you do this!"

He squeezed her fingers, stilling her, and pressed his forehead against her knuckles. "I'm here so that I may fully understand the consequences of my decision."

She wrenched from his grasp. "I will not! You must give me a minute to think. We... You are my heartsworn? You."

He fixed his eyes on the floor. "Maybe. Or maybe your blood dissolved the charm because you are a healer. Either way, I choose this."

"Why?"

He forced himself to meet her gaze. When she'd said the words to him, she'd looked him in the eye. He could be strong enough to do the same. That didn't stop his voice from breaking.

"Because, *ngariad i*, I have never loved anyone but you."

Seren's breath hitched. She sank to her knees before him, clutching his hand once again. "Please. If you love me, and I love you, and we're heartsworn, there must be another way. Owain is coming. The Unsworn are going to be slaughtered. I can't lose you."

Cadoc shut away his hopes, his desire, every future thing he'd ever wished for. "I would rather die Unsworn than be responsible for destroying the Seeress. Rhys needs you. *Everyone* needs you."

"We could carry on as we have been. Nothing has to change."

He cupped her face, and she leaned her cheek into his hand. "Seren, love, *everything* has changed. It might not happen now, or tomorrow, or this year or next, but one day, not having you would become too much for me, and I would make you mine. That cannot happen."

He could tell she was crying, her voice broken and

quavering as she gripped his hand. "What if I want it to happen? What if I choose you?"

He smiled. "You want what's best, and that means you'll let me go."

She tipped her head forward, letting her forehead rest against his. She was quiet for a long time, and he was content to hold her a few moments more.

"I... Even if I have to choose the people, you can't join the Unsworn. Cadoc, please."

"Why?"

The words came out on as a quiet sob. "Because I've seen your death."

Cadoc almost smiled. Sometimes, death was mercy.

If she wouldn't say the words, he would. He'd heard them before. He kissed her forehead, then pulled back, taking both her hands in his again.

"The Unsworn are the first to battle, the last to leave. I have no clan. I have no family. In combat, should I have the choice of preserving my own life or the life of a heartsworn dragon or a dragon who could someday heartswear, I will forfeit my own. This I vow."

Seren cursed through gritted teeth. Then, "Pledge to me."

Surprise made him pull back, trying to read her face through the veil. "What?"

"Pledge to me." There was determination in her voice. "If you ask this of me—if I agree to send you to your death—that's what I want in return. I want to know that you were mine, and only mine. If you will force me to live my life without you, I want to know you wait for me in the Stars."

If a travesty of a pledging was all he could give her, he would not say no. He brought her knuckles to his mouth, treasuring the feel of her as he kissed the lace of her gloves. "I pledge you the love of my heart, the strength of my body, and the whole of my faith."

"I pledge you the love of my heart, the strength of my body, and the whole of my faith." In her voice, those words were sweeter than the sweetest music he'd ever heard. He rose. She kissed him one more time. When she pulled away, the veil was dotted with her tears. "Please don't do this."

He bowed his head. "Even if it were possible, I wouldn't swear to another when I love you. This is what I want."

She took an unsteady breath. Then, "Unsworn, I declare you, Cadoc ap Brychan o'r Draig."

The words tightened around him, magic binding him to his vows. He stood and pulled her to her feet. Fighting the burn of tears behind his eyes, he took his hand from hers and picked up her gifts from where she'd set them. He might have found music again, but his fate had been sealed since he was born, destined to heartswear to the Seeress. His entire life had led to this moment, and he'd been blind not to see it.

One more time, Cadoc touched her cheek and grinned. "Sing a song for me when I'm gone, *ngariad i*, but don't miss me. I was never good at much but being a fool."

With a wink, he left, pretending he didn't hear her sob behind him.

For once in his life, he had managed to do what was best.

He hated himself for it.

CHAPTER 43
RHYS

R hys met with the Council in the stone circle while two hundred dragons moved in synchronized drills overhead. Kai stood beside him, pale green eyes serious. The wind tugged on soot-colored flyaways that had escaped her braid. She wore the leathers she usually flew in, even though it had been days, and Ancients, she wore them well. Fierce and regal and so much more than the girl he'd met and begun to love in a cave in the Rockies. He'd needed her then because of the heartswearing. He needed her now because...

Griffith's voice whispered into his mind: *Without her, I am not.*

Lust and infatuation and magic aside, he finally understood. He would make the Council understand as well.

Kai was right, and this—what he was about to do—Deryn had wanted it too. He was the one who had lacked the strength. He would forever be ashamed it had taken him this long to find it.

Deryn's death was a weight that bound him to the earth. Her memory dogged his footsteps, her voice teased, half heard as he walked through echoing halls. He would never escape the grip of her loss, pressing him down, suffocating him.

Iain. Griffith. Deryn. His father.

His mother.

His heartswearing.

If the Wingless fought with them, maybe they would win. Maybe he'd live long enough for grief to let him loose. Maybe he could rise up out of the dirt high enough to see hope again.

He surveyed the people before him. "Honored members of the Council, I've called this meeting where we can see our soldiers training to make an announcement. The dragons above us will not fight alone. The Wingless who wish it will be allowed to take part in the battle."

As expected, the Council broke into an uproar.

"You're just going to decree it?" Nerys, the Draig council-woman, shouted. "We have been voting on this issue for decades! You can't just sweep that all away!"

"What about your speech?" another called. "What about you telling us you are different from Owain because you rely on the Council? How can you say that then make these declarations?"

"Because you are hypocrites!" Rhys roared. Something in him had broken at last. "Because what you are whining about right now is that I have taken away your freedom *to take away the freedom of others*, and I will not have it! Do you understand?"

There was a quiet shuffling at this, then silence. After a full minute of watching them, waiting to make sure no one would speak, Rhys knew he had won.

"From now on, this Council will not make any laws for Wingless that do not also apply to dragons, and vice versa." He indicated Kai at his side. "Tell your clans that if any of them who are sworn to Wingless wish to practice, the queen and I would be glad to share some of the techniques we have developed both before and since our sundering."

There were a few more murmurs, but Rhys ignored them. He turned to the group of two dozen people who also stood in the stone circle—people who had waited patiently while he spoke, and who looked at him now with a mix of curiosity and fascination. "Councilmembers, I would also like to introduce the envoys who the Free Dragons of the Wonambi have been kind enough to send. When Owain comes, they will not take part in the actual battle, as they've sworn to remain neutral. However, they will link—perhaps with a few Wingless, also, should any of them volunteer—and provide an illusion large enough to cover the archipelago. I know one of the concerns with drawing Owain into a large-scale battle here was that humans would notice. Now they will not. If you have any questions—"

"Rhys!"

He turned, and so did everyone else present. Seren was walking down the beach so quickly that Iolani and Ffion had to scurry after her. All of them looked unhappy, but Seren was the one who had called his name, her voice desperate.

Stars, what is it now?

Rhys caught Seren when she tripped over her long skirts, and both of them landed on their knees. This close, he could see through the veil. She'd been weeping. He looked over his sister's shoulder to Ffion, but she only shook her head, all the color gone from her face. Rhys squeezed Seren's shoulders gently. "Tell me."

"Cadoc..." Her voice broke. Rhys's stomach dropped.

Iolani, calm and unruffled despite having to run across the sand, said, "Cadoc o'r Draig has declared himself Unsworn."

Rhys stepped back as if she'd struck him. He stared from

Iolani to Seren. "Blood of the Ancients, what was he thinking? Why would he do that?"

The Council and visiting Wonambi shifted uncomfortably at his outburst. Ffion raised an eyebrow in an expression of subtle reproof and cool self-possession he hadn't seen since Griffith died. "Listen to what she has to say before you start shooting fire from every orifice."

Seren's voice broke. "I've seen... Don't— Please don't let him die."

Rhys shook his head, not knowing what to say. The vision. So much had happened, he'd nearly forgotten. Cadoc, dead, staring at the sky. So real. All of Seren's visions had always been steeped in symbology. But this one had been so concrete. Why?

Could it be because Cadoc and Seren truly were meant to be heartsworn?

Rhys helped Seren to her feet. Tradition and law prevented him from doing anything about Cadoc. The Council controlled the Unsworn. After what he'd just pulled with the Wingless, he had very little political capital left. "I'm sorry, Seren. If Cadoc has really done this—" She nodded, and Rhys's heart sank farther. "Then there's nothing I can do."

Except find out why. Which he would do. Right now.

"Rhys!" Morwenna ran toward him from down the beach as well.

She stopped in front of him, fighting for breath. "The evacuees have come back. They never made it to the mainland."

The Council burst into shouting again. Rhys raised a hand and hollered, "Let her speak!"

Morwenna's face was pinched. As soon as silence fell, she said, "Owain's got soldiers all around the archipelago, patrolling miles and miles out to sea, beyond our scouts. The children, the elderly, the humans—they're all stuck here. There is no escape.

Not for any of us. Whatever the battle brings, our fates will all be the same. I imagine the only reason they haven't attacked already is because they're waiting for him."

"Shit." He exchanged glances with Kai.

Everything they'd planned had come together and begun to unravel at exactly the same time.

Rhys took a breath, looking out at the Council. "This meeting is adjourned. You know what you have to do to prepare. Go do it. The fates of our children and elders rely on it."

CHAPTER 44

ASHEM

A week after Deryn's death, after Rhys's declaration about the Wingless, after Cadoc abandoning his vee for the Unsworn stationed to the north, after waiting day by day for the attack which had not yet come, like a blow that wouldn't fall, Ashem's restless, lonely sleep was shattered by a voice he never thought he'd hear in his mind again.

Brother, I need you!

Ashem sat bolt upright in his bed. For a moment, he was in Gwynedd, and Kavar was in the next bed over, having nightmares about their parents' death again.

He put a hand to his head. He hadn't shared a room with Kavar in more than a thousand years. They were grown men. They'd tried to kill each other dozens of times.

And Kavar was in trouble.

Ashem was out of his bed in a second, barely registering that Kavar had reopened their connection. *What is it? Where are you?* And then, a final wave of reality crashed over him. *Juliet?*

Listen, Kavar commanded. *I'm bringing her home. We're*

nearly to the archipelago, approaching from the northeast. She didn't want to tell you because she thought you'd fly out to meet us and leave Rhys without protection. But the islands are surrounded, and Jiang is here. I thought I could break through the line and beat her to the island, but she's catching up. She has a dozen others with her. I can't outfly them any longer.

I'm on my way.

Ashem grabbed his singstone and jammed it over his ear, then pictured the Unsworn commander he knew had troops in the area.

Hestia, wake your soldiers. Kavar is incoming, but do not engage. He's carrying my heartsworn. He's being pursued by dragons of Cadarnle, including Jiang. Capture her at all costs.

Hestia confirmed she'd heard, and Ashem ran to Rhys's rooms—which was the nearest exit from the mountain—and leaped from the edge, transforming in the sky, ignoring the calls of the dragon who was standing guard.

Ashem homed in on his brother's location through their connection, fine-tuning it with images sent by Juliet. It wasn't until he was in the sky that he was awake enough to remember why rage was boiling in the back of his skull.

Why, when he saw his brother, he was determined to kill the bastard himself.

Kavar had hurt Juli. He'd assaulted her mind and left her to freeze for days. Ashem had tried hundreds of times to contact him. He'd tried to leave Eryri. But after Deryn's death and with Owain's imminent attack, his departure had been impossible.

Then Kavar had decided to bring her back. Poor, sensitive Kavar. None of his friends were good enough for him. He betrayed them all sooner or later.

And yet, after only a few weeks, he was bringing Juliet home.

All those thoughts were driven from Ashem's mind as he

neared the northern island just as the sun rose out of the eastern sea. A green patch of forest clustered at its center, surrounded by a fringe of white beach. Unlike the ovular central island on which Eryri stood, this one was long, low, and crescent-shaped.

As fast as Ashem had flown, Hestia and her Unsworn had beaten him there. And Jiang's dragons had already overtaken Kavar.

Four circled Kavar in the sky, hemming him in and driving him toward the water. Each of the dragons wore onyx somewhere on their body, meaning Juliet would be useless in the fight against them. A dozen other dragons circled those four, keeping the Unsworn at bay, also wearing onyx.

Ashem didn't mind. Venom would work well enough for him.

Ashem heard Jiang taunting Kavar. *I told him you were a traitor. I told him he should have killed you!*

It was a testament to Kavar's exhaustion that he didn't retort, only tried, over and over, to break free of the circle. Hestia and her Unsworn attacked from the outside, but they were rebuffed. Only one dragon got close to breaking through, the red-orange of his carnelian scales afire with the rising sun.

Cadoc.

It was a shock to see him there, fighting with a vee that wasn't his own. But he had decided he was love-lost and couldn't go on, the wind-for-brains fool.

No matter if Ashem would have made that same choice for Juliet.

Ashem had never seen someone else attack his brother. Every time they came to battle, he and Kavar were always matched against each other. No other dragon could withstand their venom, so they always had a wide berth. While Kavar had been sincere in his efforts to kill Ashem, Ashem's heart had never been in killing Kavar. By being the one to face Kavar time after time, he had ensured his brother lived.

Seeing him under attack now sparked a wrath Ashem hadn't felt since he was a child. He didn't slow, didn't warn them he was coming. He charged straight through the Unsworn and the dragons they were fighting, bursting through the line breathing a cloud of yellow that dropped one dragon instantly and had the other three—including Jiang—swerving out of his way.

Have you come to help, Ashem? It's about time you got rid of him. Jiang's voice was silky. The Lung were capable of influencing emotion, and though dragons only had the extra energy to produce magic when they were in human form, Ashem felt the tug of her words. Only belatedly did he realize this could have been a trap—Kavar might have lured him out here, set him up.

Then his brother faltered and dropped toward the sea, catching himself a hundred feet lower than he had been, and Ashem knew this was no trap. Kavar was exhausted.

Kavar is dying, Juli said into Ashem's mind.

Ashem's lips peeled back from his silvery teeth. *He will not die. Only I may kill him.*

He banked and swooped back toward Jiang and the remaining Cadarnle dragons. The Unsworn, including Cadoc, lured the rest of Jiang's scattered soldiers away over the island and made a stand there, which left only Jiang and two others for Ashem.

He'd faced far worse odds than that.

Ashem had used most of his venom in that first pass but still had enough in his saliva to do significant damage. He chose the nearest dragon and slammed into it, sinking his jaws into its shoulder. The dragon roared, flapped twice, and plummeted into the sea.

Jiang hissed, then curled her undulating form in the other direction and flew back out to sea, the last dragon trailing after her. When Ashem glanced over his shoulder, he saw that Hestia and her Unsworn had grounded and captured the dragons who'd come after them in one of Rhys's traps. Bless Deryn's soul for her foresight and care in laying the traps while the rest of them were distracted.

Seeing that things were taken care of there, he wheeled to chase Jiang down. She'd caused enough damage. Rhys didn't want many casualties, but Ashem was more than certain he wouldn't mind if Jiang was numbered among the dead.

Before Ashem could beat his wings more than once, Juli cried out.

He'd forgotten Kavar.

His turn had brought him below Kavar's altitude, and from this angle he could see the wound. A great red gash in Kavar's black belly that rained blood into the sea far below.

Ashem didn't know why dread rose in him like it did. He hated Kavar for what he'd done to Juliet. But he could not stop being Kavar's brother. Older by a minute, Ashem's cries were the first greeting Kavar had when he emerged into the world.

Damn him.

Ashem banked, leaving Jiang to run. He flew under Kavar and Juli as Kavar flapped more and more erratically toward the island. They landed, and Juli slid off Kavar's back as quickly as she could. "Change! Hurry!"

She'd been speaking to Kavar, but both brothers obeyed.

By the time Ashem was human, Juliet was cradling Kavar's head in her lap. Kavar looked gray. Ashem pressed his hands to the wound in Kavar's stomach. His brother's blood flowed warm over his hands.

For one of very few times in his life, Ashem felt afraid. He growled. "Sunder it, you traitorous worm, you cannot die!"

Kavar gritted his teeth, his breathing unsteady, his silver eyes slitted in pain. "Don't think you'll be rid of me yet. I'll live."

He was right. Ashem checked him over once, then again. He'd lost enough blood to look waxen, but the gash wasn't as deep as it looked at first.

"Ashem," Juli whispered.

He looked up, and then she was reaching for him, kissing him while his hands were covered in Kavar's blood, and something in Ashem's soul that had been out of joint slipped back into place and healed. He breathed her in, and she did the same, tangling her hands in his hair as he kissed her lips, cheeks, nose, forehead. Every bit of her he could reach while his hands were occupied keeping Kavar's life inside him.

"I think that's enough." Kavar's voice was weak, but sharp with irritation.

Reluctantly, Ashem leaned back. He took his eyes off Juli only long enough to glance at Kavar. "You're lucky you weren't disemboweled."

"Lucky?" Kavar laughed. He jerked his head down the beach. "Luckier than some, for certain. Isn't he one of yours?"

Ashem turned.

A figure sprawled on the beach. Hestia and two Mo'o worked frantically to stop the bleeding from dozens of wounds. Ashem's heart truly stopped then, seeing the figure stretched out on the beach, pale as death.

"No," he breathed. "Cadoc."

He wasn't moving. Seren's vision was coming true.

"Juliet, put your hands here. Stop the bleeding."

Without waiting to see if she obeyed, Ashem sprinted toward his dying friend.

CHAPTER 45

SEREN

Seren paced inside her golden cage just after sunrise. Days she had been locked in this part of the mountain "for her safety," escorted by guards from her rooms with their too-small windows to the golden dome and back again whenever needed. Days since she'd gone farther than the gate that closed off her audience chamber, and even that far Iolani watched her every breath. She couldn't settle, couldn't stop moving.

But all the fear and worry she'd felt in the week since she'd seen Cadoc was nothing, *nothing* compared to waking in the nauseating grip of premonition.

She laced her fingers together only to pull her hands apart and ball them into fists, then stuff her knuckles into her mouth to stifle a sob. She hadn't stopped sobbing, it seemed. Hadn't stopped remembering his touch. Picturing his face. Could not stop the aching dreams about the hard, intoxicating press of his body, the soft pressure of his kiss.

This premonition was for Cadoc. She knew it to her bones.

Today was the day he died.

Seren had thought she could let him go. She had agreed to

it, because he'd asked her to. She'd thought she could let him go for the good of the people. All her life, she'd done her best to be who they needed her to be. She was the Seeress—she had to be *more*. More aloof. Wiser. More serene.

Less of a person.

But she wasn't more or less than any of them. She was herself, and she couldn't be the Seeress if it meant Cadoc's death.

Seren cut off her pacing and dashed tears from her swollen eyes, then picked up her trailing golden skirts and strode to the locked door of the dome. "Let me out," she said to the guards on the other side.

They turned to her, surprised. "Lady Seeress?"

Seren grabbed the door and shook the gold that penned her in. "Let me out. I have to see Rhys."

They exchanged nervous glances. "Protector Iolani has left strict orders that you aren't to be allowed out until the threat of attack has passed."

Iolani. "I command you to open this door."

The guards looked uncomfortable and shook their heads. "Then get Rhys," Seren snapped. "Bring him to me. Now."

"My lady—"

"Go!" Seren shouted.

Shocked to find her shouting at them—Seren herself wasn't sure if she'd ever shouted out of anger in her life—one of the men ran out the door and down the hall.

Seren paced, wringing her hands and muttering to herself. Every moment the nausea built, her blood rushed in her ears. The windows of the room were so large she could go through one of them if they didn't let her free, but she wanted to tell Rhys. The premonition had never come upon her so strongly—not even when she'd taken off after Deryn on the ill-fated journey to see their mother.

She had given up and turned to leave through the window that overlooked the sea when the guard came back with Rhys. As soon as Seren heard their footsteps in the hall, she darted to the gate. There was no time.

Darkness sparked on the edges of her sight. A vision. Not of the future—of right then.

Noise and wind. A flurry of leathery wings and pale blue-gray scales. Of cerulean and orange and silver. A flash of carnelian claws. A slice of hot pain shot down his foreleg, joining myriad others.

"Cadoc." Her whisper was strangled. Fighting. Losing.

This was it.

"Seren? What about Cadoc?" Rhys's voice held alarm. "Unlock this door!"

"Majesty, the Lady Protector has commanded—"

"*Unlock it.*" He didn't use the mantle, but his voice was pure command.

The guards jerked like puppets and scrambled to obey. The door of her cage opened with a soft *click*. Seren surged out and grabbed Rhys by the shoulders, her fingers like claws. She couldn't breathe. "Cadoc. Rhys, it's Cadoc. He's dying. You have to save him!"

He took her by the elbows. "When?"

"Now. Right now. Owain's people are here. Some of them... I don't know. I can't tell! Two Azhdahā. A Lung. A Derkin..." Seren shook and panted. She was half in the audience chamber, half in the vision. Premonition had never taken her so strongly before. She never saw things at the same time as they happened. At least she wasn't convulsing on the floor.

A crushing sensation in his right wing. An island spiraling up to meet him. Too late.

He was falling too fast. Hit the sand hard, shattering bones and driving the splinters into organs. A flash of Ashem and Kavar, flying together.

"We're too late!" Out of her mind with fear, Seren turned from Rhys and sprinted to the massive opening that looked out on the sea, skirts flying. She didn't stop when he called her, or when the guards did. She called up the vision in her memory, looking for landmarks. Where? Where was he?

The northernmost island. Only ten minutes' flight away.

She was vaguely aware of Rhys running behind her, and the guards. They were shouting. She didn't care. Without stopping for breath or thought, she called the change as she leaped out over the sea.

A burst of light, a widening of her mind, and Seren stretched her wings. She thought she caught a hint of smoke in the air as Rhys transformed behind her, but she didn't look back.

Each second stretched to hours, each minute to days. The sea passed slowly beneath her. Any moment now, Cadoc would take his last breath. Any moment, too late.

The island appeared on the horizon, and dark again circled the edges of Seren's sight.

Cadoc was human, but he couldn't breathe. Each unsuccessful attempt to suck in air met with grinding agony in his chest. Blood bubbled in his lungs and he coughed, tasting it in his mouth, on his lips. Blackness closed in. Death sang a sweet, cold melody in his ear.

Cadoc! Seren screamed his name in her mind as she tore across the sky. The island was small, and she'd seen enough of the vision to know exactly where he was. Her shadow rippled across the white sand of the beach and across the canopy of the forest that took up the island's interior. There, on the northern beach, surrounded by Ashem and a vee of Unsworn, lay Cadoc.

Seren dove to earth, her claws barely brushing the damp

sand as she called the change, rolled, jumped to her feet, and ran. Catching sight of her, the Unsworn cleared away so only Ashem was left desperately binding the worst of the horrifying wounds in Cadoc's torso.

Cadoc lay as he had in her vision weeks ago, blood seeping from too many places to count, amethyst eyes open to the sky.

But he wasn't still, not quite yet. His eyes, clouded and confused, fell on her and widened. His mouth formed her name. Then he blinked, seeming to come to himself. He spoke, his voice weak and bubbling. "No."

Seren knelt beside him as Rhys and the two members of her guard landed down the beach. Rhys changed, ran over, and fell to his knees next to Cadoc.

"Damn it, Cadoc, no," he said, his voice rough.

Cadoc had seconds left. Less than seconds. Her heartbeat grew loud in her ears. She reached for Cadoc, but hesitated. Rhys was right there. Rhys, whom her visions had saved. Rhys, who relied on her.

"Rhys..." Her voice was broken. Torn. She could not choose between her love and her brother, her people.

Rhys drew breath. Terror descended on Seren. What if he used the mantle? What if he stopped her? What if she had come here only to watch her beloved die?

But Rhys only looked at her with pleading eyes. "Save him."

"He's my—"

"I know. He told me weeks ago. I should have listened."

Cadoc shook his head weakly, again mouthed, "No." Seren knew his heart. He wouldn't want to take the Seeress from the king. But she was not only the Seeress, and Rhys was not only the king, and both of them needed Cadoc.

She tore off the veil and her gloves, dropping them into Rhys's lap.

She inhaled, calling the magic up from her core, and touched her fingers to his forehead just as Cadoc's eyes rolled back in his head.

For an instant, she registered the feel of his skin. Slick with sweat and blood, soft and smooth beneath. She channeled magic into him, pulling bone fragments from lungs and organs, rebuilding ribs, draining blood and repairing veins and arteries. All of it in no more time than it took to blink. For a heartbeat, nothing happened.

Then Cadoc gasped in a full breath, and magic slammed through her.

Rhys braced her from behind when the power of her heartswearing would have thrown her back into the sand. The world turned white, then dark. The sound of a whirlwind shrieked in her ears.

Her mind opened, and something like a beautiful song half-remembered drifted into her, twining around her, filling all the lonely places she'd carried with her. The song enclosed her heart in comfort and security and a love so vast she could not begin to comprehend the depth and breadth of it.

She'd heard some dragons describe the first moments of heartswearing as being filled with an unfamiliar presence. But there was nothing unfamiliar here. For the first time, it felt like she was home.

Cadoc.

But his mind was slipping away. For all she'd done, he was dying. She pushed more magic into him, more light, more strength. As she pushed, something else was being ripped from her core.

The Sight. It was leaving her.

Rhys called her name, but Seren ignored him. Nothing mattered, as long as she saved Cadoc. Her body shook. Her stomach turned over. Black sparks danced at the edges of her vision, but they were fading into gray and white. Her head was splitting open. Her eyes were being burned from her skull. Seren thought she cried out. She thought Cadoc stirred.

She held on to her power, to her sanity, fighting tooth and claw. If she'd healed him, there were others on this beach who needed her. She could still serve her people.

Uncaring, the darkness swallowed her whole.

CHAPTER 46

CADOC

C adoc woke in his bed.

He wasn't expecting that. The last thing he remembered, he'd been dead.

He rubbed his face with his hands and groaned. He felt good, but different. He'd been upset, but...why?

Then he registered the hazy extension of his mind—a mental presence that cuddled close to his and was so very unconscious that he hadn't noticed it.

Someone moaned and stirred next to him in the bed. Startled, Cadoc looked down. There, sleeping on top of his covers, lay a very veil-less Seren. Instead of gold, a color he'd never seen her without, she wore a turquoise shirt and simple gray pants.

Seren. Heartsworn. Mine.

He ripped off the covers and leaped out of bed. "Blood of the Ancients!"

The door to his room swung open and Ffion came in. "Stop bellowing," she hissed. "You'll wake her. It nearly killed her,

395

healing you and heartswearing and losing the Sight all at once. You're both lucky to be alive."

Cadoc backed away from the bed, though every cell in his body screamed to stop this instant and get in there and wake his mate up in a very wicked way.

His mate. His...

She'd lost the Sight.

Cadoc balled his hands into fists, unsure whether he should laugh or weep. "I tried. Fuck me, Ffion. I would have died to avoid this. I've made another mess."

Ffion's face turned fierce. She strode up to him and shoved her finger into his chest, her other hand on her swollen belly. "Quiet, you silly fool. I've had *enough* of death. *Enough.* Do you hear me?"

Tears sprang into her eyes, and she looked down at her stomach. "This child will never know their father. None of you are Griffith, so I need all of you. You, Rhys, and Evan. You have to be here. To tell my child stories, to keep Griffith's memory alive. So don't you tell me that you would rather be dead when *he* is dead, and Iain, and Deryn. This vee is my family, and it is my child's family, and I'll not stand for you wishing it was more torn to pieces than it is."

She collapsed into him, weeping. Shocked, Cadoc caught her and held her, stroking her hair. He tried to speak, but found a lump blocking his throat. It took a long time before he could say, "I'm sorry, love. I'm so sorry."

Ffion straightened and wiped her eyes. "I love you, Cadoc ap Brychan. Don't you ever do such a desperate, terrible thing again."

He grinned at her. It came more easily than it had in months, but it didn't feel as carefree as it used to. "I don't think the Unsworn will have me."

Heartsworn. He looked at Seren in the bed. In *his* bed. He

had to be dead and this some blissful afterlife. That was the only explanation.

"Is she—?" He cleared his throat. "How is she? How long have we been asleep?"

"A day," Ffion said, not moving away from him. "She seems to be all right. She's running a low-grade fever, but we think she'll wake soon."

Gazing at Seren, he felt a craving come over him. To be with her. To touch her. To never leave her side. While he'd wanted all those things before, this was different. A hollow echo of what it truly meant to love.

He nearly laughed. *This* was heartswearing? It was like being starved for a meal and stuffing yourself with candy. He liked candy, but food was better. Love was better.

Ffion sighed and leaned against Cadoc's side. "I'll leave you alone. I just didn't want you to wake her. And I wanted to see you healed for myself. Neither of you looked very good when Rhys and Ashem brought you in."

She squeezed his hands, raised herself on tiptoe, and he bent so she could place a kiss on his cheek. Then Ffion left, and he was alone with Seren. He was so busy staring that it took him a full minute to understand what Ffion had meant.

I wanted to see you healed.

Healed.

Scarcely daring to breathe, he lifted his right hand. The skin was pale and smooth, fingers long and agile. He wiggled them. They worked. Mostly. There was some tightness that hadn't been there before, some tugging and popping that even Seren's healing couldn't fix after so long.

But by and large, he was healed.

Again, he had a flash of clarity. Heartswearing wasn't love, and a hand that worked was not wholeness. He had accepted himself as he was, and that brought him more peace than fingers that moved in a certain way.

Seren stirred, and Cadoc dropped his hand. He studied her face, drinking it in. Gold still lined her eyes, a stunning contrast to the deep blue-green of her irises as she opened her eyes and met his. "Cadoc?"

Shame washed over him. She was the Seeress. He'd taken her power, stripped Rhys of a valuable asset. For an instant, he was determined to wallow in his guilt. Deny himself.

But then she smiled at him, and every thought of self-denial fled.

He crawled into bed. Like he had yearned to do for a thousand years, he pulled her into his arms and tangled their legs together, fitting their bodies as tightly as he could. She was so soft. Softer than he ever could have dreamed. He buried his face against her neck and breathed her in and decided he would never move again.

The instant Seren slid an arm over his waist and squeezed him back, all the pain and rage and hurt built up inside him over the course of a life spent at war drained away. Her hand came to his face, and he closed his eyes, reveling in the sensation of her skin as she ran her hands over his cheeks, touched her fingers to his lips.

Wonder filled her mind, and Cadoc reveled in that too. The same feeling of all of her stress releasing, all of her joy bubbling to the surface, of her body beginning to react to his. He wasn't sure, at the moment, where he ended and she began, and he didn't care. They shared a feeling of contentment, of serenity, of *finally*.

"You're alive," she whispered.

He became more aware of her every second. Not her body —he'd been aware of that for a while. But of her mind. Her feeling of loss. Of magical blindness.

He'd done that. He'd hurt her.

Her fingers tightened in the fabric of his shirt. "No, *ngariad i*. I saved your life, and you saved mine. Neither of us are alone."

He felt the sick horror, saw a flash of himself sprawled on the beach, blood leaking from one corner of his mouth, his body a ragged mess. It triggered the memory in him—the agony of broken ribs, of his lungs filling with blood, drowning him from the inside...

They tightened their arms at the same time, breathing gone shallow and ragged. Cadoc couldn't get close enough to her, couldn't shelter her from the terror, from the loss, couldn't forget what it felt like to die.

He found her lips—oh Stars, her lips, just as luscious as he'd imagined them—and tasted salt. She was as familiar to him as music. He slipped a hand behind her neck and tilted her face up, leashing his desperation. Forcing himself to be slow, tender as he explored her mouth, nipped her bottom lip, enticed her to explore him the same. Slow, but thorough. Ancients, so thorough. He'd waited far too long to be anything less.

Seren made a noise in her throat and slid her arms around his neck, arching against him. *Want* flared in her, doubling the impact of his own. Cadoc moaned, tangling his fingers in her hair, teetering on the edge of control.

Let go, she whispered into his mind.

So Cadoc let go.

Cadoc had imagined loving Seren more times than he could count. He'd imagined her skin, her taste, her body.

His imagination was terrible. Maybe he wouldn't have felt that way if he hadn't been able to feel her reaction to each touch, every kiss. Maybe if he hadn't been inside her mind, so closely melded that he could feel her pleasure, her tenderness, her desire, her love.

Paying attention to her thoughts so he could sense if he crossed any lines, Cadoc carefully pulled Seren beneath him, settling between her thighs. She moaned and wrapped her legs around his waist, and he nuzzled her neck.

"Have you done anything like this before, love? Do you know what kind of touch you enjoy?"

Seren's cheeks turned pink. "Who would I have done it with?"

Cadoc shrugged. "Not all heartsworn are loyal to their partners. Or you might have done things on your own."

The pretty pink turned a deeper rose. "I've experimented on my own, and I know how it all works."

"Good." He palmed one of her breasts, and Seren's eyes went wide.

"It's different with you," she gasped. "It's more intense."

"Just wait." Her nipple pebbled, and he bent to gently kiss and suck it through the thin fabric of her shirt. Seren cried out and bucked her hips, grinding against where he was already hard. He gritted his teeth against the blinding wave of sensation.

"I... You're already..." she panted, and Cadoc realized that just having him on top of her, bodies pressed together, touching in all the right places, had Seren so close to coming that Cadoc, experienced as he was, shuddered and had to clamp down on his control.

Seren gripped the hand he had on her breast and slid her fingers into his hair, pulling his mouth back to hers, parting her lips eagerly so he could delve inside. Cadoc gave her what she wanted, riding the edge of both of their control until it was almost too much.

She broke from his lips and said, "I want to know what it's like to have you inside me."

"That will hurt if you aren't ready," Cadoc said raggedly. "I won't—"

"I am ready." She gave him an irritated look. "Do you think you know my body better than I do?"

Cadoc nipped her collarbone. "I will soon enough." He eased back far enough to push her shirt up and over her head. She wore nothing underneath. If dragons had gods, Cadoc would have fallen to his knees to worship all of them in that moment.

Instead, he worshipped Seren.

Her skin was a blessing. Her voice, when she called his name, was the sweetest song he'd ever heard. Her pleasure was light, a golden glow that made him want to give her more, then more, until they both sublimated in the brightness.

She pulled off his shirt, then wrapped her arms around him and held him close as he went to work on her glorious breasts, her fingers exploring, then gripping, then clawing into his back.

She could have come for him like this. He could have her falling apart in any one of a thousand ways.

"Cadoc please," she practically sobbed, "we've waited so long. I don't want to wait anymore."

He let out a helpless groan. "Let me see."

He pulled loose the drawstring on her pants and slid them down over the rounded curve of one hip, then another, and then they were sliding down shapely thighs and the luscious curve of calf and ankle.

For a moment, it was all he could do to sit back on his heels, his knees on either side of her thighs, and stare in awe at the treasure laid out before him. The very concept of beauty given flesh and form.

His heartsworn. His love. His kind, stubborn, wise, brave Seren.

"I... I am pleasing to you," she whispered. A statement, not a question, because she knew.

"Pleasing?" Cadoc choked. "No, *cariad*. No word exists in the tongue of man or dragon that can capture your glory, or all that you are to me. Let me spend the rest of my life doing nothing but bringing you joy, and I will die a happy man."

Her cheeks turned a deep rose, but she scoffed lightly. "I'm glad to see death didn't tarnish that silver tongue."

A wicked grin stole across Cadoc's lips as pulled her up so that she was on her knees. "Silver? No, love." He kissed her breathless, then shifted them until he was lying on his back. She looked slightly alarmed as he lifted and positioned her so that she straddled his face, her sweetest place right there, so tantalizingly close. "Hold onto the headboard."

"Cadoc? What are you doing?"

"Proving once and for all that this tongue is made of gold."

He pulled her down, parting her with his fingers so that he could lick around the rim of her entrance before moving up to swirl and flick his tongue against her clit.

Seren cried out, her entire body going rigid, pleasure flooding the bond as she arched and helplessly ground down on his face.

You...won't...be able...to breathe... She mentally panted, barely able to think the words as delicious tension in her core tightened even more. He could feel it. Feel her getting close. It was so good.

She tried to shift her thighs away, give him space, but he clamped his hands around the globes of her ass and held her in place.

Then let me die this hero's death. It won't take me from you. I am already in paradise.

An unwilling laugh rippled through her, ending again on a gasp as he sucked softly on her clit, then slipped a finger inside.

Maybe she had been ready before, but she certainly was now. So gloriously wet and so perfect. He circled his finger, stretching her gently while she whimpered at the combined pleasure and slight discomfort. Slowly, he added a second finger.

This is... I want... she begged inside his mind.

I know, my heart. But it's still your first time. Let me do what I can to make it easy for you.

Words failed them both for a while after that, until she was nearly weeping with pleasure again, begging him with need rather than language to claim her in the way she wanted.

Cadoc let her ease off of him and slide down his body. Seren moved down until their hips aligned, then reached between her legs and found his hard length. She stroked it softly with a finger, and Cadoc just about blacked out from pleasure, because he was that close, too. Only sheer strength of will kept him from embarrassing himself, because he wanted so badly to give her what she wanted.

She closed her fist around him, stroking gently, then slightly harder as she felt what pleased him through their bond. She lowered her body, running his tip through her slick sweetness and circling it around her clit until they both groaned.

Then, finally, blessedly, she positioned him at her opening and slipped down over him by degrees. Cadoc let her take control, cradling her face, covering it with kisses and whispering encouragement in her ear. Holding his body still by, once again, a gargantuan effort of will as she went at a pace that was comfortable for her.

He sensed when there was pain, sensed her stretch. She lifted off of him and then settled slowly down again, over and over until Cadoc was mindless, senseless of anything beyond the feel of her.

And then with a satisfied sound, she sank all the way down.

"Oh, Ancients, Cadoc, you feel..." She made a sound of sheer pleasure, and Cadoc's will broke.

He gripped her by the hips and thrust, slowly at first, but picking up speed when she began to match his rhythm. That golden glow built between them, and they were both so close, and had waited so many years.

Her face twisted in concentration and need, her breasts moving above him, was the most erotic thing he'd ever seen. When he sensed she was just at the edge, he lifted enough to take one of her nipples in his mouth and suck.

Seren threw back her head and let out a string of cries in at least three different languages as her core clamped down on him, rippling as she came, and then Cadoc was coming, too. He gritted his teeth, biting back a cry as the tension at the base of his spine released and he came into her, wave after wave, his vision going black, then white in the most blissful moment of his life.

When it was over, they curled together, warm and heavy. Her head was on his chest, his fingers in her glorious red-gold hair. He couldn't stop touching her miraculous skin. She shivered, and he sensed that it worried her how much she liked what his hands and mouth could do.

"I think you're right," she murmured. "Your tongue is made of gold." She hesitated, then said, "Why is it so good? What we did, yes, but this too. Just...being in contact."

He smiled and stroked his fingers over the curve of her waist and hip. "You've lived a lifetime hardly being touched. I intend to make up for it, if that's something you want."

She burrowed in closer, needing him in a way that was emotional, mental, and physical. Just wanting to *be*. "Yes. I want that. But you can't make up for all of it today, surely?"

Cadoc made an exaggerated thoughtful face. "We could make a decent start."

She raised her head and pressed a kiss to his cheek, then his forehead, then his mouth. "I think we have."

"*Dwi'n di garu di*, Seren. I have loved you since I was a boy."

"I love you too. I have loved you for just as long." She lifted her hand, then hesitated.

Sensing her intention and her fear, Cadoc took her wrist and moved her fingers to push dark strands of hair from his forehead. "Never be afraid to touch me. I am yours."

Her smile went straight to his heart, and despite the looming battle and worry over how other dragons would react to him stealing their Seeress, Cadoc and Seren were at peace.

CHAPTER 47

KAI

The day after Cadoc and Seren woke, Kai listened in while Henry Harrow reported to Rhys and Ashem: Owain's people were mobilizing. They would arrive the next day.

Rhys's plan to draw him to Eryri had worked.

That night, Kai gathered with the rest of the vee in Rhys's rooms and sat on the arm of the couch next to him. Seren and Cadoc, still in the throes of a brand-new heartswearing, couldn't keep their hands off each other. Ashem and Juli were more reserved, but that didn't stop Ashem from pulling Juli firmly onto his lap and holding her there.

The two couples were a sharp contrast to the rest of the vee. Morwenna and Ffion had both lost their heartsworn, and Evan had lost the woman he loved. She and Rhys, Kai supposed, were somewhere in between. They had each other, but they lacked the synchronicity heartswearing had given them for those too-brief weeks.

Kai was coping, but even with Rhys right next to her, she missed him. She'd thought she might get over being sundered, given time. Might get used to being alone in her own head again, even like it. But she hadn't yet.

Love didn't need magic to make it real, but even with all its embarrassments, inconveniences, and privacy issues, she'd rather be heartsworn to Rhys than not.

No one talked about the battle. Instead, they played cards and laughed and spoke of other things. Memories of childhood, Griffith and Deryn. For the first time since Kai had known her, Morwenna talked about Iain, breaking down into tears. Cadoc put a hand on her shoulder and Ffion wrapped her arm around the taller woman's waist. No one said what was on all of their minds—their lives, which had centered on the war for so long, were going to change. No matter whether Rhys won or Owain did, nothing would be the same.

This night was an ending.

As the dragons gathered on the floor to play another game, Juli sat next to Kai on the couch. When she reached out, Kai took her friend's hand in both of hers and squeezed. "I don't know if I ever thanked you, Jules. For getting me out of Cadarnle."

Juli had given herself to Kavar for Kai. If it came down to it, Kai would have done the same. And, it seemed, Kavar was willing to sacrifice himself for Juli. That was a twist Kai hadn't seen coming. She wasn't thrilled that Ashem's evil twin was in his spare bedroom instead of a cell, but she supposed if the others could accept it, so could she.

Juli sighed, but smiled. "Go ahead, then. Tell me how fabulous I am. Keep it brief."

Kai laughed. "Thank you. Seriously." She glanced around at the dragons. "I can't believe this is happening. We're just us, Jules. Just normal women. Except here we are, sitting around waiting for an epic battle that will decide the fate of the world."

"A dragon battle, no less. It's surreal," Juli said.

"My parents aren't happy I'm not staying on the island with them. They realized it meant I was going into battle. They are terrified." So was she. But at least she knew her family would be safe. As safe as they could be, now that they couldn't evacuate. The entire Ironscale Vee had been tasked with protecting the humans. Once the battle started, Owain's soldiers wouldn't surround the archipelago anymore. Then they'd be able to get out. Her family, the elderly, the children. Ffion, too, would join them in the morning. Pregnant dragons were too valuable to risk.

Juli shook her head. "Sometimes I still wake up and think I'm back in our apartment. Like we might head to the mountains for the weekend. Go on a hike."

"Wow." Kai laughed, leaned back on the couch, and put her hands behind her head. "Hiking. For fun? I haven't thought about fun in a long time."

"We've both been preoccupied," said Juli, voice dry.

"By dragons. Can you believe it? I can't imagine what I would've thought about this six months ago." Kai tilted her head to indicate everyone in a circle on the floor, playing cards. Ashem laid down his hand—not a very good one—and Cadoc, who had been playing a folksy song on the guitar, changed the tune to some kind of dirge. Ashem growled a threat to Cadoc's person, and Cadoc grinned.

Despite the camaraderie, there were too many voids. Silences that Deryn should have filled. An empty spot next to Ffion. The gathering was bittersweet unlike anything Kai had known. They came together for hope, but they were also making a memory on purpose.

Just in case when tomorrow came, they said goodbye to someone else.

Juli leaned forward and flicked Ashem's ear when he threatened Cadoc once again. Without looking, he reached up and grabbed her hand, squeezing it, holding on. Juli didn't let go either.

"I don't even know what I think about it now," Juli said. "I don't like danger. I don't like complications."

"But you love Ashem."

Juli raised an eyebrow, but couldn't quite hide her smile as he turned to look at her. "He'll do."

Ashem smirked.

Kai snuck a glance at Rhys. He was already watching her, his eyes that starfire blue. Her heartbeat sped up at the slow smile that spread across his face. One look, and he could turn her brain and knees to jelly.

Later, when everyone had gone and they'd made some memories of their own, Kai held on to Rhys, listening to his heartbeat, praying to whatever god or gods, the Universe, the Ancients, anyone or anything, that they would survive. That come tomorrow and a week from now and a year from now, she would still be able to hold him like this, safe in his arms, listening to his heart beating steadily in her ear.

Whatever happens tomorrow, please let him live.

Let all of us live.

CHAPTER 48

ASHEM

After saying goodbye to the others that night, Ashem stood in his spare bedroom, watching Kavar as his twin slept. For so many years, they'd wished each other dead. Now, though they were still heartsworn to the same woman, they had come to an uneasy truce.

Even so, things could not stand as they were for long.

"What are you doing? It's the middle of the night." Kavar's voice was thick with sleep. He sat up, the moon through the window painting a line of light over his silver eyes and smirking mouth, leaving the rest of him in darkness. "I'm not going to murder you in your bed, if that's what you're afraid of."

Ashem scowled. "I've never been afraid of you, Kavar."

His brother chuckled. "We both know that's not true."

Silence.

"Why have you come?" Kavar asked.

Ashem leaned back against the wall. "Owain will arrive in a few hours, as expected. I need to know whose side you're on."

Kavar was impossible to read in the darkness. "If I said I still support Owain, would you kill me?"

411

"If I were going to kill you, I would've done it already."

A flash of white teeth. "At the moment, I'm on my own side."

"How are your wounds?"

"The Quetzal woman knows what she's doing."

Ashem scowled. "*Councilwoman* Citlali's healing abilities rival the magic of the See—the gold dragon, and were come by with more study and skill. She is owed your deepest respect."

"As you say," Kavar responded flippantly.

Ashem scoffed. "Can you fly?"

Kavar nodded.

"What will you do?"

His brother toyed with the blanket on the bed. "I was thinking of going home."

Home. Tawny mountains and pistachio groves and the scent of spices on the breeze. Glorious, baking, dry heat. Ashem wouldn't mind going home, someday.

"What about Juliet?" Ashem asked.

Kavar grunted. "Keep her. For now."

"You won't join us? Fight with us?"

Kavar threw off his covers and got to his feet. "Don't mistake me, brother—I support neither Rhys nor his cause. Owain has asked one too many things of me, but that doesn't mean I'm with you. At the end of things, humans still need to be eliminated before they discover and eliminate us."

Ashem snorted, but declined to argue. It didn't seem like a good time to delve into the topic that had caused their rift in the first place. "So you will fight with Owain?"

Kavar threw up his hands. "You still don't *listen*. I'm leaving, and good riddance to kings. If I am honest, I do hope Owain kills Rhys and wipes out the human plague. But I won't be his pawn any longer." He paused, and Ashem could feel his brother sizing him up. "Are you going to let me leave, or are you going to throw me in a cell?"

Ashem folded his arms and wished he could see Kavar's face. Wished Kavar would send more information through the open bond, so he could sense what his brother was feeling. Part of him—the stupid part—wanted Kavar to stay. For things to go back to the way they had been when they were children. Perhaps they could start counting caves on the islands.

But they weren't children, and they never would be again. A heavy weight on his heart, Ashem said, "You can go."

"Good. I hope I never see you again." Kavar gathered a few things and slung a bag over his shoulder.

"We're heartsworn to the same woman," Ashem pointed out.

"I'll pick her up at the airport."

"There won't be airports if Owain kills all the humans, Kavar."

Kavar threw up his hands, but as he reached the door, he paused and looked back at Ashem. "Perhaps I'm not on Owain's side, then. I suppose you'll never know for certain." In the darkness, he thought he saw his brother smile. "Now get out so I can escape."

Hours later, Ashem was outside the mountain, flying in the predawn dark with Tane to check on their traps. At some point, he realized Kavar hadn't closed down their connection completely. He could still sense his twin, flying east over the ocean, on his way home.

Maybe it wouldn't be so long until they saw each other after all.

Ashem returned to his apartments an hour or so before dawn. He kissed Juliet awake, and she returned his kisses with a fervor that made him lightheaded. They made love, Ashem taking her hard and desperate, then tenderly. He refused to let himself think it could be the last time.

At least if he died, she had his brother and all his dubious charm.

"Don't be an idiot." Juliet smacked his shoulder as he swung his legs over the side of the bed. "I do not. Kavar and I don't want each other."

Ashem shrugged one shoulder. For all Kavar's poisoned smiles and snide comments, if Juliet wanted him, he would have her. Gladly.

He pulled on pants and a shirt and tossed Juliet some clothes, then watched her put them on with mild regret.

Juli snorted. "Only mild?"

"Don't distract me, woman. I have a war to win."

She walked around their bed and put her hand in his. "I'm sorry, who's helping the Wonambi put up a barrier large enough to cover the entire archipelago so humans don't see a bunch of dragons fighting next time they're messing around on Google Earth? *You* don't distract *me*."

He pulled her in and held her for a long moment. Battles were unavoidable. When they came up, he fought them. He survived. He would make sure she did as well. Just another job.

As Kavar was fond of pointing out, Ashem always did his job.

"Come." If his voice was rough, she didn't comment.

He led her out of their rooms and up to the chamber on the top of the mountain where they had pledged. The crystals that lined the interior walls glinted in the faint light provided by Rhys and one of his fireballs. A handful of Wonambi had arrived already, as had a handful of Wingless, including Councilwoman Sarangerel.

"What are you doing here?" Ashem asked.

Standing at her full height put the top of the tiny Mongolian woman's head somewhere around his chest. "We will fight wherever we are needed. I am not so old."

Ashem grunted. It was not a welcoming sound. But at least the ancient woman wasn't trying to join the Wingless who would actually be flying in battle with their mates.

"Thank you, Councilwoman," said Rhys, giving Ashem a quelling look. "You honor us with your service."

Ashem didn't comment, as the woman was, indeed, exceedingly old.

Tharah, the Wonambi girl who had followed Cadoc to Eryri, unwound a long string of blue quartz beads on a wire. "Are you ready?" she asked Juliet and Sarangerel.

Juliet nodded, and both women led the rest of the Wingless inside the circle the Wonambi had formed. Tharah handed Juli the end of the string of beads. The Wonambi of Australia—unlike the Quetzal and Noodinoon of the Americas—didn't have the ability to link naturally, and the quartz would allow the sharing of magic between them.

Tharah walked around to the other Wonambi, who clasped hands and wound the beads around their wrists, connecting every person in the circle. Then she stood in her place next to Juli. Rhys took the end of the string from her so Tharah could take Juliet's hand, then he wound the remainder around their wrists and melted the ends of the wire together.

"The circle is closed," Rhys said. He indicated three anxious juveniles standing outside the circle. "If you need anything, they will take care of you." He pointed to a mousy-looking girl. "Angharad is a fire Draig. If you need to break the circle, she can melt the wire to break and reform it."

Ashem's singstone buzzed, and he answered the call, listened to the scout's report, muscles growing tense. After a terse conversation, he cut off the communication. "Rhys,

Owain has been spotted approaching the islands from the north. It's time to go."

Rhys hesitated, then grasped Sarangerel's hand. "Thank you."

"Thank you," she said, "for letting the Wingless fight."

Ashem ducked beneath two Wonambi, stole up behind Juliet, and hugged her. *Doset doram. I swear that I will keep you safe.*

I know, and I love you too. She leaned her head back against his chest, and he closed his eyes, memorizing the feel of her.

In all his years of life, he never could have imagined a love like this.

He kissed her hair and followed Rhys from the chamber.

Maybe some men would have had to tear themselves away, but Ashem went eagerly to battle. Human mythology held that dragons would die to protect their treasures.

Human mythology was right.

He walked with Rhys into his rooms, where Kai was waiting in a new set of riding leathers, the white raven flying mask perched on top of her braided hair. She greeted them with a nod. "Are you ready?"

Ashem glanced to Rhys, skimming the surface of his king's mind. Rhys was a roiling ball of emotion, but his only tells were a single jump of muscles in his jaw, a second of pale-knuckled fists. The tells were enough. Ashem wouldn't have to be Azhdahā to know that the last thing Rhys wanted was to take Kai into this fight.

Rhys said, "I am."

They met what was left of the vee on Rhys's ledge just as the first hint of dawn began to gray the eastern sky. Cadoc, Evan, and Morwenna. Ffion had gone to the southernmost island, where she and handful of other pregnant dragons waited with the humans. If things went according to plan, once the battle was underway, Tane and the Ironscales would break through the weakest point of Owain's lines and get them all out. Seren and Citlali were standing by to heal the wounded in the temporary infirmary set up in the festival cavern at the base of the mountain.

"Everything is in place, Your Majesties. We're as ready as we're going to be."

Rhys and Kai exchanged a glance. Rhys took her hand, then gave Ashem a curt nod, as if Ashem had told him something he didn't already know. "My parents began this war. Now, we will end it."

Ashem inclined his head. "Stay watchful. Every single one of Owain's people is searching for you out there. His goal is to minimize casualties, and the best way to do that is by getting to you. If I could..."

"You wouldn't let me go out there," Rhys said. "I'm sorry for your sake, Ashem, that I'm not that kind of king. I believe I've compromised enough as it is."

Ashem grunted. Rhys's "compromise" was to fly the first wave of the battle with a new force of dragon/Wingless pairs that would make up the second line, dealing with any stragglers who broke through.

Protect Juliet, protect Rhys, protect what was left of his vee. Love made everything far too complicated.

Rhys gave him a wry smile. "Don't worry, Commander, I'll do what I'm supposed to."

Ashem snorted and stalked out to the ledge. The dragons of Eryri had already begun to fill the sky, some heading for other islands, some flying in formation around the mountain.

Cadoc, Evan, and Morwenna waited. Cadoc kept flexing his right hand, then shaking it out, a slight frown on his face.

Ashem paused next to him. "Thank you."

Cadoc looked up in surprise. "For what?"

"You know what, you yodeling idiot." Cadoc had nearly given his life to save Juliet and Kavar. "I'm glad you're alive. Stay that way."

Cadoc opened his mouth to say something, but Ashem had had enough of feelings. "Transform," he barked.

Everyone obeyed except Kai and Rhys, who had one final thing to do before joining them in the sky. They watched as the rest of the vee prepared to take flight.

Ashem surveyed them, offering a silent prayer that every single one of them would come to the end of the day still alive.

May the wind carry you well, he called out to them. *You know where to be. Now go.*

They took off.

CHAPTER 49

RHYS

K ai put a hand over Rhys's as he watched his family fly to war.

"We'd better do this. The sun is rising."

Rhys glanced down at her, then nodded. Instinctively, he reached for the place on his neck where the Sunrise Dragon pendant used to sit. Of course, it wasn't there.

He took her hand and led her to one side of the ledge, where a narrow path hidden in heavy foliage hugged the side of the mountain. Rhys imagined it would be a nerve-wracking climb for someone without wings. But Kai, of course, smiled and took it with ease.

The path led to the eastern slope of the mountain, to a shimmering barrier that hid a second ledge too small to be considered anything but a foothold for a dragon, though two humans fit easily enough. The ledge was unnaturally smooth and flat, like a table top. Draconic runes had been carved deep into the stone in the shape of several concentric and inter-secting circles, and those carvings had been filled with gold. Kai stopped Rhys before he could step into the center circle, which was just wide enough to kneel inside without touching the runes.

"Are you sure you're recovered enough to do this?" Kai asked. Her voice was strained.

Rhys smiled at her. "Would you command me not to do it if you knew it was dangerous?"

Kai gave him a wry smile. "That would make me a hypocrite. But maybe I would."

He leaned down to kiss her, her lips parting beneath his, his tongue sliding into her mouth, bodies molding against each other until they were both gasping. But there was no time, and he finally gathered his will and pulled away, looking into her fey green eyes, pupils shot wide with desire. "I'm strong enough. I have to be."

She nodded, then released him just as reluctantly as he did her. He turned toward the lightening eastern sky, stepped inside the circles of gold, and knelt just as the sun began to rise, grounding himself and resting his hands on top of his knees.

Then Rhys titled his head back and sang.

He didn't know the language of the Ancients. He didn't know the meaning of the exact words he intoned, calling them up from the depths of his chest in guttural, droning music. His father told him when he was a child that the words were the Ancients speaking through him, calling upon the sun. For dragons had been born of the sun and would become like it upon death—their souls turning to stars that would give birth to worlds without end.

The golden runes sparked in the light of the new day as Rhys raised power around him. Magic billowed from the runes, twisting around him in smoky halos of light. A burning began inside him. A searing both like and unlike fire. He couldn't ever decide if it hurt or not.

He lifted his arms, the song intensifying as the magic he'd

raised mixed with the light of the sun and turned inward, rushing through him. Cleansing him. The ritual peaked. For a moment, Rhys changed. He *became* the sunlight, all that was himself burning away, and the whole world blazed white.

In that instant, he thought he lost himself. He thought he'd overestimated his own strength. That sundering would, after all, be the death of him.

Then color leached back into the world. The burn of the magic faded to tolerable levels. He slumped, but didn't hit the stone. Kai had caught him, holding his large body up with her small but strong one. He wrapped his arms around her and looked to the sun just as the bottom curve of the blinding orb lifted from the horizon.

Kai cradled him close and kissed his forehead. "For a second, I thought I'd lost you. It looked like you were going to sublimate or something."

"For a second, I thought I might."

Familiar power had gathered around him like a cloak. Kai helped him to his feet and looked him up and down. "I assume it worked. You feel like a storm about to break."

He rolled his shoulders, trying to settle the weight of the magic. "It worked."

Kai looked from him to the northern sky, where hundreds of specks had appeared on the horizon.

"Good. Because it looks like it's time to go."

CHAPTER 50

KAI

K ai sat tall on Rhys's crimson-scaled back as he glided five hundred feet above the glittering sea. Ahead of them, the main body of their army flew in a formation between Owain's approaching forces and the archipelago, their lines stacked on top of each other so they formed a loose net three dragons deep that swept back on either side to guard the island's flanks.

Behind Rhys and Kai, twenty dragon/Wingless pairs who had chosen to fight together glided back and forth, waiting for the battle to start. Just to Rhys's right, bronze-scaled Thabo flew with his mate, Lindiwe, on his back. Councilwoman Athena and her mate, a Mo'o, were to Rhys's left.

Kai had been in battles before, but never to protect her home. Never with so much on the line. Her parents were on one of those islands. So was Juli. Her soulmate was with her. Their friends were around them in the sky.

She wished as she had since the sundering that she could speak to Rhys privately. Instead, they watched in silence as

Owain's army grew from specks in the sky to row upon row of dragons.

"Are they real?" Kai finally called over the wind. The Wonambi on their side, both king-sworn and free, would use illusions in a thousand different ways in the coming fight.

They should be, though they're probably bolstering their numbers in some places and hiding dragons in others. We have to be ready for anything.

"It looks like there are more of them than us."

We can hold them, Rhys said, determination hardening his mental voice.

Kai shifted, the harness clinking. Rhys had insisted that she clip in the way she used to before she'd started fighting with him—using all the straps instead of just the one that allowed her to stand and maneuver as he flew. Without the intimate connection of heartswearing, there was no way she could follow his movements closely enough to prevent being thrown around.

Owain's army grew closer, then closer. Kai trembled in spite of herself. Watching them approach was like standing still and waiting for a tsunami to crash over your head and drown you. In fact, what was she doing here at all? Why were any of them here? They couldn't win. They couldn't—

A visible wave of fear shifted through Rhys's army. Only then, seconds before the armies collided, did Kai see why.

People rode on the backs of Owain's front line. Or rather, dragons in human form. Though she couldn't tell from this distance, she immediately suspected who they were.

"Lung!" Kai bellowed. "They're spreading fear and despair! Don't believe what you feel!"

Many of the dragons steadied themselves, but it was too late. They'd weakened at exactly the wrong moment.

Ready yourselves! Ashem called.

At the last second, the Lung dropped off the backs of the dragons they'd been riding. They fell nearly to the sea, then transformed, surging toward the lowest line of defenders.

The armies impacted with a deafening sound unlike any Kai had heard. Screeches, roars, the thud of giant bodies, the rending of claws through flesh. She couldn't count how many of them went down in the initial assault on both sides.

Originally, Rhys and Ashem had hoped that Owain would allow his troops to rush forward so the net of defenders could fall back in the center. When that happened, the dragons along each flank would move around, slowly surrounding the dragons of Cadarnle.

But it didn't work. Owain's dragons were still too controlled. They refused to be drawn in as a group, instead mounting several assaults on strategic places so they could punch through the defensive line instead of being surrounded by it.

Rhys had been right about the illusions. The Wonambi of Cadarnle nearly caused a breach of Rhys's lines within the first thirty minutes by casting illusions that made it appear as if Owain was massing his strength on one side while simultaneously hiding a movement of several of his forces in a flanking maneuver.

Ashem caught them at the last moment, commanding a smooth movement of the vees that strengthened that area and held Owain back.

For another thirty minutes, at least.

After an hour on dragonback watching the fight, Kai had a throbbing stress headache and roiling stomach. She wanted to rest, but was too afraid, to tense. Death was coming for them. Sooner or later, the line would break.

And then it did. A spearhead of Draig forced their way

through, punching a hole in the defensive line. Rhys roared and surged forward.

Now!

"Attack!" Kai shouted at the same time.

Dragons and Wingless alike screamed a battle cry into the wind as they swarmed to plug the hole. It was a wonder to behold the dragons and their mind-melded riders moving in perfect synchronicity to drive the invaders back.

Kai did what she could, but without being in Rhys's mind, she couldn't read his body. It hamstrung her ability to use her fire to its fullest extent, though she still got in a few good shots.

Their aim wasn't to kill, but to take the enemy out of the fight. That meant targeting wings or eyes. She wished she had some of the Naga-venom bombs, but the glass was too easy to break, and it would do no good for one to burst on Rhys's back, putting them to sleep instead of their enemies.

They drove back the first breach, cheering when the dragons who made up the defensive net were able to swoop back into place. Then they drove back a second breach. Then a third. The day wore on, with only a few snatched moments on the beach for the dragons of Eryri to rest their wings and for the Wingless to perform rushed rituals to refill their magic. Owain's people might have fallen by the evening if he hadn't pushed Rhys's line back far enough to claim part of an island for himself. It was distant, but when Kai was on Rhys's back, she could see the small foothold they'd gained. The sand was so crowded with dragons that no sand was visible. The island looked like a rainbow iceberg floating in a tropical sea.

By the fourth breach, the dragons and Wingless were having a significantly harder time. Though they defended their home, Owain's numbers were greater.

By the fifth, they could no longer hold back the tide.

Fall back! Ashem commanded. *Close the gap!*

Rhys's lines collapsed in on the stream of Owain's dragons diving through them, and where there had been order all day long, Kai watched the battle descend into chaos. Immediately, the dragons who had broken through made a beeline for Rhys.

Raise the fog! Ashem commanded. *Begin the next phase!*

The Noodinoon in Rhys's army dropped out of formation to the island below. Thabo flew past Rhys, as did Athena and her mate.

"You've done what you can here, Your Majesties," Athena called. "Now do the hard part and take a back seat!"

Rhys growled. Not angry at Athena, but at what they had to do next. Kai pressed her knees into his back and shouted. "Come on, Rhys. She's right. You're the only thing standing between Owain and the mantle. We need to what we were told to do."

With a roar of rage that reverberated through Kai's bones, Rhys turned and left the battle behind.

CHAPTER 51

RHYS

"These traps are good to go."

Rhys nodded at Kai and resettled his wings, listening to the distant sounds of battle. He stood on the sandy beach on one of the smallest islands of the archipelago. The sky was dimming as the day moved toward sunset. To the north, the Noodinoon had raised a fog over the islands where the bulk of Owain's forces were. No longer did they fight only in the sky, but on the ground as well. Which was perfect, since that's where their traps were.

Kai wore a singstone that connected her to Ashem. So far, the second phase seemed to be going according to plan.

Somewhere out there, the rest of the Wingless and their mates continued to sweep for stragglers. Rhys and Kai couldn't patrol alone, so they'd agreed that once the initial defenses were broken, they'd join some of the King's Vee, checking the traps. Ashem's position as the commander of the army and his deadly Azhdahā venom made him too lethal a weapon to be wasted checking traps, so he'd taken command of one of the vees of Unsworn that lost its leader early in the fight. That meant he was still somewhere in the thick of things, attempting to lead as many of Owain's dragons as possible into the traps filled with sleep-inducing Naga toxins.

For the first time in Rhys's memory, everyone was working together. Since most vees—especially those filled with older dragons—were mostly of the same clan, it had been easy to assign jobs. The Wonambi of Eryri cast illusions that made Rhys's forces look greater than they were, or hid forces guarding strategic points. The Naga, skilled in the creation of magical objects, had designed the traps and were in charge of setting and resetting them. The Noodinoon held the fog, but also called up wind or lightning out of a clear sky. The Mo'o called upon the sea, casting vast waterspouts or whirlpools and protecting underwater entrances to Eryri. They were also pulling the wounded from the ocean, no matter which side they were on. Rhys wasn't interested in having any dragon drown.

The Draig, Bida, Lung, and Derkin were doing most of the fighting, keeping Owain's soldiers away from Eryri and the southern islands while luring them into fog and traps. Then the fighters took the drugged dragons—who, once unconscious, reverted to their more portable human forms—to Eryri. There, Rhys's people had converted the festival cavern at the base of the mountain to a temporary infirmary with a holding cell for Owain's soldiers in the back. Containing the prisoners was difficult, and it would take more and more of his people as the battle wore on. But the traps had already done a great deal to chip away at Owain's numbers with very few casualties.

Rhys couldn't believe his plan was actually working. He just wished he could actually see it. He understood why he had to keep away now that the forces of Cadarnle had broken through the front line, but that didn't mean he had to like it.

Now he knew how the Wingless had felt.

The traps on the other side of the island are fine as well,

Cadoc said, his streamlined carnelian head appearing through a stand of trees. Morwenna was with him. Evan stood in the clearing behind Rhys and Kai, silent and watchful. Though Rhys was fairly sure he saw the midnight-blue dragon lean in the direction of the battle more than once. Apparently, Rhys wasn't the only one feeling the pull of the fight.

Kai clambered onto Rhys's back, and he heard the faint *click* of her carabiners clipping into the harness.

Have you heard from Ashem? Rhys asked.

Kai shook her head. "Not for a little while."

It looks like Owain has taken the northernmost island, Cadoc said, craning his neck to see what he could of the battle. From this distance, the mass of fighting dragons looked like darting, jewel-colored hummingbirds.

We expected that, Morwenna said.

The fighting is done on the little island next to it, said Cadoc. *We could go around and help scoop up the wounded. See if there are any prisoners.*

That would take them temptingly close to the battle.

All right. Rhys moved toward the beach without waiting to see if any of them would follow. *We'll skirt the fighting.* But at least they'd be able to see it.

Though they'd taken some losses throughout the day, the dragons of Eryri now seemed to outnumber those of Cadarnle. Unfortunately, the number of new prisoners was tapering off now that Owain's soldiers had learned about the traps.

Even so, the white dragon's forces had been considerably winnowed down. Rhys hoped—too optimistically, he knew—to hear of Owain's capture by the end of the day. Once they had Owain, they'd get the necklace from him and Rhys would use it to repair the torn mantle.

This battle could be their last. The war could be over at any time, and he felt like they actually had a chance at winning.

They took off, soaring over the sea, skimming the waves to stay out of sight. The sounds of battle grew louder, the air filled with roars and shrieks and the scent of burning. Tendrils of fog mixed with the nauseating miasma of several different kinds of venom—all too dispersed to have any effect, but concentrated enough to make everyone feel slightly ill.

They landed on the beach of the small island and split up again. Rhys, Kai, and Evan went around the northern shore while Cadoc and Morwenna headed south, then zigzagged inland to make sure they covered the ground thoroughly in their search for dragons who were injured or unconscious.

They came across half a dozen bodies, and Rhys's heart contracted at the sight of each one. Dead.

Kai must have felt him tense, because she patted his shoulder, her hand barely registering through his thick scales. "You can't save them all. No matter how hard you try."

I should've done more.

She shifted, and he suspected she'd leaned down and put her arms around as much of his neck as she could. "That way lies madness, Rhys. We've done all we can. *You* have done all you can. It's taken a thousand years of your life, and you've given them willingly. If dragons have to have a king, they couldn't ask for one better than you."

Her words eased his heart, but not his grief. *I wish it was only about power,* he whispered into her mind. *I would give myself to Owain in an instant and let him torture me forever to save them.*

"I know. But it isn't just about power. It's about stopping Owain before he causes death on a scale neither your people nor mine have ever seen."

In the trap near the center of the island, they found three of Owain's dragons sound asleep, gassed with Naga venom. Evan

432

pulled the dragons from the trap and laid them carefully in the sling-like pouch that hung below his belly.

Aside from Owain's people, they found no survivors.

It isn't right. Evan's gray eyes flashed. *They killed our people. Now we're taking them alive and safe into the heart of Eryri. This is not a good idea.*

Rhys flicked his wings, making Kai shift around on his back. *You and I have killed more of Owain's people than any of these have killed of ours.*

Evan snorted and turned away. Rhys flexed his claws, digging them into the sand.

"You told him the right thing," Kai said.

Did I?

Rhys! Cadoc's call was faint, which meant he was probably on the far side of the island. *Look out! Demba—*

His voice cut off.

"Go!" Kai shouted.

Despite his cargo, Evan was already spreading his wings. They leaped into the air, adrenaline and rage flooding Rhys's body in a tsunami of fire. Demba had taken Griffith from them —he would not take Cadoc or Morwenna.

Owain's dragons rose from the forest where they'd been waiting, apparently in ambush, half a dozen in all. Rhys felt a vicious pleasure at the sight of the bronze dragon. He'd wanted a chance to fight Demba since the Bida killed Griffith.

He opened his mouth to scorch the hide off the Bida's bones, but the memory of Ffion's words made him snap his jaw shut.

Vengeance is not what Griffith would have wanted. More than any of us, I think, he wanted peace. When you win, that will be your hardest job. You'll have to heal us. You and Kai... You must unite us.

With a growl, Rhys pulled an orb of Naga venom from the

holder he'd strung on the harness. He threw it—not as easy for dragon arms as it was for human ones—and hit Demba between the eyes. The enormous dragon crashed to the earth. Around him, the others were doing the same.

Sedating, not killing.

Rhys landed and grasped human-shaped Demba with one claw, resisting, second by second, the urge to rip the man in two. Evan put two more prisoners in his sling. Morwenna carried the others.

Kai slipped from his back, securing the prisoners in the sling with dexterous hands. When she came back, she paused and patted his scaled cheek. She was so small from this angle, and yet she was everything.

She leaned against him, and he nuzzled into her. "You did it, Rhys. I swear, sometimes the level of control you exercise over your desires borders on bizarre."

I hate him. I want to kill him.

"I want that too. But it won't give Ffion's baby a father. Evan watched you do that. People will know you spared him. They'll see how hard you're trying to avoid casualties while Owain throws dragons to their deaths like they're nothing. We might not be on the front lines, but you're still leading. I admire you so much."

Rhys warmed at the praise. Kai climbed into the harness, and they led the King's Vee to Eryri.

Kai was right. If he could capture Demba and not kill him, perhaps there was hope to unite the people after all.

For the rest of the day, Rhys stayed closer to the battle than Ashem would've liked. It still wasn't close enough for Rhys. As the sun rolled across the sky and the battle contracted to a small area of the north island, he had less and less to do.

Despite all the fighting, Owain hadn't shown himself. His absence was ominous.

Rhys tried not to think about it as he returned to his rooms in Eryri that evening after the fighting died down for the night. The battle lines had been firmly drawn far from the mountain —it would be safe enough to sleep for a few hours. Outside, vees traded off sentry duty. His plans were working. His people were winning.

But it didn't feel that way. Not as long as the white dragon went free.

CHAPTER 52

SEREN

Seren collapsed onto a wooden chair off to one side of the makeshift infirmary, rubbing her temples. Not entirely recovered from losing the Sight, she'd had to pace herself, using magic on only the direst injuries. Even then, she could only use enough to bring them from the brink of death. It hurt her heart to leave people in pain, but Citlali had to do the same.

In the back of her mind, Cadoc hummed to himself as he checked traps and tried to steer Rhys away from the worst of the fighting.

All right? he asked.

She smiled, leaning into his strength. *I'll survive.*

There were just too many of them. It was barely midmorning on the second day of the battle, and she was ready to sleep for a week.

She looked across the rows of cots that held the injured. Deeper into the cavern, near the lake, a mass of sleeping dragons was laid out on the floor. Some of them had begun to stir. She contacted Ashem through the singstone he'd given her, and he said he would send more guards.

The battle was dragging on longer than any of them had intended. There were only so many Naga in Eryri, and they could only produce so much of their sleep-inducing venom. There wasn't much left in the festival chamber to give the dragons.

Seren hoped Owain would show himself soon. The work of the moment kept the worst of her fears for Cadoc at bay, but it never left entirely.

A cry of pain drew her attention. Seren rose on tired feet and headed for the sound. She was nearly there when shouting brought her up short. Instinctively, she waited to feel some kind of premonition. There was nothing.

Heart in her throat, she turned.

At first, she couldn't make sense of what she was seeing. Then it became horrifyingly clear. A dozen young dragons led by Gethin, the son of Councilman Powell, were attacking the guards.

They broke through to the prisoners, and Gethin headed straight for the enormous man Seren recognized as Demba. Drawing a vial from his pocket, he opened Demba's mouth and dumped the sludgy liquid down his throat.

Demba woke.

Though their heartswearing bond, Cadoc sensed her terror. *What is it? What's happened?*

For a moment, Seren froze to the spot, unable to answer. But Cadoc didn't need her to answer. They were so deeply intertwined that he saw the answer before he finished asking the question. *Seren, RUN!*

But her body was slow to respond. Around Gethin, his fellows were doing the same—rousing Owain's soldiers and handing them tiny vials of black liquid. Some stopped to toss back vials of their own.

Then they attacked in earnest.

Seren burst into action, waking the wounded who belonged to Rhys. "Run!"

Cadoc was still speaking to her. *Love, listen to me. Don't worry about anyone else, just hide. Owain isn't interested in killing, but he is interested in recapturing you. Keep yourself safe. We're on our way.*

Owain's soldiers were among the cots now. Any of Rhys's people they caught, they knocked to the ground, reversing the roles of prisoner and guard so fast that Seren's head spun. She gathered a small crowd of patients, chivvying them along in front of her as she ran.

Then, a shout. "It's the Seeress! Take her!"

Seren's stomach dropped. She ran, but a woman grabbed her braid, yanking her painfully backward. Seren struggled unsuccessfully. Then the woman shrieked and let go, and someone shoved her to one side. Citlali appeared, bloodied obsidian knife in one hand. "Let's go!"

She pulled Seren from the cavern beneath the mountain and up the winding road.

Seren half ran and was half dragged after her. "Wait! There are people here still," she panted. "In other parts of Eryri. We have to warn them."

Seren, hide! Cadoc was desperate, but she couldn't do what he wanted. Not while there were people who needed help.

Citlali's expression was unhappy, but she nodded. They and the small group of wounded and guards who had escaped Gethin and Demba's coup ran up the main road that spiraled the open shaft inside the mountain, shouting a warning. All of the dragons who couldn't fight—the old, the young, and the pregnant—had been ordered to the southern isle before the battle started, thank the Ancients, but there were always those who were too stubborn to leave.

They gathered more of Rhys's people as they climbed.

They were beginning to stumble over each other. She needed to get them out, and then she would go back for more.

They made for one of the branching tunnels that led toward a residential section of the mountain, where Seren knew there was a way out.

Gethin was already there. He stood in the middle of the exit with half a dozen of Owain's soldiers and his father, whom he must have freed from the cells.

"Lady Seren." His lip curled. "If you *are* a lady anymore. Owain would like to see you."

"Gethin, what are you doing?" His father, Councilman Powell, seemed horror-struck. "You cannot be serious."

Gethin glowered at his father. "I'm helping to end the war. I've never understood why you stayed with Rhys for so long. You want power, Father? Owain will give us power—and he'll make sure the humans know their place. That's what you want, isn't it?"

Powell gaped at his son. "If we go to war with humans, we'll all die." His eyes went wide. "It was you. The mead they thought *I* sent Rhys. That was you. You poisoned the princess."

"Now is not the time, Father."

Seren turned on her heel, but too late. Gethin lunged and grabbed her. "Get them. All of them. Owain wants every single one of these dragons taken prisoner. Leave no one to help the false king!"

Seren smashed her foot down on Gethin's instep. But the cordial had strengthened him and he didn't react except to shake her so hard she saw double.

Then Gethin let go and fell to the floor. Rhys stood behind her, eyes shadowed, a bloody dagger in his hand. Gethin stared unseeing at the ceiling, a red stain spreading from beneath him. Rhys bent and wiped the dagger on Gethin's shirt.

Seren pressed her hands to her mouth. "Rhys. Did you hear what he said? He sent the poisoned mead. He killed Deryn."

When Rhys looked at Seren, the answer was in his eyes.

Cadoc appeared at Rhys's side, a bruise forming on his cheek. He pulled Seren close and held her, his entire body shaking, the scent of cedar, lemon oil, and sweat filling her nose.

In his mind, however, Seren sensed pride in what she'd done. *And you thought you wouldn't make a good soldier.*

Around them, Evan, Morwenna, and Kai fought the rest of Gethin's companions. When they saw their leader fall, some fled, choosing to leap into the sky and transform rather than stand and fight. Those who remained were subdued quickly between Rhys's vee and the dragons Seren and Citlali had saved from the lower chamber.

Kai and Citlali began organizing everyone, keeping a sharp eye on the sky for any of Owain's soldiers.

"Eryri is compromised, thanks to Gethin. But it looks like they're concentrating their efforts on taking the mountain from the bottom up. If we hurry, we can fly for the southernmost island," Kai said.

"There were wounded who didn't make it this far," Seren said. "They've taken the lower cavern."

Rhys closed his eyes, then shook his head. "We have to take who we can. Owain doesn't want dragons dead any more than I do."

Seren couldn't stop staring at Gethin's body, lying on the stone floor. He had murdered her sister—had tried to murder Rhys. For the first time in her life, she was glad for someone's death.

Rhys leveled his now-clean knife at Powell. He hadn't fought, so he hadn't been subdued. Instead, he stood to one side, staring at his son's body as intently as Seren.

"Did you know?" Rhys demanded.

"No." Powell's bulldog face was white as a sheet. He tore his eyes from Gethin and sank to his knees in front of Rhys. "Majesty, I had nothing to do with this. I swear it. If Commander Ashem had ever had time to question me, you would have known days ago."

"We'll know now." He hauled Powell up by the arm and looked over his shoulder. They couldn't see anything from where they were, but they could hear the sound of Owain's soldiers taking prisoners and ransacking homes. "Eryri is lost to us. Kai?"

"We've done what we can here." She waved the last of the wounded who had escaped the infirmary onto the ledge. Rhys joined her, going outside. He and Powell transformed, and Kai climbed onto Rhys's back with no harness at all.

The group of refuges—so dishearteningly small—headed for the southern island, fighting their way free of a few of Owain's soldiers to get there.

Once they were clear, Seren looked back at the mountain that had been her home.

High on the peak, on the ledge outside Rhys's rooms, the white dragon watched them fly away.

CHAPTER 53
KAI

K ai walked through the too-small camp and counted the dragons who had escaped Owain's counterattack, then counted again. Just over three hundred dragons and Wingless had made it here. Ashem and his group of Unsworn had come to the island as well, along with a few other soldiers—but not nearly as many as Kai thought should have. The others, she could only hope, were alive as prisoners in Eryri or hiding in pockets on other islands, presumably dodging the patrols Owain had flying around, killing or capturing anyone they discovered. Preventing any chance of escape.

There was no way out.

The humans who'd been on the island before the fighting broke out were living in a cave complex. It had been enhanced a little by the dragons, but it was so bare it felt like a cheap motel next to the grandeur of Eryri.

The complex had been built to house only about a hundred people, so they were squishing in everywhere they could. Rhys, Kai, Juli, and Ashem shared a tiny set of rooms with Kai's parents and Liam. The rest of the vee and Seren were in another. Rhys sat with Ashem, not speaking. Kai knew he blamed himself, and many of the dragons blamed him, as well. Bringing Owain to Eryri had been his idea.

It had come *so* close to working.

They'd gone from nearly winning the war to almost certainly losing in the space of a few minutes. There was no way to get her family out.

Kai didn't blame Rhys. She'd wholeheartedly supported his plan. But while Owain might keep the dragons alive, she had no delusions that he would spare any humans who came under his control.

Every time she saw an enemy dragon circle the island, she grew more desperate. Even if they'd lost the war, she still had to get her family home. Owain could be finished here, soon. Once that happened, it wouldn't be long until he began attacking the human population.

At least if she got her parents and Liam off the island, they'd stand a chance. Perhaps she and Rhys could make it out, go to the leaders of powerful nations, and warn them. He could prove dragons existed...

But he'd do so at the cost of his own life. Kai didn't see a world in which humans knew about dragons and just let them walk free.

If it came down to that, Rhys would do it.

Hell, it probably was down to that. Shit.

Feeling helpless, she sank down on the sandy ground next to her mother and stared into the fire Rhys had lit in the small fireplace.

Leila Monahan put her arm around Kai and pulled her close. "Thank you, sweetheart."

Kai shook her head. "I haven't done anything that I deserve to be thanked for."

"You did your best. You got us this far."

"It's my fault you're here."

Her mother laughed softly. "Oh, honey. If anything, it sounds like it's either your father's or my fault that *you're* here. You said this...heartswearing...runs in families." She kissed Kai's forehead. "We'll find a way out. At least we know where you are now. Did you really think you were going to disappear off the face of the earth?"

Kai laughed without humor. "I didn't know what I was going to do." Tears formed in her eyes. "Mom, I don't think there's any hope."

Her mom rubbed her shoulder. "There's always hope, sweetheart. If anyone knows that, I do. Look how long I hoped for you to finish school. We knew you'd achieve such amazing things, once you figured out your place in the world."

Kai snorted. "Yeah, and I never did."

Mom gave Kai a crooked smile. "I know. Now you're the dragon-riding queen of a race of mythical creatures. I have to say, you've exceeded our expectations."

This time, Kai's laugh was genuine. She studied her mother's face. Leila Monahan wasn't old, but she had wrinkles around her eyes and veins that stood out on the backs of her hands. Not old, but aging, like Kai would not. Not for more years than she cared to count.

She opened her mouth to say something, then closed it again. If they all died tomorrow, it wouldn't matter. And if they didn't, there would be time.

Rhys appeared in the low doorway of the room. "Kai, I— Can we talk?" Kai took one look at his face and stood. Saying goodbye to her mother, she followed him outside, all the way down to the beach. A few of his soldiers patrolled, but they were few and far enough between for talking.

Kai caught his hand in hers as they walked. He wouldn't look at her. "Whatever you're thinking, Rhys, the answer is no."

"I'm going to give myself up in exchange for free passage for you and the humans."

Kai glowered. "Didn't you hear me say no? *Hell* no." It would be better to try and sneak him out and turn themselves over to humans.

Except Owain had them surrounded.

He turned to her, his hands cupping her face, and kissed her fiercely. "I'm not asking you. I'm telling you. I did this. Help isn't coming, *cariad*. Tomorrow when the sun comes up, I'm turning myself over. I'm going to ask Owain to allow Ashem, Cadoc, and the others to fly you and the humans to safety. Then Ashem and the other dragons will get as far away as possible. Take your family and go into hiding. Your species is going to need you. You—and all the Wingless. You're the only ones strong enough to fight dragons and long-lived enough to make a difference. You are the only beings with magic who can't be controlled by the mantle."

Kai gripped his wrists. "*No.* There has to be a way out of this. Come with us. We'll go to the humans together."

He lowered his forehead to hers, letting out a slow, unsteady breath. "Kai, my love. There is no way out. Not for me."

"We can find a way!"

He shook his head, eyes closing, and pressed a desperate kiss to her forehead. "Please let me do this. We're already sundered—you won't feel it."

"*Won't feel it?*" Kai heard how shrill her voice was, but she seemed to have lost control. "Are you insane? If you die, I will feel it every second of every day for the rest of my life. My ridiculously long life, thanks to you."

"Kai—"

"Rhys. I am not going to agree to this. Not ever. If you want to sacrifice yourself to Owain, I'm going with you."

It was his turn to refuse. "No. Absolutely not."

"Yes. I don't care if I have to swim over to Owain on the other island—I will fucking swim. Whatever happens, you and I are together."

"Kai..." There was such pain in his voice. She couldn't allow herself to hear it.

"You don't get to ask me to stay safe when you refuse to. You don't get to make your own choice and take away mine. By all means, let's bargain with Owain. Force him to allow my family to go home. But I am not leaving *you*." She pulled him down and kissed him hard. After a few minutes, they broke apart.

"Is there anything I can say to make you stay?" he asked, stroking her cheek with his thumb. "Please, *cariad*?"

His eyes were bright in a way Kai had never seen—not with starfire, but with tears that didn't fall. She swallowed back her own and shook her head.

Slowly, he nodded and took her hand. Neither of them needed to speak.

She would go with him.

They walked hand in hand to her family's rooms and lay down on a folded blanket in one corner, his arms holding her tight against him, her face buried in his chest. Eventually, the rest of her family came in and lay down in their own blankets. Liam's snores filled the air.

The night passed. Kai listened to Rhys's heartbeat, breathed him in. He stroked her hair. Neither of them slept, but they held each other until the sun rose, taking comfort in each other's warmth and strength.

In a dark corner of her mind, the door she'd locked and tried to forget creaked and groaned beneath the weight of everything piled behind it. More than once, she consciously relaxed. To stop herself from hyperventilating.

But even Rhys's arms weren't safe enough to stop her from imagining what Owain would do to her if he killed Rhys and kept her alive.

If he took her back to the dark and cold of Cadarnle.

CHAPTER 54
JULI

Juli watched the sky lighten above the eastern sea. Ashem had made sure the sentries kept watch all night. Now he propped himself against a boulder, legs sprawled. Juli sat between them, leaning back against him, his arms around her waist.

She'd overheard Rhys and Kai talking last night, and she couldn't get the conversation out of her head. "Those two are going to do something stupid."

Ashem didn't have to ask who she meant. "Of course they are."

"Well?"

"Well, what?"

Juli made a sound of disgust. "Well, what are we going to do to stop them?"

Ashem turned to Eryri, its distant peak barely visible against the night sky. "Kill Owain ourselves."

She tilted her head. It was an interesting proposition, and she was not at all opposed. "Could we?"

Ashem shrugged. "I am Azhdahā."

449

"Valid point. What about the rogues? Are any of them coming? The emissaries have had plenty of time to reach them." Juli ran a hand through the sand, pretending a casualness she didn't feel.

"I lost my singstone during the retreat. I have no idea."

"I suppose we should go while it's still dark, then. So many of the Cadarnle dragons have those onyx charms now that there's no telling who will see us and who won't."

Ashem transformed. It took Juli a long time to get the harness on by herself. By the time she managed, a sliver of the sun peeked above the horizon.

They took off, flying low, speaking into each other's minds about unimportant things. When death was certain, there was no point in wallowing.

For the first time since he'd forced his way into her mind, Juli opened her connection to Kavar. She figured he at least deserved some warning.

To her shock, he was close. Far closer than she'd thought he would be. *I thought you were going home.*

I was. Kavar's voice was a familiar silky growl. *And then I realized what you two were going to do. Before you did.*

Visions of Kavar warning Owain, of all of the soldiers of Cadarnle waiting for them, flashed through Juli's head. *What did you do?*

I found your reinforcements. They were lost, so I showed them where to go. His voice was harsh, and Juli sensed the agony he'd suffered in making the decision. Them or Owain.

He had chosen them.

Kavar may have just saved them all.

Where are you now? Juli asked. *Are you coming back?*

Stars, no. I told you both, I am not taking part in this. You are more trouble than you're worth, Juliet King. When this is over, I want whoever wins to sunder us.

Juli swallowed. She hadn't seen what Kai and Rhys went through with her own eyes, but she had through Ashem's. *Are you sure?*

Perhaps it won't hurt as much if whoever does it has the power of the entire mantle.

Juli doubted it. All of the records she'd seen indicated that sundering had always been painful. *If that's what you want.*

It is.

The sky lightened in the east, and Juli saw a black mass headed their way. Hundreds of dragons spread across the horizon.

The rogues had come. Considering Owain's numbers, it wouldn't be enough to get him to surrender outright. But it might be enough to keep them fighting another day.

She sighed. *Fine, Kavar. But only because you might have just saved the world.*

He said nothing, but the feeling in their bond was smug. Juli shook her head and told Ashem to turn around.

They had to get to Rhys and Kai.

CHAPTER 55
OWAIN

Owain watched the death of his plans approach from the east: a cloud of rogues large enough to give him pause. Rogues he had not called. Rogues who were not coming to Eryri to support him. It was a momentous feeling, like destiny sliding through his claws.

Rhys was already out there. Of course he was, because Rhys couldn't just let this end.

Owain had the numbers to fight them, but hundreds would die. Too many for their population to recover in his lifetime. Too many to even think about taking on humans and surviving.

Rhys was forcing his hand. The scales were too balanced. They would have to solve things the way he should have years ago, as soon as Rhys became an adult.

He waited for the rogues to arrive on the southernmost island of the archipelago. Gave them time to settle. He ordered his own people to clear the central island and fly for the northern island. Then Owain flew out and landed on the peak of the mountain, roaring a challenge the way dragons had since time before time. Jiang and Demba sat just below him, waiting.

It didn't take long for Rhys to answer.

He flew from the southern island, Ashem on one side, a rogue Naga chieftain on the other. As always, the Wingless woman was on Rhys's back. Owain didn't understand it. He'd sundered Rhys—given him a chance to be free—and still, he burdened himself.

Well, if he wanted the Wingless with him, so be it. That probably meant Owain could insist on bringing Jiang into the battle, but there was no need.

Let Rhys's love of humans finally bring about his own death.

Rhys, Owain called, *Son of the Usurper Ayen, son of the true king Thân, I challenge you to combat to the death. No champions, seconds, no aid from our people. Let's not end hundreds of lives when one life will suffice.* Owain paused, as if considering. *I'll even let you bring your pet Wingless.*

His cousin didn't even stop to think about it. Didn't argue. *Agreed. Ashem Azhdahā and Naakesh of the Free Naga witness it.*

He'd made it so easy. By himself, Rhys was a fearsome fighter, but with the girl, he would be burdened. Distracted. All Owain would have to do was land one good hit, and her death would seal the red dragon's.

Owain bared his teeth and indicated his own people, stationed slightly below him on the mountain. *Lung Jiang, Queen of Dragons, and Demba of the Bida witness it.*

Rhys flew forward, and Owain leaped from the mountain peak. Soon, it would be his.

All of it would be his.

Finally, he was going to have the power he'd been born to wield. He would return his people to the glory they deserved.

CHAPTER 56

KAI

When the dragons decided they were going to fight, they didn't waste time. Owain came right for them. Kai pulled down her white raven mask and tightened her grip on Rhys with her knees.

Rhys stretched, beating his wings for altitude. Sticking close to the side of the mountain, he wheeled and dodged Owain's first blast of flesh-freezing breath.

Kai crouched at the base of Rhys's neck, just above his wings. Her carabiner was clipped into the harness in the way that allowed her to maneuver, and she tried to breathe normally. She had no way of connecting with him like she once had, but she had ridden on dragonback enough times that she could fight.

Rhys angled into a steep climb, leaving Owain behind. Kai stood and turned so she hung facing the receding ground. She raised her palms and called on her storm of flames, sending fireball after fireball at Owain.

The white dragon's eyes widened in shock and he barrel-rolled out of the way.

Rhys peaked and dove, aiming a stream of fire at Owain's side. Again, Owain dodged. Kai raised her hands to shoot another fireball as he went by, but Rhys's wings were in the way.

After that, it was hard to keep track of all the hits and near misses. The white dragon seemed to be everywhere at once, breathing ice or raking his claws in a glancing blow down Rhys's side. He was faster than Rhys, Kai realized. Whether from natural abilities or cordial, she had no idea. She suspected the latter.

Finally, Rhys scored a hit. Three long, shallow gashes on Owain's white flank welled with crimson blood.

Kai shot more fire, but she missed time after time. Without her connection, she was afraid of accidentally hitting Rhys's wings.

Owain pursued them around the mountain, breathing ice at Rhys's tail. Rhys roared in pain, and Kai saw that Owain had frozen the tip. He smashed his claw against it. The last foot and a half of Rhys's tail was shattered and gone.

Bile rose in Kai's throat. Owain was toying with them. Taking Rhys apart piece by piece.

Kai aimed another volley of fireballs at Owain. She was so focused on fighting that she wasn't paying attention to Rhys's movements. He lurched to one side as Owain breathed another cloud of ice, sending Kai tumbling through space for a few short feet before her harness caught her.

Damn it, damn it, damn it! Her worst fears were coming true. She was a liability here, not an asset. Now Rhys was flying crooked, trying to block her with his body while Owain gained on them, eating up the precious altitude Rhys had worked so hard to gain.

Kai gripped the rope and pulled herself up onto Rhys's back through adrenaline and sheer force of will.

But it was too late.

Owain zoomed past and slashed his two-foot claws full across Rhys's face.

Rhys roared and struggled to right himself. Blood sprayed in the air and sheeted down the side of his face.

"No!"

Rhys shook his head back and forth, and Kai saw the damage. Owain had taken Rhys's eye. Just as Rhys, through Kai, had taken his months ago in the Rockies.

It's okay, she told herself. *We'll survive this and Seren can heal it. He'll be okay.*

But Rhys was not okay. Owain raked past them again on Rhys's blind side. Kai tried to shout to him, tell him where Owain was, but the wind snatched her words. If they'd been heartsworn, they could have done this. She could have been his eyes.

As it was, Rhys didn't dodge in time. Owain shredded one of his wings. They went down.

Rhys did his best to steady them as they fell, but there wasn't much he could do. Thinking quickly, Kai used her magic to burn through the strap that held her to the harness. As Rhys crashed to the earth, she leaped free.

Kai landed in the sand and rolled, the wind knocked out of her. Rhys looked around for her wildly, not seeing that Owain was almost on him.

"I'm here!" Kai shouted. Dimly, she noticed that dragons had taken to the sky again. Despite Rhys's and Owain's orders, they were fighting. She thought she saw Ashem. Cadoc. Even Seren and Ffion.

They and the rogues circled Eryri, keeping Owain's dragons back.

Then Owain smashed into Rhys.

Kai scrambled away as the red and white dragons raged

above her, battling and clawing and roaring so she thought she would go deaf—if she wasn't killed outright.

Fear crescendoed inside her. Rhys was torn and bloody, unable to use one of his foreclaws because of the crash, unable to see from one eye. Kai called fire to her hands, but before she could shoot it at Owain, the white dragon turned and shot superchilled air in her direction. Kai leaped out of the way and the cold blasted past her, coming close enough to crackle her sweaty hair into strands of ice, but not close enough to maim or kill.

The white sand of the beach gave beneath her feet as she ran, trying to get a better angle on Owain. There were frozen droplets on her face, and she realized they were tears.

She wouldn't be enough to help Rhys.

With a roar, Owain smashed his claws across Rhys's face. Rhys's crimson head jerked to one side so hard Kai thought his neck had broken. For a moment, her world froze. He staggered to one side and fell, spraying sand and blood.

"Rhys!" Kai screamed, racing toward him, reaching for him with her mind as she had done time after time. But there was nothing. Like shouting into empty darkness.

Flames rippled across the beach, and Rhys became human. The watching dragons roared.

Icy wind whipped past her. Owain had changed as well, becoming the blond, cold-eyed man who haunted her nightmares. He stalked forward, pulling a necklace from his neck. Rhys's father's necklace. The Sunrise Dragon.

His cold eyes found her, and she stopped. The door in her head was open. Days of torture. Of hurting her to hurt a man who wasn't even there.

"Move away, Wingless. He is not yours anymore. Go home and live the life you wanted for as long as you can."

Kai was frozen in place, trembling. Panicking. Memories

shrieked in her ears. Beatings. Electrocution. Cutting. Pain. *Pain.* She needed to run. To escape. He would break her this time. He would kill her.

Her eyes fell on the Sunrise Dragon, the shine of sun on the gold pendant slicing through the darkness.

If Owain touched Rhys's skin with that, it was over. He would suck the mantle away in a matter of moments. He would be unstoppable, and it would be over.

There was part of Kai's old self—a weak, desperate part, the part that had dropped out of school, let her life slide, hid and run from responsibility—that wanted nothing more than for this to be over.

No. She was not who she had been.

Kai scrambled around Rhys, behind Owain. He spun and shot icy blast after icy blast toward her. She shot back, pinching off balls of fire and hurling them as quickly as she could manage, spinning the fire inside her faster and hotter and tighter.

Snarling, Owain gave up chasing her and turned instead for Rhys, who lay only a dozen feet away.

Rhys had been hurt enough. With a roar, Kai sprinted after Owain and leaped onto his back. She wrapped her hand in the chain and tore the Sunrise Dragon from his grasp just as he stumbled and fell across Rhys's prone body. Kai landed on top of them both with a yelp of pain. The weight of her body plus Owain's smashed her fist, driving the corners of the pendant deep into her palm.

The world halted. Time itself sucked in a breath. The men beneath her might have been carved from stone. In her hand, trapped between Owain's hand and Rhys's bare arm, the pendant hummed. The vibration turned into a heat. Not the friendly heat of fire, but the heat of a star. So intense that she cried out again. It felt as if the skin of her palm was melting.

The vibration spread from the pendant to the chain, from the chain to the skin of the two men. And then...

And then...

Power.

It thundered and howled, flooding her like a river overflowing its banks. Like she stood at the bottom of a waterfall, trying to drink and drowning instead. Pure and hot and *everything.* Her body shook. She opened her mouth, a scream forcing itself up her throat. Her arms and legs seized, muscles cramping.

So much energy. So much power.

So much, so much, so *much*, and it had nowhere to go. Like when she'd lost control and set a gym on fire.

Except this power couldn't escape.

Abruptly, it settled. Like seeing a bonfire snuffed like a candle. The flood was gone. It had become an ocean within her, burning from the inside. But not like fire. Like light. Like possibility.

Like nothing and no one in creation could stand against her.

Queen of Dragons.

Kai rolled off the men, the Sunrise Dragon still gripped in her fist. She was dazed. She couldn't think, couldn't move.

Couldn't do anything but lie in the sand as Owain pulled himself off Rhys and stood, looming over her. He drew a dagger from his belt, sharp and black and covered with white runes. Instead of coming after her, Owain knelt on Rhys's chest, pinning his unbroken arm. Owain grasped a handful of dark red hair in one fist.

Rhys blinked his remaining eye, just coming back to consciousness. Owain jerked Rhys's head back, exposing his throat. "Give me the artifact, Wingless."

Roars and shrieks from the sky. Some dragons were still fighting, but many of them had stopped.

They only circled, watching the spectacle below.

"No!" Kai pulled herself up to her knee. Her head felt strange. Too large, somehow. Full of half-heard, whispering voices.

Owain pressed the dagger into Rhys's throat, and blood welled around the tip of the blade.

Something was building in her, something that buzzed and scorched her tongue.

It couldn't be what she thought it was. She was Wingless, not a real dragon. She was Kai Monahan from Rifle, Colorado. Surely she'd only brushed the power of it as it flowed through both of them.

"Give it to me," Owain repeated. "If I have the Sunrise Dragon, I have the mantle, and no reason to kill him. Give me the artifact, and Rhys lives."

Kai didn't move.

Owain twisted Rhys's broken arm, and Rhys cried out.

"Give it to me, or I will do to him every single thing I did to you." A rime of frost feathered down the blade.

As the frost touched Rhys's skin, he gasped, "Run, Kai."

He spoke again, rapid, liquid whispers in Welsh, directed at Owain. Pleading whispers. Kai strained to hear him over the crashing waves. She didn't have to understand the language to know that Rhys wasn't pleading for himself, but for her. Always, only for her.

Owain grinned up at Kai, a horribly cold version of Rhys's smile. He pressed the dagger down a little harder, and Rhys's fingers dug into the sand, his eyes fixed on her.

"You know what he wants, Wingless? He's asking me to leave you alive. He knows that he's dead. There's nothing he can do. He is lost."

Kai shook herself, her focus fuzzing and blurring around the edges. Everything was too bright. "No," she whispered again. Something pulsed inside her, like a sun just barely out of reach. If she tried, she might brush it with her fingertips. If she tried...

"Time is up," Owain snarled.

His fingers tightened around the blade.

Desperate power boiled over, rushing from Kai in a burst as she screamed, "STOP!" No more death. No more war. No more pain. None of it.

Owain went still. The battling dragons ceased. An eerie silence fell.

Owain's eyes widened. His muscles bulged and rippled as he tried to force the dagger into Rhys's throat, but he couldn't move.

Kai pulled herself, swaying, to her feet. Slowly, painfully, she uncurled her hand. The corners of the pendant had bitten deep, staining her hand and the necklace in blood.

She was so tired and scared that her brain hadn't comprehended it at first. Because it shouldn't be possible. She hadn't thought—and knew Owain couldn't even begin to comprehend —that a Wingless might be able to hold the mantle.

But why not? After all, she was a dragon, even if she had no dragon form. The power was hers. It surged through her. Even though she'd just issued a command with no ritual, she felt it buzzing in her bones.

She looked to the sky. The dragons there had stopped as well.

She shouldn't have been able to command a dragon already under Rhys or Owain's control. But perhaps a whole mantle made them all hers. All the dragons in the world, under the control of one being for the first time in a thousand years.

Her.

Kai lifted her eyes to Owain. Focused on those pale eyes. Telling him to stop had merely been the first part of her command. What came next? That was for all of them.

Her lip curled as she issued the rest of the command, raising her voice, spreading her power until she could *feel* the dragons all around, drawing them in, accessing some part of them that forced them to bend to her will. Kai clutched the pendant tight and drew on the new, dazzling, hideous power inside her. She had to protect Rhys.

She had to protect them all.

"THIS WAR BETWEEN DRAGONS IS OVER. THERE WILL BE NO MORE FIGHTING AMONGST YOURSELVES FOR POWER OVER THE MANTLE. THERE WILL BE PEACE."

Jerking like a badly made puppet, Owain rose from Rhys's chest and stepped away. Rhys gasped and rolled to one side. With a groan, he sat up. Blood and sand covered the entire side of his face, and she could hardly bring herself to look at the ruin that had been his eye. Still, she threw herself on him as carefully as she could. He caught her with his unbroken arm, wrapping it around her. Kai buried her face in his chest. Alive. He was alive, and it was over. She had the mantle. Owain couldn't hurt them. They'd won.

They'd won.

Without warning, Rhys threw her to one side. Shocked, Kai rolled once before catching herself.

Owain and Rhys were grappling, fighting over Owain's dagger. Like an idiot, Kai hadn't realized the loophole in her command. She was Wingless—not human, but not truly a dragon, either. She'd protected Rhys, but not herself or those like her.

Rhys tore the dagger from Owain's grasp and plunged it into the blond man's chest with a sick, wet *thunk*.

Bound by Kai's command, Rhys could not have hurt Owain to end the war.

But to protect her, he could.

Another loophole. She had to close them fast, so she shouted, "No more violence!"

Owain gave a surprised grunt, looking from Rhys to the dagger in his chest and back to Rhys. "Cousin..."

And then he fell into the sand, pale eyes staring as blood soaked the sand beneath him, crimson against white. One of the dragons overhead let out a keening scream that pierced Kai's eardrums. Jiang half fell, half dove toward the beach, jade body writhing.

Kai leaped in front of Rhys, but there was no need. Jiang wasn't coming for them.

The jade dragon crashed to the beach. In an instant, she was human. She knelt at Owain's side, brushing hair from his face. Ignoring the blood, she lifted his torso, cradling it and wailing in a language Kai didn't know. She looked dazed and half insane. Kai knew something like that feeling, and despite everything, she had a moment of uncomplicated compassion for the woman who had lost her mate.

Then, silently, Rhys collapsed.

Kai panicked and crawled to him. "Rhys?" He didn't answer.

She raised her eyes to the gold dragon circling with the others. "Seren!"

The gold dragon dove for the beach. Around them, other dragons were landing.

"Save him," Kai cried. All the peace and power in the world meant nothing if he died.

Seren knelt at Rhys's other side. Kai watched, her heart in her throat, as Seren placed her hands on his forehead. "He's almost gone. I don't have enough. I've been healing so much. I need—"

The Wingless councilwoman, Athena, slid off her mate's back and dropped beside Seren on one side, and a woman Kai didn't know by name came to the other. They each put a hand over Seren's. Without waiting to ask, Seren closed her eyes. From beneath her fingers, a golden light burst.

Rhys coughed and rolled onto his side. Kai turned his face toward her. He blinked two starfire-blue eyes.

Relief and exhaustion crashed over Kai. For the rest of today, she didn't care what they did. As long as everyone stopped trying to fucking kill her and the people she loved.

Power buzzed inside her, hot and confusing and unwanted. She opened her blood-crusted hand and looked at the pendant. In the center of her palm was the imprint of a sun.

Kai shuddered. She had the power to control every dragon on Earth. The thought made her sick. "Rhys, oh my—what do I do?"

She didn't expect him to answer, but he said in a sleepy voice, "Keep them from killing each other."

"I don't know how to do that!"

Except she was pretty sure she did. That she already had. "I don't want to do this by myself."

"*Gyda'i gilydd,*" he murmured. "*Beth bynnag a ddaw.*"

Kai laughed, tears falling from her eyes. Something inside her kept chanting *alive, alive, alive.* "I don't know what that means," she said.

Seren smiled at her. "Together. Whatever comes."

CHAPTER 57

RHYS

It took days for things to gain even a semblance of order. Rhys organized everything from where all the extra dragons would sleep to meals to setting up judges he trusted to fairly arbitrate disputes. He also helped Kai. Not that he'd ever held the full power of the mantle, but he'd lived with a piece of it for long enough to give her pointers.

Every time she walked in the room, the air grew heavy and electric, as if she carried the energy of a hurricane wherever she went. When he'd commented on it to Ffion, she laughed and said that's what he used to feel like, except not quite as powerful.

They were so busy with meetings, cleanup, sending most of the humans home, and keeping the Cadarnle and Eryri dragons from killing each other that he and Kai rarely had a second alone. He'd thought they'd been sleep-deprived during the battle, but that was nothing in comparison.

Three days after the end of the war, delegations arrived from the rogues—those who had sent aid and those who had not. More dragons to house and mouths to feed and disputes to settle.

Rhys had thought peace would bring...well, peace. Instead, it was as if he and Kai had upended the world. Everyone was scrambling to find their places within it, and even a mantle-backed command against violence wouldn't hold forever.

Now that there were no longer two kings, the clans started to come back together. In his father's time, the united clans had been far more powerful and far more of a headache than the divided clans during the war. Eventually, when things were settled, he'd have to call for a reelection of councilmembers to make sure everyone was equally represented.

Wouldn't that be fun.

Finally, a week after Kai had taken on the mantle, Rhys found himself, her, and his vee gathered in his rooms.

For once, no one was pounding on their door.

It reminded him of the night before the battle, except things were a little more subdued. Instead of talking or playing cards, everyone seemed content to sit in the same room with everyone else.

At least this much of their family had survived.

Kai snuggled into Rhys's side where they sat on the couch. Across from them, Ffion sat in a rocking chair, staring into the fire. The rest of the vee ranged around on couches, chairs, and the floor. Kai's brother Liam was there as well, standing off to one side with Morwenna.

"Ffion?" Kai asked.

"Hmm?"

"Do you know what you're going to name your baby?"

Ffion smiled, one hand resting on her belly. Dragon pregnancies lasted longer than human pregnancies, but not by much. Rhys still had a hard time believing she was pregnant, sometimes. He'd known her since both of them were little more than babies themselves, and now she was having one. They'd been so busy surviving, he was just now realizing he'd missed out on growing up.

He looked down at Kai, wondering what their children might be like.

Then he remembered. They couldn't have children.

"Griffin, if he's a boy. Like his father, but still himself. If she's a girl, I was thinking, if Rhys and Seren don't mind, I'd like to call her Aderyn."

Rhys found he couldn't speak past the lump in his throat.

Ffion sniffed and wiped at her eyes, but didn't sink into a quiet despair as she had so often since Griffith's death. She truly had decided to live.

"What about you two?" Ffion asked. "Things have quieted down. Are you going to try to fix your heartswearing?"

Kai blinked rather owlishly. The physical pain of the sundering had become less of a problem in recent days, though he wasn't sure when. But it had left behind the psychological pain he imagined went with a phantom limb. "We haven't talked about it."

Kai frowned up at him. "Do we need to talk about it?"

Tension he'd thought they were past sprang up between them and seeped into his voice. "I don't know, *cariad*, we're doing fine like this, but—"

"What? You don't want to be heartsworn to me?" Kai demanded.

"Kai, you know I—"

She grabbed his face and kissed him. "I'm kidding. Of course we're going to try to fix it. If you want."

He pulled her into his lap, leaning down so he couldn't see anyone but her. His lips hovering an inch above hers, he whispered, "I want."

She closed the distance between them, and he kissed her

thoroughly, only breaking off when Cadoc threw a pillow and Ashem muttered, "Get a room."

Rhys laughed, but a knot of unease grew inside him. There was still a chance that no matter how strong the wanting, it wouldn't work.

"Do we do this now?" Kai asked, the same unease reflected in her eyes.

Rhys lifted Kai to her feet, stood, and offered his hand to her, drawing her into the center of the room, surrounded by their friends. "Now."

CHAPTER 58
KAI

K ai stood in the midst of the vee, facing Rhys. She tried to hide the way her hands trembled. But by the way Rhys squeezed her fingers, he knew.

Since the battle, she'd done the ceremony once to recharge the mantle under Rhys's extremely vigilant supervision. Actually using it to command all dragons had depleted it greatly. When she asked how she'd been able to use it in the first place without doing the ceremony, Rhys and Ffion both suspected that it had shifted to her from him and Owain with the amount of power they both held at the time.

"How do I do this?" she asked, looking from Rhys to the others as if one of them had actually healed a sundering before.

"When I tried, I sensed that there was still something between you," Seren said. She looked exhausted. Since the battle, she'd been working herself to the bone, healing anyone and everyone who came to her. Thankfully, plenty of Wingless had volunteered to help. "Like chains that had been broken. I think you need to forge them back together."

Kai nodded, wishing she had some carabiners to click. "So... I guess I'll just concentrate and see how it goes?"

The power of the mantle still overwhelmed her, but it didn't frighten her anymore. Not in and of itself. What it could do... That was frightening. If she wanted, she could command every dragon in the world to jump into the sea. Or do the hokey pokey.

Or kill. Or hurt themselves. It wasn't right.

Whatever had driven the ancient dragons to create the mantle must have been dire indeed.

Putting those thoughts away, Kai inhaled and closed her eyes. Broken chains. She thought she knew what Seren meant. At the moment she and Rhys had been sundered, she thought she'd seen those chains herself.

She leaned her forehead against Rhys's, felt his arms around her, and dug deep.

Maybe if this didn't work, she could use the Sunrise Dragon to pass the power back to him and he could do it. In a couple of years or whenever it recharged.

At first, Kai didn't sense anything. Easing herself into the power of the mantle was like settling into a bath that was barely too hot. The power was so strong it burned, and she had to do it slowly. She let the room fade, then her worries, until there was nothing but her and Rhys.

And there, between them, the glimmer of something broken.

They *were* chains, she saw. When she'd been sundered, she'd thought they were made of gold. But now she could see they were made of light, or magic, or spirit, each with its own purpose, its own subtle signature. Grasping one of her broken ends and matching it with one of his, she pressed them together.

Nothing happened.

She waited. Still nothing happened.

Letting the last of her fears subside and giving in to her instinct and her love for Rhys, she poured power into the broken bond. More and more, until a fine sheen of sweat covered her face. The links softened. Then, with a tug Kai could feel in the center of her soul, it came together. Her breath caught, and so did Rhys's.

She could do this.

She picked up another chain, then another, working until the sheen of sweat turned to drips and her body shook with strain. Rhys held on to her, steady as a rock. As she repaired each of their broken bonds, something coalesced as if from fog, a presence that became clearer and clearer with each new connection.

She welded the last chain together and let go of the power, going limp. For the moment, she was utterly drained.

Without warning, the power of the mantle that had raged inside her like a leashed hurricane ran down the repaired bonds. No longer raging, it settled somewhere between them, as calm as a still pond.

Rhys inhaled sharply, but both of them knew what had happened. Somehow, when Kai poured the power of the mantle into repairing their bond, that's where it took up residence.

Not torn, but shared.

Love rolled into her mind, and a voice so familiar to her she wanted to cry.

Together, cariad, *whatever comes. No one can object to you being queen now. Not because of me. Because of you.*

And then she did cry, and he held her, body and soul. After so long alone in her own mind, she forgot how good it felt to be this close to him. Yes, they loved each other without the bond, and sometimes being in each other's heads was not at all convenient—instalove was not all it was cracked up to be—but they both wanted this, and that was what mattered.

She had healed their heartswearing. Rhys cupped her face and kissed her softly. "I love you, Kai."

She sighed, kissing his lips, then his nose, then his lips again. "I love you too."

"So," Cadoc said, breaking the profound silence. "When are you two going to start having babies?"

Rhys chucked the pillow he'd thrown right back at him.

CHAPTER 59

SEREN

S eren stood at the doorway of her former audience chamber and waved goodbye to the last of her patients. The room, large and airy, had served as a much more pleasant infirmary than the darkened festival cavern down below. Over the past several days, she'd healed as many dragons as she could, starting with the worst injuries and working her way up to the minor ones.

Cadoc came up behind her and wrapped his arms around her waist. She leaned in to him, sliding her bare hands up his muscled arms. She had never thought she could find such peace in another person, or that another person could find such peace in her.

A member of Clan Draig passed in the hall, happening to catch a glimpse of them. He sneered and spat on the floor. Cadoc stiffened, but Seren stilled him, turning so she could slide her hands up the back of his neck into his hair and force him to look down at her. "We've got to give them time."

Not all dragons were as accepting of the loss of the Seeress as Rhys. She had been, after all, a symbol. An untouchable figure. The fact that Cadoc was so very interested in touching her had brought out the worst in the dragons who had treasured the Seeress—not Seren—most.

Cadoc pressed his forehead against hers. "As long as I have you, *ngariad i*, I'm willing to weather whatever they throw at us."

Seren smiled and kissed him, then broke off. "Aren't you supposed to be down in the festival hall?"

Cadoc, a couple of willing dragons from Cadarnle, and some of the rogues had taken to giving nightly performances in the cleaned and restored cavern, which Rhys and Kai hoped would boost morale and begin the process of healing their very broken people.

He grinned wickedly and winked at her. "Five more minutes and my entrance will be the spectacle it deserves to be." He hooked his fingers over the strap across his chest that held a guitar on his back. "I have an idea. Sing with me. Kai is going to, I think."

The thought made Seren slightly queasy. "Isn't performing with you a little..." She'd been about to say "below the queen's dignity," but realized at the last second how insulting that would be. Which was why the mental connection of heartswearing was sometimes highly inconvenient. He knew exactly what she'd been going to say.

Cadoc scoffed. "I am the epitome of dignified."

Rather than reply and dig herself in deeper, Seren silenced him with a kiss. She would have kept it light, but he put a hand on the back of her head and pulled her closer, turning the kiss demanding and deliciously dark.

She pushed him away, laughing. "Come. I know how you hate to be kept from your music."

He stubbornly held on to her. His amethyst eyes as serious as she'd ever seen them, he swept hair from her face and ran a thumb along her jaw to her lips. "You are my music. And I will never be parted from you again."

He was considerably more than five minutes late.

CHAPTER 60

JULI

Juli was half relieved, half terrified when Kavar came back to Eryri two weeks after Owain's death. She clutched Ashem's hand as the silver-eyed man approached them across the white sand, the ocean muttering in their ears.

"You're sure?" she asked when he came near enough. Kavar nodded.

Juli swallowed, and Ashem tightened his grip on her hand. "All right, then. They're waiting for us."

They walked to the stone circle, where Kai and Rhys had taken to holding court when it wasn't raining. Everyone had gone for the evening, and they were alone among the standing stones. A salt breeze rustled the plants that grew along the shore of the lake, and the air was full of the songs of insects and frogs.

Tensions still ran high in Eryri, but for the moment, many of the dragons seemed relieved that the war was over. Oh, there would be dissenters. Jiang, for example. Who had disappeared. Kai could have used the mantle to call her back. With its full power, Jiang didn't have to be in hearing distance for Kai to issue a command. But Kai had her hands full with other things. She'd done enough magic to prevent Jiang from harming anyone, and for now she was content to leave it at that.

Juli reached out with searching tendrils, brushing the minds of a few dragons who walked along the beach. So many tensions brewed beneath the surface here. Sundering would put her out for a week or more. She felt like she was leaving her friend in a den of vipers.

But Kai, she'd learned over the past few days, was more than capable of taking care of herself. Kai stood, fully robed in the regal silk and bejeweled trappings of a dragon queen, on a boulder beyond the circle's edge, skipping stones into the lake with a similarly attired Rhys. They turned at Juli, Ashem, and Kavar's approach. Kai sat. She was so short and the boulder so large that her feet dangled off the side. She kicked them lightly against the stone, her red and gold silk robes rustling. Despite everything Kai had been through, in that moment she looked so very much herself.

Kai Monahan, her best friend, Queen of Dragons.

It fit.

"Are you ready?" Rhys asked. Juli and Kavar nodded.

Rhys looked to Ashem, who scowled. Even though he wasn't the one being sundered, his position was hardly enviable. He desperately wanted Juli to himself—and desperately wanted to spare her pain.

"So, we're going to try something." Kai sounded nervous. "You two are more or less handing Rhys and me a scalpel and asking us to do surgery. But I noticed a couple of things when I repaired our bond. I think people in the past have always sundered by ripping the connections apart. But I think they might be able to be...sliced. Which doesn't sound any better, but trust me, it will be a lot cleaner. And since there are two of us, I think instead of cutting in the middle and letting the broken connection snap back at you, Rhys and I can sever each connection at its source at the same time. No snapping. No backlash. Maybe—hopefully—less pain."

Juli swallowed, speaking with a crisp confidence she didn't feel. "Let's do it, then."

Kavar and Juli faced each other. He spoke deep into Juli's mind. *If I had heartsworn to you first, you would have loved me. You could have been mine, Juliet King.*

His voice was wistful, not sarcastic. Juli gave him a small smile. Maybe he was right, but it didn't matter. She had committed to Ashem months ago. Perhaps it wasn't romantic, but choice held relationships together just as much as emotion. *I might have. But I am my own, and I choose Ashem.*

And so, after a glance at each other, Rhys and Kai began.

It didn't *not* hurt. On a scale of pain, Juli would probably put each severed bond somewhere between a paper cut and Owain's henchman breaking her finger. But when they were finished, it was done. She waited for the pain to grow, like Kai had said happened to her and Rhys. She waited for the aftershocks.

There were none. And when she reached for Kavar, he was gone.

Kavar met her gaze and smiled. He looked pale and clearly shaken, but ultimately all right. He gave her a sardonic bow. "Juliet King, it's been hell. May we never meet again. Ashem..."

Kavar swallowed whatever pithy thing he'd been about to say.

"Let me know when you're settled," Ashem said.

"Perhaps." Without a backward glance, he walked off into the night.

Juli and Ashem said goodnight to Rhys and Kai. Then, truly alone for the first time in far too long, they walked toward the mountain.

"We'll have to visit him on holidays," Juli observed. Then she sighed. "I've never met someone I wanted so badly to kill and mother in all my life."

Quiet, woman, Ashem said into her mind. *This family is perfectly comfortable being dysfunctional. I don't want to hear his name for a century.*

Juli raised her eyebrows at him. "I dare you to call me that again."

The corner of Ashem's mouth lifted ever so slightly. He leaned forward and whispered in her ear, "Woman." The way he said it, luscious and dark and husky, made goose bumps run down her spine.

She shoved him away, laughing a little.

"How is your magic?" he asked. "Has it diminished?"

Juli tested her limits, stretching her mind into the night and brushing over all the sleeping and quiet minds in Eryri. "No. I don't think so. Kai didn't lose her power when she was sundered. Neither did Rhys's mother. Whatever physiological changes occur in the body during heartswearing must be permanent."

"Fascinating."

Juli banked her power and put up the shields that made her sanity possible. She had gotten good at blocking out the noise, weaving through crowds in Cadarnle.

Kai would need her in the days and weeks to come, but for now, she was ready for a rest—and to relearn what it meant to be with Ashem without his brother hovering in the backs of their minds.

Juli sighed and wondered if Ashem was still connected to

Kavar. The other man's absence, surprisingly enough, was bittersweet. She'd wanted to bring Kavar home for Ashem. To reunite him with his brother, the only other remaining member of his clan. They had done much to fix things, but not enough.

Maybe someday, they could finish what they'd begun.

CHAPTER 61

KAI

R hys and Kai stood on a precipice, where earth met the edge of the sky. Kai's toes curled over the rim of stone, and the finely crafted jewelry decorating her bare feet and ankles glittered in the rising sun. She leaned her head against Rhys's chest, and he tightened his arms around her.

They watched Evan, Kai's parents on his back, grow distant and small. The goodbye had been tearful, and she wondered when she'd have a chance to see them again. They were the last of the humans to depart. Liam was staying. Kai had warned him to be careful who he touched—humans could heartswear tended to with long enough exposure to dragons.

Liam didn't seem to care. He was fascinated by the dragons. Kai thought he might even want to heartswear—if he ever stopped following Morwenna around.

That would be bizarre. How would her parents explain how two of their children *and* their daughter's best friend simply fell off the face of the earth?

Kai sighed. "The world is shrinking, Rhys. We can't hide

forever. It might take another hundred years. Two or three hundred if we're lucky. But the humans will find us."

A flash of something crossed Rhys's mind—an island filled with dragons. Dark waters rising. He banished the image and dipped his head, inhaling the scent of her hair, then laid his cheek on her head. "I know." The thought had haunted both of them since the dust started to clear. In winning the war, they had protected humankind from dragons.

But they had no way of protecting dragonkind from humans.

Kai reached back and slid a hand over his shoulder, her fingers caressing his neck, lingering on his cheek. Thoughts of the mantle made her uncomfortable. They'd had to use it a few times already, mostly to stop brawls and prevent murder. It felt wrong, to be able to take away free will.

Someday, she'd like to find out if they could get rid of it altogether. But would that leave humans open to dragon attacks? What was right? What was responsible?

"One step at a time, *cariad*." He twined his fingers through hers, brought her hand to his mouth, and pressed a reverent kiss against her skin. Through the bond, she sensed that they could live for another ten thousand years and he would never take this for granted. Not even one time. She turned her face, snuggling into him.

Neither would she.

"We have time," Rhys murmured against her hand. "We'll figure out a way."

"We can try." Kai shook her head. "I'm not going to worry about it now. I just want to *be* for a little while. Breathe. Sometimes I still can't believe we're alive."

Something echoed through her soul. A word. A yearning. *Freedom.*

He loosened his grip. Kai grabbed his arms before he could

drop them entirely. "No. I'm freer here, with you, than I've ever been in my life. That's not what I meant. What I wanted was..."

Rhys grinned, catching a flash of sky in her mind. The wind through her hair. The feeling of the world beneath her. He stepped back, giving himself room, and called the change.

Not bothering with a harness, Kai scrambled up his side and held on to the spike in front of her, gripping his spine with her knees.

If she fell, he would catch her. Every time.

Sensing her readiness, his heart beating in rhythm with hers, Rhys grinned a dragon grin and launched into the sky.

ACKNOWLEDGMENTS

The creation of these books has been such a journey. Thank you to my former agent, Marlene Stringer, and those at Carina Press who oversaw the original version of this book in 2015. Many readers may also want to join me in thanking this book's first editor, Libby Murphy, who convinced me not to kill Kavar.

Thank you also S.M. Carrière, who was very helpful in translating much of the Welsh used in the original version of this trilogy. Other thanks from the first writing of this story go to my critique partners Charlie N. Holmberg, Kim Vanderhorst, and Erin Summerill.

As for the 2023 version, Charlie N. Holmberg remains the reason it exists and has my everlasting gratitude. Charlie, you're the best. Thank you so much for your generosity and belief in me. Thank you, Kristy Gilbert, the editor of the 2023 version. I'm starstruck that I got to work with you, and I'm in love with the way you helped me revitalize these books. You've helped me create something I'm proud to call mine.

Thank you to Mikki, Tricia, and my D&D group. My friends have been the only thing keeping me sane since 2020. I love and appreciate you all.

Most profoundly, thank you to my husband and my kids. You people are the only reason I don't run off into the woods on the days the writing is hard. Love you.

ALSO BY CAITLYN MCFARLAND

Dragonsworn Trilogy

Soul of Smoke

Shadow of Flame

Truth of Embers

Daughters of the Shattered Moon

Echoes of Night

ABOUT THE AUTHOR

After spending most of her adult life in UT, Caitlyn McFarland has returned to the Midwest and currently lives by a lake in Missouri with her husband and three daughters. She has a Bachelor's degree in linguistics from Brigham Young University. When she's not writing romantic fantasy, Caitlyn can be found wandering the woods, crafting, or playing TTRPGs.

www.ingramcontent.com/pod-product-compliance
Lightning Source LLC
Chambersburg PA
CBHW020515110726
47899CB00004B/1119